Curious?

A Woman's Introduction to Gay Romance

Dreamspinner Press

Published by
Dreamspinner Press
4760 Preston Road
Suite 244-149
Frisco, TX 75034
http://www.dreamspinnerpress.com/

Edited by Elizabeth North

Cover Photos by Dylan Rosser
Cover Design by Mara McKennen
Illustrations by Paul Richmond   http://www.paulrichmondstudio.com

ISBN: 978-1-61581-073-4

Printed in the United States of America
First Edition
April, 2010

eBook edition available in Adobe PDF, MobiPocket and MS Reader formats
eBook ISBN: 978-1-61581-074-1

Table of Contents

Introduction

They say curiosity killed the cat.

I say that it left her with a satisfied smile.

The last few years have seen an incredible increase in the number of women reading gay male romance. Why? What is it about two men falling in love that women find so alluring?

I've heard answers as simplistic as: One hero is good; two heroes are better. I believe it is even simpler than that. Women read romance novels because we all live in the real world where bad things happen to good people, and it's nice to visit, for a while, a place where love overcomes all obstacles. In our society and throughout time, two men frequently face and conquer unthinkable obstacles to be together. Reading stories of love and redemption, action and excitement, tears and laughter, small acts and large deeds, that speak to our hearts, souls, and minds gives us hope, rejuvenates our souls and allows us to believe in happily ever after.

In *Curious,* we've chosen stories that run the gamut of M/M romantic fiction: from initial curiosity to the first blush of love, from awkward first times to finding fulfillment, and from heart-warming forever devotion to hot and sweaty sex. Think of it as a romance buffet: take a little bit, try a little dab, and find the flavor of M/M romance that satisfies you.

Aren't you just a little curious?

Elizabeth North

Gambling Men: Ante Up
Amy Lane

Quentin looked sideways at Jace and tried to read his tells. They'd known each other for five years—ran a successful day trading business actually—but Jace had a poker face to beat them all. And he did beat them all. Frequently. But on this night, even in the crowd of their stockbroker buddies, telling raucous jokes and pounding vodka, Quentin needed a sign, a glance, a wink, a twitch… *something*… because what had happened between him and Jace earlier that week… well….

It could leave a guy feeling insecure; that's for damned sure.

Jace ran a finger under his collar and freed the stays from his black tie and then took a deep gulp of his vodka from the cut-glass tumbler. He looked up over the edge of the glass and caught Quentin's eyes—crystal blue sparking off dark brown—and Quentin flushed.

Okay—so Jace *did* remember.

"Good game, Quent."

Jace's voice echoed hollowly off the tile in the gym. They were the last two off the racquetball courts, and all but one of the employees were gone for the night. Quentin looked up at his old college buddy and flushed with pleasure. They'd been playing since their senior year, and Quentin felt like he so rarely did anything better than Jace.

"You let me win," he said gamely, running a hand through his thick brown hair. It had been hanging in his eyes from the shower.

• • •

1

"I don't let anybody win," Jace replied mildly. His scalp-trim was already dry, and his vodka-blue eyes were twinkling. It was the truth. Jace was a cutthroat competitor; everybody knew it, and Quentin had always worshipped it.

"Then I must be getting better!" Quentin said brightly, although he knew for a fact that he wasn't. He didn't expect a reply; banter had never been their strong point, so instead he started rummaging around in his locker for his toiletries. Deodorant—always a plus, right?

"Hey—can I borrow some of your Pit Stop?" Jace's voice came from right behind Quentin's ear, and Quentin almost jumped. Jace sounded... odd. Breathy. Different.

"Yeah, no prob... lem?" Quent squeaked on the last part, because Jace just reached over his shoulder, the front of his lean chest pressing so tightly against Quentin's back that Quent could feel pointy, air-hardened nipples pebbling against his slick skin.

"Thanks, brother," Jace murmured, and Quentin felt a moment of dizziness as his partner's voice brushed his ear. Jace had never been a "touchy" kind of guy, and Quentin had never thought his hero worship of his old roommate anything more than admiration for a gifted friend.

Jace's erection prodded at Quentin's ass through their towels, and Quentin took a risk and leaned back... just... just... just enough to rub a little, see if that hard lump under the terrycloth really was what he thought it was.

Jace pinned Quentin's shoulders to the locker so quickly Quentin didn't have time to breathe, and without a word, without hardly a deep breath, Jace ground up against Quentin hard enough to leave bruises—and Quentin gasped and grunted... and rubbed back. Jace's movements grew more frantic, more frenzied, and he dry-humped his friend—his business partner—desperately, and Quentin wished... wished... wished *for a hand on his cock*, even his own, to ease the painful, frustrated ache that had blossomed in his groin.

He wished for that right up until Jace bit him, hard, at the tender joining of neck and shoulder, and then grunted and came, the semen seeping between the towels to soak into the skin of Quent's hip. The bite alone did it, sent Quentin over the edge, and he climaxed without even touching his own cock.

They stood there for a moment, breathing heavily, and then Jace backed away, saying, "Ooops... my bad. I forgot I had some of my own."

And that had been it. For most of a week, they had worked in the same building, played ball at night, and that moment—that gasping, breathless moment of sex and come—had ceased to exist.

Until right now. Until Jace looked over his cut-glass tumbler with vodka-blue eyes and showed his cards—low cards, a flush of hearts.

Through the electricity of their glances, Quentin barely registered that his cards beat Jace's. "I won," he rasped breathlessly among the crowd of catcalls from the other men at the table. And then, hoping this meant something: "You must have let me win."

Jace grinned recklessly, and Quentin felt his knee—just a bump really, or a promise. "I told you on Tuesday, Quent—I never let anybody win."

AMY LANE teaches high school English, mothers four children, and writes the occasional book. When she's not begging students to sit-the-hell-down or taxiing kids to soccer/dance/karate—oh my! she can be found catching emergency naps, grocery shopping, or hiding in the bathroom, trying to read without interruption. She will never be found cooking, cleaning, or doing domestic chores, but she has been known to knit up an emergency hat/blanket/pair of socks for any occasion whatsoever or sometimes for no reason at all. She writes in the shower, while commuting, while her classes are doing bookwork, or while she's wandering the neighborhood at night pretending to exercise and has learned from necessity to type like the wind. She lives in a spider-infested and crumbling house in a shoddy suburb and counts on her beloved mate, Mack, to keep her tethered to reality—which he does while keeping her cell phone charged as a bonus. She's been married for twenty plus years and still believes in Twu Wuv, with a capital Twu and a capital Wuv, and she doesn't see any reason at all for that to change.

Visit Amy's web site at http://www.greenshill.com. You can e-mail her at amylane@greenshill.com.

Bad News Brett

Sean Kennedy

The crack of a wooden bat against a ball made Brett Nicholls nostalgic for a childhood that he had never had. As he and his partner made their way to the batting cages, he paused for a moment to rest against the railing and watch the children scattered about on the infield. They were in the middle of a play—the ball soared into the sky, and one ponytailed girl waited confidently beneath it with her glove at the ready. It hit her palm with a resounding smack, and her team-mates whooped as they ran in to congratulate her on her save. A wistful smile tugged on Brett's lips. He turned when he felt a hand against the small of his back.

Tex Johns looked at him quizzically. "What are you thinking about, Brett?"

Brett shrugged. "Do you know the closest I ever came to a baseball game when I was a kid was reading a *Peanuts* strip or catching a rerun of *The Bad News Bears* on TV?"

Tex smiled, his gorgeous dimples on full display. Only someone named Tex could get away with such dimples. His smile was not a mocking smile, however, just one of commiseration and concern. "Well, your mother was overprotective. Maybe when we're parents, we'll understand that a little more."

They began walking again, while Brett tried not to grin like a loon at the thought of them having kids one day. They had been together for five years now, and among their friends, it might as well have been fifty, as they had become the "old married couple" the others looked up to. Perhaps it was only logical to start thinking of the next steps: commitment, family, all those things.

"You're still thinking," Tex said. He wore a faded replica of a Rangers team jersey, and a sports bag was flung over his shoulder. Brett couldn't help but be a little turned on by the jock beside him, a slight fetish that always seemed to arise in him whenever his partner was dressed that way.

Brett looked back out at the kids in the field. "I guess my mom *was* a little overprotective. Maybe it comes with the territory of only having one child."

Tex snorted. "Yeah, my family didn't have *that* problem." He had five siblings, and although all were loved, they had pretty much been given free rein to do whatever they wanted to do. His parents should have gotten frequent usage points at the local hospital for the number of sports injuries that sent their kids there.

"That's good, though," Brett told him earnestly, thinking of the wall of shame back at Tex's childhood home, where the Johns children were represented photographically in every year of their life. The quantity of older pictures that were dedicated to all the siblings in various sporting uniforms would have made anyone believe they could have started their own professional league: the von Trapps of sport.

Unbidden, the thought of a little miniature version of himself or Tex following them out onto the field in the future, dragging a bat behind them in the dirt, came to Brett's mind. He hoped that their kid would be like the girl he had watched earlier, fearless and elated, ready to take on anything that came their way. But even if Brett became as overbearingly protective as his own mother, Tex would be there to tease him out of it.

"Maybe my mom should have been a little bit more like yours," Tex laughed. "The number of times we were in the emergency room between the six of us, I'm surprised Child Services never came calling."

Brett would have liked to have seen someone try to report Tex's parents and the chaos that would have ensued. They raised them tough in the Johns household, and Gail and Herb Johns were even tougher.

They made their way to the batting cages and took one at the far end of the row. Tex crouched to unzip the bag and began unpacking the equipment he had bought for them only a few weeks before. Brett had been complaining about Tex's obsession with sports and the amount of time he now spent meeting for practices and games with the league that had just started up among a group of their friends—time that could have been spent with Brett instead. Tex had countered that Brett just might appreciate baseball more if he actually experienced hitting a ball, and that occasionally dribbling a basketball with a few friends in college wasn't the real thing compared to truly playing a team sport.

So Brett had taken up his challenge, which Tex really hadn't been expecting. He was actually quite touched that Brett would do something he seemed to hate in order to spend more time with him. When Tex came back from the sports shop laden with purchases, Brett was skeptical about running around a field after a ball, especially when there were much more fun activities that could raise a sweat involving Tex. But there was something stirring about slipping on the leather of the mitt for the first time, feeling its strange heaviness upon his palm.

"Smell it," Tex had instructed him.

Brett had raised an eyebrow but obeyed. He couldn't quite figure out the emotion in the rush that came over him at the scent of the leather combined with the softening oil, but there was something almost visceral in his response. "It smells like… summer."

There was really no other way to describe it.

Tex had given him one of his blinding smiles and a quick kiss to the top of his head. "Let's test that baby out."

Over the next couple of weeks, they had played catch as if they were kids, throwing the ball back and forth in their backyard. Brett astounded Tex with the speed at which he could throw the ball, although his aim was far from perfect. Their elderly next-door neighbor, Mrs. Lester, had grown tired of them knocking on her door and asking for their ball back, so she gave them permission to leap the fence and get it whenever it sailed over. She secretly liked having two "such nice young men" living beside her, and if the intrusion of a stray baseball every now and again was the only trouble they caused her, she had nothing to complain about.

Which led them to the batting cages. Brett had grown tired of merely playing catch; it was time to introduce him to the bat as well, and combine the two. Tex tapped his Louisville Slugger against the tip of his sneaker as Brett ran down to activate the ball machine, looking tall, gangly, and as if he would trip over his own feet if you gave him the chance. The pneumatic whoosh warned of the impending launch of the ball, and Tex expertly sent the first pitch back to the opposite side of the cage with a crack of his bat. Brett jumped aside automatically even though the ball went nowhere near him.

"And it's a homer for Tex!" he called encouragingly.

Tex shot him a grin and held the bat at the ready again.

Brett sat with the fence at his back, watching his partner work up a sweat, the slight sheen on his skin highlighting the movement of sinew in his forearms. Once the machine emptied itself of the balls, Tex jogged down and restocked it. Brett jumped to his feet and picked up the bat Tex had chosen for him. It was metallic, yet lightweight, and a bright red that Tex knew Brett would appreciate. He approached the line in the dirt with some trepidation and tried to stand as he remembered baseball players did in movies and games he had watched with Tex (although his mind had usually been more on distracting Tex).

Tex hid his smile as Brett took up an awkward stance, as if he was about to try and defend himself from a mugger rather than hit a ball. He moved behind him, and Brett instinctively leaned into the familiar weight.

"What am I doing wrong, boss?" Brett smirked.

"Nothing, if you *don't* want to hit the ball," Tex teased. One hand came to rest on Brett's hip, and his foot snaked between Brett's legs to push them farther apart. Brett allowed himself to be manipulated into what felt like a strange position, but Tex obviously knew what he was doing. "Keep your feet parallel to the plate, for a start."

Brett looked down at the strip in the dirt. "There's no plate."

"That line is your plate," Tex said patiently, used to Brett and his insistence on taking things literally from years of experience of living with him.

"It's a funny-lookin' plate, that's all I'm saying."

Tex ignored him and his attempts to rile him and moved his hand from Brett's hip to his stomach. Brett bit his lip, restraining a sharp intake of breath at the intimacy of Tex's hand pressing him in and the sudden warmth of Tex against his back. He couldn't believe he was getting turned on in a batting cage of all places. Laughing nervously, he said, "I never thought baseball would be this fun."

"Only in training," Tex responded soberly.

Brett knew he was only teasing but played along. "Fuck."

"Later, babe," Tex muttered with a grin meant only for Brett. "Just keep leaning back slightly so that your weight is more over your back foot." His hands pulled on Brett's hips, and he rocked them slightly.

Brett briefly closed his eyes, thoughts of baseball far from his mind.

Unfortunately, Tex was staying on subject. "Try and keep your hips square with your shoulders, and tuck your chin in a bit to your shoulder." His hands travelled up Brett's body and along his arms. He moved Brett's hands slightly apart on the bat but left his hands over them, steadying them. "That's it. Now, swing."

He rocked against Brett so he would get an idea of the motion he was meant to make. Brett followed, but he began to feel a little heat racing through his body as Tex continued to rock against him, swinging him forward. He rubbed back against him just a tiny bit, and Tex's chuckle was hot against his ear.

"You're evil."

"No, I'm not," Brett said softly, rubbing once more.

Tex tried to keep them on track. "How does that feel?" he asked, obviously meaning the swing of the bat and the follow-through.

"Good," Brett squeaked in reply, wishing they were home so he could turn around and start ridding Tex of his suddenly-unnecessary clothing.

"Then we're ready."

"We are?" Brett tensed while waiting for the ball machine to kick in, but Tex was still behind him, helping him ease into the first few swings.

"We're just going to tap the first few," Tex instructed, and Brett nodded. The familiar sound of the pneumatic launcher started, and Brett barely had time to register exactly when to hit the ball, as all he saw coming towards him was a blur of white. But Tex was at the ready and guiding him, and Brett felt himself swiveling at the hips, then heard the crack of the ball as it connected with the bat.

"I did it!" he whooped.

"You sure did, babe," Tex murmured, his breath warm against Brett's ear again.

They remained glued together for about ten balls, and then Brett felt Tex leave him. He was on his own now, and of course, he missed the first ball because he was dwelling on that fact instead of concentrating, and the ball flew right past him.

"Don't stress out," Tex called from behind him. "Relax."

It was easy for him to say—after all, he had been doing this all his life—but Brett did as he suggested. The next ball glanced off his bat, but it was more of a dull thud than a sharp crack. Tex continued to call out encouraging advice, and Brett's confidence grew, although he still missed the occasional ball.

One came at him on a curve, and he managed to hit it, but it bounced off the bat at an awkward angle and spun off behind him. He heard Tex yelp in pain, and Brett turned in time to see him go down without an ounce of grace.

"Tex!" Brett yelled, dropping his bat and running to him.

"You beaned me pretty good, babe," Tex groaned from where he lay sprawled in the dirt.

"I'm so sorry!" Brett had to duck as he tried to attend to him because he heard the sound of the ball machine launching again, and without anybody there to deflect the ball, both he and Tex were directly in the firing range.

"It's okay." Tex rubbed at the right side of his head gingerly. "These things happen in sports. You know you haven't been giving your best if you don't end up in an emergency ward." He grinned as he remembered his older brother Ryan accidentally releasing an arrow too early and putting it through his thigh the year the Johns siblings experimented with archery.

"You want to go to the hospital?" Brett asked, worried and contrite, ducking as another ball flew perilously close to his head.

"No, don't be silly." Tex laughed but winced. "But we should at least move out of the cage while the machine is still going."

Brett waited for the next ball to launch, knowing they would have about forty seconds' grace to get out of the line of fire. He helped a woozy Tex to his feet and guided him out of the cage to a nearby bench. "Lie down," he instructed. "I'm going back in."

Tex stretched out, enjoying having Brett look after him as he watched him race back into the cage. A ball thumped against the back fence and Brett ran in, grabbing the fallen equipment and the bag Tex had carried in earlier. He escaped just as another ball let fly. As he slammed the cage gate behind him, he frowned at the sight of Tex lying on the bench with a hand shielding his eyes from the sun.

"How are you feeling?" Brett asked as he began rummaging in the bag.

"I'll survive, B," Tex said amiably. "I've had worse."

Brett tried not to think too hard about that, especially as this was the first time *he'd* ever injured his partner, and he unzipped the cooler bag tucked away with the equipment. Tex had thoughtfully included a six-pack, and there were two blue refreezable icebags keeping the drinks cool. He pulled one out and tenderly lifted Tex's head as he slid in beneath him and repositioned his partner's head in his lap.

"My favorite pillow," Tex quipped, closing his eyes with contentment.

"Down, boy." Brett smiled as he rested the bag against Tex's neck, where the ball had glanced off. It was beginning to swell, and Brett's smile quickly turned into a grimace as he surveyed the damage he had caused. Tex winced at the sudden cold, but Brett lightly stroked his hair. "Just go with it for a while."

Tex felt he could almost fall asleep there, on the bench in the late afternoon sun in the warmth of Brett's embrace. The coolness against his head, the comfort of Brett's lap, and the heat of the sun upon his body were having a remarkably soporific effect upon him, even if the "bed" beneath him was not built for comfortable slumber.

"Were you expecting me to injure you today?" Brett murmured.

"Those batting cages are death traps," Tex said in mock seriousness, trying not to smile. "I'm surprised there aren't more fatalities in them each year."

"You mean to say you've heard about batting cage fatalities?"

Tex pondered this. "I think I saw it in census statistics, sure."

"Really? A killer ball machine?"

"Well, it was probably people being killed by other people on playing fields. Maybe because they brought the wrong beer to the game."

"Well, that was really what I was trying to do to you. I'd noticed you brought Miller."

"You love Miller," Tex wheezed. "Don't make me laugh. It hurts."

"Maybe we should get you checked out. What if you have a concussion?"

"I wasn't hit in the head. It was more the neck." He applied pressure to the icebag to emphasize the point.

"Ouch."

"I can think of ways you can make it up to me."

"Oh?" Brett smiled wistfully.

"Yeah, you can rub my feet and bring me snacks when we get home."

"You make that sound like a punishment!" Brett teased him.

Tex reached behind him and whacked Brett lightly on the shoulder. "What did I tell you about making me laugh?"

"To never stop?"

With his arm still up in the air, Tex stroked Brett's shoulder, although he was in an awkward position to do so. "That'd be right."

"Come on, let's get you home."

Brett was true to his word and mollycoddled Tex for the rest of the night. Tex also made sure to take full advantage of his guilt, occasionally sighing and rubbing the swelling on his skin. Unfortunately for him, Brett's patience and guilt waned when they woke up in the morning and the swelling had reduced significantly.

Inspecting himself in the mirror while Brett was brushing his teeth, Tex said, "I hope you haven't been scared off the game."

Brett shook his head. "I can only get better, right?"

Tex wrinkled his nose. "God, I hope you can't get worse!"

He yelped as Brett whacked him.

"Uncle! Of course you'll get better!" Tex finally managed to say between fits of laughter. He headed off to the lounge room as Brett rinsed his mouth.

Joining him on the sofa, Brett climbed on top of him. "You better make sure you pick me first to be on your team at practice, Tex Johns. I'm not reliving high school all over again. It's not my fault I'm crap at sports. Your parents named you Tex, for Chrissakes; you were destined to be a jock."

Tex kissed him, relishing the taste of spearmint toothpaste on Brett's lips. "I was born to be your jock."

The kisses, gentle against Brett's skin, grew more heated. "Thank God for that."

"Oh, and one more thing?" Tex paused to look into his eyes. "Of course you'll be first pick—you always are to me."

Brett's reciprocated kisses and fumbling hands over his body were all the reply he needed.

That weekend, Brett didn't achieve anything spectacular like a homerun that won the game for their team. He managed to make it to second base but got caught out when the next batter's ball headed straight between him and third. It didn't matter, though.

Back when he was a kid and his mother had stopped him from playing sports, Brett had never known what he was missing out on, but he had all the time in the world to discover it now. And when Tex presented him with his own baseball jersey that night, Brett knew that the look on his face was the same as the girl he had watched catch the fly ball a few nights before: elated and fearless, ready to take on the world.

SEAN KENNEDY lives in the second-most isolated city in the world, so it's just as well he has his imagination for company when real-life friends are otherwise occupied. He has far too many ideas and wishes he had the power to feed them directly from his brain into the laptop so they won't get lost in the ether.

Visit Sean's web site at http://www.seankennedybooks.com/.

Choices and Changes

S. Blaise

Brendan hesitated in the suddenly vast-seeming hall. Others moved around him, secure in their destinations, chattering loudly as they called to friends. The food-laden tray felt like a heavy weight in his hands. Every table seemed crowded and lively; everyone seemed to have somewhere to sit except for him. This was a hundred times more awkward than trying to find a desk during class. Finally, he spotted it, calling out to him like a beacon in the darkness: a table with only one other boy sitting at it. The fact that this table only had one occupant when all the others were full perhaps should have given him some warning, but all he could feel was relief that there was another person sitting alone. Brendan approached the table, his palms slick against the plastic of the tray. He suddenly felt sick and wondered if he would throw up. The thought of doing that, and everyone in the cafeteria seeing it and laughing at him, only made him feel worse. If that happened, he'd leave school and beg to be taught at home. No way he'd be able to survive that.

"Can I—can I sit here?" he asked, his voice rough and barely above a mumble.

The other boy looked up from the book his nose had been buried in to regard him with an apathetic stare. "Dunno, can you?"

Brendan almost felt like he could cry, not sure how to answer. Someone cool and popular would have had a snappy, funny comeback, but he wasn't cool or popular, and he knew he never would be. Finally, the boy relented, turning back to his book with a shrug and a muttered "whatever". Brendan

* * *

took that as permission, sinking gratefully onto the hard plastic chair opposite the other boy, who continued to act as though he wasn't there, reading and managing to eat his lunch with one hand. *Sweeney Todd*, Brendan noted.

"Um, my name's—Brendan Wallis," he said, figuring he should at least make an effort to introduce himself. He only got that cold stare flicked at him again, and then those pale green eyes returned to the pages. He decided to give up and started to eat his lunch.

Darting glances at the boy opposite him, Brendan wondered why he was sitting on his own. He had dark brown hair that was a little too long, hanging down and obscuring his eyes as his head remained bent to the page he was reading. His skin was pale, and he wore a grey T-shirt and black jeans. He was thin, almost scarecrow-like, his bony shoulders hunched and sharp elbows resting on the smooth, unforgiving table. He wasn't bad-looking though; he could probably have been popular if he tried.

Brendan began eating his own lunch, looking down at his stomach, which protruded over thighs twice the size they should be. He would never, ever be that skinny. The boy looked like he would fit inside Brendan's body with room to spare. His own hair was a short, spiked dirty blond that he thought made him look like a porcupine, and his blue eyes were nestled in his fleshy face. He kept eating, looking around while the boy continued to pay him no mind. Brendan envied his casual, uncaring attitude, being able to simply sit there and read while noisy hordes of teenagers moved around him. He just hoped that the presence of the book didn't mean the boy was a nerd. He didn't look like one, which was reassuring.

He learned, as the teacher took attendance in the very next class, English, that the boy's name was Sebastian Gallagher. He learned later, from the whisperings of his classmates, that Sebastian, or "Seb", had been in a juvenile detention centre, was a devil-worshipper, and had either killed his own father or was on the run because his father wanted to kill him. Brendan thought he just seemed to want to be left in peace to read his book

The next day was the same ordeal: lunch tray, packed hall, nowhere to sit. Brendan spotted Seb sitting alone at a table again and walked over, his anxiety only slightly lessened from yesterday.

"Can I sit here?" he asked, his voice still trembling a little.

"'Can' is for whether or not you physically can do something. If you're asking permission for something, you say 'may I'," Seb told him in a bored tone, not looking up from his book.

"Oh. So… *may* I sit here?"

Seb shrugged. "Free country."

Brendan smiled, taking a seat.

The next day, he didn't even ask, simply sat down. Seb continued to ignore him, but it was still better than sitting alone. The day after that, Seb still had his nose buried in his book, but Brendan thought he could feel Seb glancing at him from time to time.

"Hey."

Brendan glanced up, looking around, but no—it seemed Seb really was talking to him.

"You doing anything after school?"

Brendan swallowed. "Um—not really. Why?"

"I want to dye my hair blue, and I'll probably need someone to help me."

"Uh, why?"

"I don't want to risk fucking it up by doing it on my own."

"No, I mean, why dye your hair blue?"

The nonchalant shrug again. "Why not? So, you gonna help me?"

Brendan wasn't sure if that were really a valid reason, but he couldn't think of any argument against it. And it meant that he was being invited to the other boy's house, which kind of made them friends, didn't it? Being friends with a juvenile delinquent, devil-worshipping possible murderer wouldn't be too bad. Hopefully it would mean that he'd get hassled less, at least.

"I'd need to call my mom first to let her know. And I have to be home by six."

Seb shrugged once again, but there was also the merest hint of a smile as he returned to his book, gone before Brendan had fully realized it was there.

The first thing Brendan noticed as he was led into Seb's apartment was the books—lots and lots of books. There was a bookshelf covering one whole wall, as well as others tucked into nooks and crannies; the apartment was infested with them. Seb must have taken notice of the look on his face.

"My mom owns a bookstore," he said, as if it explained everything.

Leaving their bags and shoes by the door, they walked further into the nest of books. "So, you really like to read, huh?" Brendan asked, feeling like a tool as soon as the words had cleared his mouth.

"It's my mom's fault. She used to work in a library; sometimes she couldn't find a sitter, so I'd have to come to work with her and sit quietly. Pretty much all there was to do was read."

"Oh. What about your dad?"

"I murdered him," Seb said, totally straight-faced.

Brendan stared at him a moment, then snorted and punched his arm. "Yeah, right."

Seb's grin was sharp and brief as lightning. "Okay, so I know the crap they're saying about me in school. Actually, I don't know anything about my dad. My mom never talks about him. Maybe *she* murdered him." He grinned again, leading the way to his room with Brendan trailing behind.

"You think your mom could have killed your dad?"

"Hey, it happens. Maybe she snapped one night and hid the body in the library, in one of the sections where hardly anyone goes."

"Sure. Or maybe she cut the body into pieces so it would be easier to hide but saved his skin and had it made into a book."

Seb turned from digging something out from under his bed, his eyes gleaming. "Yeah. With his blood as the ink. Maybe she's a serial killer who does that to all the guys she meets, and my dad's just one of her unfortunate victims. You know, she quit the library to finally buy her own bookstore— maybe it's all just a cover to get rid of the evidence."

Brendan shook his head, grinning. "If you say so." He noticed the box Seb held in his hand, one showing a picture of a feisty-looking girl with hair a shade called "stellar blue", a deep, almost navy color. "Are you sure your mom won't mind you dying your hair that color?" he asked, not wanting Seb to get in trouble. For that matter, he didn't want to get in trouble for helping, either.

The shoulders bunched and relaxed again as Seb went for the bathroom. "There's not much she can do about it. And she's working all the time anyway, so it won't really matter. Don't worry about it."

Seb pressed the box into his hands. Brendan studied the instructions, fear that *he* would be the one to screw it up gnawing at him. Meanwhile, Seb laid a ratty-looking towel on the tiled floor and slung another one over the bath. Brendan looked up as Seb pulled off his T-shirt and tossed it by the door, wrapping the second towel around his shoulders like a shawl. He kneeled down, leaning over the edge of the bath and glancing back at Brendan.

"Showerhead's up there, and you can detach it. Just turn the dial to turn it on. You ready?"

Brendan nodded. "Y-yeah."

It was oddly soothing, washing another's hair, though he had to try hard not to think about the position they were in, with him leaning over Seb's prone, shirtless form. There were plenty of other things to concentrate on, like spreading the dye evenly, not getting too much on Seb's skin or in his ears, and avoiding spraying him in the face with the water, which wasn't easy. His bowed back was smooth, the knobs of his spine standing in relief. Brendan could almost see his ribs and felt jealous again. Why couldn't he be so skinny? It wasn't fair.

At lunch the next day, he sat down at what he now thought of as "their" table. Seb's hair had come out looking really good, even if he did say so himself, though the color kind of clashed with his eyes. Seb had gotten a few stares and the whispering had increased; he'd even been called to the principal's office. He'd faced it all with a characteristic shrug, saying his mom had said what was done was done and they'd just have to wait for it to fade and grow out. Seb had said he was grounded, but since he didn't really go out anyway, it wasn't a big deal. But now, at lunch, it was Brendan's turn to steal awkward glances.

"Um," he began, getting Seb's attention. "Um, my mom said to ask you if you want to come to dinner. I told her about going to your house yesterday, so now she wants to meet you, but you're grounded, so it's okay, don't worry about it."

Seb stared at him a moment, then shrugged. "Sure, I can come."

"But you're grounded."

"My mom keeps saying I'm not making enough friends, so this should get her off my back for a while. Besides, she doesn't usually get home 'til late, anyway, so she worries I'm not eating right."

Brendan grinned. "Oh, okay, cool. So I'll just see you after school again?"

Seb nodded. Having Seb there at dinner would probably make him look even worse, but he found that he didn't really care.

"IT'S nice to meet you, Seb. My goodness, you're so slim! Isn't he slim, Brendan?" Marjorie Wallis said, practically pouncing on Seb when they were introduced.

Brendan simply nodded his head, sighing quietly to himself. His mother had become a health food nut, talking constantly about articles she'd read and features she'd seen about obesity and how it could lead to a multitude of health problems later in life. Not to mention all the times she'd say he needed to lose weight if he wanted to make friends and get a nice girlfriend. Maybe she'd stop bugging him now if she saw he had made a friend, though from the way his mother was looking at Seb's hair and clothes, she didn't seem to be entirely certain about the kind of friend he'd made.

Dinner was, as usual, a depressing affair for Brendan, his mother once again trying to stuff him full of vegetables. There would probably be some kind of fruit for dessert. His dad never talked much at dinner, usually being too tired from work, and his mom was always asking questions like what he'd eaten during the day and if he was making friends at school. At least he had someone else now to share in the misery. He noticed Seb glance at him and his mountain of green on the plate. Seb's plate was piled with the potatoes and stew they were having for dinner. He tried not to laugh as, when his parents weren't looking, Seb pushed half of what was on his plate onto Brendan's, taking some of his vegetables.

"You're so slender, Seb, dear; is there a special diet you're on?" his mother asked.

"No, I was starved as a child and beaten if I tried to eat too much," Seb deadpanned.

Brendan muffled a snort in his napkin. "He's kidding, mom," he reassured her.

"What an—interesting sense of humor you have."

Seb nodded. "Did you know in the past, only poor people were thin and sickly-looking, like me? Being overweight was seen as a sign of prosperity, and some cultures see it as a sign of strength."

Brendan hid his smile at his mother's expression.

"You doing anything Saturday?" Seb asked the next day at lunch, his voice quiet.

"Don't think so, why?"

"My mom has the morning off. She said you should come to lunch since you had me over for dinner."

"Sure. Okay."

"You remember where I live?" Brendan nodded. "Just come round about twelve."

On Saturday, he found himself again at Seb's door, feeling as unaccountably nervous as he had the last time.

"Brendan, hello, come and sit down." Lucy Gallagher waved him over to the table where Seb was already sitting. "My, you're a big boy, aren't you? I wish my Sebastian could get some more meat on his bones. He's so skinny! It can't be healthy."

The two boys looked at each other, their lips twitching. Mrs. Gallagher couldn't figure out what was so funny to make both boys laugh that much.

They hung out even more after that, drifting together naturally until they were practically spending every day in each other's company, most of the time without realizing it. Brendan supposed it was an odd friendship, the fat boy and the (somehow still slightly cool) loner, but he didn't care. Seb was really smart without being a jerk about it, didn't make fun of his weight, and had a good, if odd, sense of humor. Hanging around with him made Brendan feel kind of cool by association too. School was not as much of a nightmare as he thought it would be, which helped him relax, though he still hadn't quite achieved Seb's level of "couldn't care less" attitude.

Seb found him barricaded in one of the bathroom stalls one day. The other boy climbed onto the toilet of the stall next to his, peering down at him over the top of the flimsy partition.

"What're you doing in here?"

"Nothing. Go away." He tried very hard to keep his voice from shaking, keeping his face down so Seb couldn't see his red eyes.

"Have those losers been picking on you again? Want me to mutter some mumbo-jumbo around them like I'm saying a spell?" he grinned.

Brendan managed a weak smile, which soon fell. "It's—it's P.E. next. They're always worse during P.E., and the Coach either never sees it or lets them get away with it."

"So let's skip."

Forgetting about hiding his face, Brendan's head jerked up, staring at his friend. "But—we'll get in trouble!"

"We'll say I wasn't feeling well, and tell my mom you took me to your place, since she was at work."

"But—what if someone phones my house? To check."

"So we tell your mom that you took me to my place."

"But—but—" It was crazy. No way would it work.

"I'll write a note to bring in tomorrow from my mom saying I was ill and you stayed with me until she came home. Look, it'll work out fine."

"You can copy your mom's handwriting?"

"Sure. How do you think I get out of doing P.E. all the time? I wrote a note saying I have anemia and strenuous exercise can cause me to faint." He smiled triumphantly. "Now come on so we can get out of here."

Brendan was almost too scared to do it, certain that they would get caught, but they made it out of school without anyone yelling or chasing after them. He started to relax, feeling almost giddy at the unexpected freedom.

"So, where to now? Back to your place?"

Seb shook his head. "Nah, can't risk a neighbor seeing us. We're at your house 'cause I'm ill, remember? Come on, I know a place."

They ended up in a narrow back lot with trash littering the ground, but at least there were a couple of boxes to sit on. Seb pulled something out of his backpack pocket, a plastic bag with cigarettes and a lighter in it.

"You want one?" he offered.

"Where'd you get those?" Brendan asked, not sure whether to be impressed or disgusted.

"My mom smokes; I sneaked them from the pack in her purse one night. She won't notice, she'll just think she smoked them and forgot or a friend took them." He lit one, taking a drag and exhaling in a way that looked easy.

"Smoking helps you lose weight, right?"

Seb shrugged. "I dunno."

"I'll have one."

He coughed a few times in his first smoking attempt, Seb chuckling at him, but he soon got the hang of it. They sat in a comfortable silence, Brendan feeling like a badass from an action movie, puffing on a cigarette in a dirty back alley. Of course Seb really looked the part, and so effortlessly too. In a real action movie, Brendan probably wouldn't even make a comic sidekick.

"So, what? They were calling you names again?" Seb asked, staring at the wall opposite them.

Brendan shuffled his feet, not wanting to think about it. "I don't care about the nicknames so much anymore. I'm used to them. But why does even my own name have to be so stupid?"

"Your name's not that bad."

"Compared to yours, it is."

"'Sebastian' is a stupid name," Seb snorted.

"But 'Seb' isn't. 'Seb Gallagher'—you sound like a rock star or something. At least you can shorten your name to something that sounds awesome. I can shorten my name to Bren. Makes me sound like a girl."

"What about Dan?"

Brendan made a face. "There's already a Dan and a Danny in our class; we don't need any more. Besides, it's—I don't know—weird."

Seb's lips moved, silently trying out variations of Brendan's name. There weren't many. "How about Bree?"

"Bree?" Brendan asked, uncertain. It still sounded kind of girly, and yet not. He said it to himself a few times. "Yeah, I guess that works," he said grudgingly, still not completely sure.

Seb smiled. "Okay. From now on, I'll call you Bree."

Brendan—Bree—made a face and kept smoking. Bree. Bree Wallis. It was still a little strange. Bree and Seb. Seb and Bree. That seemed to work better.

BRENDAN couldn't say exactly when or how things had started to change, but he was sure Seb was acting differently around him. His friend was quieter and more irritable. Brendan would talk about what to do after school or at the weekend, only to be blown off. He didn't know what to think. Had he said or done something? Was there a way to fix it? Or did Seb just not want to be friends with him anymore? Maybe he was finally sick of having the fat loser trailing around after him all the time and wanted to make some real friends. They still ate lunch together, but they didn't talk. Brendan stopped suggesting things for them to do, and they regressed back to the silence of when they'd first met, Seb hardly looking at him. Summer was coming up soon, and Brendan had looked forward to long, lazy days with the two of them just hanging out together. Now, he didn't know what he'd do.

It was a few days into summer break when he got an unexpected call. His mother had been pestering him to help out in the yard or with fixing up the house if he had nothing better to do. His skin had burned bright red, then morphed to a golden brown, his hair turning blonder, and he even felt he was starting to look more bulky than chubby. He'd come in for a drink of water and managed to grab the phone on its fourth ring.

"Hello?"

"Hey." The quiet voice was so unexpected he couldn't think how to reply. "Bree? You there?"

"Uh, yeah. Hi."

"Look, sorry I haven't—sorry I've been—"

"It's okay. Don't worry about it." And it was. As long as Seb was talking to him again, nothing else really mattered.

"Could I come over?"

"Sure, come over whenever you want."

"Now?"

"Um—"

"It's kind of… please?"

"Yeah, okay, if you want," Brendan replied, a little surprised.

"See you soon."

Brendan let Seb in and led him to his room, sitting on his bed while Seb perched sideways on his desk chair. He grabbed a bag of chips from one of the junk food stashes hidden around his bedroom, grabbing a handful for himself after Seb declined. His friend still seemed to be withdrawn, barely glancing at him.

"You got a tan," Seb said quietly.

"Oh. Yeah, mom's been using me as her personal yard slave. Thinks the exercise will help me lose weight. I wish she'd shut up about it. Keeps talking about how I need to watch what I eat and be more active. As if it's not bad enough seeing all the guys in shorts and T-shirts going swimming or to the beach. If I went in the sea, I'd probably be mistaken for a whale."

"Maybe you should listen to your mom though. Try and make more of an effort."

"I have tried!" Brendan protested, aware that he was whining just a little. "Nothing works. Face it; I'm stuck like this. No girl will ever want to date me. You don't know how lucky you are. You have this attitude that's just so cool, like you couldn't give a fuck about anyone. You have the whole badass, mysterious, aloof thing going on. You could probably have any girl you wanted. I'm just a fat loser and I'll be that way forever."

He didn't notice the angry expression on Seb's face or his clenched fists until he stood up, glaring. "You're so *stupid*, you know that? You keep moaning about how fat you are and how you want to lose weight. You try for maybe a day or two, but when you don't see results straight away, you just give up! The only thing holding you back from looking the way you want is *you*. Why don't you join a gym or start going swimming? How about you stop eating all this crap you've got in your room all the time? If you really wanted to change, then you'd put the work in and do it.

"And lucky? You think I'm *lucky*, Bree? You have—you have no idea why I act the way I do. No idea. And stop putting yourself down so damn much! You're a great guy. You could have a girlfriend and lots of friends too if you let people get close enough to get to know you more. You're—you're the lucky one. You think there's something wrong with you because you're fat, but at least you can *change* that." Brendan was shocked to see tears sparkling in Seb's eyes. They were brushed angrily away. "I act so cold to everyone because I'm scared. I'm scared *shitless*. Scared that they'll realize what's wrong with me and that I'll be the one getting picked on and called names."

"What are you talking about?" Brendan demanded. Seb's ranting didn't make any sense. "There's nothing wrong with you."

Seb choked out a laugh. "There is. And unlike you, there's nothing I can do about it. I've tried; believe me. You said I could have any girl I want, but that's the thing: I *don't want* them. I don't want any of them; do you understand?"

Brendan gaped at the other boy. He'd thought he'd known him, and now he seemed to be a stranger. Little things he'd never paid attention to suddenly made sense: Seb's reluctance to do any kind of sport at school or go swimming, the way he never drooled over cheerleaders or talked much about actresses or models…. Seb wiped his face again, then ran one hand through his hair.

"And you—I know I've been acting like a jerk towards you. But I—the reason I—"

And suddenly Seb was there, so close to him, one leg kneeling on his bed and their faces barely an inch apart, the distance closing in record time. His eyes stayed open as Seb's lips were pressed to his, and he found himself thinking, *the blue hair dye really* doesn't *match his eyes.* It was awkward and mostly one-sided, Seb's dry lips scraping against his with a hint of wet, slippery tongue behind them. And it was still, somehow, the most amazing thing to happen in his life so far. But then suddenly the warm, rough pressure was gone. Seb was staring at him with a panicked look on his face.

"I'm—I'm sorry," he croaked out, and then literally ran from the room and out of the house.

• • •

Brendan didn't know what to do. Go after him? Try to call him? Had it really been that bad? Oh, God, his first kiss and he'd probably tasted of chips! He groaned, flopping down on his pillow. His first kiss had been with a guy. Not just a guy, but his best friend. Should he pretend nothing had happened? Could he really do that? Maybe he should just wait. Wait and see how Seb acted the next time they saw each other. They'd have to see each other again at some point. Deep down, he knew he was being cowardly, but couldn't think of what else to do.

They didn't see each other the rest of that week, or any of the next. Brendan wanted to call Seb, but he couldn't think of what to say, had no idea of how Seb was feeling or if he'd want to talk. And then his parents dragged him on vacation. He wondered if Seb had tried to call him or gone to his house. Before he knew it, the weather was getting colder, the new school year was starting, and they still hadn't seen each other.

Seb wasn't in homeroom, where the other students greeted each other and talked about their vacations, or in any of the morning classes. As the lunch bell rang and he looked around the hall, still not seeing Seb, he finally decided to ask someone. He went to the school office, where the secretary looked at him with kind eyes and a questioning smile.

"Um, where's Seb?" he asked.

"Seb?"

"Sebastian Gallagher, he was in my year."

The woman typed a few keys on an ancient-looking computer. "He doesn't seem to be enrolled, dear; are you sure you have the right name?"

He felt a sharp panic start to grip his chest. Had something happened to Seb? He would have been told, wouldn't he?

"Who are you looking for?" a female asked behind him. He turned to see his English teacher with a mug in her hand.

"Sebastian Gallagher, Carol," the secretary answered for him.

"Seb Gallagher? He moved, didn't he? His mother was having trouble with that store of hers. I think she sold it and was going to work in a partnership with a friend or something in another city. Didn't you know?"

Brendan shook his head dumbly. "Thank—thank you," he managed to stutter out, stumbling away.

❋ ❋ ❋

Seb was gone? Seb had just gone, without even telling him? He felt his eyes beginning to burn and rubbed them angrily. He found an empty classroom and slumped into a chair. Seb hadn't even wanted to talk to him again. Not even to say he was leaving. They'd probably never even see each other again. He choked back a sob, the misery welling up inside him. How would he survive the next few years without him? He dug into the pocket of his baggy jeans, retrieving a slightly smushed candy bar from the depths. He sat, holding it in his hands, staring at it like it was some rare artifact—or an object of loathing. Tears continued to run silently down his face, falling on the bright plastic packaging.

SEB surveyed the room with disinterest, trying to hold onto the flimsy food-covered plate and his barely-touched glass of wine, attempting to work out how to eat from one without spilling the other. Hadn't someone solved this age-old predicament? Weren't there little clips to use for the glass, or something? At least others around him were having the same problem, and it was amusing to watch them. You could always tell who the models were at these things; they were the ones that never ate, only drank. Probably enough so they didn't have to work so hard to barf later. Seb hated these kinds of functions, but a friend from college who had helped him get to where he was now, editor of an "alternative" but high-profile magazine, had invited him, so he felt obligated to attend. He'd said his hellos; he'd figured he could spend an hour or so wandering around and taking advantage of the free food and drink, then get the hell out of there.

The collar of his shirt was making his neck itch, and he didn't have a hand free to scratch it. Wearing a tux was annoying, but at least he looked damn good in it. He'd grown a few inches taller and filled out since high school, discovering in college that running helped him think. He had made it a regular part of his morning routine ever since. His hair was a little longer at the back, and his face had matured, holding a serious, experienced air that came from the working world and being given the power to tell a large group of people what to do on a daily basis. He could still give cold, unwavering stares with the best of them. In fact, he was sure he'd improved on that skill since high school, and he found it came in useful more often than not.

His eyes fell on the group holding court practically in the center of the room. They all seemed to be focused on one man who stood taller than all of them. Seb licked his lips. The man's back was to him, but what a back it was. Atlas-like shoulders, a thick waist, and legs like small tree trunks. The perfect-fitting tux jacket hid his butt, but Seb was willing to bet it was firm as a rock. And speaking of being firm as a rock, Seb's dick was steadily heading in that direction. He swallowed his drool before any of it could trickle out. He'd split up with his last boyfriend months ago and hadn't been getting any since. "Atlas" obviously played some kind of sport—and perhaps raided small coastal villages in a longboat in his spare time. He had a woman clinging to his arm like a tree to the side of a cliff. Seb vaguely recognized her when she turned to snag another flute of champagne. She was some model or singer, or possibly one of those women who seemed to be famous for no apparent reason whatever apart from sleeping with someone or having a rich daddy or something.

She wore a long dress of silver that sparkled and shimmered in the light and looked as though there was barely anything beneath it. It hung from her thin shoulders as if on a coat-hanger. If Atlas's legs were tree trunks, hers were more like toothpicks. Her arm, linked to one of Atlas's, looked like a string against a rope. He fought the urge to grimace. And men found this attractive? This sallow, near-skeletal look? Obviously, if they had sex, she'd have to ride him, as any other way he'd probably break her in half or something. Seb fought the urge to grimace again. Het sex. Bleugh.

Atlas finally turned around as Seb was mentally denigrating his choice of bed partner. Seb took a good look at his face—and nearly dropped his plate and glass. No, it couldn't be. He must be mistaken. But the more he looked, the more certain he was. Brendan Wallis. Bree. His first real friend, his first crush, the boy—now a man—he hadn't seen in nearly twenty years.

He was barely recognizable. His face was much leaner; he had visible cheekbones now, and his body—damn, his body looked just as good from the front as the back. He was tanned and muscular, his hair still short but blonder than Seb remembered. But no, there was that smile. And from what Seb could tell from across the room, his eyes hadn't changed a bit. He had heard of the headline-making quarterback, of course, but he would never have equated Brendan "Brick Wall" Wallis with his Bree. The man had certainly outgrown his high school nickname of "Mallow Man" and was living up to his current one. Well, good for him. He'd finally gotten what he wanted: good looks and a place in the "in-crowd" with a gorgeous girl on his arm. Seb turned and walked away, making sure Brendan couldn't see him and that nobody would notice him or what he was doing. How could he face Bree now? Especially when he looked like that? He was obviously successful and happy; the last thing he needed was a reminder of his loser friend from high school who had ditched him like a coward. Bree had probably forgotten all about him, anyway, and Seb wouldn't blame him. God, he needed a cigarette.

He leaned against the shadowed wall of the balcony, the night air cooling his skin, blowing smoke from the last of his cigarette up to the not-quite-full moon. He'd taken his time, in no hurry to go back inside. He still wasn't. He crushed the remains of his cancer stick under the toe of his shoe and debated having another. It was cool and peaceful where he was, the sounds of the party muted, and so far nobody else had come out to disturb him. He retrieved his cigarette packet from his pocket again and fished out another. He placed it between his lips and thumbed the wheel of the lighter, raising sparks but no flame. He tried again and again with the same result. He shook it, kept trying, only getting more and more irritated.

"Come on you stupid, cheap piece of shit," he muttered around the cigarette still held in his mouth.

As if by magic, a flame appeared before him. He realized it was coming from a silver lighter being held in a large, masculine hand. He followed the arm attached to the hand upwards, straight to the face of the very person he'd been trying to avoid. Feeling uncomfortable, he leaned toward the light, letting the tip of his cigarette catch and inhaling.

"Thanks, Bree," he mumbled, and froze, cursing himself. Maybe the other man hadn't noticed? Hadn't recognized him? It was a feeble hope. Bree had never been stupid, even if he was a footballer now.

He heard Bree exhale slowly as he leaned against the wall of the building. "Only one person in my life ever called me that," he said, sounding thoughtful. "This guy I knew in high school. He was my best friend, but he moved away without even saying goodbye."

Seb looked at the ground, out into the darkness beyond the railing—anywhere but at the man beside him. He hunched his shoulders, an automatic, defensive gesture, as he sucked again on the thin stick of tobacco and paper between his fingers. He cleared his throat. So that was how Bree wanted to play it? "Maybe he was—scared. Maybe… maybe he'd done something and figured you didn't want to talk to him. That it would be better to just leave."

"Huh. Well, that was a pretty stupid assumption of him to make," Bree said flatly.

Seb exhaled smoke again. "Yeah. But when you're kid, you do and say a lot of stupid things."

Bree chuckled. "True. Is that what happened, Seb?"

The soft, tentative tone only made him feel worse. "I wanted to call you again…. Didn't know what to say. And then mom's business was folding; she talked about moving…. I finally tried phoning and went to your house, but no one was there. I thought about leaving a note, but I didn't know when you'd be back or what our new address and number would be or even if you'd want to speak to me again. I should have done more, I know. I really regretted that, losing contact with you."

"Yeah, me too," Bree said after a while. "Though I have to thank you, really. It was that talking-to you gave me that I kept thinking about after I found out you'd gone. It was what got me off my lazy butt and really gave me the drive to start getting serious about losing the pounds."

"Really?" Seb asked, not quite believing it.

"Really. I was so angry with you—and myself. I'd had enough. Started exercising my ass off. I joined the football team, and by senior year, I was a star quarterback with scholarship offers."

"Wow. That's really great, Bree. I saw your date in there tonight, Mr. 'I'll Never Get A Girlfriend'."

"Yeah…."

Seb noticed the hint of something in his friend's voice. For someone with so much going for him, he didn't exactly sound enthusiastic about it. "Something wrong?"

"No! I—I don't know." He chuckled ruefully. "You know the old saying about how some people can never be happy with what they've got." Seb was silent, letting him talk in his own time. "I love playing football and being in the shape I am now. I think of how I used to be, all that junk I ate, and I feel sick. But now, I have people all around me, I'm dating a top model, and all I'm thinking is, 'Is it me they like? Or is it the fact that I'm a footballer? That I'm good-looking? Do they know the real me? Would they like me so much if they did?' I just don't know what to believe."

Seb looked at him a moment. "Pffft. You say some stupid shit. Looks can only get you so far. Why wouldn't people like the 'real' you? As long as that's what you show them and not some stupid façade." His eyes fell back to the railing. "I know I did," he muttered, almost to himself.

He took a deep breath. "Back in high school, I didn't want anyone getting too close in case they figured out I was gay and told the whole school. I knew my life would be a nightmare then. I still wanted someone to talk to, though, to hang out with, but a girl was out of the question 'cause people would think we were dating and, to be honest, girls made me nervous. I figured if I made friends with a good-looking guy there was a chance I might be attracted to him, and he'd either blow me off or tell everyone and I'd be screwed. So I chose you. I figured you'd be 'safe'. We could be friends without me worrying about falling for you and making it weird between us. The stupid thing was, I found myself becoming attracted to you anyway, despite how you looked. Spending time with you was just—really great. It started to get so that I couldn't wait to see you every day, and when I realized I—I freaked. I tried to stay away from you, but that hurt even more. Seeing you look so miserable because of me… I couldn't take it anymore. And then I went and completely blew it all by kissing you."

"You didn't blow it," Bree said, so softly that Seb barely heard him. "That kiss—it's still the most memorable one I've ever had. And I've kissed my fair share of people since then, believe me." He smiled wryly. "Even when I was dating someone, I'd keep thinking about you. I'd wonder what you were doing, if you ever thought about me. I wanted to see you again, to show you that I'd done it, I'd gotten fit just like you'd said I could if I tried."

Seb couldn't drag his cigarette out any longer and dropped it to the ground. Brendan was suddenly much closer, practically looming over him as Seb bumped into the wall at his back. He wanted to run his hands along those massive shoulders and muscular arms, to feel them wrapped around him and be held against that broad, warm chest.

"What about your girlfriend?" he managed to ask, the tiny voice of his conscience managing to be heard over the much louder one of his libido.

Brendan frowned, shaking his head. "I came out here to get away from her; that should tell you something. You'll notice I don't smoke. I only carry the lighter because she does; seems I have a thing for smokers." He smiled, his tone lightening for a moment. "She's one of the people I'm pretty certain is with me for appearance's sake, and I don't want people like that around me. Especially not a lover. When you kissed me, I realized why I wanted to spend so much time with you too. Why it hurt so much when you weren't talking to me. I have regrets too—that I wasn't brave enough to contact you again, even to return the kiss you'd given me. Though I'd like to do that now, if it's not too late."

Seb smiled as Bree grinned down at him. He'd had a crush on the boy Brendan had been; perhaps now he could finally have a chance to fall in love with the man he'd become. He reached up, the lips against his strong, confident, and enticing. This kiss was miles better than their first, and he planned to make sure it lasted longer too. Bree's arms stroked his back and held him close, as though he'd never let go. All those years ago, he'd been worried that admitting his feelings to Bree meant things between them would never be the same. And he'd been right. Now, at long last, they would be better.

S. BLAISE has loved reading and creating stories for as long as she can remember, but first got into the "male romance" genre through fan fiction. She found slash and yaoi quite by accident (honest!) and began voraciously reading stories online in many fandoms, finally getting up the courage to have a go at writing some fanfics herself before shifting to original fiction. She has lived on both sides of the Atlantic and so can write about Caribbean summers as easily as Scottish winters, since she has experienced both.

She loves sci-fi/fantasy, murder mysteries, comic books, anime and yaoi manga, which she spends far too much money on while still having so much more to get. She's a creature of nocturnal habits but really wishes story ideas would stop jumping around in her mind at three in the morning when she is finally trying to sleep.

Visit her blog at http://sblaise-08.livejournal.com.

Equinox

M. Jules Aedin & Anna J. Linden

Matthew watched the country roll by outside the car window and sighed. The view of the craggy coastal landscape was beautiful; each gap in the rows of towering redwoods afforded a glimpse of the glittering Pacific Ocean to his right, and the rich, earthy scent of the trees drifted into the car to heighten the experience.

At that moment, he hated it all. It wasn't home.

You're wrong, Matthew, my boy. This is the only home you've got now.

He made a cursory attempt to shove those fatalistic thoughts from his mind, but they'd taken root there months before, and it would take more determination than he could currently muster to kill them like the poisonous weeds he knew they were. The pain was still too raw.

This week was spring break of Matthew's sophomore year in college. Most people went home to their families over spring break or hung out at the beach with their friends or went on vacations to Mexico. Matthew couldn't do any of that. He couldn't afford a trip, and when he'd gone home over the winter holidays, it had been… less than pleasant.

Scratch that. It had been a total fucking disaster. But then, he suspected nothing nice ever happened when two very conservative parents found out that their only son was gay.

It wasn't that he'd expected them to be calm in the face of his confession, to accept him with open arms and assurances of love and approval

• • •

no matter what and all that sentimental stuff. He'd even been ready for it when his mother had started to cry. He *hadn't* expected them to throw him out of the house and tell him not to come back until he could "change his ways".

But that was what had happened, and he hadn't been back since. He hadn't heard from them, either, and the monthly transfers of spending money into his bank account had stopped. Fortunately, he had a full scholarship, and he'd managed to get a part-time job to pay for food and supplies. As long as he hadn't let himself wallow in dark thoughts and self-pity, he'd been okay.

And then he'd found out that his dorm would be closed over spring break. Since most of the students were gone that week anyway, his small liberal arts university was trying to cut back on expenses. One minute, Matthew had been looking forward to having his dorm room to himself for an entire week of peace, privacy, and relaxation. The next, he'd found himself facing the prospect of being homeless for nine days straight.

Thank all that was good in the universe for Samantha, his friend from the school's Gay-Straight Alliance club. When he'd told her about his dilemma, she'd offered to let him tag along to her family's home in the heart of the California redwoods. She'd assured him that her parents were very open and accepting people. She talked about her older brother and how his being gay had never been a real problem for him all the time at club meetings. His family loved him, if the pride and adoration his sister showed when she talked about him were any indication. He'd never been kicked out on the street with his father's screams echoing in his ears.

"What are you thinking about so hard over there? There are, like, trenches in your forehead."

Samantha's voice snapped Matthew out of his brooding. He tried to force his facial features into a semblance of unconcern, but he could tell it wasn't very convincing. "Just, you know, taking in the view. That's why you took this route, isn't it?"

"Then you must *hate* the view, if that was your reaction to it. You got something against trees, wine country boy?"

That made Matthew grin for real. Sam constantly teased him about the fact that he came from Napa, or "the land of the drunken yuppies", as Sam liked to call it.

"We have *some* trees in Napa." Sam raised a skeptical eyebrow. "Okay, so these ones make ours look like bushes." He tilted his head to look up, and up, and up at the towering redwoods that crowded the highway. He'd have had to stick his head out the window to see the tops of the nearest ones. It was dark and green under the canopy of the forest. Tendrils of mist coiled around the huge trunks. He couldn't decide if it was creepy or enchantingly beautiful.

He looked back at the winding road before he could get carsick. "Are you sure your parents'll be cool with me just showing up like this?"

"Yeah, definitely, they won't mind at all." Sam must have seen Matthew's hands twisting together in his lap, because her tone grew concerned again. "Hey, don't worry, okay? They'll all love you; take my word for it. Probably even more than they like me."

Matthew laughed and settled back in his seat, still unable to shake off all of his nerves. He didn't want to make Sam feel like she had to spend her entire spring break keeping him company, but he had no idea how he was going to occupy himself for a whole week in an unfamiliar place.

IT TURNED out he really needn't have worried about Sam's parents. As soon as he stepped inside the family's gorgeous cabin in the woods, Dennis shook his hand and greeted him warmly, and Judy pulled him into a tight hug before asking what he wanted for dinner. He relaxed enough to make the Herculean effort it took to ignore his remaining anxiety and enjoy himself.

An hour later, he was carrying a huge bowl of salad to the dining room table and laughing at Sam's crack about keeping him on as a servant boy when the front door opened. Only then did he remember Sam telling him that her brother would be over for dinner.

"Hey guys, the fun's here, party can start!"

Matthew had a few seconds in which to fight down an urge to run to the bathroom and puke from sheer nerves at the prospect of meeting the fabled brother. He'd never had any siblings of his own, but he thought most little sisters didn't hold their brothers in such high esteem.

Then the owner of that laughing voice came into the dining room, and Matthew froze, all fight-or-flight instincts forgotten in an instant.

Sam's brother was *hot*. He was about as short as Matthew's 5'9", but a tight T-shirt and khaki shorts revealed muscles more toned than Matthew's. A shock of blond hair fell across deep brown eyes that looked into Matthew's from across the room and crinkled a little at the corners as he smiled.

"Never mind—looks like the fun is already here." The guy walked across the room and stuck out his hand. "Hi, I'm Aaron. You must be Sam's friend from school."

The fact that Matthew's brain had apparently turned into useless mush was making it difficult to form coherent sentences, and he had a horrible feeling that his mouth had been hanging open. He shook Aaron's hand, then somehow found his voice. "Matthew. From the Gay-Straight Alliance club."

Aaron grinned in a way that lit up his entire face.

Sam came back into the dining room with a bread basket. "Oh, cool, you guys have met. Matthew, don't believe a word he says about me. I could never live up to the hype."

"Ah, what a cute little rebel my baby sister is." Aaron went over and slung an arm around her shoulders, kissing the top of her head. She poked him in the ribs in retaliation, then threw her arms around his waist and hugged him hard.

Matthew knew he'd been feeling tense about this trip, but he hadn't realized just *how* tense until he started to relax during dinner. Sam's family was so warm that it was impossible to stay shy around them, let alone nervous. And he had to admit, it was kind of nice to be spending his break with someone, even if that empty dorm had seemed so appealing.

"So, Matthew, how old are you?" Dennis asked during Matthew's second helping of lasagna.

"Nineteen. Actually, I'll be twenty soon."

"Ah, the big two-oh! So that would make you, what, a sophomore?" Matthew nodded. "Any idea which major you'll go for?"

"Be careful, Matthew," Sam chimed in. "Just make something up, or he'll pester you about going into anthropology until you bleed from the ears."

Matthew laughed. "That's okay; I like social sciences. I like studying people, figuring out what makes them the way they are."

"Aaron's always been like that too," Judy put in, scooping more lasagna onto Matthew's plate. "Did you know that he works with children? He does puppet shows at all the local schools, sometimes for troubled youth programs. All the kids just love him."

"Aw, Mom." Aaron grinned, looking uncharacteristically shy.

"What? You do wonderful things for those kids, Aaron; I'm allowed to brag."

"Well, they do most of it themselves. I just give them a little push."

Sam bumped him with her elbow, making a bite of lasagna fall off his fork. "Jeez, get some humility, why don't you." She shrieked as Aaron started tickling her.

Judy's plea of "Children, will you try to behave when we have a *guest?*" was drowned out when Matthew joined the attack by tickling Sam's other side. He might or might not have been doing it so his fingers would brush Aaron's.

After they calmed down, Sam said, "So, Aaron, the gang and I were going to take Matthew down to the river tomorrow and have a bonfire. You should come."

"You sure your big bro won't be crashing the party?" Aaron teased.

"No, you dork, you should definitely come." She raised her eyebrows significantly. If Matthew hadn't looked up at the tone in her voice, he wouldn't have seen it.

Aaron raised his own eyebrows. "Right, sounds like fun. I'll definitely be there."

Matthew suddenly found himself looking forward to the next day like he hadn't in a long time.

CROSSING his arms tightly over his chest in an attempt to preserve body heat, Matthew watched in awe as Aaron unhesitatingly stripped off his shirt and dove into the river, a pair of swim trunks his only protection from the cold. After a worryingly long time, he resurfaced in the middle of the calm stretch of water and crowed, shaking his head back and forth like a dog. The water droplets made his blond hair shimmer in the sunlight.

"What the hell, you lived through that?" Matthew called, laughing, his voice echoing off the water. "How are you still moving?"

"I'm of hardy mountain stock, city boy. A little water can't defeat me!"

Matthew chuckled and walked out onto a rock that jutted into the flow of the river. He squatted down to stick a hand under the clear water and shivered.

"Holy crap, I'm not even going to defend my honor. If I went in there, I'd get hypothermia."

Aaron swam over, looking so comfortable that he might as well have been in a heated swimming pool, and perched his crossed arms on the rock at Matthew's sandaled feet.

"Don't do it," Matthew warned, grinning.

"Don't do what?" Aaron's wide-eyed expression of innocence was so patently feigned that Matthew laughed, and Aaron took advantage of the moment to cup a handful of water and splash it onto Matthew's foot.

Matthew yelped and scrambled back a bit from the edge, sandals squeaking on the slick granite.

Aaron cackled. He seemed content to tread water there, arms still crossed on top of the rock. "Come here for a second."

"No way, man. You had your chance."

"Crap, that was my only one?" Aaron pulled his lips down in a ridiculous pout and batted his eyelashes.

Matthew snorted. "Your Jedi mind tricks won't work on me."

"Guess I'll just have to use my natural wiles, then." Aaron dropped the pout. "I promise I won't do anything. You've just got something on your face."

Matthew could have argued that he could clean his own face, but he wasn't completely stupid. He carefully approached the edge of the rock again, bending down to kneel at Aaron's level. Aaron might talk big, but there were goosebumps on his arms that made the golden hair there stand up a little.

Matthew was so intent on controlling his impulse to reach out and run a hand over that soft-looking down that he was caught almost unaware when Aaron's hand smoothed over his cheek, sweeping his floppy brown bangs aside in the process and leaving a wet streak on his skin.

"There, got it."

Matthew tried to keep his eyes from crossing in sheer pleasure. Aaron's hand was soft but callused, strong and reassuring in some indescribable way that made Matthew feel warm to his toes despite the ice water that had just drenched them.

If Aaron noticed any sign of Matthew's inner struggle to keep from melting into a puddle of goo right there on the rock, he didn't show it. He pulled another smile from his seemingly endless arsenal and said, "You have the greenest eyes I've ever seen."

Matthew couldn't think of anything to say for a second, and by the time his brain finally started working again, Aaron had left the rock to go persuade Sam's boyfriend, Ryan, to get in the water.

Clearly, Matthew was hallucinating, because it seemed like Aaron was actually *flirting* with him.

Well, even if he was, it was probably just in a casual, innocent way. Just humoring his sister's friend.

They lit the bonfire at twilight, everyone putting on jackets and getting blankets out of their cars. Sam insisted on spraying everyone with bug repellant, recounting horror stories about the mosquito hordes that hung out around the river. She'd also brought the ingredients for s'mores, so they roasted marshmallows. Aaron ate his straight off the metal skewer, not bothering with chocolate or graham crackers. Matthew couldn't help but watch as the man licked excess white stuff from sticky fingers, and the sudden and vivid fantasies that sight brought to mind were so embarrassing that he blushed profusely. He hoped it was dark enough that nobody noticed.

When the marshmallows were gone, Aaron went to Sam's car and grabbed a blanket.

"The hardy mountain man is finally cold, huh?" Matthew teased.

"I think the hardy mountain man's nipples are about to freeze off." Aaron grinned and threw the blanket around both of their shoulders, scooting so close to Matthew that their legs pressed against each other from hip to ankle. He shrugged at Matthew's questioning look. "It was the last one. You looked cold."

Matthew looked down at his lap. "Thanks."

One of Sam's friends started playing a slow song on an acoustic guitar. Everyone listened, chatting occasionally but under no pressure to make conversation. It was probably the most peaceful Matthew had felt since the day after Christmas.

He was staring into the flames, watching a log turn blue with heat, when he felt Aaron's hand on his thigh under the blanket. It didn't move, just rested there. Aaron didn't give any indication of what he was doing except to glance at Matthew and smile. After a few seconds, Matthew smiled back. He didn't emerge from his dreamy haze until he fell asleep hours later back at Sam's parents' house.

THE next day, Aaron came over to hang out and play video games with Matthew, Sam, and her boyfriend. Sam claimed it was because she missed her brother, but Matthew was finally beginning to suspect her of ulterior motives. The more time he spent with Aaron, though, the more he wanted to thank her for her scheming.

Aaron was less flirty than he'd been at the river, but any illusions Matthew might have had that the man was just really friendly and tactile had been thoroughly dispelled as soon as he'd felt the hand on his thigh the night before. He'd be the first to admit that he didn't have much experience dating men, but he suspected that even gay guys who were just friendly didn't touch each other like that.

That night, they went to a pizza place that ran a Sunday night all-you-can-eat special. Servers walked around offering different kinds of pizza by the slice. The place was packed with locals and tourists, all laughing and shouting over the sounds of arcade machines and the baseball game on TV. Near closing time, a server brought a tray with the last two pieces of a huge cinnamon roll. Sam and Ryan took one, and Aaron and Matthew shared the other. Matthew caught Aaron watching him intently as he licked icing off his fingers.

This was turning out to be the best spring break he'd ever had.

THEN Monday came along, breaking up the fun in the way that only a Monday could. Dennis and Judy were at work, Aaron had a job lined up for the day, and Sam had plans to go to an all-day music festival with Ryan. They'd had the tickets for months and weren't able to get another one for Matthew. Sam apologized profusely, but Matthew insisted that it was no problem and practically shoved them out the door. Then he turned around and was confronted with the empty house. He had no transportation, even if he'd known where to go. He sighed and settled on the couch to flip through TV channels and try not to feel sorry for himself.

Just when he was contemplating making himself a sandwich for lunch, Aaron came breezing in the door, holding what looked like a fancy waffle iron. He rushed through the living room into the kitchen, not looking at the couch. "Hey guys, just dropping off my grill. Mom's doing paninis tonight." Coming back through, he noticed Matthew and skidded to a stop. "Oh, hey, you're all alone. Where'd everyone go?"

"Sam and Ryan went to that concert. It's just me, myself, and I." Matthew made a half-hearted attempt to smile, but today, even Aaron's unexpected appearance couldn't cheer him up completely.

Of course, Aaron wasn't fooled. "Well, I know from experience that you're great company. So what's got you looking like you want to eat thistles?"

Eat thistles? That was a new one. And really cute, for some reason that Matthew couldn't pinpoint.

It distracted him enough that he forgot to make up some bland lie. "It's nothing, just…." He sighed. "It's my birthday today."

"Oh." Aaron flopped down on the other end of the couch. "Man, when you said it was soon at dinner, you meant *really* soon. You should have told us; we'd have done something for you."

"That's why I didn't say anything. I didn't want anyone to go to the trouble."

"It wouldn't have been any trouble," Aaron said quietly.

Matthew picked at a cuticle on his left hand. "I just didn't want to make it seem like I expected something. I already kind of feel like a burden." Realizing how that might sound, he hurried on. "I mean, don't get me wrong, your parents are great, you're all—" he looked up suddenly to find Aaron's brown eyes watching him intently—"great." The corner of Aaron's mouth turned up, and Matthew's breath quickened a bit. "It's just that you've all given me so much by letting me stay here. I don't need anything else."

Aaron smiled and reached out to ruffle Matthew's hair—not in an annoying, big-brother way, just sort of running his fingers through the strands. Matthew resisted the urge to let his eyes flutter closed.

"Has anybody ever told you that you're really cute?"

"Uh…." Matthew swallowed convulsively. "Your sister's been known to say that."

Aaron smirked. "Well, great minds think alike."

Matthew snorted, most of his melancholy magically gone, replaced with a butterflies-in-the-stomach kind of exhilaration. No day could be all bad if it included Aaron flirting with him.

"Hey, I've got an idea, if you want to get out of the house for awhile. It's not exactly a birthday party, but it might be fun."

Matthew looked up, unable to keep the enthusiasm off his face. "Yeah?"

"Don't look so happy until you hear what it is."

"Dude, anything to get me out of the house. I'll be your slave for a day if that's what it takes."

Aaron's eyes sparkled in a way that Matthew couldn't figure out. It was probably just a default state for him. "That's not far off the mark, actually. Feel like schlepping things around for my puppet show? We can make you my personal assistant. You can hand me stuff and make sure nothing falls over. It's kind of hard to do it all by myself sometimes."

A chance to see the job that Aaron was so passionate about? Matthew didn't even have to think about saying yes.

HE ALMOST missed his cue to hand over the elephant puppet, absorbed as he was in the little story Aaron was enacting with the flamingoes and the stork. The large paper screen was set up at the front of the classroom, illuminated from behind by several white lights. Aaron was crouched on the floor below it, his body hidden by a black drape. The puppets were made of black cardboard and held by thin sticks, and the way that Aaron moved certain parts of their bodies independently of each other made their silhouettes amazingly lifelike.

Matthew was completely enchanted. For one thing, he'd never known that shadow puppets could involve so much more than making a dog's head on the wall with your hand and a flashlight. For another, Aaron was amazing with the class of second-graders sitting in a semi-circle around his makeshift "stage". He somehow managed to retain their rapt attention, dispel the occasional brewing disruption, and tell an entertaining story without ever missing a beat.

Matthew felt like one of the kids as Mr. Stork learned that it was okay to be different from all the pink-feathered flamingoes. He laughed when they laughed and was touched by the sweet, simple message.

When the show was over, the kids filed out of the classroom for lunch and Matthew helped Aaron pack up.

"Whew." Aaron mimed wiping his brow as he straightened up from the last case of light stands. "Thanks so much, you were a huge help."

"No problem, it was fun." Matthew hefted the puppet box into his arms and followed Aaron out to the parking lot. "Your show is awesome! I've never seen anything like it."

"Cool, I'm glad you liked it. I hadn't seen anything like it until college, myself. My philosophy professor used to do it in Europe. Puppets are popular over there." Aaron unlocked his Corolla and starting fitting things into the trunk. When he bent over, his pants pulled tight across his ass, and Matthew had to fight to keep his mind on the conversation.

"I think you're making them popular here too. The kids loved them." He could feel the heat creeping into his cheeks. "You're great with them."

"Thanks. I really appreciate that." Aaron flashed that thousand-watt grin of his, and Matthew ducked into the passenger side of the car before his knees could give out. Aaron got behind the wheel. "So, the day is young; you wanna go do something?"

"Are flamingoes pink?"

Aaron laughed as he pulled out of the parking lot.

AARON drove down a twisty road through an area of incredibly dense forest. They emerged into a clearing where a long street bordered by small businesses sat like a tourist trap version of the fairy city in the middle of the

* * *

woods. They parked at one end and walked, poking around in all the kitschy little shops selling cheesy handicrafts and every object that could possibly be made out of redwood or cedar.

One store offered several racks of jewelry made with different gemstones. Matthew was idly spinning the racks when Aaron's arms encircled his neck from behind and fastened a necklace on him. He looked in the little mirror on the side of the rack and saw a thin black cord holding a simple green stone, probably jade, understated and elegant.

Aaron stared at him for a second and actually licked his lips. Matthew couldn't tell if it was unconscious or if Aaron knew exactly what he was doing, but it made him want to follow the path of Aaron's tongue with his own.

"I thought so. That looks great with your eyes."

Matthew couldn't bite his cheek in time to keep himself from grinning like a lunatic.

Aaron watched Matthew's reaction in the mirror. "Do you like it?"

"Yeah, it's cool." And so was the way Aaron looked at him while he wore it.

Aaron insisted on buying the necklace for him "for his birthday", and Matthew was beginning to wonder if his face would be stuck in a permanent smile. His cheek muscles were starting to ache, but he couldn't bring himself to care.

They bought ice cream cones from a bustling café and carried them to the head of a walking trail that led off into the trees.

"This is one of my favorite places in the world." Aaron led the way onto the narrow path, talking over his shoulder until there was room for them to walk side by side. "I used to come here as a kid and pretend it was another world. All I needed was the trees."

"That sounds like you. The kind of kid who could occupy himself for hours with just his imagination."

Aaron chuckled. "Yeah, that was me. Still is me, really. I wander around here by myself whenever I need peace and quiet."

And that was when it hit Matthew: this was Aaron's *place*, his personal sanctuary. Matthew had had one in Napa, an apple orchard down the road from his parents' house. He didn't know what to think of the fact that Aaron was sharing this with him. Maybe it wasn't such a big deal to Aaron. Maybe he brought people here all the time. Matthew didn't want to hope that it might mean something more than a friendly gesture, but he couldn't help it.

The forest was gorgeous, perfumed with the scents of redwood and damp earth, dimly lit without being dark. Beams of sunlight made their way past the overhead branches in small patches, and sparkling motes drifted through them like fairy dust. The path cut a ravine through the huge ferns blanketing the ground. With the trees muffling all outside noise and enclosing everything in a surreal kind of stillness, it *was* like some other world.

They climbed over a huge log that had fallen across the trail at some point, the wood slowly becoming one with the ground.

"Watch out for the soft parts; they can break under you," Aaron called up to Matthew, who had gone first and was perched three feet above Aaron's head.

Matthew could see that it would be difficult to climb down the other side with the remnants of his ice cream cone in one hand, so he ate it hurriedly, cramming the last of it into his mouth and maneuvering to a spot where he could jump to the ground.

Aaron scrambled over after him. There was a brown leaf sticking out of his bright blond hair. Matthew reached up to pluck it out before he could think better of it, his fingers brushing silky strands. He twirled the leaf between his thumb and forefinger, watching it instead of Aaron, which was why the sensation of Aaron's thumb rubbing across his chin startled him.

Aaron raised his thumb to his own mouth and, before Matthew could process what was going on, sucked the tip of it between his lips. It came back out with a soft sound.

"You had some ice cream on your face." His voice was low, oddly serious.

Matthew actually gulped. Loudly. "Uh, thanks."

He started to turn away, walk down the path, grab desperately at the shreds of his control, but Aaron gently cupped the side of his face with one hand.

"Oops, don't think I got it all." And he bent his head and *licked* the corner of Matthew's mouth.

Matthew froze in shock and stayed that way until Aaron bent his head again and brushed his lips over Matthew's in an incredibly soft kiss.

"Is this okay?" Aaron asked quietly, looking into Matthew's eyes and rubbing his thumb back and forth over Matthew's cheek.

Matthew breathed an incredulous laugh. "Are you kidding me?"

Aaron's grin was stunning. Matthew leaned in to taste it, and Aaron obliged. It was probably cliché, but when Aaron's mouth opened beneath his, he could swear it tasted like sunshine and double fudge brownie. Aaron was gentle—not careful, not going easy, just sweet and slow. They kissed for so long that Matthew eventually had to pull away for a breather. Only then did he realize that his hands had slid up to tangle in Aaron's hair.

Aaron closed his eyes and exhaled a shaky breath. "I've wanted to do that since Saturday."

"What stopped you?" Matthew watched Aaron's face as his eyes snapped open in what looked like surprise.

"You know, I don't really know."

"Oh, good. Then I'll assume it won't happen again."

Aaron chuckled. "I'd say that's a safe assumption." He leaned in for another kiss.

They strolled along the rest of the path holding hands, laughing at practically nothing and detouring into shaded spots to make out. Matthew's T-shirt was eventually covered in dirt and moss streaks from the frequency with which he was pinned to huge tree trunks, and Aaron's hair was mussed because Matthew could not stop running his hands through it.

Somewhere between watching a banana slug ooze along a fallen log and spending five minutes exploring Aaron's neck with his tongue, Matthew was struck by a revelation.

"You! Winnie the Pooh!" He threw back his head and cackled.

Aaron huffed out a bewildered laugh. "Matthew, Tigger. This isn't some kind of weird role-playing thing, is it?"

Matthew wiped tears from his eyes. "No, no, I just figured it out. When you found me on the couch, you said 'eat thistles'. You meant like Eeyore!"

Aaron actually went a little pink, which was a new and interesting look for him. It was so cute that Matthew wanted to kiss him, so he did, and man, that was a great feeling.

Aaron still looked a little embarrassed when they broke the kiss, but he was grinning hugely. "I work with little kids all day; what do you expect?" He stepped in even closer and looped both of his arms around Matthew's waist, pulling their bodies together.

Someone could have come walking down the path at any second, but Matthew felt utterly safe. He leaned his forehead against Aaron's and took a deep breath, reaching up to tug gently on the strings of Aaron's sweatshirt hood. He wondered if his face looked as flushed as it felt but realized that he didn't care. Let Aaron see the effect he was having on Matthew, that head-rush-swoopy-stomach sensation. Matthew let out his breath slowly, feeling like he would float away if he didn't. He slid his arms up around Aaron's neck and hung on tight.

MATTHEW returned to Sam's parents' place on Monday night still punch-drunk. When he woke up on Tuesday, he half-suspected the previous day of being one giant hallucination born of boredom and self-pity.

But then Aaron came over for dinner again after a full schedule of puppet shows. He sat next to Matthew during the meal and occasionally put his hand on Matthew's thigh under the table. This made it extremely difficult to concentrate on the conversation, but Matthew figured that as long as the family couldn't actually see the impromptu fantasy marathon going on in his head, he was doing okay.

Aaron gave him a covert goodnight kiss in the foyer, and Matthew desperately wanted to follow him home for more. Really, he could think of no good reason not to, but in the end, his nerves fused his feet to the porch and he watched Aaron drive away, feeling a bit like a pathetic, abandoned puppy. He needed more time; that was all.

Except that he didn't *have* time. He was leaving in a few days.

He lay awake for hours that night.

On Wednesday, it rained, and Aaron didn't have any jobs lined up, so they decided to hang out at his place to play video games and watch movies and make out. When they walked in the door, a small white missile propelled itself off the couch and tangled itself in Aaron's legs before Matthew had time to figure out what the hell had happened. Aaron crouched down and started wrestling around with the missile, which turned out to be a white Labrador puppy.

"Matthew, meet Picasso. I found him at the animal shelter a month ago, and he's owned me ever since."

Matthew, dumbfounded by the cuteness and trying to be manly and indifferent about it, watched the wrestling and steadfastly passed up the chance to roll around on the floor with Aaron and a freaking puppy. "Why Picasso?"

"Because he can't hear a dang thing. Can you, boy?" Aaron scratched behind the dog's ears, and Picasso's short legs folded, sprawling him out on the carpet in delight.

Matthew was surprised into laughter. "Doesn't that make him a little hard to take care of?"

"Well, sure. But it makes life more interesting. Besides, look at this face." Aaron held Picasso's head in both hands and turned so Matthew could see. "Could you resist that?" He blinked goofy puppy eyes to match, looking ridiculous and adorable.

"The dog's or yours?" As soon as the question popped out, Matthew wished he could reel it back in. He blushed. *Smooth, real smooth.*

Aaron's eyes gleamed with something Matthew had never seen before. He wasn't sure what it was, but he definitely liked it.

"Can't resist my charms, eh?" Aaron reached up and tugged on Matthew's arm until Matthew bent over far enough to kiss him. It went on for so long that the dog whined and butted his head up under Aaron's chin.

It didn't take long for Matthew to give in to Picasso's charms too. By early afternoon, he lay on the couch with his head on Aaron's lap and the puppy curled up against his stomach. He tried to focus on the movie while Aaron stroked his hair, but it was difficult not to zone off in a state of half-conscious bliss.

Above him, Aaron chuckled at something on the screen. For some reason, it reminded Matthew of how he'd laughed at the puppets on Monday.

"Hey, you have another show on Friday, don't you? Can I come watch again?"

"Sure, that'd be great. You were a lot of help last time."

"I don't know how you manage to do all that by yourself all the time." Matthew rolled slightly so he could look up at Aaron's face, carefully shifting the puppy without waking him.

"Well, I definitely won't be able to lug all that stuff around forever. Not to mention stay on my toes all the time with those kids." His fingers threaded through Matthew's hair, and Matthew would have purred if he'd been able.

"Really? What do you think you'll do instead?" He couldn't imagine Aaron not having enough energy for whatever he wanted to do.

"I was thinking I'd take a more direct route to helping the kids, maybe go into counseling. My degree is in social work, but I don't want to have to take kids away from their parents, even if they'd be better off that way."

"You don't want to be the bad guy." Matthew reached up to put his hand over the one on his head.

"Yeah, maybe."

Matthew took his hand back and turned his head to watch the movie again. Despite the pride he felt for Aaron's desire to help people, it gave him a strange sinking feeling in the pit of his stomach. There was so much conviction and happiness in Aaron's voice when he talked about his plans for the future. Matthew sometimes couldn't summon enough conviction to decide what he wanted on his pizza.

"Looks like you've got it all figured out," Matthew said softly, not really seeing the TV screen but staring at it anyway.

"What do you mean?"

Matthew shrugged. "Well, you've got a job you love, a house. You're totally okay with who you are. I don't even know what I want to major in, let alone what I want to do with the rest of my life. My family—" He spent about two seconds fighting back the melodrama and lost. "My family doesn't even love me anymore. They kicked me out when I told them I was gay." Oh shit, he was *not* going to start crying, not here. He hadn't even cried when he'd taken a bus back to campus the day after Christmas and eaten cold Pop-Tarts for dinner because the stores were all closed and he didn't have anything else in the dorm. He sat up and crossed his arms over his chest. The puppy yawned and hopped off the couch to go do puppy things.

"Hey, don't stop there." Aaron reached out and cupped Matthew's face in his hand, stroking his cheek. "Listen, you know you can talk to me, right?"

"You don't have to do that."

"What? Why not? I want to."

Matthew rubbed his eyes with one hand, trying to look like he was tired and not wiping off tears. "I don't want to be some *case* to you, another poor little lost child. You don't have to *counsel* me."

"Matthew, look at me." Aaron put both hands on Matthew's shoulders and turned him sideways, pulling one foot up onto the couch so they could face each other. "I do *not* see you that way. You're not a child. In fact, I think you're pretty damn mature for your age. I don't usually go out with people six years younger than me. But even if you're mature, you don't have to have your entire life figured out by the time you're twenty. Hell, I'm lucky to have it figured out at *my* age, and I reserve the right to change my mind at a later date."

Matthew couldn't look Aaron in the eye, but he reached up and put one hand over Aaron's on his shoulder.

"I just want you to know that I'm here if you want to talk about it, as a friend. But only if you want to. Okay?"

Matthew nodded, feeling like a jerk. So much for being mature for his age. But he couldn't be sorry he'd said all that. He hadn't realized it until practically the moment the words were out of his mouth, but he *had* been worried, somewhere in the back of his mind, behind all the warm floatiness he'd been feeling for the past few days. Worried that he was just some pity case. Just another deaf puppy.

Aaron picked up Matthew's abandoned video game controller and held it out to him. "Now take this so I can kick your ass at *Halo* again."

Matthew finally cracked a smile. "Kick *my* ass? I didn't know you were delusional." He faked goggle-eyed disbelief, and Aaron cracked up.

Aaron did, in fact, kick his ass. Matthew threw down his controller and groaned, rubbing his strained eyes with both hands. Aaron went to the kitchen to get chips and salsa, and before he even had time to sit back down, Matthew started talking.

"My parents have always been pretty religious. Their church is really conservative, and they buy into all the usual hate propaganda stuff. I stopped believing it myself when I was about fourteen, but I never really talked to them about it. I never dated anyone in high school or even got very involved with anyone secretly."

He took a deep breath, pulling at a loose thread on the sleeve of his T-shirt. Instead of snapping off, it unraveled further. He hoped that wasn't a sign or something. "Then I went off to college, and it was just so... eye-opening. I finally felt like I could be whatever I wanted to be. I was still afraid to tell my parents anything, because I knew how they'd react. I *knew*." He sighed. Aaron sat quietly, just listening. "But I just couldn't take it anymore when I went home last Christmas. I couldn't stand that they didn't really know who I was. Anyway, long story short, they kicked me out. At least I have a full ride for school, or I'd be kinda screwed."

Aaron didn't say anything for a few seconds, but before Matthew could get twitchy, Aaron pulled him into a two-armed embrace. Matthew stiffened, then relaxed, letting his head rest on Aaron's shoulder.

Aaron kissed the top of his head gently. "You're really brave, you know that?"

Matthew snorted. "I'm not brave, I'm scared to death. I'm even scared of.... " He realized how it would sound, but he couldn't take it back when it was already halfway out. Apparently it was his day to over-share, so he might as well go for the big one. "I'm even scared of whatever's going on between us." He desperately wanted to ask what that was, exactly, but he didn't want to dig himself any deeper into the new hole he'd created.

"You're brave *because* of your fear, Matthew, not despite it. And why are you afraid of what's between us?"

"Because you're so damn sure of yourself and you're older than me and you're probably really... experienced." He was blushing yet again, but he barreled on ahead. "And I still don't know how to be comfortable being 'out' or whatever. I've never even...." Oh crap, there was the limit. He was *not* going there, not without leaving his dignity on the floor in shattered pieces.

Thankfully, Aaron didn't press the matter. He spoke quietly into Matthew's sudden silence. "You know, I have to admit, my being gay has never been much of a problem for me. I can't say that I know what you're going through, exactly, but I can imagine it. I think everyone's experience is different, anyway." He rubbed one hand slowly up and down Matthew's shoulder. "It was a little weird for me to come out to my parents, even though I knew they'd be fine with it. They knew way before I actually told them. But what I've learned so far is that new things in life are usually only scary in the beginning. I think that pretty soon, being gay will just be another fact of life for you, like having brown hair and freckles. You just have to give yourself time to adjust."

Matthew didn't know what to say. He wasn't sure he believed what Aaron was saying, but he wanted to. Being with Aaron was like suddenly seeing the world in Technicolor after a lifetime of black and white.

"As for this thing between us… well, that's a little more complicated. But don't be afraid of it. We'll deal with it as it goes along, do what comes naturally to us." He paused and pursed his lips thoughtfully. "It's kind of like my shadow puppets."

Matthew snorted. "How is it like the puppets? You're not going to demonstrate anything with them, are you? Because that would be a level of kinky I don't want to explore."

Aaron flashed a shit-eating grin. "No, I wouldn't do that. Then I'd get a little too excited in front of the kids whenever I did a show." Matthew shoved his shoulder and laughed. Aaron held up his hands in surrender. "No, it's just that relationships, like shadow puppets, take a little practice to master."

Matthew stared at him, desperately trying to keep a straight face. "You're so full of shit."

"Mm, but at least I'm cute."

"Don't get too cocky," Matthew retorted, ruining his feigned nonchalance by leaning over and kissing Aaron deeply.

The kiss grew more and more heated, and eventually Aaron grabbed Matthew by the hips and pulled him up until he was straddling Aaron's lap, one knee on the couch on either side. Matthew suddenly felt Aaron's erection through both pairs of their thin khaki shorts, and it made him break the kiss and gasp.

"See what you do to me?" Aaron rasped into Matthew's ear. "How could you think for a second that we wouldn't be good together?"

Matthew made a sound close to a whimper and mashed their mouths together again. On impulse, he shoved a hand between them and pressed down on Aaron's hard cock. It was warm under his palm. Not letting himself stop to think, he wrapped his fingers as far around it as they would go through the khaki. Aaron groaned into Matthew's mouth, grabbed Matthew's ass with both hands, and thrust his hips up, grinding their crotches together.

Matthew bucked his hips at the friction, surprising himself with his own lack of control. The leather of the couch squeaked under his calves. A strained sound escaped his throat without his consent.

They stayed that way for a long time, kissing and grinding and hanging on to each other until Matthew couldn't take it anymore. He expected Aaron to take the lead any second, but it didn't happen, and Matthew didn't want to come in his pants like the teenager he wasn't supposed to be anymore. So he dragged his mouth away from Aaron's long enough to locate the button of Aaron's shorts and flip it open. He drew down the zipper and slid his hand inside Aaron's boxers, encountering silky heat and the wetness of precome.

Aaron groaned and tipped his head back onto the couch cushions. "Holy shit, Matthew."

Matthew leaned forward and sucked the smooth skin of that exposed throat, then put his mouth by Aaron's ear.

"Aren't you going to help me out?"

Aaron's eyes flew open and locked onto Matthew's. His mouth fell open slightly. Then the surprise was replaced by a mischievous grin.

"Is that what you want?" He practically tore at Matthew's shorts and underwear to get inside them and pull out Matthew's own leaking cock, giving it a couple of good, hard strokes.

Matthew's own hand on Aaron stilled, and a strangled sound escaped his throat.

"Guess so." Aaron wrapped an arm around Matthew's hips and dragged him even closer to bring their cocks together and jack them both with one fist.

It was fast, a little messy, and kind of uncoordinated, but it was the best thing Matthew had ever felt. His knees dug into the couch cushions on either side of Aaron's waist and he wrapped both arms around Aaron's neck, just hanging on for the ride. He was about to embarrass himself by coming as fast as… well, a virgin. Since that was pretty much what he was, he couldn't bring himself to care. Not when Aaron bucked his hips up and swept his thumb across the head of Matthew's dick. Not when he leaned forward and rasped heady things in Matthew's ear.

"Oh, God, Matthew, you're so beautiful, wanted this since the first time I saw you. Come on, baby, come for me...."

And right on command, Matthew did. The force of it surprised him, slamming into him almost unexpectedly. He shuddered and clung to Aaron's shoulders, breath coming in huge gasps. Not more than a few seconds later, Aaron cried out and shot all over both their T-shirts.

Matthew stayed where he was, face buried in the crook of Aaron's neck, until he could gather enough strength to push himself up. He stared, dazed, into Aaron's half-lidded eyes.

Aaron reached up to run his clean hand through Matthew's hair, uncharacteristically silent.

Matthew dropped back down onto Aaron's chest, unable to summon the energy or the inclination to move any further. Aaron didn't seem to mind.

"You know something?"

Aaron's "Hm?" sounded sleepy.

"We're definitely not in Kansas anymore."

They both bounced up and down as Aaron laughed.

"SO, MATTHEW." Sam looked up from the eggs she was frying and spoke across the kitchen to where Matthew sat in the breakfast nook. "You and my brother."

Matthew choked on his eggs and grabbed for his glass of orange juice. When he could breathe again, he clung to any shreds of plausible deniability that might have been left to him.

"What?"

Great, Matthew. Razor-sharp response, there.

"What do you mean, 'what'? Matthew, I'm insulted that you think I'm stupid enough not to have noticed." But the grin she tried to hide as she turned back to her eggs suggested that she was far more amused than insulted.

"I don't… I mean, I'm not.… " Oh, who was he kidding? There was no hiding anything from Sam. He should have known. He dropped his head into his hands, rubbing his eyes. "Are you mad? I didn't mean to—it just kind of… happened."

She whipped around to stare at him incredulously. "What are you talking about? Why would I be mad? I think it's awesome."

"He's your brother, so I understand—wait, what? Awesome?"

"Hell, yeah! Are you kidding? I couldn't have *picked* a better boyfriend for him!"

Matthew's blush probably spread to his ears. "Well, thanks, but I'm not really his *boyfriend*. I mean, we've only known each other for a few days."

"Matthew, do you know how many times I've seen Aaron spend a few days in a row with only one person?"

Matthew played along. "How many?"

"Zero. None. Zip. I mean, he's definitely a people person, but that's just it. He likes to be around *lots* of people, not just one. He has lots of friends, but I don't think he's ever had one best friend, even when he was a kid. And nowadays, he spends so much time on his job that he hardly ever goes a day without doing a puppet show or preparing for one."

It was so much information that Matthew latched onto one part of it like a man with a life raft. "Oh, crap, you don't think I've been distracting him from his work, do you?"

Sam looked like she was trying not to laugh. "Yes, I think you have been distracting him. And I think it's been good for him." She brought her eggs over to the table and sat down. "In fact, I know he doesn't have any shows today, so I think you should bring him to the coast with me and Ryan. We'll make it a double date."

If Matthew choked again, he would probably need medical attention. "Even *Ryan* knows?"

Sam just reached over and patted his hand. Matthew groaned.

THE fog shrouded the land around them so thickly that Matthew might not have been able to tell they were near the ocean at all if not for the crash of the nearby waves and the occasional cries of seagulls. Sounds carried so easily in the still, wet air that he could hear Sam and her boyfriend talking from far across the rocky beach like they were on the end of a staticky telephone connection.

Matthew's longish hair curled frantically around his face in the moisture. He brushed it out of the way, but it fell back into place. Then a hand swept through his curls and lifted them out of his eyes.

"Let me help with that."

Matthew tipped his head back far enough for Aaron to lean forward and kiss his mouth. Then he remembered that they were in public and checked to either side of them for an audience.

Aaron dug his fingers into Matthew's scalp, then stepped in closer and wrapped his arms around Matthew's waist. "Don't worry; nobody can see us in all this fog. And even if they could, Sam and Ryan are the only ones here."

Matthew relaxed into Aaron's embrace. "Sorry, I didn't mean to panic." He put his hands over Aaron's, clasped on his stomach. "It doesn't matter if someone sees."

Aaron dipped his head to press a kiss to the skin under Matthew's ear. "It's okay, babe; I understand."

Matthew's stomach twisted into knots at the endearment. He hoped Aaron didn't expect him to make any intelligent conversation for a while after that. All he could do was bask in the new and unfamiliar glow of contentment. They spent a couple of hours wandering around on the beach, investigating tide pools and the crazy rock formations carved out by the waves. One hollow provided a handy, secluded cave for a slow and languorous make-out session.

The fog created a curtain around them, a bubble separate from the rest of the world. The illusion held until Sam and Ryan came looking for them, catching them kissing with their feet dangling in a pool.

"Whoa, looks like it's time to go home before you scare the fish," Sam teased.

Matthew couldn't look her in the face the entire ride home.

THE ubiquitous north coast rain returned on Friday, so Matthew spent the portion of the day not taken up by Aaron's puppet show curled up on the couch at Aaron's house. Kissing and playful touching eventually turned into something more intense. Matthew was awash with anticipation, expecting Aaron to take the lead any minute and take things to a higher level. But when the time came, nothing went further than it had on Wednesday. They fumbled at pants and underwear, jacked each other off, and then Picasso whined for attention from the floor and that was that.

It wasn't that Matthew wanted to rush things. He definitely didn't want to seem like an overeager kid to Aaron. But he wanted Aaron *so badly*. It was cliché, but he'd never felt this way about anyone before, and it was starting to feel like Aaron didn't return those feelings to nearly the same degree.

A worry that had been niggling at the back of his mind finally pushed its way to the fore: what if Aaron only saw him as a spring fling, a bit of temporary fun with no strings attached? He didn't seem like the type to play the "fresh meat" game, to mess with a naïve kid's feelings and then toss him aside. But maybe he didn't see it that way. Maybe everyone was just supposed to assume that spring break relationships weren't meant to last. Maybe Matthew just didn't know what he was doing.

Well, he was a big boy; he could live with that. He *could*. But he wasn't about to waste the time he had left, not if he could help it.

FOR all his conviction, Saturday was turning out to be a disaster. It was the last full day that Sam and Matthew would have before returning to school early Sunday morning. Sam's parents were hosting an all-day barbecue for a huge group of their friends—and Sam's—but Aaron would only be showing up near the end due to his full show schedule at the county library. Matthew couldn't skip out on the barbecue to help with the show, since he shared guest of honor status with Sam. He tried hard to enjoy himself, but the wait was agonizing.

When Aaron finally arrived, it got worse. Every time he caught sight of that golden hair shining in the glow from the luau torches that circled the twilit yard, his heart sped up. He wanted nothing more than to drag Aaron off to a secluded corner of the house and spend the rest of the night there.

But Aaron, social butterfly that he was, spent most of the party chatting with the other guests. Occasionally he would glance across the yard and catch Matthew's eye, winking or miming falling asleep from boring conversation. But he didn't seek Matthew out intentionally until things started winding down and people began trickling out in small groups. They met at the hors d'oeuvres table, where Matthew had been munching on carrots and dip and trying not to look sullen and abandoned.

"Hey." Matthew could swear Aaron watched the motion of his tongue as he licked ranch dressing from the corner of his mouth, but maybe that was wishful thinking.

"Hey." Aaron shoved both hands in his jeans pockets in an oddly standoffish move. "So, you're going back to school tomorrow, huh?"

"Yeah. Gotta check into the dorms before Monday."

"Right, right. Been a hell of a week, hasn't it?"

"Yeah, that's kind of an understatement."

Aaron chuckled. "Well, I'm heading out, so I guess I'll see you?"

A panicked voice screamed in Matthew's head, but he wouldn't let it escape. "Sure."

Aaron seemed to expect him to say something more, but Matthew was frozen. He didn't know what to say to make Aaron take him home. To make Aaron want to keep him. In the end, he just followed Aaron to the front door and watched him walk away with the streetlights illuminating his hair like a halo.

He wandered into the guest bedroom he'd been using, threw what little of his stuff still remained to be packed into his duffel bag, and flopped down on the bed with a huge sigh.

He hadn't moved from that position when Sam tapped on his open door. "Hey, kiddo, can I come in for a sec?"

He sat up and tried to look like he hadn't a care in the world. "Sure, what's up?"

Sam ran a hand through her hair casually and came to sit on the bed next to him. "So, I know this is none of my business, but I kind of noticed that you seem a little sad."

Matthew opened his mouth to object but realized that, with Sam's insightfulness, it was a losing battle. Instead, he just shrugged. "You know, going back to school and everything."

Sam raised an eyebrow at him. "School? That's all you've got? Honey, you can hide your puppy dog eyes from my parents, but you can't hide them from me. I saw the way you were looking at Aaron all night."

"I do *not* have puppy dog eyes!"

Sam ignored this. "Was it because he wasn't paying much attention to you? Matthew, that was probably just because he didn't want to make you uncomfortable."

"What do you mean, uncomfortable? Him ignoring me made me feel *uncomfortable*."

"Well, he didn't realize that. Knowing Aaron, he probably didn't want to force you to get all PDA in front of all those people. He knows you're not really used to that."

Matthew stared at Sam with his mouth open. He could have kicked himself. "Oh, my God, Sam, I'm such an idiot. What should I do?"

Sam dragged him into a one-armed hug. "You should go tell him how you feel."

"But I'm leaving tomorrow!"

"Which is why you should do it tonight."

Matthew gaped for about the millionth time in the last five minutes. Then he shot up off the bed and practically ran out the front door, calling a "Thanks, Sam!" behind him.

He jogged the few blocks to Aaron's duplex, panting by the time he reached the front stoop. There was nothing left to do but ring the doorbell. Who'd have thought that pushing a button could be so hard?

Aaron opened the door, looking a little rumpled in the clothes he'd worn to the party. Matthew spared a few brain cells to wonder what the man had been doing to achieve that look, but the majority of his mind was occupied by a strangling mixture of longing and panic.

"Matthew, what…?"

Before he could continue, Matthew found his voice. "Aaron, I'm so sorry, I'm a complete idiot, I didn't realize you were just trying not to pressure me at the party, and I didn't mean to be such an asshole. Well, I did, but only because I thought you were being an asshole. But I like you, I like you a lot, and I don't want to say goodbye yet. Can I come in?"

Aaron blinked, blinked again, and dissolved into quiet laughter, one hand thrown over his mouth.

Matthew glared, blushing. "It's not funny; I'm nervous." Then he mentally reviewed his little speech and pressed his lips together to keep from smiling. "Okay, it's a little funny."

Aaron reached out and pulled him into a tight hug, leading him inside and closing the door behind him. "Oh, Matthew, what am I going to do with you?"

"Well, I had a few ideas." He leaned in to kiss the silly grin off Aaron's lips.

Aaron responded hungrily, squeezing Matthew's waist with both arms and kissing him fiercely, sucking on his tongue and moaning into his mouth.

Matthew did his best to guide them, stumbling and groping, to the bedroom. Aaron seemed to have no objections, letting Matthew push him backwards until the backs of his knees hit the bed and he fell onto it, bringing Matthew down with him. Picasso woke with a start and made a frustrated noise as he jumped off the bed.

Suddenly, Aaron pushed on Matthew's shoulders until their mouths disconnected with a loud sound. "Wait, wait! You're a virgin, aren't you?"

Matthew gaped, speechless.

"I mean, that's what you were going to say that one time in my living room, wasn't it? That you've never had sex?"

"I...." Matthew flailed for something to say that wouldn't be a lie. "I've had sex!"

Aaron raised one eyebrow.

"With girls." He chewed on his lip. "Okay, one girl. In high school. It didn't go very well." Aaron didn't say anything, just rubbed Matthew's shoulders absently, waiting. "Okay, it wasn't really sex. She gave me a hand job in the limo after junior prom. But that didn't count! I want you to be, you know, my first."

Aaron leaned up and licked the place where Matthew's teeth were turning his lip white. "Are you sure you want this? Now?" His voice came out ragged, and he jerked his hips up into Matthew's once, like he just couldn't help himself. "I don't want you to feel rushed."

• • •

Matthew snorted. "*I* came *here*, remember?"

Aaron's eyes darkened, and he grabbed Matthew by the hips and rolled them both so that Matthew was pinned to the mattress under him. "Oh, you'll come here, all right," he growled. "More than once, if I can help it."

Matthew shivered. Then he reached for the hem of Aaron's shirt and tugged it off, Aaron raising his arms obligingly and then doing the same with Matthew's shirt. Matthew ran his hands over that expanse of silky flesh and yelped when Aaron slid down to suck on his nipple.

He pulled away from Aaron's mouth long enough to gasp, "Do you have condoms and lube?" He'd watched enough gay porn to know how this was supposed to go, but it still made him blush to say the words.

Aaron licked the shell of his ear and growled, "I'll get them." He shoved himself up far enough to reach over to the bedside table, open the drawer, and fumble around inside it.

While Aaron was occupied, Matthew fumbled with his shorts and tried to pull them off, but Aaron's hands on his stilled him.

"Let me." A sudden pang of worry hit Matthew right in the solar plexus. He realized that this was the first time he would be fully naked in front of someone who wasn't one of his parents or a random guy in the high school locker room. He'd never been particularly self-conscious, but this was Aaron. What if he didn't like what he saw?

But as soon as Aaron eased Matthew's underwear down past his hips and Matthew's cock bobbed free of the material, he let out a groan of anticipation, and Matthew forgot to worry in the face of his desperate wanting.

Aaron licked the head of his cock, and all vestiges of coherent thought flew out of his mind. Warm, wet heat wrapped around him as Aaron took the entire length into his mouth, and the back of Matthew's head hit the mattress hard as he moaned.

Aaron seemed content to make him come this way, and as much as Matthew wanted to wait, he couldn't have controlled himself if his life had depended on it. Not when Aaron started bobbing his head, pressing his tongue to the slit on every upward motion. Matthew tugged on Aaron's hair as he felt the wave building inside him, but Aaron kept sucking even as Matthew cried out and shot down his throat.

Aaron's hands shook slightly when he climbed up to hold Matthew's head in his hands and kiss him long and deep. Matthew's cock twitched again when he realized that the salty taste in Aaron's mouth was his own come.

Aaron sat back on his haunches, straddling Matthew's calves. He rolled a condom onto himself, then squeezed a liberal amount of lube into his hand and coated his cock with it, stroking himself slowly and thoroughly. Matthew practically drooled at the sight. Then he gasped as Aaron reached down and stroked a finger over his hole. His hips strained up for more of the touch.

"Shh, easy." Aaron's finger circled his hole, then pressed slowly inside. Matthew squirmed. It didn't hurt yet, but it was definitely a weird feeling.

The burn started when Aaron slipped another finger in, then a third. Matthew whimpered a little, tensing up. Aaron rubbed a hand over his chest, then gave his cock a few swift strokes.

"Come on, baby, relax. Breathe for me."

Matthew forced himself to take a few deep breaths, and his muscles relaxed in increments. The burn started to fade, and Aaron thrust his fingers in and out.

When Matthew started bucking his hips, Aaron drew his fingers out, and Matthew winced at the sudden emptiness.

"It'll probably be easier for you if you turn over."

Matthew hesitated, then shook his head. "Wanna see you."

Aaron's eyes darkened and he made a sound low in his throat. He raised Matthew's knees up, positioned himself between them, and ever so slowly pushed his hips forward.

Matthew panted in short, shallow breaths. The sting of Aaron's fingers hadn't been nearly as bad as this. He knew it was supposed to hurt at first, but the reality of it still startled him. His hole burned as it stretched around Aaron's cock, and he couldn't stop the noises that escaped him.

Aaron kept up a string of reassuring words, urging Matthew to relax and breathe, pushing in so slowly that his thighs shook. Matthew thought it must be agony for Aaron to hold back, so he exerted as much control as he could muster over his screaming muscles, taking in a deep breath and letting it out. And suddenly, something loosened inside him, and Aaron slid in until his balls bumped Matthew's ass.

They held that position for a long moment, Aaron gripping Matthew's thigh with one hand and stroking his cock with the other. The combination of Aaron's continued murmurs and the pressure on his dick finally let Matthew relax enough that Aaron sensed the change and pulled out a tiny bit.

When he thrust back in, the burn receded to a much more pleasant ache. On the second thrust, they both moaned loudly, and Aaron started a slow and easy rhythm.

The ache grew less intense with every movement, and when Aaron suddenly shifted the position of his hips and hit something inside of Matthew that made him see stars, he arched his back and cried out. Aaron leaned forward to drape himself over Matthew's torso, licking Matthew's neck and nipping his earlobe. His hand kept up a steady rhythm between them on Matthew's cock, and Matthew wrapped his arms around him, running his hands up and down Aaron's back.

"Oh, God, Matthew, so good. Come for me again, come with me inside you."

The words and Aaron's cock hitting that spot inside him on every stroke pushed him over the edge, helpless and moaning. Aaron stared into his eyes, thrust hard a few more times, and followed, crying out his name.

It was the most intense thing Matthew had ever felt. Aaron rolled to the side as he collapsed so as not to crush Matthew, and they lay there side by side with their legs tangled, panting. Picasso, who'd been whining on the floor for a while, jumped back up and settled himself against Aaron's other side with a soft huff of breath.

Sex always seemed to make Aaron oddly silent. He reached out to stroke Matthew's sweaty hair away from his face, then pulled him close until the entire lengths of their bodies touched. Matthew settled his head on Aaron's shoulder.

He lay there listening to Aaron's breathing even out, feeling the rise and fall of his lover's chest under his hand, and fought the urge to cry. He didn't know what to do next, how to get on with his life. He couldn't believe he'd ever thought he could handle letting Aaron go.

MATTHEW threw his books into his messenger bag with a heavy sigh. He wasn't sure if he was relieved or disappointed that it was finally Friday. On one hand, the week since he'd returned to school had been one of the longest of his life. On the other, the weekend loomed in front of him like a vast and empty desert to be crossed.

He hadn't talked to Aaron since Saturday night, when they'd fallen asleep holding each other. He'd slipped out early on Sunday morning after writing a vague note. He assured Sam that he and Aaron had said their goodbyes, and they left a short time later. He'd left his phone number and email address, but he hadn't heard from Aaron. Apparently, it really had just been a spring fling. He kept telling himself he was fine, he didn't care, but none of his self-assurances warded off the black fog he'd been walking around in all week.

He knew he shouldn't have disappeared like that. He should have at least left a better note. But he just couldn't bring himself to face the man he was falling hard for if it turned out to be the last time they ever saw each other. Not if Aaron was just going to toss him aside like his parents had. Matthew preferred to keep the memories of Saturday night unspoiled.

He was so wrapped up in those memories when he reached his dorm that he didn't notice the familiar car parked in front of it until he almost walked right into its owner.

"Hey, where are you going, space cadet?"

Aaron was backlit by the sun, so Matthew had to blink a few times to bring him into focus. "Aaron? What are you doing here?"

"What do you mean, what am I doing here? I missed you." Aaron stepped closer and wrapped him in a tight hug. Matthew breathed in the scent of him and really shouldn't have been surprised by how relieved he felt. "I didn't even get to see you off. I at least want to spend the weekend with you."

"Sorry, I shouldn't have run off like that." Matthew leaned in for a long, deep kiss, hoping it was enough to show how glad he was that Aaron was there. "It won't happen again."

"Oh, good." Aaron grinned at him and kissed the end of his nose. "In that case, why don't we figure out how your RA feels about your boyfriend visiting for the weekend? We may have to get a hotel room."

The look on Aaron's face made Matthew think the hotel might be a good idea no matter what his RA had to say. But before that….

* * *

"Boyfriend?" The way his face ached with the force of his smile, he knew Aaron couldn't possibly think he was upset about the terminology.

Aaron pressed his hips into Matthew's and nuzzled his hair. "You didn't seriously think I was going to let anyone else have you, did you?"

Matthew laughed, feeling almost giddy. "No danger of *that* happening."

Funny how Aaron showing up could take his dark little world and make it blossom like the first day of spring. It might be too early to tell, but Matthew couldn't help hoping. Maybe this could work out after all.

Growing up Southern has been an interesting experience for M. JULES AEDIN, whose philosophy is best summed up by Joni Mitchell: "I don't know who I am, but life's for learning." When not reading or playing video games or writing (or doing all three at once!) Jules is generally trying to pretend to be a responsible adult and at least do laundry once in a while.

Visit her web site at http://mjules.net/ and her blog at http://mjaedin.livejournal.com/.

ANNA J. LINDEN is a bookworm, Internet junkie, and all-around geek, and she wouldn't have it any other way. Her closest friends would probably describe her as "harmlessly crazy," but she prefers the term "free spirit." She lives in California, but (contrary to popular legend) she doesn't get to wear shorts all year long.

Visit Anna's blog at http://ajlinden.livejournal.com.

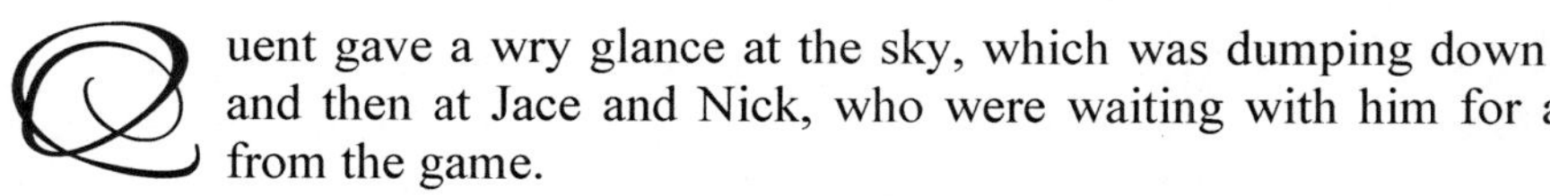

Gambling Men: Deal
Amy Lane

Quent gave a wry glance at the sky, which was dumping down rain, and then at Jace and Nick, who were waiting with him for a cab from the game.

"I'm *not* walking!" Nick muttered, and Quent wanted to groan. He would have walked. Of the three of them, Nick lived closest to the bar that housed the poker game. If Quent knew Jace would be at his back, he'd run the entire distance through the pissing rain to be in the same room with him. Alone. Stripping off their wet clothes in the steaming hallway. Alone.

As it was, they were waiting in the rain in front of the club with Nick, and Quent wasn't sure if his hope was real or *just* that. A hope.

The two girls giggling shyly at them were real. They were hardly dressed, especially for a night like this, and Quent saw blue toes with red toenail polish peeking out from the little strappy sandals one of them wore. Jace's cheerfully rolled eyes gave Quent a little more hope.

"You always were a chivalrous bastard," Quent muttered as the cab pulled up. The three gentlemen took a step back, and the girls shimmered their way into the back of the cab, leaving the men in the rain.

Again.

"Damn," Nick muttered, shaking his head. "You'd think they would have offered to share the back, at least!"

"With the three of us?" Jace's voice held nothing but wry amusement. "We would have been in each other's laps. Quent's muscle mass alone would have pressed me to the floor!"

Nick made a moue of distaste for the bottom of the taxi cab, and Quent pushed his dripping dark hair from his eyes to mask the heat that built up in him with the thought of pressing Jace to the floor of anything.

Ah, God... if only—

The thought was interrupted when the cab pulled up, and the three men squashed their tightly muscled bodies into it, Quent in the middle.

Nick chattered all the way to his apartment about the girls and how badly he wanted the two of them together, and Jace replied with laconic, one-word statements, keeping up the joy of the night.

Guys, playing poker, drinking vodka—didn't get much better than that, right?

Quent sat in the middle and wondered why the heat from Jace's thigh seemed to sear right through his wool slacks when he couldn't feel the heat from Nick at all.

Finally, *finally,* Nick was out, and he was walking cheerfully past his doorman, apologizing for dripping into the building. Quent made to move, to give Jace a little more room, but Jace's hard hand gripped the inside of his thigh and squeezed.

Quent's lungs went on perma-freeze.

Jace gave crisp instructions to the cabbie, and Quent's gulped a chest full of air and stopped breathing again. Jace's place. No stop at Quent's. Both of them, going to Jace's. Jace's index finger traced a sure path along Quent's inseam, and Quent's slacks were suddenly too. Damned. Tight.

"I told you," Jace murmured into the hollow of Quent's ear, "I never let anybody win."

Quent turned his head and found that he was close enough to bump his lips along Jace's jaw. So he did. "So why play this game?" he asked. "Why now? After five years?"

Jace tilted his head a little so it rested on Quent's shoulder. For a captain of the stock market, a bloodless shark who ripped the throat out of anything that stood in its way, the gesture was curiously vulnerable.

"You never tipped your hand," Jace said softly. "I didn't even know it was in the cards."

Quent closed his eyes and turned his head until he could feel the puff of Jace's breath on his cheek. They were both flushed and hot, and the cab was steaming and close from their body heat and their wet clothes, and the foggy windows gave them an intimacy, an isolation from the rest of the world. The cabbie might not have existed. Jace's hand moved strong and certain, up Quent's thigh… up… up… and then it brushed Quent's cock through his slacks.

Quent let out a whine, because just that suddenly, he was ready, his cock was blood-full, his chest was tingling, and his vision was dim with desire. "I didn't know what game we were playing," he rasped.

Jace's trapped Quent's cock against his thigh and squeezed, and Quent sucked in a rattling breath. That grip was strong, almost painful, heavenly. Jace pressed his lips against Quent's jaw again and nipped lightly.

"Not a game, Quentin. Never was."

We Are Stardust

M. Jules Aedin

obin Danvers was walking along the side of the highway with all his possessions strapped to his back and the August sun pounding down on him mercilessly. He was hungry, thirsty, and the road-dust was clinging to the sweat dripping off his face and neck. He'd lost his job, his home, his family, and his girlfriend the day before.

It was the best day of his life.

Until that moment, he hadn't realized that all the things he'd found security in might have been a kind of burden. He'd been a good boy, done everything his parents had asked of him. He'd been a straight-A student, a model employee at the soda shop his uncle owned, and the picture of gentlemanly restraint with his girlfriend, Alice Miller. They'd held hands exactly three times and kissed exactly once.

But when he'd seen the advertisement for *An Aquarian Exposition* in upstate New York, in some little town he'd never heard of, he'd been consumed with a need to go. He wasn't sure why, but it called to him. He'd asked for the time off from work and before he'd even gotten home from the store, Uncle Jimmy had called his parents and told them. Robin's father had been waiting in the living room, wanting to know why Robin was taking a vacation.

It only briefly occurred to Robin to lie, even knowing how his parents felt about hippies, but he'd only lied once before in his life, when he'd eaten one more piece of candy than his mother had told him he could have, and he'd

• • •

felt so guilty about it that he'd confessed almost immediately. He knew he didn't stand a chance of lying about something like taking a road trip to a hippie music festival in New York.

His parents' first order that he change his plans was phrased politely. So was his refusal. The second order was firm. Robin's voice trembled when he refused that one. The third was an ultimatum. Robin didn't answer that one at all; he couldn't. The idea that his parents would disown him, forbid him from coming home ever again just because they didn't approve of the crowd or the music that would be at the festival shook him to his core. He thought being their son—their devoted, faithful son—would have counted for more than that.

By the time he went for a walk with Alice Miller after dinner, she'd already heard. Robin could only guess his mother had been on the phone about it, and by now the news would be all over town. He'd be poked fun at for months for wanting to go to a hippie concert.

"You're not really going, are you?" Alice gave him a curious look, walking half a step to his right. They weren't even close to touching; their behavior was something both their parents would approve of if they looked out the window and saw them.

Alice had blonde hair that curled a little at the end of her ponytail and soft blue eyes that reminded Robin of clean-washed skies after a springtime rain. Her lips were always a perfect shell-pink, curving sweetly over straight, white teeth. She was the prettiest girl on the block and had said once that she liked dating Robin because he was the only boy she'd gone with who hadn't tried to put his hand under her sweater. She liked that he was a gentleman.

"I don't know," he answered, scratching at the back of his neck where his short-sleeved sweater was starting to itch. "It looks like it's going to be really cool."

"I thought your parents said you couldn't take the car. How would you get there?"

He shrugged. "There's always hitchhiking."

"Robin Danvers, you can't do that! Somebody might think you're a hobo—or a hippie."

"My hair's not long enough to be a hippie." It was true; his hair didn't even touch the tops of his ears, cut close to his head on the sides with a light fringe of floppy bangs in the front.

"It doesn't matter. Nice boys don't hitchhike."

Something about that rankled—like she was saying he was too dumb to do it, too naïve. He tried to sound cold and aloof when he said, "Maybe I'm not such a nice boy."

Alice giggled. "Robin, you're the nicest boy I've ever met." When he scowled, she brushed his arm just lightly with her hand and said, "It's a compliment. Don't look so sour."

He didn't respond more than to give her a thin smile—even he could feel that it was a tight and miserly expression—and ask her about her sister's upcoming wedding. He barely listened as she rattled on about fabrics and fittings and flower girls. He was merely relieved that he'd succeeded in diverting her attention from him.

When they were on the far side of the block where neither of their parents could see them and a high hedge blocked them from the Hendersons' view, Alice leaned close and kissed him, those shell-pink lips pressing against his briefly before he pulled back.

"It's all right," she said, smiling. "We're going steady. You can kiss me." She gave him a coy look with those baby-blue eyes. "You can put your hands on my waist if you want."

He did, awkwardly, and found that he could only think how uncomfortable he was when he had to crane his neck to kiss her and how unpleasantly warm her breath was as it skittered over his skin in the summer heat. Sometimes he was sure other boys only talked about how cool kissing was because it was expected of them—that's what Robin did, anyway.

They didn't dare linger more than a few moments by the Hendersons' hedges; if they were out too long, their parents would suspect that they hadn't just taken an innocent walk around the block.

On the way home, Alice chatted about all the neighborhood gossip, and Robin thought about New York. When he dropped her off at her door, she gave him a very serious look.

"If you go to New York," she said, "don't bother looking me up when you get back."

* * *

That night, lying in bed and listening to the muffled sound of his parents snoring behind the closed door of their bedroom, Robin examined his life. He was coasting, really, doing what was expected of him. If he stayed on the same road he was on now, he'd end up in the family business, married to Alice Miller, living a block or two over from his parents and raising a couple of well-groomed, mannerly children who could be mistaken for overgrown china dolls. Of course, that was all assuming he survived the war. He had just turned eighteen; he'd be getting his draft notice soon, he figured.

He'd never thought of having any other kind of life until just recently. He'd never considered that he might want something else, something more, something *his*. He didn't know how he knew, but something in him said that this festival, this Aquarian Experience in New York, was the only open gate in miles and miles of the fence keeping him penned into other people's dreams. It was his chance to find some dreams of his own.

The entire time he was packing, he told himself he wasn't really going to go through with it. When he got dressed, put on his shoes, he told himself he wasn't leaving, that the next day he'd call his uncle and cancel his vacation time. When he climbed out his window, he told himself he was just going for a walk around the block.

By the time he hit the highway, plodding along under a thin crescent moon with only the headlights of passing cars to show him the way, he couldn't lie to himself anymore.

He was going to Woodstock.

CAT ELLIS was halfway through a toke when he saw the kid. He sat up—as best as he could with three other people sprawled across him—and pointed out the window.

"Hey!" he yelled over the sound of The 5th Dimension on the radio. "Pull over!"

Lily Mankowitz, one hand on the wheel and one hand waving a cigarette as she sang along with the radio, didn't hear him at first. Cat leaned forward, the flowers in Lily's hair brushing against his face as he put his mouth by her ear.

"PULL OVER!"

Lily squeaked in surprise and jerked the wheel of the Volkswagen bus to the right, slinging people out of their seats and onto each other or the floor. There was a general commotion, arms and legs flailing, and somebody yelled, "What the fuck, man?" as Cat crawled over a tangle of bodies and opened the door of the van, practically falling out onto the grassy shoulder of the highway. He handed the lit toke back through the door, and somebody took it from him.

Glancing down to make sure he wasn't about to step on anything sharp with his bare feet—his shoes were somewhere in the van, maybe—Cat made his way back toward the guy he'd seen sitting on the side of the road, the one he'd made Lily stop for.

"Hey, man," Cat called out. "You all right?"

The kid looked up at him, expression mildly alarmed but mostly confused. There was a pink strip across his nose and cheeks where the sun had gotten him. It made him look incredibly vulnerable. His hair and clothes were a style that had gone out of fashion a decade before, and his shoes didn't look comfortable for walking. There was a bag beside him in the grass that looked too empty to be holding anything useful like food or water. When the kid didn't answer, Cat tried again.

"You okay, man? You look like you could use a drink of water."

The kid's eyes widened. Relief? Fear? When he licked his lips, Cat noticed they were chapped and peeling. This kid was a danger to himself.

"C'mon, I think we got somethin' to drink in the van."

The kid hesitated but finally got to his feet. Cat watched him carefully in case it looked like he was going to collapse.

"Where are your clothes?" the young man asked.

Either the kid was sunburned worse than he'd thought, or he was blushing. Cat laughed and looked down at himself. He was wearing jeans; what more did the kid want? A shirt, shoes?

"What are you, a restaurant owner?" Cat grinned. "Gonna kick me out?" He spread his arms. "You can't kick me out of *out,* can you?"

"I'm sorry," the kid said, not meeting Cat's eyes. "That was rude. I didn't mean—"

"It's all right, man. What's your name?"

"Robin Danvers. Pleased to meet you, Mister…?"

"No mister. Cat Ellis."

"Cat? As in—meow?"

"Cat as in short for Christopher. Where you headed, Robin Danvers? What happened to your car? You don't look like the hitchhiking type." He turned and started walking back toward the van as he spoke, gesturing for Robin to keep up with him, which he did.

This time Cat was sure the kid was blushing, but there was a spark to his eyes, as if Cat had pissed him off with that question.

"Well, I *am* hitchhiking," he said. "I'm going to Woodstock."

Cat thought about teasing him, giving him some hitching tips—like sticking out his thumb, for starters—but he settled on the latter half.

"Woodstock, huh? Hear there's some kind of hippie fest up there. You goin' to join a rock 'n' roll band?"

"Maybe." Robin's chin lifted in defiance.

Cat grinned. "Well, you're in luck, kid. That's where we're headed." Cat stuck his head into the van, where several people were sprawled in varying states of consciousness. "Hey, somebody throw me a can of somethin'. Kid's thirsty."

A can came flying toward him, courtesy of a guy who called himself Samba and carried a pair of bongo drums with him everywhere. Cat handed it to Robin, who took it and reached for the tab. Cat tried to stop him, but it was too late. Soda spewed all over both of them, making Robin cringe and Cat laugh.

"Sorry, kid, didn't think about it gettin' all shook up until it was too late."

"No, I should have… it was my fault."

Cat watched as Robin took a sip of the cola and made a little face at its temperature. They didn't have any way to keep the cans cool in the van.

"You don't like me calling you 'kid', do you?" Cat said suddenly. Robin gave him a wide-eyed look that he was beginning to think was the guy's default expression. "I noticed you frownin' when I said it."

"Oh. Well, it's all right, just… I'm eighteen, you know? I'm not a kid anymore."

A smile tugged at Cat's lips. "All right, man."

"'Man' works." Robin tried on a smile, and it didn't look half bad on him.

Cat shook his head. "I got somethin' that works better." He winked. "Hey everybody," Cat yelled as he stepped back up into the van, reaching his hand back. Robin stared at it for a second before taking it cautiously. Cat grinned and pulled, dragging Robin into the van. "This here's Bobby Danvers. He's goin' to Woodstock with us!"

The announcement was met with cheers and greetings from the rest of the van's occupants, and Lily started pulling the van back onto the road just as Brenda got the door closed.

"Hey, Bobby," Samba shouted from the backseat. "You know any good songs, man?"

"I know 'Moon River'," Robin said, perking up a little.

"Aw, *man*," Samba groaned, and light laughter rippled through the van. "We gotta teach you some better shit than that. Hey, Lily, turn up the radio. Let's teach this cat some tunes!"

WHATEVER Robin had thought hippies were like, he wasn't sure he'd expected anything like this. There were eight of them crammed into a van that seated seven, but nobody seemed upset about it. Everyone was relaxed and happy—most of all, no one seemed to have any boundaries. Limbs were sprawled across laps and cans of soda and bags of snack food were passed around and shared, along with what Robin suspected was marijuana. He'd never seen the stuff before, but he'd heard that it was the drug of choice for hippies. He didn't partake, but with the thickness of the cloud in the van, he'd be surprised if he didn't get high just from smelling it.

Some of them were philosophers. Others seemed to want to take the world as it came and enjoy things without thinking about them too hard. Robin didn't join in any of the conversations or debates unless he was specifically addressed, and then he tried not to say too much. He didn't know what would offend people, what would put distance between him and his new friends. Besides that, he wasn't sure exactly what he thought, anyway. He hadn't really had to think about it before.

After a while, they seemed to catch onto that and didn't ask him any direct questions, though he never felt excluded from the discussions. In fact, more than once, he caught Cat glancing at him and smiling. It always made a warm burst of something spread through him, like standing in the sunshine on a perfect spring day.

Time seemed to lose its edges, melting away and bleeding out like water through sand. Scenery passed by through the windows of the van, just moving pictures framed in bits of conversation that floated through his consciousness without catching on anything.

"…transcendental meditation, they say it's better than a trip, man…."

"…mean sure, we ball sometimes, but it ain't like she's a tract of land. I ain't got an owner's deed or nothin'…."

"…gonna change the world like that…."

He became aware of a voice above him, silky-smooth, somehow rich and golden, melting like salt and honey over his ears. Fingers were sifting through his hair, softly lifting and petting.

"Can't you feel it, though? Like we're on the edge of something changing—like, if we just take two steps to the left, we could just… slip right into the fabric of the universe, all harmony and everything."

"Man, are you tryin' to tell me who to vote for or what, 'cause that's bullshit."

"No, no, get your mind out of this whole—politics and war and shit. That's just the shadows on the wall, man. I'm talking about… inside us, outside of us. Like us, but bigger. Like—there's a whole universe out there, full of life and consciousness and wisdom, and we're just little pieces of it that got dropped here on earth by some meteor or God or somethin'. Like our souls are made out of little pieces of the stars."

The fingers in Robin's hair tightened as the speaker's voice gained passion, and he realized he must be lying in the lap of whoever was talking. He opened his eyes and could see Cat's wildly curly hair, the boyish face with the stubborn chin. He was leaning forward, gesturing with the hand not in Robin's hair, his eyes sparking and eager. Just then, Robin thought maybe he was right; maybe there were little broken-off fragments of stars inside them.

* * *

He thought he could feel their jagged edges pressing up against his heart, shining with a sweet, peculiar ache.

Whoever Cat was talking to dismissed him with a snort, and Cat sat back, shrinking into himself. The look on his face twisted Robin's stomach into knots; he could see the stars in Cat's eyes dimming, like the smog from the city had rolled over them.

"Stars?" he whispered, one hand coming up to touch Cat, to get his attention.

Cat looked down and seemed to see Robin for the first time, as if he'd forgotten Robin was in his lap. "Yeah." His voice was low; his eyes were soft and tender. "We're all just stardust, tryin' to get back home."

Robin closed his eyes, tiny sparks of sensation rolling through him as Cat's fingers went back to combing through his hair.

For the first time in his life, he felt like he could breathe. He knew what Cat meant by trying to get back home, and he had a feeling he was closer to it now than he ever had been before.

IT WAS the middle of the night, and Cat was driving when they got to White Lake. In the passenger seat beside him, Lily was curled against the window, her breath fogging the pane. Somewhere behind him, he could hear the soft sounds of snoring—Samba, Jefferson, Richard, Brenda, Molly, and Robin.

Bobby.

Cat's hands tightened on the wheel as the van slowed to a crawl. There were cars everywhere, blocking the road in both directions. The traffic crept along, and Cat thought it would be faster if they just got out and walked. On the other side of the small town—a crossroads, really, in the middle of nowhere—he realized that everyone seemed to have had that thought. Across the grassy shoulder and further on into the fields, vehicles were strewn haphazardly, like matchsticks dropped from the hand of a giant.

With a mental shrug, he followed suit, turning the van off the road and across the grass. He hit a shallow ditch first, making the van lurch and waking almost everyone, judging by the muffled noises of protest in the back seat. Driving across the bumpy field woke the rest of the passengers, and Lily squeaked as he slammed the van into park and turned it off.

"We're here," Cat called out. He was answered by mumbles and requests for silence. Then a chin landed on his shoulder, and he nearly jumped out of his skin.

"Are we sleeping in the van or are we camping?"

Robin didn't sound nearly as sleepy as Cat had expected, but his voice was soft and warm and made Cat shiver. Out the windows of the van, he could already see the pale shapes of tents, strewn through the field as haphazardly as the vehicles. Most were right beside a car or a van, both presumably owned by the same people.

"Probably both," Lily answered for him, shifting against the window. "There won't be room in the tent or the van for all of us, so we'll probably just split up between them." She gave a jaw-cracking yawn and wriggled until she was comfortable. "But we'll wait 'til tomorrow to set up the tent. We can all manage in here for one night."

Cat stretched, feeling places on his body protest the prolonged immobility, and knew he couldn't stand the idea of staying where he was for one more minute.

"I'm gonna get out and walk around," he said. "Stretch my legs a little."

He hopped out of the van and was only a couple of steps away when he heard the rough metallic sliding sound of the side door opening. He looked back in time to see a figure stumble out of the van and close the door again. Robin stood there grinning at him shyly, short blond hair sticking up crazily all over his head and making Cat think of a haystack.

"Mind if I walk with you?" Robin asked. "It's a little… crowded in there."

"Sure." Cat shoved his hands into the pockets of his jeans, wiggling his bare toes in the grass. The summer dew was condensing on the blades, and it felt cool and welcome against his skin after he'd been trapped in the van all day.

They walked in silence, weaving around vehicles and people sleeping on the ground wrapped in blankets or sleeping bags or just their own clothing until Cat started to feel like they were playing hide and seek. Stars winked at them from a sky that seemed to stretch out forever overhead, and a pleasant breeze tickled their skin wherever it could reach.

When the field melded into a forest, they kept going, drawn by sounds of a celebration just up ahead. They found the party at the edge of the trees, the flickering glow of campfires casting a festive light on the faces of the campers. There was a chain-link fence running around the perimeter, but it was already pushed down enough that Cat and Robin climbed over with no trouble. Some of the campers were sleeping, but many were talking, laughing, singing. Someone had an acoustic guitar, strumming along to a tune Cat didn't recognize. Likely the guitarist didn't recognize it either; he was probably making it up as he went along.

"Holy Toledo," Robin said beside him, making Cat want to laugh at the outdated slang. Where had he grown up, in his parent's bomb shelter basement? But the sight that had prompted such awe from Robin was stunning indeed.

"Shit," Cat said reverently.

The field swept away into a natural amphitheater, semicircle hills cradling a valley perfect for sound. At the bottom of the grassy bowl, Cat could see the pale, raw wood of the stage and the looming shadows of the cranes that had been used to build it. Towers were set up further up the hill, criss-crossed beams holding up speakers and lights.

All through the field, people were stretched out on blankets or their own clothes, using backpacks and the bodies of friends for their pillows. Cat could hear it now, the charged atmosphere like electricity crackling just behind the breeze. Another guitarist down near the massive stage was strumming and singing; Cat could barely hear the notes carried to him on the night wind. The sounds of traffic made a constant screen of white noise in the distance, and Cat didn't know how anyone could sleep with this much excitement in the air.

"Let's go," Cat said to Robin, already trotting down over the grass toward the stage.

"Go where?" Despite his confusion, Robin was right there, voice a little breathless as he jogged to keep up.

"*In.*" Cat laughed, not knowing how to explain it more than that. All he knew was that something was going on, something was *happening*, and he needed to be right in the middle of it. Having Robin there with him sounded like the best idea in the world.

IT WAS strange at first, sleeping on the ground with so many other bodies, many of them casually nude or so close as not to matter, and not just the men. There were women sporting loincloths and nothing else, the rest of their bodies shamelessly bare. He'd caught himself staring at first before Cat nudged him in the ribs and laughed.

"See something you like?"

"Ah—no—I mean… I've just never… it's not.…" Robin felt himself turning pink. He was shocked by the nudity, but the lush, round curves of the women's bare breasts didn't tempt him. Instead, he found himself stealing glances at the young men, many of whom were just as nude. He was drawn especially to Cat, who was wearing nothing but worn brown jeans that hung low on his hips, cinched with a wide leather belt. Robin could see Cat's hipbones, the subtle crease where his thighs met his abdomen. If the pants slipped any lower, he might as well not be wearing anything at all.

But Robin had been tired enough to ignore his culture shock, at least long enough to fall asleep. Cat was curled up against him much like his namesake animal, all but purring with contentment. Robin could tell that everything about this was practically Utopia for his new friend. Even though it was all new and a little overwhelming for Robin, the excitement was contagious. He could already feel anticipation buzzing through his veins; he barely got to sleep at all, too conscious of where he was, why he was there, and of the firm, warm body pressed against his back.

He woke alone in the midst of the crowd as the sun came up the next day, spreading its warmth over his face. Surrounded by strangers on all sides, Robin couldn't see Cat anywhere. He wondered at the lonely disappointment that swept over him at the realization. Twenty-four hours previously, he had expected to be at this festival by himself, not knowing anyone. How had he become so attached to one person so quickly?

Trying not to let it get to him too much, Robin stood and stretched, grimacing when his joints popped like gunfire in rapid succession. He wondered where he might be able to dig up some food and was struck again by the thought that he had been woefully unprepared for making this trip. He had a couple of oranges in his bag, but that was back in the van with Cat and Lily and the others. He looked around, trying to get his bearings, trying to figure out which way he needed to walk through the maze of human bodies to get back to the van.

He had just started stepping over people, apologizing quietly as he went, when he heard a woman yelling at the top of her lungs.

"Bobby! Hey, Bobby! Over here!"

It barely registered, and he didn't look up, concentrating on not stepping on anyone. He was straddling a sleeping man with long red hair when he heard a different voice, one he recognized. Cat's.

"Bobby Danvers!" The call was followed by a loud, sharp whistle, and by this time, several people were waking up, looking around to try to help find the person being called for so raucously.

Robin looked up and had to smile. Cat and Lily were standing at the top of the hill several yards away, waving enthusiastically at him. He thought he could see Samba behind them, and maybe the other people in the van whose names he was having trouble remembering. He waved back and started picking his way up the hill, moving more quickly now that he had a destination in mind. Something inside him soared at the knowledge that his new friends hadn't abandoned him, but he didn't examine it too closely.

"Hey, man," Cat said with a broad smile as he approached. "You were still sleepin' when I got up, and I didn't wanna wake you. Long day yesterday. I needed to help these cats get their shit here, though. Sorry you had to wake up alone."

Robin was shocked to feel his throat close up with emotion when Cat acknowledged the feeling of disorientation he'd experienced upon waking, and he tried to smile and make light of it.

"I wasn't alone," he said, though his voice wasn't quite steady. "There's hundreds of people here."

Cat flashed a bright smile that said he wasn't fooled, and Robin shrugged.

The rest of the day was spent wandering around, meeting people as they trickled in, watching the crew set up technical items on stage, and listening to pieces of songs as they floated on the air from one amateur musician or another. It wasn't until that afternoon, when they heard the loud noise of the helicopters coming in, that Robin actually remembered there were going to be concerts. Announcements were made over the microphone that the musicians were being flown in because of the ridiculous amounts of traffic, which was backed up for more than twelve miles.

Cat and Lily were passing marijuana back and forth between them, and Molly and Samba had little brown squares of paper with liquid dropped on them.

"What's that?" Robin asked quietly enough that only Cat could hear him.

"Acid," Cat answered. "LSD. Somebody said that particular batch ain't so good, though, so if you wanna try it, you might wanna wait 'til we find some better."

"Not good?" Robin was a little worried. Molly and Samba were blithely putting the stuff under their tongues. "Are they gonna be okay?"

Cat shrugged. "Probably. They know the acid's bad, though, so it's their trip, y'know? They wanna experiment, it's their thing. Me? I'd stay away from it. Acid's cool, but it can come back and hit you at the wrong time." He blew out a lungful of thick blue smoke. "Weed's better for you." He offered the joint to Robin, but Robin shook his head.

"No, um, thanks."

Cat smiled, sliding his arm around Robin's shoulders. Robin couldn't help but notice that Cat still wasn't wearing anything but his pants and nearly shivered when Cat tugged him close to his bare chest.

"That's cool, man. You do what you want. That's what it's all about."

At ease with Cat's acceptance, Robin relaxed into his half-embrace, telling himself just to get over the little jumps and jitters in his stomach. *This touchy-feely stuff is normal for hippies*, he told himself.

Then he caught Cat's sidelong look at him, a sly glance through thick eyelashes that scorched over the edges of his nerves hotter than the August sun. He swallowed thickly as he felt his body start reacting the same way it had in the locker room showers in gym class, only this time accompanied by a crescendo of fluttering butterfly wings in his belly.

There was a crash of sound from the stage area that sounded like a microphone check, and Robin looked in that direction. Cat followed his gaze and took another hit on the joint.

"Wanna go?" he asked. "Sounds like they're starting."

Half-eager and half-reluctant to get out of Cat's embrace, Robin tried for a casual shrug. "Sure. I mean, whatever."

* * *

Cat gave him a steady look and then burst out laughing. "You got it, man." He handed the joint to Lily, his last inhale streaming out between perfect, shapely lips. "Lil, here ya go. Me an' Bobby are gonna go check out the stage."

"Okay." She took the marijuana from him and gave them a happy smile. "Have fun."

Cat headed off toward the stage, letting his arm drop from Robin's shoulder as he did. Robin tried to tell himself he wasn't disappointed, that it was too hot outside for a lot of physical contact, but he was still thinking about it by the time they found a spot on the hill to sit together, watching and listening and just soaking up the music.

Robin had to admit he didn't pay much attention during the first few songs. He didn't recognize the musician—somebody had introduced him, but the name didn't stick—and the song was just talking about the war, and about bombs. Robin was just sitting back, watching everybody else, especially Cat. It went on for hours, and Robin was getting lost in the music, in the sunshine and the fresh air and the thousands of bodies around him, all of them seeking their own path, just like he was.

The last song of the set started—still by that same guy, and Robin still didn't know his name, but he knew he'd remember that brown, wise-looking face forever. It was an explosion of guitar and some kind of hand-beaten drums, and the *voice*, belting out the word "freedom" again and again—Robin felt something inside his soul explode like two live wires had been touched together. He was on his feet in a moment, aching and straining toward the music like he could take it inside himself and breathe it, taste it.

He wanted to dance, but he didn't know how, and he just stood there, trembling, needing to move and frozen in place. He felt a hand on his shoulder, felt breath on his ear, and barely managed to hear Cat's shout over the music.

"What's wrong?"

Robin shook his head. How to explain, using few enough words that Cat stood a chance of hearing him over the music?

"Wanna dance," he finally shouted back.

"So dance!"

"Can't!"

Then one of Cat's hands went to his hip and the other slid around to his stomach, and he felt Cat's body press up against him, pushing his sweat-soaked shirt against his back. He shivered at the dampness and at Cat's nearness. He felt Cat's lithe body behind him, felt the way he moved with the music, and tentatively moved his hips to match.

"Yeah! That's it!"

Cat's enthusiasm was nearly deafening, and then he realized he was moving. *They* were moving, dancing like they were limbs on the same body, writhing together, tangled. Cat's hands on his hip and stomach guided him, encouraged him, and then they were just there, just holding him.

Robin threw his head back, feeling it connect with Cat's shoulder behind him. Cat's long hair tickled his cheek, his neck, and the heat of their bodies sliding together was scorching in the August heat.

And all the while, above and underneath and through it all, were the music and the refrain of *"Freedom, freedom."*

Robin had never understood the word like he did at that moment. Right then, it seemed less like a word, an abstract concept, and more like a pair of wings unfurling inside him. Then Cat kissed the shell of his ear, and he was sure he could fly.

"I SAW that."

Cat turned around, arching his eyebrows at Lily, who stood a couple feet away, licking grease off her fingers from the hamburger she'd managed to buy from one of the vendors. Cat was on his way to the lake, which had turned into something of a communal bath, wondering just where Robin had gotten off to.

"You saw what?"

"You and Bobby." She grinned slyly at him. "Don't think I didn't."

Cat had an inkling of what she was talking about but decided to tread carefully. Some hippies weren't as open-minded as others. "I'm with Bobby all the time. Which time are you talking about?"

She lowered her voice and leaned in, eyes sparkling. "When you kissed him."

Cat sighed. He couldn't say that he hadn't kissed Robin without sounding like he was protesting too much, but he hadn't actually been able to kiss more than his ear yet. "Yet" being the operative word.

Lily snickered and took another bite of her hamburger, looking smug. "Don't worry. I don't care. But if you're looking for him, he's over there somewhere." She waved vaguely with her hand; Cat couldn't even tell which direction she was indicating. "Last I heard, he'd been roped into rounding up all the marshmallows he could find. Who knows why."

Cat muttered his baffled thanks and started to move off toward the lake. Lily's voice stopped him.

"If it makes you happy, baby, there ain't nothin' wrong."

Cat paused to give her a grateful smile over his shoulder. "You got it, babe." He flashed her a peace sign and left her to her hamburger, feeling a little lighter as he got to the edge of the lake. It wasn't like public opinion would be able to stop him, but it always felt nicer to have support than mockery. He got altogether too much mocking as it was for his long hair and his "strange clothes", as his mother had called them the last time he'd seen her.

He put it all out of his mind as he stripped out of those clothes and splashed into the lake. The water was cool enough to make him yelp in surprise at first, to the amusement of a girl soaping up her body a little ways away.

"You get used to it," she said, smiling. "You need this?" She offered him the bar of soap, and he took it with thanks, scraping up a lather to rub into his skin and hair.

He'd just gotten his hair soaped up and was going to rinse off when she spoke again.

"Where are you from?"

"All over," he said with a smile. "Originally Boston, but my parents are a little too high society for my fashion sense. Been all over the east since then, looking at heading west sometime soon. How about you?"

"Alabama." She rinsed the ends of her long hair in the water. "But yeah, I've been all over, too. Was in Memphis last year."

Chills that had nothing to do with the cool lake water shot up Cat's spine. Last year in Memphis was when Dr. King had been assassinated. It must have reflected in his expression, because she gave him a wry smile tinged with sadness.

"I wasn't *there*, but I was in town. Close enough to hear the sirens. It was crazy." She took the soap back when Cat offered it to her, and Cat quickly dunked himself in the water before the suds could get into his eyes. When he surfaced again, she was walking up out of the lake, her long wet hair clinging to her skin.

Cat pushed off the silty bottom of the lake and floated on his back for a while, soaking up the sun and the sweet tug of water over his limbs. Somewhere nearer to the shore, he could hear laughter and talking, the sound of the film crew that was recording the festival, a couple of reporters from the major news stations alternately cajoling people into interviews and spitting out colorful epithets at one thing or another. Cat stayed away from all of it, wanting the time just to soak up the connection with the universe, to think about what was happening in the world and absorb it.

This will be the time people look back on, point to, learn about in history books, he thought. Everything felt bigger than he could contain, and he had a sudden longing for someone to share it all with him. He wished Robin were there in the lake, floating beside him, feeling the way the world around him seemed to knit itself into his soul with the music for thread. Then he thought of how Robin probably would have reacted to being naked with everyone else and laughed, getting water up his nose for his trouble.

He swam out of the lake when he felt his skin beginning to warm a little too much, not particularly wanting to spend the rest of the festival too sunburned to move. He found his jeans right where he'd shucked them but couldn't get into the idea of putting them back on. Denim against wet skin was never comfortable.

He was staring at the offending article of clothing, bare-assed naked on the shore of the lake, when a boy and his girlfriend wandered past with their arms around each other, both of them nude, carrying cloths in their hand.

"Just go natural," the girl advised, laughing, and Cat grinned at her.

"Not that I wouldn't love to, but I've got a friend it would probably scare to death."

The boy tossed him the cloth he was holding. "Here, take this. I thought I'd use it, but I think I like it better like this."

Cat shook out the cloth, seeing that it was one of the simple loincloths a lot of people were wearing. He grinned. "Groovy! Thanks, man."

"You got it." The boy gave him a thumbs-up and kept walking, and Cat tied on his new, freer bit of almost-clothing. He carried his jeans with him, just in case he ended up needing them again, and wandered off in search of his friends.

To his surprise, Robin was right where Lily said he would be—somewhere in the general vicinity of the camping tents set up on the perimeter of the woods—with a group of people who appeared to be heating a shovel over a campfire.

"Hey, Bobby," Cat said, sidling up to him. "What's happenin'?"

Robin looked over at him, full of excitement, until his eyes slid down Cat's nearly-nude body and widened at the loincloth. After a loud swallow and an awkward pause, Robin's gaze shot back up to Cat's face and stayed firmly fixed there—except for the time or six it wandered back down his body—as he explained what was going on.

"We're making the world's biggest marshmallow," he said, voice almost steady and some of the excitement returning to his eyes. "We've got all these marshmallows, and we're gonna melt 'em down on the shovel until they're just one *big* marshmallow."

"Yeah?" Cat grinned. "And what are you going to do if it catches on fire?"

Robin's brow furrowed. "I hadn't thought of that."

Cat patted him on the back, a friendly gesture, but Robin's eyes went wide and startled again, as if Cat had groped his ass. Come to think of it, that wasn't such a bad idea. The kid could use a push in the right direction.

"You have fun with your marshmallow," Cat said after a minute. "I'm gonna go find some nice sunshine to soak up."

He was barely eight feet away from the campsite before he heard footsteps running up behind him. Then Robin fell into step with him, scratching nervously at the back of his neck.

"Give up on the marshmallow?" Cat asked, trying to keep the teasing out of his voice. The look Robin shot him told him he hadn't been successful.

"Sunshine sounded like a good idea."

In fact, the sun was setting rapidly. The days were long in August in northern New York, but they did end eventually. There was music blaring from the stage, wrapping itself all around Cat, and there was a glow of red and gold over the lake he'd just been skinny-dipping in. A swell of bliss bubbled into his throat, and he took a deep, lingering breath, just holding in the air and the music and the magic.

"Thank you."

Robin's voice was so quiet that Cat almost didn't hear it. He turned just enough to see Robin's face, that beautiful skin and hair tinged with gold from the low-hanging sun.

"For what?" Cat's voice was just as quiet, but Robin heard him.

"For stopping, for picking me up. For bringing me here and staying with me." Robin swallowed visibly; Cat watched his throat work. "I don't know where I'll go when this is over, but this is the first time in my life I've felt like I'm really alive."

Cat stopped walking, and Robin followed suit. Streams of people flowed around them, not bothered by the tension Cat could suddenly feel in the air, a balloon of delicious pressure, telling him to move. He studied Robin's face silently for a moment, arguing with himself over whether or not to act on his instincts, before he took a step forward. Robin didn't flinch, didn't move back, and Cat reached up to touch his face.

Robin's eyelids fluttered closed, and his lips opened on a trembling sigh. Carefully, slowly, Cat leaned in, tilting his face up at the same time he pulled Robin's down, and pressed their lips together softly. Robin shook under his hands like a tree in a windstorm, but Cat held the contact for another tenuous moment before he let go.

When Robin opened his eyes, Cat took a deep breath and said, "You're welcome."

THE next day, Robin found himself following Cat out to a part of the field where grass grew as high as Robin's waist, away from the other festivalgoers.

He had only the vaguest ideas of why he wanted to be alone with Cat, but he had a feeling Cat knew enough for both of them.

They'd slept curled together the night before, the same as they had the first night, only everything was different. They were drifting by the time the last note from the last band faded away, the skies overhead twinkling with stars. Their limbs were twined together, and this time Robin knew why he was so conscious of Cat's body against his in a way he'd never been conscious of Alice Miller's.

They'd woken together at sunrise, their noses brushing, their eyes blinking as they struggled to focus on one another's face, so close together in the dim light. Cat had kissed him, Robin had pressed in close, and Cat had whispered, "Let's go somewhere a little less crowded."

Robin had seen other couples wandering off into the high grasses or the woods, hands linked, bodies brushing together as they walked in careless intimacy. It hadn't been hard to guess why they'd been seeking solitude, even if the privacy was partial at best.

And now here he was with Cat.

"Here?" Robin wished he didn't sound *quite* so horrified and naïve.

Cat looked around at the grass surrounding them and laughed. "Where were you thinking? A hotel? One of the ones that's full, maybe, that we'd have to walk to anyway because all the roads are blocked with traffic?"

Cat's eyes were sparkling; he wasn't being mean, just pointing things out in his way.

Robin couldn't help looking around to make sure no other early morning couples were headed out toward this spot where Cat had led him.

"I guess, I mean… we won't… Nobody's going to bother us?"

"I should hope not." Cat laughed. "Unless they're looking to join in, but I think most folks around here are more polite than that. They'd ask *before* we got started."

Robin hoped like hell he wasn't blushing, but he bet he was. His face felt hot, and he didn't think it was just the sunburn talking.

"Even though we're two guys?"

Cat did look a little unsure at that. Hippies were all about free love, but there were still a lot of them that put limits on what genders could be involved. In the end, though, Cat's life philosophy won out, and he shrugged. "Free is free, you know? Nobody's getting hurt, and everybody's happy. Trying to put limits on love is like trying to put a fence around the ocean."

Robin couldn't help the smile that took over his mouth. It felt like a sun rising inside him. That was just so… Cat. It made him feel light and safe, the knowledge that Cat might not know everything, but given a little thought, could come up with some pretty reasonable ideas.

Cat reached out and brushed his fingertips across the edge of Robin's mouth. Robin thought Cat looked pleased too, and he liked knowing that he wasn't the only one riding this bright feeling.

"You've got a beautiful smile, baby," Cat murmured. "It's so… *pure*. Like there's nothing there but happiness."

Robin felt embarrassed, wanting to duck his head and hide that smile, but he liked the way Cat was looking at him, and he didn't want to miss it.

"I *am* happy," he said. "I like this. I like being here. I like you."

He shrugged, looking around again. Now that he wasn't preoccupied with the thought of why they'd come out this far into the tall grass in the first place, he could take in more of it. He could see tents through the trees, crowds of people sitting in front of the huge stage, the lake with people splashing through the water in careless nudity. Instead of feeling different, out of place, he suddenly felt very connected. "Even though I don't know what I want to do after I leave here, I'm not worried. I'm happy *now*."

"Now's all we've got, really," Cat said reasonably, reaching out tentatively and wrapping his fingers around Robin's. "All we really need."

Robin let Cat pull him in, let Cat bring his face down for soft, seductive kisses. His hand slid across Cat's bare side, down over the hip covered only with a leather thong holding on the loincloth, and couldn't help laughing.

Cat pulled back from the kiss, studying his expression. "Something funny?"

"The night I sneaked out of the house to come up here, I went for a walk with my girlfriend. She kissed me and told me I could put my hand on her waist." He rubbed his thumb over the bare, summer-colored skin he was touching to emphasize his point. "I was kind of glad she was wearing a sweater." He leaned in, kissing Cat's mouth softly. "I'm really glad you're not."

Cat's lips curved against his, and Cat's hand slid under his shirt. "What'll your girl say when you go back home?"

Robin's smile fell away. "She's not my girl anymore, and I'm not going back home. My parents told me if I came here, I shouldn't bother coming back. Alice said the same thing."

Cat's hand came up and wound through Robin's hair, petting him. The sensation was comforting and arousing all at once.

"Poor baby," Cat crooned, his eyes sparkling with mischief. "A motherless child, such a long way from his home." Robin recognized the lyrics from that freedom song he'd heard on the first day and grinned. Cat saw the expression and kissed him. "For the record, I don't know where I'm going when I leave here, either. I was thinking west. They say California's got somethin' groovy goin' on. Haight and Ashbury in San Francisco, callin' it the Summer of Love."

Robin let Cat kiss down over his jaw, pulling the other man's body in close to his and thinking how grateful he was that he'd come to New York. Kissing Alice Miller had never felt like *this*.

"Can I come with you?" He said the words into Cat's neck, half-hoping the other man wouldn't hear him. But of course, Cat had. The warm, lithe body in his arms went perfectly still, and he could feel Cat's breath puffing against his own throat.

"I'd like that."

It was a whisper, but Robin heard it and shuddered with relief.

The universe opened wide and welcomed him in, and he let himself be swallowed by the sun, the sky, and the music.

Cat pulled him down toward the ground, and Robin went willingly. Their arms wound around each other, and Cat's thighs opened to cradle him.

Maybe he wasn't so far from home after all.

• • •

Spontaneous
Chrissy Munder

I

ike Vincent squinted beneath the brilliant overhead lights. This wasn't a gas station; this was a mothership landed in the middle of the deserted Michigan landscape. He blinked in amazement, his dark brown eyes blurred with the sudden oversaturation of light as he fed his credit card into the slot of the gasoline pump. The dazzling display had been visible even from the expressway, and for a change had alerted him *before* he passed the exit sign.

The smart thing would have been to top off his gas tank prior to starting on his journey, but he hadn't been thinking clearly once he had okayed his unexpected vacation with his boss. No, Mike corrected himself, not unexpected. Spontaneous. Did sarcasm count when you were the only one to hear it? Thankfully, Mike's small and practical economy car went quite a few miles before requiring a fill-up.

Mike fiddled with the nozzle of the gas pump and brushed his dark hair out of his face. He had never been able to figure out how to use the slidey thing on the handle to fill his tank without having to stand and watch it, no matter how many times Derek impatiently showed him. The couple of times he tried had left an expensive puddle of fuel on the ground.

• • •

His eyes roamed from the bright lights of the gas station's lot to the dark expanse of highway visible from where he stood in the calm quiet. Despite the early hour, the last several miles of road had stretched before his headlights in an uninterrupted ribbon, his vehicle the only sign of life. Even the nocturnal creatures waiting by the shoulder, watchful eyes glowing red with reflection, disappeared to their dens.

Great. Mike grimaced. There was nothing and no one out here but him and his thoughts. He had hoped the impromptu drive to Michigan's west coast would clear his head, maybe even enable him to leave his confusion behind in a cloud of exhaust. Instead, his brain kept churning over the same questions. They stayed with him like the bug carcasses stuck to his windshield.

Mike focused on the distraction. Why did the biggest bugs always hit and smear dead center in his line of vision? The entire passenger side surface loomed smooth and enticing. The mutant-sized Michigan mosquitoes could choose to commit hari-kari on that welcoming expanse, but no. They had to land right smack in the middle of his share of the windshield. Mike stared at the thick, greenish-white goop his wipers had spread over the glass. One lone bug leg stuck out of the middle of the mess and waved at him.

Gross.

Mike hated bugs. He hated deer that leapt across the roadway in front of him in their search for the perfect cornfield on the other side just as twilight fell. He hated driving at night, and he especially hated whichever idiot had thought it a fun game to hit the orange and white safety barrels marking the endless stretch of road construction he'd driven through for the last forty minutes.

At least the resulting slalom course had forced Mike to stay alert. He couldn't afford to let his attention drift, risking a run-in with any of the barrels scattered in his way. He might damage a tire rim or, even worse, spin out and end up off the side of the road. The denseness of the forest on either side of the highway guaranteed the probability of hitting a tree. With Derek still listed as his emergency contact, things would get complicated. Mike wondered if an accident might prove the exception to Derek's timeout on their relationship.

To Mike, a timeout meant you stuck a two-year old in the corner for bad behavior. He'd seen his friends use the technique often enough with their kids. He wouldn't vouch for the effectiveness, but his buddy John had told him the procedure worked better for the parent's sake than the child's.

Apparently experience proved things looked different after a little timeout, at least when it came time to rethink the wisdom of maiming your offspring.

So what did it mean when your boyfriend of six months told you that you were boring, totally predictable, and as practical as the car you drove? Oh, and by the way, he was taking a timeout from the relationship. Which in Derek's case didn't translate to standing in the corner, or even moving into the spare bedroom until they had a chance to talk things out.

Mike understood timeout meant goodbye in Derek-speak. He couldn't say his heart felt broken, but Mike's pride had taken a few dents as, once again, he felt like the nerd he had been back in high school and his crush told him he was too smart to be a fun date.

Mike's personality shouldn't have come as any great surprise to Derek. Not only was Mike a systems engineer specializing in research and development, but they had met at a science fiction convention, after all. Granted, Derek was there to do a special interest piece for a local television station, while Mike had been an attendee, but Derek had been the one to do the pursuing in their relationship. It would seem the thrill had all been in the getting, not the having.

The pump clicked and Mike started as the nozzle jumped in his hand. Mike went through the rest of the motions, cursed when, just like at home, the self-serve unit refused to print out a receipt, and then reached for the squeegee at rest in the mostly-dry reservoir affixed to the side of the pole. Hardly enough fluid to moisten the spongy surface. Mike grimaced and determinedly tackled his windshield.

A loud rattle pulled his attention away from the dried bug guts. Mike glanced over at the gas station's attendant as he wheeled a large cart out to the pumps. His shaved head kept time, bobbing to whatever noise pounded through the ear buds of his MP3 player.

The attendant looked young, probably no more than twenty or twenty-two to Mike's thirty-two. Baggy jeans threatened to slide off his skinny hips, and only the practiced shuffle of the new generation of multi-slackers kept them up, but he had wiry appeal. A flash of biceps caught Mike's attention as the guy pulled the top off the trashcan and tossed the plastic bag full of trash into the cart. Hey, Mike told himself, he was pissed off at the male species, not dead.

"Excuse me."

The sound of Mike's voice over the clatter of the cart made the attendant jump, and he glanced up, obviously disgruntled Mike had disturbed him.

"Yeah?" he muttered around his yawn, his utter disinterest displayed by the way he dropped only one side of his earbuds as he pushed the cart toward the next trashcan.

"You got any more window cleaner?" Mike asked with an impatient gesture at his windshield.

"Uh, I don't know." The attendant yawned again. "I guess there should be somewhere."

"Can you look?" Mike held on to his temper with difficulty as the young man slowly shuffled back into the station.

Mike added anyone under the age of twenty-five to his list of things he disliked and felt surprised when the young man actually shuffled back out carrying a plastic jug of blue liquid. He handed the jug over to Mike and stood to the side, his hands shoved deep in his pockets while he swayed to the beat of the music only he could hear.

"Slow night?" Mike asked through gritted teeth as the attendant waved his hand to disrupt the cloud of bugs attracted by the lights.

"Seriously dead, and like, it's only ten. I'm never going to stay awake tonight if it stays like this." Mike poured cleaner directly from the jug onto his windshield and tried to ignore him. "What's the Michigan state bird?"

"What?" Mike stopped scrubbing, and then he got it. "Oh, yeah, the mosquito. Very funny."

"You liked that?" Another yawn, this time accompanied by a smirk as the attendant shifted his feet. "How can you tell it's spring in Michigan?"

"You see the first construction barrel on the highway." Mike grimaced as he gave up the punch line for the familiar joke about his home state, too true to be funny.

"So, like, where you headed?" the bored attendant asked, apparently having chosen Mike as his evening distraction.

"Pentwater," Mike mumbled under his breath, the bug guts finally gone as he turned to the rubber strip on the other side of the squeegee to dry the glass. He appreciated the extra cleaner but wished the young man would go back to emptying the trash.

"By yourself?" Picking up on things didn't seem to be the guy's strong point.

"So?" Mike scowled at the disbelieving tone.

"Won't that be, like, boring?"

Mike dropped the squeegee back into the reservoir with a splash. "Look," he gritted out through his teeth, his frustration spilling out and over as he voiced the thoughts, his only company on the drive. "I'm not the one who decided after six months I needed a timeout from my relationship. I'm not the one who decided I was boring compared to the new little twit who offers massage therapy at the gym, and I'm not the one who took off to Cancun with that same little twit instead of working on fixing our relationship!"

As his voice echoed in the empty lot, Mike pressed his lips together in an effort to hold back the rest of the words clamoring to be heard and looked at the attendant standing wide-eyed in front of him. At least he didn't look bored anymore. They stared at each other in the sudden silence, even the background buzz of nighttime insects hushed, until the young man finally offered his opinion.

"Like, bummer, dude."

II

MIKE waited in hopeful anticipation for the punch line to this morning's cosmic joke. Not that he would hear it over the rousing chorus of hammering, sawing, yelling, and, well, he didn't even know how to describe the noise audible through the room's open windows.

"No," he whimpered as he gave up all attempts at sleep. Mike pulled the pillow off of his face and squinted at the alarm clock on the wicker nightstand beside the bed. The blurry, red, digital numbers couldn't be right. He hadn't seen this hour of the morning in years.

"Oh, my God." Was there no mercy in the world? Mike moaned as he pulled the covers over his head. A nice and fluffy duvet and sheets with some heft to them; maybe they would work to block the noise better than the pillow did.

Not.

So much for the stellar start to his vacation. Mike could picture the entry in his blog: *Day one: I woke filled with the desire to commit murder and mayhem. Where's my axe?* Pushing aside his craving for bloodshed and ignoring the way his boxers had twisted high up on his leg to let everything flap in the proverbial breeze, Mike rolled over and struggled to peer through the sheer drapes covering the windows.

When that didn't work, he stumbled to the closest open window and rubbed his eyes as he stared out. Cleary visible in the early morning light, the booming construction site he had been too sleepy to notice when he arrived last night bustled with a full accompaniment of workers.

Lots and lots of workers. They swarmed over the incomplete structure and scurried along on the ground below like an industrial-size colony of ants, every one of them busy with some type of implement, or tool. All of them were making noise.

Lots of noise.

No simple cottage remodel, this spelled out "project" with a capital "P". Right next door to the bed and breakfast where Mike planned to stay for the next week, the very same bed and breakfast that had advertised nothing but fresh lake air and the sounds of summer. Noticeably absent in said

* * *

advertisement had been the part about the smell of diesel equipment and the sounds of hammer and saws and the rest of it.

"Oh, hell," Mike muttered. See what a little spontaneity got you?

Caffeine. Mike needed caffeine. Then, and only then, could decisions be made. Spurred on by the proper incentive, Mike forced himself to walk over to the small refrigerator in the corner of the room. There, in the position of honor, sat his baby. His pride and joy. The only lover who had never let him down throughout the long years of school and work.

His coffeemaker.

Other than clothes and his laptop, the shining, silver monster was the only thing Mike had packed once he decided to prove he could do spontaneous as well as the next guy. He had taken took off for parts unknown based solely on a television commercial and, of course, some quick research on the internet, which, for him, could be viewed as pretty damn spontaneous.

Mike ignored the ominous flickering of his room lights when he flipped the on switch. While the unit happily burbled and hissed, he ran his hand through his dark, wavy hair, shaking out the nighttime tangles, the humidity from the lake already taking its toll. A quick glance told him the pot hadn't finished brewing, so he walked into the small bathroom and splashed some water on his face. He deliberately avoided staring into his bloodshot brown eyes.

So much for his morning routine.

By the time the pot of lifesaving liquid finished brewing, Mike had slipped into a pair of shorts and a T-shirt, both left over from his college years. Not much had changed, despite his attempts at the gym. In Mike's estimation, he need more bulk for his over six-foot height.

He felt almost human by the time he had finished his first cup of strong, black coffee. By his third, despite the strange power fluctuations, the laptop was open, Mike had checked his email and even posted a comment on his favorite science fiction movie blog. The clock on the nightstand announced a more humane hour and thus ended the debate over cup number four.

Time to talk to management.

* * *

"WHAT do you mean, there's nothing you can do?' Okay, based on the way his voice rose at the end of the sentence, perhaps Mike should have opted for the extra dose of caffeine.

"Well, I am sorry, dear, but the construction is slated to continue until the fall. Those condos aren't even close to being done yet." The elderly woman running the counter was made of sterner stuff than Mike originally thought, because she wouldn't budge, not even under the full force of Mike's glare.

Mike didn't understand it. He quelled programmers with years of experience with that glare. Here, it made no impact whatsoever. He scratched at the mosquito bite on his arm. The elderly woman continued straightening and twitching at the forest of greenery trailing from the potted indoor plants on the counter no matter how indignant Mike let himself become.

"The project had a lot of locals stirred up, I can guarantee you that. Did you know we even had a 'no new condo' commission try to halt the groundbreaking? But progress will persevere."

Time to try reason. "But nothing was said about a major construction project when I made my reservation. Your brochure promised nothing but peace, quiet and the sound of the lake."

"We still have all that." With a final pat to the greenery, the calm blue eyes smiled up at Mike. "You'll just have to walk down to the beach to get the full effect."

Whatever meds the old gal had taken this morning, Mike wanted some. It didn't matter what argument Mike tried, she smiled and ignored all his extremely valid and concise points. Her calm, unchanging expression seemed practically robotic, and it definitely creeped him out. He reached down to rub at the itchy spot on his calf.

"Look, just give me a refund on my credit card, and I'll find somewhere else to stay. There's no way I can spend a week listening to all the noise." Mike glared suspiciously at all the greenery and tried not to think about pod people.

"Oh, no, dear." Mike watched the tufts of gray hair bob up and down in one direction while the wrinkled wattle under her chin swung back and forth in another. "I'm sorry, but there are no refunds. It said so directly on the bottom of the paperwork you signed last night. Small print, you know. Didn't you read it?"

"No." It took some effort, but Mike unlocked his stiffly clenched jaws. "It was dark, and I was tired when I arrived."

"That road construction is a real difficulty, isn't it?" A wrinkled hand reached out to pat Mike's hand instead of the plants this time, ignoring the way it clutched at the counter. "It took my grandson close to three hours last week to go less than two miles. I shouldn't say it, seeing as how I depend on them for my business, but all the tourists don't much help things, either."

"I'm sure." Mike struggled to keep his polite smile. What the hell did she call him, if not another tourist? Anyway, it wasn't fair to expect him to take the loss and pay to stay somewhere else. "About my room—"

"Well, I can try to see if there is something on the other side." The old gal pursed her lips in thought. "There's a couple from Kalamazoo who mentioned they might have to leave early." She leaned forward and lowered her voice in confidence. "I think one of them is married and their spouse came back from a business trip sooner than expected."

Mike stared blankly at the old woman and scratched harder at his arm. "How in the world would you know?" He ignored the wave of paranoia that made him wonder if the rooms were bugged. He hadn't worked on any government contracts lately, had he?

"Oh, my." Another one of those beaming smiles made his jaw twitch in response. "You'd be amazed what you can hear if you stop and listen."

Faced with such sheer, unrelenting pleasantness, Mike began to think he had entered some kind of bizarre Twilight Zone. Perhaps a geriatric twist on the *Children of the Corn* movies? Maybe his sleepy vacation village would turn out to be the original *Village of the Damned*?

"I know." Mike's mental list of movies he would never confess (other than on the Internet) he watched every time they came on television was interrupted by his hostess once again. "Why don't you take one of the folding loungers and head down to the beach and I'll see what I can come up with?"

"Well—" Mike couldn't believe he even thought about agreeing. What happened to all his drive and focus? Were the plants giving off a brain-controlling pheromone?

"You'll see. Things will look better after some time in the sand." Her gray head titled sideways, the blue eyes sparkling. "They always do."

* * *

Mike dazedly found his way back to his room. He didn't know what just happened, but time spent at the beach with nothing to disturb him sounded like a good idea. The best idea he had heard in weeks, actually, even if it did come from a Stepford Grandmother.

Mike changed into his swim trunks and grabbed a towel and his T-shirt. He resolutely refused to pull out his bag and gather up sunscreen, one of the research journals he had brought along, or do anything else remotely resembling planning. He would be spontaneous if it killed him.

Taking a final glance around the room, Mike let his gaze linger with disgust at the window. He froze. Was it even possible to break into a sweat at the same time? All Mike knew for sure was one hundred percent of his attention was suddenly riveted to the most perfect ass he had ever seen. There it was, displayed before him in all its splendid glory, firm and high and framed front and center in the middle of his window.

III

MIKE knew he had a plan when he entered his room. He was sure of it. But he couldn't focus on anything but the image in front of him and the faded jeans that clung so lovingly to the taut flesh beneath. He whimpered at the hint of a pucker at the back seam of the material, designed to deliberately tease him with the defined separation.

Holy moly. Mike held his breath as the body the oh-so-fine ass belonged to unfolded and treated him to a smooth and elegant expanse of tanned back. Any closer and Mike bet he could see trickles of sweat running down the firmly defined muscle. Why in the hell wasn't he any closer?

Beach. He had decided to go to the beach. He should turn around and head there right now. He should probably do anything other than stand in place like Lot's wife. But despite the mental commands Mike gave his limbs, he kept staring at the vision so confidently balanced on the roof across from him.

Turn around. Turn around. Even deprived of northerly blood flow, Mike's brain still managed the mental chant, and Mike automatically reached down to adjust himself as he drew closer to the window, his T-shirt and towel dropping to the floor, forgotten. Surely the front view wouldn't be a good as the rear. Because, really? That would be totally unfair.

But unfair must have been the word of the day, because when the figure on the roof turned with lazy grace to pick up a hammer, Mike found himself faced with a front view as good as the back. Hell, maybe even better. A leather tool belt slung across narrow hips pulled the front of the jeans low, dangerously low considering the sudden press of Mike's insistent arousal. He couldn't help but moan at the discovery the guy could claim membership in the small club of honest-to-God real blonds.

Mike couldn't tell what color eyes this walking wet dream had, but the rest of him matched everything Mike had ever dreamed of in a man. From the top of the battered straw cowboy hat to the bottom of the work boots visible beneath frayed denim, the man embodied nothing but sweat-covered perfection.

Abs, Mike thought dreamily. Those were abs to die for, with a hint of roundness in the belly Mike could imagine running his hand over. Hell, who

* * *

was he kidding? That belly was made for Mike's lips and definitely for the caress of his teeth. Man, could he imagine how that belly would taste after a day in the sun, salty and sweet all at the same time.

The blond in the bandana standing beside the vision laughed, and his shoulder nudged the other man, turning him slightly and allowing Mike a glimpse of a line of dark ink circling the defined bicep. Heaven. Somehow between last night and today, Mike had died and gone to unadulterated, lust-filled heaven.

"HEY, Eben."

Sam's voice had him turning around even though he had already started down off the roof. Break time had finally arrived, and Eben Bowman was more than ready for something wet and cold. All he had to decide was whether to pour it over his head or down his throat.

"Eben, man, you listening to me?"

"What?" Eben navigated the maze of metal and wood beams with the ease of long practice. "No, I'm not listening to you. I'm thirsty. Let's go."

"Check this out first."

The laughter in Sam's voice should have been a warning. Sam Carlton may have been his best friend going all the way back to high school—the two of them were practically twins after all this time—but there were days when he was still nothing but a pain in the ass.

Like today.

"What?" Eben demanded as he bent down to pick up the hammer that wasn't where he had left it. "Didn't I tell you to stop using my stuff? You've got your own tools to ruin."

"Your tools are never so happy as when I use them. It's pitiful how clean you keep them. A man's tools were meant to be used hard and put up dirty." Sam pushed his bandana further back up on his forehead, the fabric darkening as it absorbed more sweat. He winked as the press of his shoulder nudged Eben to the right. "Happy Monday, big boy. Take a look at the view."

"The lake? Are you nuts? I know what the damn lake looks like." But it wasn't the lake below attracting Eben's attention. Nope, try the expanse of pale skin belonging to the man leaning out the window of the bed and breakfast next door. Huh, it looked like Old Joe had forgot to finish installing the window screens again.

One part of his brain noted he'd have to tell his grandmother about the screens; the other part let Eben's light green eyes wander from the top of the shiny dark head to the hidden waistband of the blue shorts. Just maybe both parts let his gaze linger on the mat of dark chest hair in between. Lord, did he love a man with a bit of chest hair.

"Isn't that your grandmother's place?" Sam asked. Eben didn't have any time or attention to waste listening to him, too busy estimating the height of the half-naked man based on the way he filled the window frame. Eben had what you might call a "thing" for tall guys. And pale guys. And guys as lean as this one appeared to be.

"Uh huh." The gap between the condo project he and Sam were working on and the bedroom window across the way was a fair distance, but if he pushed the brim of his dad's old hat back from his forehead and squinted in the mid-morning sun, Eben thought he could detect a hint of stubble on the firm jaw. Eben liked stubble. Especially when tall, pale, lean strangers were rubbing it against your—

"You listening to me?" Sam again. Always butting in when he wasn't wanted.

"Should I be?" Eben mumbled. For one all-too-brief second, his eyes met those of the man in the window before the opposite pair of eyes widened and the man quickly backed out of sight.

"You always did like the tall, geeky types, and from the way he's falling out of the window to get a look at you, he's interested as well. Too bad you and Barry the jerk are still seeing each other." Sam paused for effect. "You *are* still seeing each other, aren't you?"

Since the tall stranger didn't seem to be making another appearance, Eben turned back to his friend. "You realize you show more interest in my love life than my grandmother, don't you?"

"And you realize you're avoiding my question, don't you?" Sam countered with skill earned through years of experience dealing with Eben. His friend might be stubborn, but Sam had learned how to outlast him.

"Why do you want to know?"

"Why don't you want to tell me?"

The two friends stared at each other until Eben gave in with an exasperated sigh. "No, we aren't still dating." Eben rolled his shoulders, uncomfortable with the confession. The last part of his sentence trailed off into a mumble.

"What?" Sam had one hand cupped behind his ear.

"Come on, Sam. Give me a break, why don't you? You heard me." Eben looked at the other guys on the roof and then headed down the ladder to ground level. He hated it when Sam embarrassed him like this. Eben didn't worry the rest of the guys would give him grief about his preferences, but they would sure ride him about the breakup.

"Whose idea was it?"

Sam scrambled down the ladder after him, and Eben ducked as Sam's booted foot narrowly missed his head. "Slow down, will you?"

"Does your grandmother know?"

"No, she doesn't know." Eben fit the insides of his boots to the outside of the ladder and slid the rest of the distance to the ground in his hurry to get out of Sam's way. "And I broke things off." A damn good decision, based on his reaction to the man he'd just seen.

"Uh huh."

Eben wondered how so few words could hold such meaning. "Really," he insisted as they walked over the dusty lot to where their trucks were parked. "I didn't fit into his world, you know? He always seemed so embarrassed if we ran into anyone he worked with."

Sam put his hand on Eben's shoulder with a solemn look of concern. "I told you he was a jerk. You poor thing. When will you find someone who will love you for your brain, not your body?"

"You're a dick." Eben knocked Sam's hand off his shoulder and opened the cooler in the back of his truck. "I don't know why I put up with you."

"You love me." Sam reached past Eben and grabbed the soda from under Eben's hand. "Just admit you've always secretly longed for me and that's why you can't seem to find yourself a real boyfriend."

"Renee's been making you watch the *Lifetime Channel* again, huh?" Eben took off his hat and opened a bottle of water. He tried to prepare himself for the shock to come as he tipped the bottle and poured the cold water over his head and neck, but failed. "Son of a bitch!"

"You can tell?" Sam asked mournfully as he drained his soda in three big gulps and rummaged in the melting ice for another. "I think I'm going into Arnold withdrawal. Do you know she absolutely refuses to watch *Commando* or *The Running Man*, even after I told her they're really love stories?"

"Unbelievable." Eben shook his head, water flying off his blond hair in a crystalline spray. He could always distract Sam by bringing up his girlfriend of the moment. "Try *True Lies* instead."

"Then she'll ask me if I think Jaime Lee has a better body than she does, and I'll have to lie my ass off." Sam shook his head. "I'm telling you, relationships are hard work. Do you remember when sex used to be fun?"

"Tell me about it." Eben muttered under his breath. Barry hadn't really touched his heart, but the experience had deepened his wariness when it came to men. Maybe Sam had a point. Maybe, instead of a relationship, Eben needed a summer romance with someone he knew wouldn't be sticking around.

Maybe even someone tall and pale with a sexy bit of stubble on his jaw.

* * *

IV

IT *WAS* better in the sand.

Mike shifted on the vinyl lounge chair. The sun beat down from the clear and cloudless blue sky, reflecting off the already heated sand and baking him where he reclined in between. Sweat ran down his back and disappeared, absorbed into the white sand.

The state park's surprisingly sandy camping area appeared full of RVs and tents, but only a small crowd dotted the beach. A few brave souls kept busy dancing in and out of the waves where the water met the sand. They exclaimed at the brisk temperature; the water was freezing, despite the heat of the day. Others chose to walk along the shoreline, crumbling footprints in the damp sand the only sign of their passing.

Mike stuck his toes experimentally into the water, and then quickly retreated to the lounger. His balls would be stuck in his throat for months if he waded into water that cold. Maybe he'd come back and try again, say after a few more years of global warming.

He sat back and let his eyes close, enjoying the rhythmic sound of the water and the birds cawing overhead, viewing the humans on the beach as interlopers even while keeping a beady eye out for any unattended food. Kids ran up and down with their usual amount of boundless energy, and the smell of coconut oil filled the air.

Wow. Look at him relax.

It had been a short walk along the channel to the state park. Recognizing the lure of the water, both sides of the channel connecting Pentwater Lake to Lake Michigan were lined with a concrete walkway. Tourists kept pace with recreational boaters as they slowly chugged their way through the no-wake zone and out to the big lake.

Mike's attention had been torn between the variety of boats in the channel and the houses to his right as his flip-flops slapped along the sand-covered concrete and the folding lounger bounced on its carry strap on his back. He bet even the decrepit, gray-shingled cottage with the sagging roof was worth a pretty penny based on location alone.

Like all the tourists, Mike couldn't resist walking out to the channel marker at the end of the pier. While not lighthouses, the structures on each side of the channel were equipped to warn approaching craft at night and in bad weather. Based on the blanket of graffiti covering the one he stood beside, it doubled as the favorite hangout for the local disaffected youth.

Enormous slabs of rock, brown and discolored with weathering, lined the outside of the breakwall, and Mike could see the debris left behind by some inconsiderate fisherman. Teenagers ignored the posted warnings, jumping off the concrete pier into the middle of the channel, barely missing a group of kayakers as they paddled determinedly past.

The graceful motion of the small crafts looked like fun, but Mike didn't think he'd be comfortable with nothing but a thin piece of fiberglass between him and the water. Lake Michigan looked much bigger than he expected. If anything, it reminded him of the ocean, a vast and endless expanse of water stretching far to the horizon.

From his vantage point, he could see the rocky hills of Ludington further up the coast in the hazy sunshine. One of the other tourists standing on the pier had told Mike about a hydroelectric plant there he could tour. That sounded interesting.

He wondered whether the man he had seen on the roof liked the water. Probably, if he lived close. How spontaneous would it be to ask the gorgeous blond out to dinner? Not that Mike felt he still had anything to prove in that department. Mike considered his newfound serenity. If this was the effect one day of vacation and a good-looking man could have, what would he be like after a week?

Right now, Mike planned to kick back and relax. The only thing he wanted to think about was the absolutely amazing man he'd had the good luck to see this morning, and if he had anything to do with it, the man he would see again tomorrow.

Mike closed his eyes under the dark shield of his sunglasses and relaxed further back into the chair with a satisfied grunt. He'd have to remember to tell his hostess he didn't want to change rooms after all. A soft breeze blew inland off the water and, slowly but surely, Mike's breathing deepened as he fell asleep.

● ● ●

"WELL, you know what Old Joe is like, dear." Eben knew what to expect as soon as his grandmother patted him on the cheek and gestured at the hammer on the counter. "Thank goodness I have you to help me out."

"Come on, Nana. I've been at work all day." Eben knew it wasn't polite to whine at his grandmother, but it had been a tiring day and he was more than ready to head home. "Let Joe finish them all up tomorrow."

"But my guests could get carried off by mosquitoes in the middle of the night. That wouldn't be good for business." The steely glint in those familiar blue eyes was a sure sign no good deed goes unpunished. Eben regretted stopping by the bed and breakfast instead of joining Sam at the bar, especially when there wasn't any sign of tall, pale, and stubbly, or Michael Vincent, as the only new guest was named in the bed and breakfast's register.

"It's not like they got carried off last night," Eben muttered, his shoulders slumping with resignation. So much for his not-very-subtle plan to meet the man who had caught his eye.

"It's not like you have anything else to do when you get home." Eben wondered how a smile that sweet could still be so cutting. "From what I hear, you're single again."

"How did you find out?" Eben ignored the disapproving sniff following her last comment, and, giving in to the inevitable, he picked up several of the window screens set to the side of the front desk. She had obviously been primed and waiting for him. "Let me guess: Sam called and told you, didn't he?" Eben shook his head. "It's amazing I have a love life at all between the two of you."

"We only want you to be happy." Pleased Eben had given in, she hurried out from behind the counter to slip the hammer into his tool belt. "It would be nice if you would make a little effort to help us out."

Satisfied at having the last word, she waved him off, leaving Eben to grumble to himself as he slowly climbed the stairs with his burden.

OW. MISTAKE. *Big* mistake.

Mike held his arms outstretched and stared at his naked body in the mirror of his rented bathroom. He shuffled slightly from side to side, wincing as the skin pulled with the motion. His back was okay, but from the front, he looked like a giant red candy gummy worm, the ones with the clear part in the middle. He was even kind of gooey and oozy too, at least where he had managed to put some lotion on his abused skin.

Why had he ever thought not taking his sunscreen to the beach would be considered a show of spontaneity? Obviously because, hey, nothing said "I'm a wild and crazy guy" like massive third-degree burns all over one side of his body. Mike looked at his chest in dismay. Okay, maybe they weren't third-degree burns, but his skin appeared red and swollen and jeez, did his nipples hurt.

So now what? Mike hadn't been able to cover all of the red with lotion, and actually, the parts that *had* gotten the lotion didn't feel any better. At least he had kept his sunglasses on; otherwise, his eyeballs might have cooked in their sockets. The knock on his door distracted him, and Mike grabbed a towel in irritation, holding it up front of him as he shuffled painfully to the door.

"Yeah?" Mike yelled through the door. He didn't want to risk moving any more than he had to.

"Maintenance." If Mike didn't know better, he'd swear there was a long-suffering sigh after the word. "I'm here to put the screens in the window. It'll only take a minute."

Mike wondered how fast he'd have to move to open the door and dash back in to the bathroom. "Any chance you could do the others and come back?"

"Sorry, you're my last one." This time the exhalation sounded tired. "Trust me, I'll work fast."

It was Mike's turn to sigh. He had finally figured out where all his mosquito bites came from and didn't want a repeat. He could only imagine the hell he'd endure if he got even one bite on any of his sunburned parts. He unlocked the door and then shuffled back a step. "Come on in."

"Sorry about this." The wood floor creaked beneath the heavy work boots. "But my grandmother wanted to make sure these screens were put up tonight."

Busy making sure his towel wasn't in danger of giving whatever wizened old gnome who did maintenance for the Stepford Grandmother a free show, Mike didn't look up until the workman passed him, and then he had to accept this wasn't his day. Not only did that ass not belong to some old geezer, but he recognized it as well.

"Oh, wow."

Blinded by the quick glimpse of the sweetest ass he had ever seen, it took Mike a second to register it wasn't the view outside the window that warranted the low whistle of appreciation. It was his half-man/half lobster-red body.

"Are you okay?" The handsome blond Mike had seen on the roof earlier in the morning set down the screens and gave Mike a concerned glance. "You sure got some sun since I last saw you."

"Uh, yeah." Mike's throat tightened, and the saliva flooding his mouth suddenly dried. This guy acted like they knew each other. Granted, Mike had stared much longer than was polite this morning, but that hardly constituted an introduction. Of course, what did he care, when being this close, the view looked even better than it had earlier?

Now he could see his dream man's eyes were a light, almost lake-water green, and the blond hair was cropped ruthlessly short in a futile effort to control its wayward curl. It was a shame that his belly was covered, but Mike could remember how fine it had looked in the sunlight, and the rest of the man lived up to his initial, dazed impressions as well. "Yeah, I'm fine. Just a little sunburned." And embarrassed at his current condition, but Mike wasn't going to mention that part.

"More than just a little. That's gotta hurt." While Mike appreciated the obvious concern in the pleasant voice, he wished the good-looking blond would stop circling him. There was something vaguely predatory, and definitely arousing, about the close scrutiny, and the last thing he wanted to do was get hard while only wearing this towel.

"I don't think you need to go to the hospital, but let me go get you something to put on that burn. It would be a shame for skin as nice as yours to blister." For a breathless second, Mike thought he felt one of those big hands lightly brush against his back, and he shivered at the touch. "My grandmother has the greatest stuff; it will put you right in no time."

● ● ●

"No, really, I'll be okay." Mike inwardly cringed at the thought of having to go the hospital, and it must have showed, because the blond nodded and ignored his protests.

"I'll be right back."

V

EVERYTHING blurred. One minute Mike stood there dumbly, as embarrassed as he'd ever been in his life. The next, he soaked in some kind of oatmeal/herb bath while the sexiest man he'd ever seen wielded a hammer in the other room.

Mike didn't have time to do anything more than shuffle back over to the bathroom before he heard the hurried sound of the heavy work boots as they took the stairs two at a time. He couldn't help but wonder if this were a delusion brought on by too much sun, because otherwise, this was so pathetic.

His dream man was on the other side of the door, and thanks to his own stupidity, Mike was totally out of the running. Assuming there even was a running, of course. His internal debate over whether or not to open the door to his room was cut short when the door was unceremoniously pushed open.

"Here you go." Pale green eyes blinked up at him. One large and work-battered hand held out two cloth bundles, both tied at the top with a yellow ribbon. "Run yourself a lukewarm bath and let these soak in it with you. You'll be ready to have fun in no time." A quick wink accompanied the optimistic announcement.

Mike blinked in turn. He went ahead and took the soft bundles and held them up to his nose as his grasp released an aromatic fragrance.

"They've got oatmeal and herbs in them. Trust me." White teeth flashed in an endearingly crooked smile, and Mike realized it wasn't that his intelligence had deserted him—it simply knew when to surrender gracefully.

"When you get out, I've got this cooling stuff to put on you that will take away the rest of the sting."

Put on him? With erotic images of those large hands rubbing cooling gel onto his body flashing through his mind, Mike took the tube of green gel in his other hand. This had to be a joke, right? Who was this guy, and why did he act like he was interested in Mike? As if in answer, one of the large hands thrust toward him.

"Sorry. I forgot my manners." Another one of those crooked smiles. Mike decided he could cheerfully spend the next month counting the freckles scattered across the bridge of the beaked nose. "I'm Eben. Eben Bowman. My grandmother runs the bed and breakfast. We saw each other earlier this morning?" At Mike's continued silence, the smile faltered. "I help her out with some of the maintenance stuff."

The disappearance of the smile woke Mike from his daze. Ignoring the pain from the movement, he tossed the tube of green gel into the hand with the oatmeal stuff and took the extended hand in his own. "Sorry, I just—" Mike paused again, stumped at trying to come up with a polite way to say "I just noticed your rainbow bracelet" without sounding like an idiot.

The braided and dyed hemp had faded, but against the tanned skin of Eben's muscular forearm, it was still an obvious statement. Despite his physical discomfort, Mike smiled and allowed himself to enjoy the feel of the work-roughened hand a little longer than polite in light of his new knowledge. "I'm a little out of it. My name's Mike."

"I'm pleased to meet you, Mike." The freckles took another dance across the bridge of Eben's nose, and if it hadn't had been for his sunburn, Mike would have been ready to dance right along with them. "Why don't you get in the tub and I'll get these screens in."

And wasn't that the best offer Mike had all day?

HIS tiredness forgotten, Eben hummed as he fit the last screen into the window frame. He knew he was pushing things, but his quick glance at the reservation schedule warned him Mr. Michael Vincent was only in town for a week. Eben would have to work fast if he wanted the time to be spent with him.

He couldn't believe his luck. The sunburn could be considered a setback, but Eben knew the home remedies from his grandmother would fix things up in a jiffy. Then all he had to do was convince Mike that Eben was ready and willing to show him the sights of Pentwater and the surrounding area. Assuming, of course, Eben's interest was returned.

Sam said it was, and Sam was rarely wrong when it came to matters of physical attraction. All in all, things were looking pretty fine from where Eben now stood. If he was lucky, he'd get a good week in, and if he was even luckier, maybe even a summer romance.

Hey, it could happen.

Eben could hear faint splashes from the bathroom and allowed himself the luxury of imagining how the soft, pale skin would look when slippery and wet. He didn't even feel bad sneaking in a quick mental caress of Mike's back. How could he resist?

For someone so lean, Mike carried nothing but muscle, and Eben appreciated the time spent at the gym. The screens were almost finished—what would happen if Eben walked into the bathroom and offered to wash Mike's back?

"Eben?"

Oh, hell. Eben's sensual fantasies disappeared at the familiar voice. "What?" he called out in response, pulling up his tool belt as he walked toward the door and pushed it open to reveal his grandmother's anxious face.

"There's a problem with the electrical in the yellow room again. Do you have time to take a look?"

"I thought Joe took care of that?" Eben tried not to show his annoyance. It really wasn't her fault he'd rather stay here and contemplate the joys of playing hide the soap with Mike.

"Obviously not, since they called down to the desk, and I climbed up here to find you." Her tone snapped more than usual, and Eben immediately felt bad for his sourness when he remembered his Grandmother's arthritic knees.

"Fine. I'll be there in a minute." Eben watched as his grandmother headed back toward the stairs, and only then did he let his disappointment show as all of his plans came crashing down around him. "Hell." Unable to put it off, Eben knocked on the bathroom door.

"Mike?" Eben cleared his throat nervously.

"Mmmm?" The husky reply, muffled by the wood of the door between them, went right to Eben's dick. Eben pressed his forehead against the door and thought about his grandmother's swollen knees and Old Joe's gouty foot. Anything he could to distract himself from the knowledge that Mike glistened wet and naked on the other side of the door, and there was nothing he could do about it.

"Uh, my grandmother needs me to check on something for her." Eben ran his hand over his close-cropped hair in frustration. And Sam and his grandmother wondered at his lack of a love life. "Would it be all right if I came back when I'm done to check on you? If it's not too late? I could bring you some iced tea or something." Eben squirmed. He sounded so lame. "So, uh, I'll be back, okay?"

He waited for a response from the other side of the door. His heart was pounding so loud when Mike did say something that Eben couldn't hear what it was, but he knew damn sure he wasn't going to assume anything but a positive answer.

MIKE floated in the lukewarm bath. He wiggled, the water sloshing up and around as he tried to find a comfortable place for his bent legs. With his height, it was a rare tub that allowed him room to fully stretch out, but he wasn't going to complain.

Stepford Grandmother she might be, but whatever had been in those cheesecloth bundles was amazing. He wouldn't have believed it, but the stuff actually seemed to be working. His skin didn't feel as tight, and it wasn't as hot to his tentative touch.

The only thing the moment lacked was a cold beer and Eben to wash his back. Granted, he might be moving a little fast for a first meeting, but those thoughts were tame compared to everything else Mike wanted to do with the handsome blond.

Mike let his imagination drift along with hands. He had left the light off when he had gingerly lowered himself into the water, and it was easy to let the quiet peace lull him into envisioning Eben in the tub right along with him, their legs tangled and soft hairs scratching against his calf.

He let himself wonder how Eben kissed, how he tasted. How those strong hands would feel against his back as wet skin glided across wet skin. If he concentrated, Mike could imagine the press of Eben's muscular chest more fully against his as they slipped and slid into more satisfying alignment.

Mike's hand teased up and down in a motion made slow and languid by the resistance of the liquid surrounding him. He deliberately thought about Eben's slightly crooked smile, the freckles across his face, and wondered how many more were scattered across the tan skin. His elbow moved and water dripped off his arm, spilling over the side of the tub and onto the tile below as he replayed his first sight of Eben in his mind's eye.

* * *

The heat of his sunburn paled in comparison to the heat of the flesh swollen and pulsing in his hand. Mike groaned, remembering his furtive thrill as the weight of the tool belt had dragged the waist of Eben's jean so dangerously low, the wiry blond curls asking for his attention.

Mike's long body trembled, and he gripped his cock with a tighter, steadier motion. He slid past the point of lazy enjoyment; raw need building as he worked his hand faster and faster despite the twinges of discomfort from his chest and shoulders. He imagined Eben watching him, visualized the play of greedy pleasure across his face, and Mike came in a shuddering moment that went on and on until he lay back, gasping, dazzled by the intensity of his orgasm.

He slid down, his head and face sinking below the water. His eyes closed until the need for air brought him back to the surface, and he sat up again, dark hair slicked back from his face. His body felt light and open and, Mike laughed as he swished his hand under the water to clean it. Now that was a cure for sunburn he could enjoy.

• • •

VI

EBEN knocked softly on Mike's door. It was late, later than expected, and far later than polite to come calling. But he couldn't go home without checking on Mike. His grandmother had given him one of her familiar scowls when he'd poured out two glasses of tea, but he had scowled right back. Based on the mess Old Joe had made of the wiring in the basement, it would take a lot of favors to put things right.

But enough about Old Joe. Eben mentally crossed his fingers Mike was still awake and wanted to see him and at the same time regretted the fact he hadn't had a chance to clean up after work. He raised his arms, the glasses of tea suspended above his head, and gave his armpits a quick sniff. Eben shook his head. Not good. Maybe he should leave.

Mike opened the door before Eben could decide, and all thought of leaving disappeared at his first sight of the faint creases the pillow had left behind on Mike's cheek and the expanse of naked flesh. It took Eben a moment to see past the enticing mat of chest hair and realize Mike wore only a close-fitting pair of shorts.

"Hey." Mike smiled sleepily, and Eben felt helpless to do anything but smile back. He wanted to run his hand through the tousled mass of dark hair and smooth it down. Then he wanted to be the one to muss it all back up again.

"Oh, man, did I wake you up?" Smooth move, as Sam would say. "I wanted to see how you were doing."

"And you brought me something to drink." Mike's face brightened, and he reached out eagerly. "Great. I feel like the Sahara." He raised the glass and drank it all down while Eben watched, inwardly groaning at the wave of lust that washed over him at the movement of Mike's throat. "Wow, that's good."

Hypnotized by Mike's hand as he wiped the remaining moisture from his lips—and why hadn't Eben noticed those full lips earlier? —Eben silently handed over the second glass of tea. Mike sighed with satisfaction after he drained that one as well and then looked down at the empty glasses in his hands.

"That was rude, wasn't it? Come on in."

Eben silently followed Mike into the room.

"You look a lot better; maybe I should go." Eben shifted uncomfortably. He hadn't expected the air of intimacy between them. The lateness of the hour, the darkness of the room and the obviousness of the bed only contributed to his awareness of Mike.

"Sit down." Mike rubbed his hand through his hair and over his face. "Tell me about what you were doing while I passed out." He sat on the bed and gestured toward the chair.

Eben lowered himself down, nervously crossing and uncrossing his leg. "My grandmother has this old guy who helps her out. Well, he's supposed to. Half the time he doesn't get anything done, and the other half he makes a mess." Eben relaxed as he started talking, and he leaned forward, his hands gesturing as talked. "The wiring in this place is old to begin with, and Joe's modifications haven't exactly been up to code."

Mike shook his head, and Eben held up his hands. "Not that you have to worry or anything. It's nothing that will burn the place the down."

"It's okay." Mike smiled, and once again the drowsy peace on his face hit Eben low in his gut. "I'm not worried with you around."

They stared at each in the soft light of the bedside lamp. Only two things kept Eben from pouncing, one being his own sense of fair play and the other the obvious discomfort visible on Mike's face. Eben swallowed past the lump of desire in his throat and jumped to his feet.

"Where'd you leave the gel? In the bathroom?" Once in the relative safety of the small room, Eben gripped the counter and stared at himself in the mirror. He had a whole new sympathy for John Travolta's character in that Quentin Tarentino movie. He could do this, he told his reflection. He was going to go out there and be polite, rub some gel on Mike's sunburn, and then go home and furiously jack off.

God. He only hoped he could wait that long.

Any resolve Eben had was tested once he washed his hands and walked out of the bathroom to find Mike sprawled out on the bed. Hooboy, was Mike tall. And slim. And utterly desirable, despite his glow-in-the-dark redness as he stretched some more and sighed happily when he saw Eben with the tube of green gel.

● ● ●

"If that stuff works as well as the soaking stuff did, I'll be a happy man."

And if you weren't sunburned and this was a tube of lube, so would I. Eben chastised himself and smiled weakly. "I sure hope so." He flipped open the top of the tube and squeezed some of the green goo onto his fingers. The similarities were unmistakable, and he practically whimpered. At least, until he gingerly rubbed it on Mike's arm and heard the resulting hiss of pain.

"Sorry," Eben apologized, chagrined at the thought that he had caused further discomfort. "My hands aren't the softest."

"No, really. They're great." Despite his words, Mike flinched again. "I'm more tender than I thought, and that stuff is cold. It's like when—uh, never mind." Mike suddenly stopped talking, and Eben laughed at the look on his face.

"Oh, thank God. I thought I was the only one with a dirty mind." Tension released, Eben felt a lot more confident as he applied the gel in long, slow strokes across Mike's belly. He tried not to watch Mike's nipples react to the stimuli, but the stiff peaks drew his eyes as he lightly brushed the gel over them.

"I can't believe the way my nipples hurt." Mike groaned, then laughed. "Can you imagine if they start peeling?"

"You keep putting this stuff on and you'll be fine," Eben replied breathlessly. Oh, yeah, he could imagine all kinds of things.

"So am I going to get to take you out for dinner, you know, to say thanks?"

Eben didn't know how Mike could sound so casual, spread out on the bed beneath Eben like he was, but somehow he did. "I've got to pick up some parts in Bay City tomorrow, but I'll be back on Wednesday." Eben knew he sounded eager, but how was he supposed to play it cool with Mike laid out like a banquet? And why had he agreed to drive across state?

"Great." Mike smiled and sighed with enjoyment, both actions leaving Eben hard and aching. The repetitive motion of Eben's hands had a soothing effect on Mike, though, and his eyes closed despite his desultory efforts at conversation. Eben finished applying the gel to the reddened parts of Mike's skin and let his fingers trace the faint lines on Mike's face as they softened and disappeared under the touch of Eben's hands.

This wasn't how he might have hoped the evening would go. Somehow, it was even better.

THE fiery ball of summer sun hovered for one last second above the horizon before it dipped below the water and disappeared, leaving the sky streaked with shades of soft pink and a darker magenta reflected in the water below.

Mike sat cross-legged on the rough concrete of the Pentwater breakwall with the rest of the tourists and smiled with enjoyment. The water was surprisingly smooth, and there were still some die-hards swimming on one side of the pier. He turned his head to the other side to watch the line of sailboats out for an evening turn on the lake glide through the channel.

A quick glance at his watch directed Mike's attention toward the entrance to the pier. Even at this distance, he recognized the blond head as it pushed past the tourists walking back to their hotels and campgrounds. Eben arrived right on time, and Mike stood to greet him.

"Sorry, am I late?" Mike appreciated the fact that Eben actually seemed worried. He had stopped for a shower, and his blond curls were still damp. Mike savored the clean scent of his aftershave and while he regretted the loss of the low-slung jeans the blond had been wearing at work again today, the khaki shorts and moss-green polo brought out the rich color of Eben's tan.

"You missed the sunset, but I guess you've seen it before." Mike smiled as Eben gave him a slow and appraising glance.

"I have, but never with you." The flirtatious vibe was unmistakable, and Mike's smile grew even wider. "You're looking a lot better than the last time I saw you."

"Feel that way too." They had waved to each other across the distance this morning. Eben had called and left a message with a time and place for them to meet, but they hadn't really seen each other since the first night. "I'm almost back to the right color. Your grandmother could make a fortune with that stuff. What is it, anyway?"

"You probably don't want to know." Eben's smile was still as amazingly crooked as before, and Mike felt himself falling less into lust and more into out-and-out like. "Sometimes I wonder about her and all those plants."

Mike laughingly agreed, and they stood in comfortable silence. Mike's arm lightly brushed against Eben's shoulder as they watched the variety of sailboats, both big and small, float smoothly by. He didn't know where he had gotten the nerve to ask Eben out—probably he had been delirious from his sunburn—but he was damn pleased he had.

"Sorry about not picking you up; Nana would put me to work if she saw me." Mike thought it sweet, the way Eben ducked his head as he apologized.

"It's fine, really. I understand." After two additional days spent interacting with Eben's grandmother, Mike definitely understood. "So, what's on for the evening? I still would like to buy you dinner."

"Have you ever been to a drive-in?" Eben asked, looking up to catch a glimpse of Mike's relaxed face. "There's a classic science fiction double feature in Muskegon. They're playing John Carpenter's *The Thing* and then *Lifeforce.*"

"Really?" Mike exclaimed. "I love Kurt Russell in that movie, and I haven't seen *Lifeforce* in ages. Do you like science fiction?"

"I love it," Eben replied. "I've seen both movies more than a couple of times before, but I thought the drive-in could be fun even if you didn't care for the films." His long fingers reached out and lightly stroked the palm of Mike's hand. "I'd like a chance to get to know you better."

"I can't remember the last time I went to a drive-in movie." Mike let his fingers curl around Eben's. "Will there be mosquitoes?" He was amazed at how nice it felt to hear Eben was looking for more than a one-night hit-and-run. Mike might only be on vacation for the week, but he wasn't going to plan the end of his acquaintance with Eben before it even had a chance to begin. Where there was a will, there was a way.

Eben pretended to consider the question. "It is Michigan, you know."

"How about beer?" Mike teased. "The last time I went to a drive-in, I was sixteen, and our beer was confiscated at the front gate."

"For you, I could be persuaded," Eben teased right back.

"How about making out under the stars?" Mike ignored the other people on the pier and moved even closer to Eben. He knew his voice had roughened, but the thought of spending hours making out with Eben like a couple of teenagers instead of jumping right into sex was surprisingly intense, especially since he already knew how those hands felt on his skin.

"Absolutely," Eben breathed, and Mike's stomach tightened in anticipation at the warm glow in Eben's eyes.

"Well, what are we waiting for?" Mike let his hand trail up and down Eben's arm, lingering on the dark band of ink and trying not to smirk at the resulting gooseflesh. Without hesitation, Mike lowered his head and lightly grasped Eben's face in his hands.

He was all over this spontaneous stuff.

Eben's lips opened beneath his, and suddenly there was the first experience of taste and texture to savor. Eben's tongue curled to twist around his, and while it was slow and exploratory, it was also more than casual. Eben kissed him like he'd been waiting for this very moment. Their lips clung; then they broke apart and grinned at each other.

"Have I asked yet where you live when you aren't on vacation?" Eben wrapped his hand firmly around Mike's as they slowly walked back to the end of the channel.

"Not that far." Mike squeezed Eben's hand. "Not for a spontaneous guy like me."

* * *

The joke in CHRISSY MUNDER'S family is that she was born with a book in her hand. Even now, you'll never find her without a book or seven scattered about. Forced to become a practicing realist in an effort to combat her tendency to dream, her many years of travel and a diverse assortment of careers have taken her across most of the United States and shown her that there are two things you can never have enough of: love and laughter.

Visit her web site at http://www.chrissymunder.com/ and her blog at http://chrissymunder.livejournal.com/.

* * *

The Meaning of Significant Digits

Ashlyn Kane

Alex dug his keys out of his pocket, juggling a six-pack of beer and a couple of bags of chips in the other arm. Sometimes it was just plain inconvenient having a key to Dev's apartment—like now. If he didn't have one, Dev wouldn't bitch every time he rang the doorbell. He'd actually have to come open the door for him.

Most of the time, though, he didn't mind. Dev had like fifteen different international sports channels, and Alex didn't. If he wanted to watch Mexico play in the World Cup (and he obviously did), he'd have to do it at Dev's. Plus, this way they could gossip about the wedding.

Finally getting the door open, Alex kicked it closed behind him and dropped the chips on the sofa. He could hear Dev shuffling around somewhere, so he toed off his shoes and headed to the kitchen with the beer.

"Look, it's not like that." Dev's soft, faintly accented voice drifted in from the bedroom.

He must be on the phone with someone, Alex thought, sticking his head in the fridge to check it out. Ohh, Dev had made fresh salsa. Thank God for that, because the stuff white people called "salsa" didn't even come close. Judging by the number of containers in the fridge, he hadn't stopped there. A quick peek revealed homemade hummus, couscous, and a saran-wrapped

* * *

plate of pitas. And judging from the heavenly aroma wafting through the apartment, he'd made curry, as well. Damn, Alex loved having a friend who could cook.

"No, come on, how could I do something like that? It would ruin the tone of the whole day."

It sounds like a serious conversation, Alex thought, grabbing the plate of pitas. The game started in fifteen minutes, and he wanted to make sure everything was ready. Peeling away the saran wrap, he put the pitas on the top rack in the oven and set it to broil.

"Are you crazy? No way. The wedding is next week. How awkward would that be, standing in front of a church with him? I've handled this stupid crush for this long. I think I can manage not to ruin the most important day of Elijah's life; thanks for your input."

Alex froze halfway back to the living room, heart sinking a little. Had he just heard that right? Dev, sweet, funny Dev, the guy who had shown him around when he'd first moved to the country in eleventh grade, the guy who'd almost single-handedly pulled Alex out of the worst depression of his life, had been carrying a torch for Elijah all this time? Alex swallowed. That was pretty heavy. Especially considering Elijah was getting married a week from today.

Dev walked out of the bedroom half a minute later, no trace of the strain Alex had heard in his voice evident on his face. "Hey, I didn't think you'd get here so soon."

"Bitch, are you saying I'm not punctual?" Alex joked as naturally as he could, setting the bowl of salsa on the table. He was hurt that Dev hadn't trusted him with the information, but on the other hand, it made some sort of sense. After all, Alex had been known to tease Dev from time to time about his reluctance to date.

"I'm saying you're early by North American standards. By Mexican Standard Time, you're like, six *hours* early. I'm a little freaked out."

"Like you're ever on time for anything," Alex pointed out. "Besides, I'm never late for football."

Dev made a face. "We'd better get our collective ass in gear for next week, or Amanda will castrate us."

Amanda was Elijah's bride-to-be. As far as girls went, Alex thought she was pretty okay. She didn't watch soccer, but she did play foosball and she could hold her liquor. She was also five-foot-nothing of pure terror when she was angry. "Let's be early."

"Good plan." Flicking on the TV, Dev dropped down onto the couch, putting his feet up on the table. He seemed so completely normal that Alex was having a hard time processing what he'd just heard. "You going to get those pitas out of the oven before you burn them?"

Alex rolled his eyes. "Remind me why I put up with you again?"

"Because I make you fresh salsa from scratch and your mother likes me. Oh, and because I helped you pass your biology final."

"Oh yeah. I knew I kept you around for a reason." Oh well. He was the one who had put them in the oven in the first place. Alex headed to the kitchen, returning a half a minute later with the warm pitas on a plate and trying to come up with a way to broach the subject. "So."

"So?" Dev flipped the channel until the World Cup logo came up. "What, you want to make a bet? Because honestly, my money's on Portugal."

"Jerk. I would take that bet, but all my cash is tied up in Elijah's wedding gift." That was a lie, but Alex's father had been a gambling man, and Alex wasn't about to follow in that loser's footsteps. He loaded his pita up with hummus, gathering his courage. "Anyway, that's not what I was going to say."

"Spit it out, then, *hermano*; I haven't got all day." Dev had been throwing miscellaneous Spanish words into his English sentences more or less since they'd met, and it had mostly ceased to be irritating, even though Alex couldn't speak a word of Bengali that wasn't a curse.

Fuck it. Tact was for wimps. "I heard you talking on the phone when I came in. You got something you want to tell me?"

Dev didn't exactly go pale—his complexion wouldn't allow it—but he did seem to shrink a little, which was ridiculous, as he wasn't that big to begin with. "What exactly did you hear?"

"Enough." Alex shrugged, trying not to be distracted by the music from the television or the triple-time beating of his own heart. "I know you've got a thing for Elijah."

Dev's whole body sagged on the couch, but instead of looking miserable about it he just seemed relieved. "I guess the jig is up, huh?"

● ● ●

Alex blinked rapidly, wondering why his eyes suddenly wanted to tear up. "You could say that. Why didn't you ever say anything?"

"To Elijah? When would I have done that? When he told us he was going to propose to Amanda? Or after she'd said yes?" Dev rolled his eyes. "He's straight. I know that. It's not a big deal, dude. I can live with it."

"Yeah, but…." Alex shrugged. What the hell was wrong with him? He was way more emotionally invested in this than he'd thought. "You have to stand up in his wedding in a week. I don't even want to *think* about how much that's going to suck for you."

"I've come to terms with it," Dev said firmly. "Seriously, I'm fine. Shut up and watch the game."

But Alex couldn't concentrate on the game yet. His mind was completely boggled over how Dev could have kept something this huge bottled up for so many years and just be willing to pine away for the rest of his life over Elijah, who, though a dear friend, wasn't even that good-looking. Not as good-looking as Alex, anyway. And, yeah, he was a great guy, but he'd also been with Amanda for *years*. Dev had had more than enough time to get over it.

Maybe he hadn't really tried, though. Maybe Dev had given up hope of ever meeting someone else. That would be just like him. "Okay, okay, I've got an idea. We've got a week, right? A week to get you over Elijah before the wedding. We can do that. And we will. Starting tomorrow."

"Alex, you don't have to do that. I told you."

"Forget it; I can always tell when you're lying. Your accent gets stronger. We are doing this." Finally satisfied, Alex put his feet up on the couch. "Now, pass me the salsa. The game is starting."

"GOD, I'm coming already," Dev grumbled under his breath. Who the hell would bother pounding on his door at eight-thirty on a Sunday morning, anyway? That was what doorbells were for. He was still wiping the sleep from the corner of his eye when he opened the door.

"Oh, good, you're up," Alex said cheerfully.

Dev blinked. Something fishy was going on. Alex was not a morning person. There was no way he was really standing there on Dev's doorstep this

* * *

early on a Sunday. Plus, Alex had a key. It had to be a dream. "I'm going back to bed," he announced. "Feel free to do whatever you dream apparitions do."

"Not so fast, Sleeping Beauty. I made a promise and I plan to deliver. Get dressed; we're going out."

"But it's eight-thirty," Dev pointed out in a tone dangerously close to a whine. He was beginning to suspect he might actually be awake. Alex's usual dream guest spots tended to involve less talking and more nudity. "In the morning. On a Sunday. Where could we *go?*"

"Breakfast," Alex said succinctly. Breakfast was the one Western meal they both agreed on. "Golden Griddle. Come on, let's go."

Dev looked down at himself blankly to make sure he hadn't actually gotten dressed in his haze of new consciousness, and then he looked back up at Alex. "Why?"

"This is step one," Alex informed him in an overly friendly tone, ushering him back toward the bedroom. Dev's sleepy body treacherously allowed this without objection.

"Of how many?" he asked, almost afraid of the answer.

"Twelve, obviously. It's not worth doing if you can't do it in twelve steps. Step one is comfort food. Now hurry up and get dressed, you lazy shit. I'm hungry."

"God, you're pushy," Dev grumbled, rummaging for a clean pair of boxers in his dresser drawer. "Anybody ever tell you that?"

"Every guy I ever dated," Alex confirmed. Dev remembered something about that, but he wisely kept his mental tally of Alex's ex-boyfriends to himself. "Seriously, man, my stomach's gonna eat itself if I don't get pancakes soon."

"Whatever." Dev rolled his eyes, thinking that this was in fact a highly improbable outcome. He cut a sideways look at his best friend across the room. "Can a guy get some privacy?"

"That's the other thing those guys complained about. I don't trust you not to go back to bed, amigo."

Neither did Dev; the problem was that he wanted to take Alex *with* him. He seriously doubted he was going to come out of this week any less in love

* * *

with his best friend, but then, Alex thought it was Elijah he was after. "Of the two of us, *you're* the lazy one," he pointed out.

"Which is why I am a licensed actuary, and you babysit little children all day. Yes, I see your logic."

Dev grit his teeth as he stripped his boxers and didn't bother resisting the urge to fling them in Alex's face. "I'm a biology teacher, asshole."

Alex peeled the underwear off his face just as Dev stepped into a fresh pair. "You say potato, I say potahto."

Dev zipped up his jeans and started the quest for clean socks. After a moment, he gave up and slipped into a pair of beat up Birkenstocks instead. "Remind me again why I put up with you?"

"'Cause you love me, dummy. And because I am a bitchin' BFF who buys you pancakes. Shirt, please. Seriously, you are the palest brown guy ever."

Unfortunately, at least the first part of that blather was true—hence the problem. Dev pulled a T-shirt off of the hanger. "Like you can even tell the difference. All right, I'm ready. Let's go."

"Finally. They'd better not be out of whipped cream when we get there, that's all I'm saying."

Dev rolled his eyes and followed him out the door.

THEY were both in a better mood after coffee and all-you-can-eat pancakes (with, in Alex's case, prodigal amounts of real whipped cream). Alex was busily cleaning his plate of all remaining traces of said cream with a strawberry when their waitress showed up with the bill.

"Do you need anything else, Mr. Patel?" Tina asked, smiling brightly. Dev tried to remember if he'd taught her last year or the year before.

"We're all right, sweetheart," Alex cut in. He winked and flashed his dimples at her as he took the check.

Dev gave Tina his best put-upon expression. "Perhaps a muzzle, if you have one handy?"

"Sorry." Tina laughed. "We're fresh out. There's a Pet Valu next door, though. You could try there."

Alex handed over his MasterCard, and Tina gave another bright smile. "I'll be right back with this."

Dev thanked her and sighed as she walked away, stretching out his legs under the table. "So, step one was comfort food. Dare I ask what the second has in store for me?"

"Step two includes getting you right drunk, but that's too trashy for a Sunday morning, so it'll have to wait."

Dev rubbed the bridge of his nose. "Step three, then."

"Ah, yes. Step three." The waitress returned with the bill, and Alex signed it. "Step three involves vigorous physical activity."

Dev waited until his former student had walked off, blushing, before hissing, "Please do not tell me you got me a prostitute."

Alex grinned. "What did I tell you about respecting the Sabbath? Besides, a pretty boy like you doesn't need any help in that department. Come on, finish your coffee and I'll show you."

He'd foolishly let Alex drive—mostly because he had a sweet classic 1960s-era Chevy Nova SS that Dev was half in love with—so he didn't have much of a choice. When Alex parked the car in the lot adjacent to one of the city's many soccer fields, Dev raised an eyebrow. "Physical activity?"

Grinning, Alex pulled a flat yellow disc from the back seat. "Ultimate frisbee."

"You set up a game?"

"Shirts versus skins," Alex confirmed, leering. "Exercise boosts good endorphins, Mr. Biology Teacher. You should know that by now."

"Uh huh," Dev agreed skeptically. Alex wasn't fooling him. "And the sweaty half-naked men?"

"We're just an added bonus," Alex smirked, stepping out into the sunlight. He reached over his head to grab a fistful of his T-shirt. "I promised I'd play skins."

That figured. Alex was about the world's least self-conscious person, maybe because he'd practically grown up shirtless. Dev glanced down toward the soccer field, where a dozen or so guys were already warming up. "Right."

Alex grinned. "Last one there's a rotten egg."

THE doorbell rang again at nine o'clock on Monday morning.

"I think you're missing the point of summer," Dev grumbled, wiping a drop of milk from his cereal off of his chin. "It's the two months of the year teachers get to sleep in without anyone interrupting. It's part of the code!" He rubbed the remainder of sleep out of his eyes and added, "Also, you are not a teacher and therefore don't have summers off. What gives?"

Alex was already inside, because he thought it was funny to ring the bell and then open the door himself. He doffed his shades and pushed past Dev in the hallway, resplendent in board shorts and an indecent tank top. If he'd been one of Dev's students, Dev would have given him detention. "I took the week off to continue your treatment. Are you seriously not dressed yet? This is disgraceful. I won't have you wasting your summer like this."

"Oh my God, you're going to micro-manage my vacation. What step are we at?"

"Four. Beach. Good for vitamin D and—"

"More hot sweaty shirtless men. Yeah, got it." Dev scrubbed a hand through his hair. By the end of the week, his willpower was going to be shot to hell. "Just lemme shower." He was pretty sure a day of staring at Alex's chest wasn't going to help get over him. Maybe this was some kind of karmic retribution for lying to him in the first place. He really needed to start thinking before he spoke.

A quick, admittedly cold shower later, and he was ready to go. Or so he thought.

"Don't you have anything less formal?"

"I wasn't aware there was a dress code to go to the beach." Dev sighed. He was wearing khaki shorts and a button-down short-sleeved shirt. He was a teacher, damn it. This *was* informal!

Alex pointed. "Back into the bedroom. Swim shorts and a T-shirt, Dev, seriously. You're a smart guy. You can handle it."

It took some digging, but eventually Dev came up with an outfit Alex couldn't find fault with, though the T-shirt was so old it was snug across the chest.

"Tomorrow we're going shopping," Alex said darkly in a tone that brooked no argument.

Dev grabbed a beach towel as they headed out the door, taking a deep breath as he locked it behind him. It was going to be a long week.

"OKAY," Dev conceded, flopping down dripping wet onto his towel, "it's possible you had a point about the wasting of summer thing."

"Someday you will learn not to question my authority on these matters," Alex smarmed from the towel next to Dev's. He was lying face down with his eyes closed, head pillowed on his arms. It left Dev with an unparalleled view of a lovely expanse of supple tanned skin interrupted only by the infuriating board shorts, which were wet and, well, clingy.

"Probably the same day you start listening to my advice on dating," Dev rejoined half-heartedly. At least Alex seemed to be ignoring the company of other men present for the time being.

Alex snorted. "That'll be the day. I'd like to get laid again sometime this century, thanks." He rolled over onto his back, sunglasses still firmly in place.

Dev flushed, reaching into the cooler for a beer so he wouldn't be tempted to further explore the clinginess of Alex's shorts. "I'm not that picky."

"Yes, you are." Alex sat up, looking over seriously across the tops of his Ray-Bans. "Is that why? The Elijah thing, I mean. That's why you never really...."

"No. Yes. Maybe?" Dev cracked open the can and dug his toes into the sand. "There never seemed to be much point. I always knew within a week or so whether someone was worth keeping around, you know?"

"Yeah, I know what you mean."

Surprised, Dev almost choked on the first sip. He shot a glance sideways, but Alex was looking at the water, not at him. Alex was sort of notorious for being a man-eater. Dev had been so flustered trying to remember the name of his most recent flame at one point that he'd refused to meet new boyfriends until they had passed the two-week benchmark. Alex hadn't introduced him to anybody new in more than a year. "If you know it's not going to work out, why do you bother?"

Alex shrugged. "Maybe I'm hoping one of them will prove me wrong." He ran a hand back through his hair so that it stood up in damp clumps. "Nothing ventured and all that."

Dev guessed that maybe he had a point. After all, Dev's method was failing pretty miserably. Operation Wait Around Until Your Best Friend Notices You're Perfect For Each Other had been ongoing for years. "You're probably right."

"Of course I'm right." Alex stood, brushed off his shorts, and offered Dev a hand up. "Come on, it's too hot to sit on the beach. The lake is calling your name."

"I'm pretty sure that's my beer you hear," Dev whined, but he allowed himself to be pulled to his feet anyway. It was pretty hot, after all, and if Alex was going to be all wet again, he wanted to be as close as possible. Pathetic as it was.

"Do you know what kind of bacteria live in that lake water these days?" It was a token protest; both of them knew it. The lake had been cleared for swimming weeks ago.

"Acute Devitis?" Alex suggested, shoving him toward the water.

"I cannot believe I got you through twelfth-grade biology," Dev groaned. "The suffix -itis connotes the infection itself, you-you—"

Dev stopped. Alex had started reciting the numbers of *pi*. That was so annoying. Probably as annoying as Alex found Dev's random biology tangents. "All right, all right, I get the point."

Alex ignored him, reciting louder now. He could have been making it up, for all Dev knew about *pi* after the first two decimal places. He dipped his foot in the water and sent a wave at Alex, splashing him from the thighs down. "Hey, did you know there was an official movement to make *pi* equal three?"

"Even an act of Congress can't change the meaning of significant digits," Alex scoffed, splashing him back. "Come on. I'll race you to the buoy."

DEV got up at eight-thirty on Tuesday, showered, shaved (Alex's early morning interruptions had resulted in three days' stubble growth), and was dressed by five after nine. He read the paper as he ate breakfast, refilled his coffee mug, and did the crossword. When the apartment was still silent at quarter past ten, he got up and went into the living room to look for his phone.

Alex was sitting on his couch, flipping through last month's issue of *Scientific American.*

"This is bordering on stalking," Dev warned him when his heart had crawled back down from his throat and was no longer in danger of escaping if he opened his mouth.

"Oh, sure. I try to be nice and let you sleep in for once."

"After this week, I'm never going to sleep again," Dev grumbled. He took a fortifying breath. "You said shopping, right?"

"Step five," Alex confirmed, tossing the magazine onto the coffee table and stretching. The exposed sliver of skin on his stomach was tanned bronze from the sun. "Look fabulous, feel fabulous."

"Why do I feel like I'm going to regret this?"

"Because for whatever reason you still have no faith in me. How much time have you spent mooning over Elijah in the past three days?"

The same amount of time he'd spent mooning over Elijah in the past seven years: "None." Dev managed to make it sound sulky. He'd spent most of it drooling over Alex, who had once again failed to notice. This was seriously verging on the pathetic.

"Exactly. It's working! Trust me."

"There's a game on this afternoon," Dev mentioned as casually as he could.

Alex rolled his eyes. "As much as it pains me to say this, TiVo it. We'll watch it later. Besides, I thought you were bitter because Bangladesh got beat out by Tajikistan."

"I'm bitter for a lot of reasons," Dev protested. Besides, that had been three years ago in the qualifying rounds. Preliminaries took ages, and Bangladesh hadn't qualified in the thirty-six years since it had joined FIFA.

"That's the spirit. Come on. Let's go before the teenagers wake up."

●　●　●

"I see enough of them during the other ten months of the year," Dev agreed. He loved his students, he really did, but he'd *just* got rid of them. He wasn't ready to face them again yet, at least not en masse.

Alex smiled and dug into his pocket, pulling out his keys. "You want to drive?"

Dev took them from his hand. The metal was warm. "Seriously?" Alex never let anyone drive his car.

"You can drive home, too, as long as you're on your best behavior."

Dev rolled his eyes. "Let's get this over with."

The mall was like a ghost town when they arrived, shop attendants still sleepy-eyed and mainlining coffee. Alex herded him into the Gap ("I'm too old to shop at the Gap!" Dev protested. "You're gay! Quit being such a pansy!" Alex rejoined), American Eagle ("I'll come out looking like my students!"), Banana Republic ("You only want to go there because the sales guys are cute." "Yes, and?"), and Tommy Hilfiger. Alex ordered him into six pair of swim trunks, a dozen T-shirts, five polo-style tops, six pair of nearly identical khaki shorts, a pile of practically disposable flip-flops and seven pair of cheap sunglasses before he declared the trip a success.

"Well, that was fun," Alex said, dropping into one of the crappy chairs at the food court.

Dev followed suit, setting his bags on the table, and took a long sip of his milkshake, surprised to find he didn't disagree. "Hey," he started, but he was interrupted by Alex reaching across the table and poking a fingertip into his cheek. "What are you doing?"

"You're smiling," Alex said triumphantly, more than a little smug. "I knew you couldn't be immune to retail therapy."

"Shut up." Dev laughed, smacking his hand away. He felt like himself for the first time in weeks, though, so he wasn't going to complain. "I am human. I'm allowed to have a couple of bad days."

"Uh huh," Alex said tolerantly, spooning up a mouthful of ice cream and Oreo. "So anyway, you were saying?"

"Hmm? Oh." Dev put the shake down, grinning. "You wanna play?"

"Seriously?" Alex's eyes lit up. "Man, we haven't played that game in ages. I'm not sure I remember the rules."

"Liar. I'll go first." Dev switched seats so that he and Alex were side by side and then scanned the steady stream of passers-by for a likely candidate. The object of the game was to pick a man out of the crowd and then imagine the circumstances in which you might find yourself sleeping with him. "Okay, okay. Red hat, blue T-shirt."

Alex followed his gaze, picking the man out from the crowd. The man Dev had indicated was youngish and passably cute, taller than Alex usually liked, broad at the shoulders but thin at the waist. "That kid is barely out of high school, Dev."

"No whining; you know the rules."

Alex made a face. "Fine. He's maybe a two on the Kinsey scale, so I'm thinking drunken one-night stand. Possibly just after he lost his job."

"Ooh. Nasty." Dev grinned. "Your turn."

Alex picked out a well-dressed middle-aged man with a briefcase and a cell phone. "Easy," Dev said, draining his milkshake. "Phone sex hotline. A guy like that would be too busy to have a real relationship."

"And we all know you don't do casual," Alex teased.

Dev pulled his straw out of the cup and flicked it at him. "In this last scenario I worked at a phone sex provider. I am using my imagination." To get back at Alex for his jab, he picked the least attractive man he could find.

"Ugh." Alex made a face. "Okay, okay. We're the last two people on Earth, and I'm catatonic."

"I don't think that actually counts."

"Drunk, then," Alex amended. "When'd you get so mean, anyway?"

Dev schooled his features into innocence. "If you don't want to play…."

"Jerk," Alex said, but he was laughing. "Okay, okay. Blue tank top, three o'clock…."

ALEX still hadn't put the last touches on the plans for Elijah's bachelor party, so Dev knew he wouldn't be around until later in the day. He spent Wednesday morning sleeping in and then donned one of his new pair of swim trunks for a few laps in the pool at his apartment complex.

* * *

Alex showed up just in time for dinner, a carton of Ben & Jerry's pistachio flavor under one arm and a bag of DVDs in the other hand. When Dev let him in with one eyebrow raised, Alex just said, "Everybody knows that sappy romantic movies and ice cream are an integral part of the healing process," in his usual cheerful voice. "Step six."

Dev stared. "You brought a stack full of romantic comedies?" he asked incredulously.

Alex snorted, pressing past him into the living room. "Please. I brought *Die Hard*."

Dev considered his options. John McClane was looking better and better. Plus, Justin Long was totally hot. "I'll get the spoons," he said, and put the chicken tikka in the fridge while he was at it.

ALEX rubbed his hands on his jeans, cursing himself for a fool. It had taken him until Tuesday to realize why Dev's sudden revelation had him so off-kilter and why he was so invested in this side project to get Dev over Elijah. Now that he thought about it, it was painfully obvious what was happening. He should have had it figured out years ago.

Sighing, he reached for his keys and unlocked the door to Dev's apartment. He really should have bought a place in town himself, but the lure of having a yard for the first time had been too great, so he'd moved into the suburbs. Now every time he wanted to do something with his friends, he had to drive in.

This wasn't exactly "something with friends," though, Alex admitted to himself. This was a date, even if Dev didn't know it yet. Resisting the urge to tug nervously at the collar of his shirt, Alex shut the door behind him. "Honey, I'm home!"

"You didn't even live in this country when that show was on the air," Dev said drily from where he was sprawled on the sofa. "Wow, are we going somewhere?"

"Yes. It's once again time to leave the nest." Alex flashed his winningest smile. If he was going to do this, he wasn't going to hold back. "Get dressed! We're going out."

Dev only rolled his eyes a little before getting up and heading farther into the apartment. "Someplace with a dress code?" he called back.

* * *

"It's a surprise. Hurry up; we have to leave in ten minutes." Alex shifted from foot to foot, wondering whether he should continue, and then thought: *To hell with it.* "Wear the dark blue jeans."

"Yes, mother!" Dev yelled dutifully from the bedroom. "Would you like to pick out my underwear too?"

"Can I?" He tried to sound casual but had a feeling he missed the mark.

"No!"

"Don't tease me, then!" Alex shot back. "Chop chop, clock's ticking."

"What exactly have I signed up for?"

"Step seven is a surprise. Call it the final step in the program. Really the drinking should have come first, but I doubted my capacity to get you shit-faced twice in the same week and the bachelor party is tomorrow."

"You know me so well." Dev popped out of the bedroom again, dressed in jeans and a light blue collared shirt. "Is this okay?"

Alex swallowed. He'd seen Dev in that shirt before, of course—hell, he was the one who made Dev buy it—and he'd requested the jeans, so he really had no excuse. It shouldn't have been such a shock to his system, but, well, things were different now, and he was noticing exactly how well Dev's clothes fit. "You'll do," he managed without leering. "Grab your wallet, and let's go."

It was only a quick drive from Dev's apartment to the popular local comedy club, during which time they discussed Mexico's chances at the World Cup title on Sunday. Alex paid the cover charge, praying Dev would just assume this was a natural part of Alex's plan for his "recovery," and made sure to get seats up close to the stage.

A waitress came by to take their order before the first act, a local Indian comic Alex had heard Dev mention before. Comedians' general rule of thumb was that you were allowed to mock your own ethnicity and white people, but this guy spared no one, and an apt impression of a middle-aged Mexican woman had Alex and Dev exchanging glances before laughing so hard they had to grab the table for support.

"Your mom," Dev choked out, gasping for breath.

Alex was too busy laughing to answer him. By the time the emcee came on to announce the second act, a freckle-faced redhead who had to sit on a bar stool so that the patrons in the back could see her, Dev was completely relaxed and happy, stealing Alex's French fries when he thought he wasn't looking.

The redhead introduced herself as Alison, hooked her toes around the legs of the barstool, and immediately launched into a rant about golf. "My father-in-law played a hundred and ninety rounds of golf last year. Do you know how much golf that is? Keep in mind that it's too damn cold to play five months of the year, which leaves two hundred and fifteen days when it's warm enough to play, assuming it's not pissing down rain. The man claims it's to keep him from being bored." She paused. "Seriously? Anyone who's ever been forced to watch golf on TV knows how boring it is. Even the announcers sound like they're falling asleep. Golf's not even a real sport; it's just a good walk spoiled! Golf is like the official game of people who aren't good at hockey."

Alex had lived in Canada for ten years, and he still didn't get the whole hockey thing, but the golf rant? Oh, yeah.

"And actually, that brings me to my pet peeve about sports in general. Every single sport has got some kind of complicated terminology that's only comprehensible to people who give a shit. To everyone else, it just sounds vaguely dirty. And to prove my point—sir, what's your favorite sport?"

"Hockey," the man answered immediately.

Alison rolled her eyes. "Obviously. Well, that'll work. And how about you, sir, what's your favorite sport? Don't say hockey."

"Baseball, I guess," the guy at the next table over answered.

Alison's face lit right up. "Baseball. You guys are making this easy for me. Okay, Mr. Baseball and Mr. Hockey, why don't you join me on stage? We're going to play a little game."

With a lot of audience encouragement, the two men finally made their way to the stage, where Alison introduced them as Rick (baseball) and Shaun (hockey). "This is the way it's going to work, guys. I'll give you a sports term that relates to your sport. Then you explain what it means to the audience using plain English and as few sport-related words as possible. The guy with more audience laughs gets a beer. Ready?"

Both men indicated their readiness, and then Alison sat back on her bar stool. "We'll start simple. The first one's from hockey: five-hole." She held the microphone in front of Shaun's face.

"Uh," Shaun said. "The hole between the goalie's legs." He flushed as he realized how that sounded, and the audience laughed.

Dev glanced over at Alex, eyes twinkling. *God,* Alex thought, feeling butterflies in his stomach for the first time since he was a teenager, *how did I miss this for so long?*

"Good," Alison said, "only next time, don't use the word 'goalie'. Rick, it's your turn: squeeze play."

Alex grinned as Dev snorted in amusement and tried to concentrate on the comic. It would definitely be interesting to see how this could be explained without using the words *bat* or *bunt.* "Uh." Rick scratched at the back of his neck. "That's when a player holds a stick with two hands and hits the ball lightly so another player can score."

"Very good," Alison said over the tittering crowd. "Now you've got the basics down, let's try something a little more challenging."

Rick and Shaun stumbled their way through obstacles like triple play, butt-ending, grand slam and icing before the match was declared a tie, and the waitress brought them their beers to general applause. By then, the rest of the tension Alex had seen manifesting in Dev's posture over the last few days had disappeared, and he was leaning back in his chair, smiling and laughing, and their friendship felt stronger than it had in years.

Alex hoped that would be enough for him if his new plan backfired on Saturday.

"I AM so, so drunk," Elijah said morosely. "I am the drunkest person in the whole world."

Alex exchanged a smirk with Dev over the top of Elijah's head. They didn't get to do that often; Elijah was almost a foot taller than they were. It wasn't like either of them were particularly sober, but they weren't the guest of honor; not everyone in the bar was buying them drinks.

"Yeah, amigo," Alex agreed consolingly, wrapping his arm carefully under Elijah's shoulders, "you got the title, all right. Think you can stand?"

Elijah sighed, looking down at his legs dangling off the barstool. "My legs are drunk too."

Alex saw Dev duck his head and heard him snort as he dragged Elijah's arm over his own shoulders. It was impossibly awkward to get him up and moving; on top of his height, Elijah was built like a tank. Apparently, that wasn't helping him hold his liquor any, because the bartender had looked over at him a few minutes ago and indicated that it was time for the party to leave, pronto.

It was one-thirty in the morning, anyway, and if he didn't want to be hung over at his own wedding tomorrow, it was probably time to quit.

Oh yeah, Alex reflected; if Amanda knew half the stuff they'd got up to tonight, she'd have their balls for breakfast.

As if reading his mind, Dev huffed a laugh as they finally managed to drag Elijah out into the cool July night. "If Amanda finds out about this, we are screwed."

Elijah sighed, "Amanda," in a tone that made Alex and Dev crack up laughing so hard that they almost dropped him on the sidewalk. "Guys, I'm getting *married* tomorrow, I'm-I'm—"

Throwing up on the street, apparently. Alex winced as he and Dev held Elijah's heaving shoulders while he emptied the contents of his stomach—mostly liquid—into the gutter. "Where's the camera when you need it," Dev sighed wistfully.

"It's better that there's no evidence."

"True."

By way of a small miracle, they managed to get a cab, though squeezing Elijah into the back seat required Dev climbing in first to coordinate. Even then, when they finally got him inside, he landed face-down in Dev's lap. Dev speared Alex with a glare before he could so much as laugh and managed to lever Elijah back into a sitting position so he could secure him with a seat belt. "Don't say a word."

Alex smirked as he climbed into the front seat. "Wouldn't dream of it." He gave the driver his address, promised him an extra twenty for going so far out of the city, and sat back to watch the world go by.

He'd never admit it to Dev, but by Tuesday, he'd scrapped his original twelve-step program and rewritten the last few steps. Sure, there were some staples that couldn't be avoided (tonight, for example), but he hoped Dev never asked what had happened to steps eight through eleven. Step eight had become a covert attempt to subtly present Dev with alternative options for his affections (i.e., Alex). Nine was the plan to transfer those affections. Alex refused to think about step ten until after steps eleven (also drinking—it really should have bracketed this whole experience) and twelve (the wedding and therefore the ultimate test) were behind them.

Or he was *trying* not to think about it, anyway, but he'd woken up hard and sweaty for the last three mornings in a row, so at least part of his body wasn't listening.

In the back seat, Elijah had apparently reached the wisdom dispensing stage of drunkenness. He was leaning on Dev's shoulder and gesturing expansively with his hands as he slurred. "One day you guys are going to find someone and you'll understand." In the rearview mirror, Alex saw Elijah smack Dev in the chest with an enthusiastic gesture. He met Dev's eyes, and they shared a wry grin.

When they finally pulled into Alex's driveway after twenty minutes of Elijah expounding on the many benefits of having a life partner (seriously, Alex was never going to be able to look Amanda in the eye again), Dev hurried around to the other side of the car, but he was too late; Elijah had already spilled out onto the concrete. Alex handed him the keys and paid the driver as Dev tried to coax the drunken groom-to-be off of the ground and into the house, where they could ply him with liquids and put him to bed. "You owe me so much for this. You have no idea," Alex heard him mutter as he worked the front door open.

"You guys are my very best friends. I mean *the best.*"

You better believe it, buddy, Alex thought. They left him sprawled on the guest bed with two bottles of water.

"I set the alarm on my phone for six," Dev told him bleakly, chugging down a half-liter of water himself.

"What say we just kill the groom and call the whole thing off?" Alex said, glancing at the clock on the wall. Six o'clock was way too close for comfort.

"No good." Dev sighed. "Amanda will kill us. Slowly and with extreme prejudice."

⁎ ⁎ ⁎

The man had a point, damn it, and while death would probably be preferable to the way Alex was going to feel in the morning, he was kind of attached to Dev. "My head hurts," he sighed, downing a painkiller. "I'm going to bed."

IT WAS over as suddenly as it had started.

Dev loosened his tie, leaned back against the wall, and watched the celebration unfold all around him. Alex's speech had been characteristically funny and personal and mercifully brief, the maid of honor had wept her way through a few completely incomprehensible sentences and a toast to true love, and now the drinking and dancing portion of the evening was under way. Elijah and Amanda were swaying on the dance floor like they didn't even know there were other people present, a study in contrasts of white on dark. Dev felt himself smiling in spite of his exhaustion.

"So?" Alex asked from beside him, passing him a glass of wine. "How'd we do?"

He took a long sip before he answered. "With what?"

"You know, with your… thing."

Dev looked from Alex to Elijah and Amanda lost in their own little world, his throat suddenly tight. "Well," he said finally, "I'm not in love with Elijah." In fact, the only real outcome of the week they'd spent together was that he was now more in love with Alex than ever.

Alex cocked his head to one side like he was evaluating the truthfulness of the statement. "That's good," he said. Then he took Dev's wine glass away and set it on the bar. "Come on, let's celebrate."

"By slow dancing?" Dev asked when it became clear that that was indeed Alex's objective. "Isn't that kind of weird?" Not that it would be the first unnerving or unusual thing that Alex had said or done this week, not by a long shot, which was part of the problem, really. Dev couldn't help but hope there might be something behind it, but it was hard to tell if Alex really was treating him differently or if it was all wishful thinking.

"You're weird," Alex shot back, lacing their fingers together. "Seriously, how come you're not happier?"

"I'm happy!" Dev defended, although truthfully his palms were beginning to sweat a little. Alex was too close to lie to, and after all he'd done the past week, it wasn't really fair to continue to do so. "Listen, I have a confession to make."

He could actually *feel* the shift in Alex's body language, suddenly stiffer, more serious. "Okay."

"I never had a thing for Elijah." The words came out easier than he'd thought they would.

"What? But I heard you—"

"You overheard me talking on the phone, and I let you make that assumption," Dev broke in. He needed to keep up the momentum. "But it was never Elijah that I was talking about."

"So it was Amanda, then?"

"Amanda is a *woman*," Dev pointed out, thrown by the interruption. "A very small, scary woman who is *not a man*. I'm *gay*, and you-you are totally having me on," he sighed, deflating. "That was mean. I'm trying to pour my heart out to you here."

But Alex's body had loosened up again and he was smiling, and it wasn't like Dev could ever stay mad at him anyway. "Sorry."

"That's okay."

"So if it wasn't Elijah, and it wasn't Amanda," Alex prompted.

Dev took a deep breath. He'd lost most of his nerve and all of his momentum, but he was still stuck. Alex would know either way. He might as well be brave. "It was you," he admitted, the long years of hiding adding weight to his tone. "It's still you. You knew, didn't you?"

"Didn't have the first clue," Alex said, so openly Dev knew he wasn't kidding. "Until maybe Tuesday. And then…." He shrugged, squeezing Dev's fingers. "I was kinda hoping."

Dev's breath left him in a wordless rush, and he thought he might have blacked out for a moment, because the next thing he knew they were kissing, slow and sweet, to the soundtrack of his racing pulse.

There was a catcall or two when Alex finally pulled away, eyes wide and mouth swollen, tongue flicking out over his lips. "You think Amanda will slaughter us if we slip out early?"

Dev glanced down at their still-laced fingers and thought about the meaning of significant digits. "I think she'll understand."

⁂

ASHLYN KANE is a twenty-four-year-old supergeek who graduated cum laude from the University of Windsor with an honors degree in English language and literature and magna cum laude with a bachelor's degree in education. When she's not writing, reading, or editing, she's keeping an eye out for any teaching jobs in the area. She is addicted to classic rock, science fiction, and TV on DVD.

She has a fiancé, a little brother, and a bitchy cat.

Amy Lane

Jace's breath puffed softly in Quentin's ear, and the enforced intimacy of the cab only made Quent's mind race more.

He'd never touched a man that way.

He'd wanted to, sure—ever since a circle jerk in the tenth grade. He'd looked at the boy next to him, a taut, blond hurricane of a kid who bound friends to him like static electricity, and had been fascinated. He'd seen how the kid's eyes rolled back, how he palmed his slender, longer cock differently, how he'd surreptitiously licked his hand when he was done, and Quentin had wanted… had wanted…

Things.

Things he hadn't let himself want with Jace, because Jace was a bloodless competitor, a shark, the leader of their partnership, the electric-ball-center of their all-het peer group.

If Jace hadn't wanted those things back, Quentin would have been screwed.

And now Jace *did* want those things back, and Quentin was going to get screwed anyway. But in a good way.

He shivered, his cock aching, and Jace grunted in his ear. The cab came to a halt, and Jace was gone into the rain. Quentin followed him, barely able to walk, barely able to stand still as Jace paid the driver and then hustled past the doorman and to the elevator.

They didn't touch in the elevator. They stood, one in either back corner of the empty lift, and didn't look at each other. Quentin snuck a look at Jace as the floor meter counted to fifteen and saw that his fierce blue eyes were glued to the meter, as though he could make the lift go faster just by concentration alone. Quentin's entire body went cold and then flushed warm with excitement, anticipation.

Jace was going to turn that fierceness on him.

When they got to Jace's apartment, he gestured casually for Quentin to go first. Quent hung his raincoat and suit jacket on the hook at the entryway and moved toward the impressively large front room. He glanced to the bare, stark window looking out into the brightly lit city below them. He listened idly to Jace's noises behind him and wondered what happened next.

He was unprepared to feel hard hands on his shoulders, whirling him about and pressing him against the wall.

Neither of them had turned on the lights, and for a moment, Quentin was lost in the glitter of Jace's ice blue eyes, peering at him in the dark. His throat was Sahara dry, and he had to struggle to speak.

"I don't know how to do this."

Jace's hard mouth went soft in the corners. "Just do what you do at work, buddy."

"Follow your lead?"

And now that lean mouth went *entirely* soft, and his sharp eyes hooded. "Follow my lead."

Quentin closed his eyes and nodded, and Jace shook him a little at the shoulders.

"Look at me," he commanded, and Quentin sucked in a breath and did just that. "Good." Jace punctuated the praise with a kiss at Quentin's jaw, and Quent kept his eyes open even as he tilted his head and revealed his neck.

"Now touch me," Jace hissed against Quent's throat. He was placing nipping, gentle, tongue-point kisses at the edge of Quentin's collar, and Jace dropped his hands to unbutton Quent's shirt while Quentin raised them to do what Jace demanded.

Jace's back was taut, lean, and muscled beneath Quent's hands. Quentin took a fistful of shirt under Jace's jacket, pulled hard, and palmed the smooth skin at his waist. Jace "Mmmmmm"d at Quent's throat, and Quentin tilted his head back and groaned.

Quent's hands found Jace's shoulders, and he pushed impatiently at his tuxedo jacket until Jace dropped his hands and it fell to the floor in a puddle.

Jace returned the favor by yanking at Quentin's shirt until the buttons exploded across the floor and shoving up at Quent's undershirt. Quentin made a sound—protest, acceptance, whatever—and Jace went down on one knee and sank delicate teeth into the tenderness of Quent's stomach.

Quentin shoved himself back against the wall to keep his knees from buckling. Against the soft skin of his taut stomach, he felt more than heard Jace's evil chuckle.

"That was a little girl's sound," he grumbled, fumbling at the stays in Quent's slacks.

"I'm not…" Oh God. Jace was nuzzling the skin under the waistband of his boxer briefs. "Not… a… girl…." Quent panted.

Jace shoved slacks and underwear to Quent's thighs, and his prick bounced out, fully engorged and slapping Jace lightly on the cheek.

"I've noticed," Jace said dryly, a wicked light sparking in those hooded blue eyes. He stuck out an evil, pointed tongue and dragged it from the fur underneath Quent's cock to the broad, flaring tip, paying special attention to the taut little harp-string of flesh under the head.

Quent made that little girl's sound again and caressed Jace's head. The buzz cut tickled Quentin's palms, but Jace leaned into the touch—right before he opened his mouth fully and engulfed Quentin to the root, closed his mouth, hollowed his cheeks, and sucked, pulling his head back with agonizing slowness.

Quentin lifted the palm of his hand and bit down, hard, to keep from crying out.

Jace pulled his head back, held Quent's cock in a hard lean hand, and reached up with his other hand to jerk Quentin's arm down.

"Scream for me," he commanded roughly, and he deep-throated Quentin again.

Quentin screamed. He whimpered. He begged. And still Jace kept up that agonizingly slow, hard mouth-caress on Quentin's body until will alone kept Quent pressed against the wall. Jace opened his mouth for a moment and took his finger to the end of Quent's cock, skating it around the slick pre-come at the end.

"Your noises are making me hard," he said roughly, his voice matter-of-fact. "You know what I'm going to do to you when we're done here, right?"

Quentin moaned softly, and Jace traced that wet, glistening finger back down the underside of Quent's cock, down the underside of his balls and finally hovering, almost tickling, at Quent's entrance.

"Tell me," Jace commanded, and Quentin had no choice but to find words.

"Fuck me," he gasped. "You're going to fuck me…."

That finger eased its way in, and Quentin grabbed onto Jace's shoulders to keep his knees from buckling.

"Oh yes," Jace promised. "But first…." The finger withdrew, then breached again, and Jace engulfed Quentin and pulled away. Jace spoke again, his breath hissing along the nerve endings of Quentin's cock.

"Come for me," he whispered, and then he took Quentin into the back of his throat one more time.

And Quentin did.

Mending the Break
Jaymz Connelly

Pale sunlight filtered around the edges of the curtains drawn haphazardly across the bedroom window. The muted sound of downtown London's early morning commuter traffic wouldn't have been enough to disturb Quinten Lake if he hadn't already been awake. The discomfort of his still-healing injury meant that his sleep was fragmented and restless, and more often than not, Quin was awake and staring at the ceiling above his bed before the alarm sounded.

Quin very carefully rolled over in bed and readjusted the pillow under his knee in an attempt to alleviate the deep, throbbing ache in his leg.

For what must have been the millionth time, he wished he'd never gone on the damn skiing trip. It had been fun, though, at least until he'd gone left instead of right and collided rather abruptly with a bloody tree.

One shattered kneecap later and his holiday in the Swiss Alps had been cut painfully short.

But even that wouldn't have been so bad—two years ago.

Sighing heavily, Quin draped his arm over his eyes, as if that would be enough to block out his memories. The last time he'd had a broken bone, it had been infinitely more bearable because of Jai. A brief smile curled Quin's lips. Jai of the magic hands.

* * *

But he couldn't think about that any more. He'd lost the right to Jai's hands and every other part of him.

Uncomfortable with the direction his thoughts were heading, Quin pushed himself up to a sitting position and carefully swung his legs over the side of the bed. He braced his crutches before standing up on his good leg, and then headed out to the kitchen, hoping a bit of activity would block out his thoughts of Jai.

Jai, who was everything he'd ever wanted in a lover. Jai, who put up with all his stupid moods and who could always jolly him out of a funk, until the last time, when Quin had behaved truly, unforgivably badly.

The last two years had done absolutely nothing to lessen the remorse Quin felt for his actions, or his ache for Jai. None of the men he'd dated since had ever measured up to what he'd had with Jai. Not that he'd given them much of a chance, driving them all away with his moodiness—

He slammed his fist down on the counter and struggled to stay upright on his good leg as one of his crutches clattered to the floor. Quin clung to the edge of the counter, panting for air, until he managed to catch his balance again. Pushing himself up slowly, he glared at the uncooperative crutch, wondering how he was going to manage to pick it up without falling on his head or hurting his leg.

He grabbed the sugar bowl from the counter and raised his hand to fling it at the wall in a glorious release of shattered china and sugar but managed to stop himself, gripping it until his hand turned white. However satisfying the crash, he would then have to clean up the mess by himself, and he could barely manage to retrieve his crutch as it was.

"Rat-tempered bastard."

That was what Jai had called him after one of their furious arguments. He'd always said the angry sex and the make-up sex were worth it, and Quin rather enjoyed the excitement of the frequent squabbles himself, so it had never seemed worthwhile to try to curb his temper.

Carefully, he set the bowl down and sagged against the counter, his rage draining away and leaving him tired and empty.

If only he'd managed to learn to think before blowing up he might not be here, trying to repair the broken shards of his life all by himself. He'd thought about trying to call Jai to apologize, but he had never been able to bring himself to actually do so, and then it was too late. How do you apologize for being a complete prat six months after the event? And then it had become a year, and then two.

Quin snorted self-deprecatingly as he carefully leaned over to pick up his crutch, hanging onto the lifeline of the counter all the while.

He made himself coffee and settled at the kitchen table. Maybe he was building up his former lover to be better than he actually was, but he truly didn't think so. Even after all this time, it physically hurt to think of the pain he'd caused Jai with his thoughtless words and behavior.

Pushing himself up out of his chair, Quin shook his head impatiently. He had to stop thinking about Jai. There was nothing he could do about it now, and it certainly wasn't going to help him get ready for his first physiotherapy session.

THE quiet ticking of the clock was the only sound in the room. Quin lay on the treatment table, wondering how long it was going to take the masseuse to show up and give him his reward for working his arse off in therapy. Right now, his knee was aching so badly, Quin figured if he didn't get some relief soon, he would simply go home and take half a bottle of painkillers and damn the consequences.

The door to the treatment room opened, and the bottom dropped out of Quin's world.

"You're not a masseuse."

"No, the sex change operation was a failure," Jai said calmly as he closed the door, glad he'd taken the opportunity to prepare himself to face his former lover.

Quin sat up and swung his legs over the side of the examination table.

"I can't really massage your leg in that position, sir."

"'Sir'? You're calling me 'sir'?" Quin asked incredulously. He stared at Jai, drinking in the sight of his former lover. His heart pounded a staccato rhythm in his chest, and he felt a bit lightheaded, but he told himself that was just because he had sat up too fast or because of the ache in his leg.

"Well, you *are* a client."

* * *

"I don't need this shit," Quin muttered, not wanting to let Jai see how much his impersonal attitude hurt. He stood up on his good leg and then froze when Jai's hands rested on his shoulders, sending a shiver of desire racing over his body.

"Sit down, Quin," Jai pleaded.

"I…." Quin sat, afraid that if he didn't, his leg would give out under him, and then Jai would know exactly how much this unexpected encounter was affecting him. "They said someone named Kelly was going to give me my massage."

"She was. But she went home early because she wasn't feeling well. What have you done to yourself this time, Quin?" Jai lifted Quin's legs up onto the table as he spoke, his manner calm and professional.

Quin propped himself up on his elbows and stared at his former lover. Jai looked good, so damn good. He was broader in the shoulders and trimmer in the hips than Quin remembered. His black hair was shorter than he used to wear it, and Quin almost smiled as he remembered the time he'd coaxed Jai to let it grow a bit and discovered that it was nearly as curly as his own. The split obviously hadn't hurt *Jai* as much as it had hurt him—or Jai was just better at hiding it.

"Would you prefer that I get another therapist to give you the massage?" Jai asked when Quin remained silent for too long.

"I can handle it," Quin said quickly, wondering if he really could. The sensation of Jai's warm hands on his shoulders lingered, even though they'd long since been removed. He ached so badly to feel Jai's arms around him again.

Jai stepped away from the table and crossed his arms over his chest to hide the way his hands were shaking. He really needed to get a grip on himself before he touched Quin again. It was over, he reminded himself fiercely. Had been over for two years now, and he was never going to let Quin have that much power to affect him again.

"You look well," Quin said softly, tearing his gaze away from Jai to focus on the chart of the human body that was tacked to the wall.

"You look like hell," Jai replied, frowning slightly as he noticed the way Quin's hands were clenching into fists and then releasing, one of the giveaways that Quin felt threatened. In truth, he thought Quin looked wonderful, even with the lines of pain etching his face and the dark shadows beneath his eyes. The slim body of his former lover was still enough to make his groin tingle with desire, and the messy curls that cascaded to Quin's shoulders made Jai's fingers itch to feel the silky-soft strands once more. "I won't hurt you, Quin."

"It'd be worth your license, wouldn't it?" Quin said sourly. He lay back on the table, desperate now to have the session finished before he blurted out something even worse. "Just get on with it, Jai."

"I can still get someone else," Jai offered, even though he didn't want anyone else touching his Quin. But Quin *wasn't* his anymore. He hated watching the beloved body go rigid with tension. "Don't tighten up like that, Quin; it isn't good for your knee. You need to relax so you don't do further damage," Jai said. He couldn't bear to see Quin hurting, even after all this time. "Quin?" he said softly when the other man stayed silent, looking anywhere but at him.

"I said I can deal with it!" Quin snapped.

Not willing to push it any further and determined that he would enjoy this opportunity to touch Quin as much as he could while still remaining professional, Jai stepped up to the table, composing his face into a mask of professional concern as he reached for the massage lotion. "Where does it hurt the most, and how badly?"

"My whole bloody leg is aching like a toothache," Quin ground out, closing his eyes tightly so he wouldn't have to watch Jai. He bit his lip to suppress a gasp when Jai's strong hands stroked over his leg, starting the treatment slowly.

Remaining silent, Jai carefully massaged Quin's leg, paying special attention to the muscles that had begun to knot after the exercise Quin had done. Jai could feel Quin's leg quivering beneath his hands, but he wasn't sure if that was entirely due to the exertion he'd been through with the physio or if it was in response to his touch.

Steeling himself to be rebuffed but unable to bear the awkward silence any longer, Quin spoke. "I thought you were working in Southwark."

"I left there a year ago," Jai replied, smiling a little when he realized that Quin had his eyes tightly scrunched shut. "Am I hurting you?"

"No."

"So how did you do this?"

"Isn't it all covered in my medical reports?" Quin snarled, reluctant to admit just how stupid he'd been.

"Yeah, you had an accident while skiing and shattered your kneecap," Jai replied. "How did you do that, Quin? You're an excellent skier."

"Would you believe a tree jumped out in front of me?"

Jai laughed and shook his head in spite of his determination not to let Quin affect him. "Kamikaze tree, was it?"

"Oh, yeah," Quin agreed with a wry grin. "Mr. Fir definitely came off second-best there."

"Didn't leave a mark on him?"

"Not even a bit of bark scraped off," Quin said in disgust.

"You're usually pretty good at spotting those wayward, feral trees."

"I was a bit distracted," Quin admitted sheepishly.

"Had your eye on a hot snowboarder?" Jai asked in a hard voice, steeling himself for the answer.

"Was thinking about the last time I'd been skiing," Quin replied reluctantly. "With you."

"You trying to blame this accident on me?" Jai teased.

"No." Quin sighed. "It was all my own fault. All of it."

"It takes two, Quin," Jai said, realizing they weren't talking about the skiing accident anymore.

"So they say," Quin agreed. He opened his eyes when Jai's hands stilled and was immediately lost in the endless depths of his gaze.

Jai stared intently at Quin, reading the pain and regret in his former lover's dark blue eyes. "That's it for today, Quin," he said softly, not wanting the session to end but unable to drag it out any further.

"Okay," Quin said, pleased when his voice didn't betray how much he dreaded walking away from Jai again. He let Jai help him up and then pulled on his jeans, inserting his foot into his shoe without a word. Balancing himself on his crutches, Quin headed for the door, leaving Jai standing silently beside the treatment table.

* * *

With his hand on the doorknob, Quin turned back to face Jai and licked his lips nervously. "We'd had huge blow-up arguments before, Jai," he said quietly. "Why did we break up this time? What—what was so bad about this argument that we didn't think it was worth going on?"

Jai stared helplessly at Quin, unable to find the words. And then it was too late, because Quin had vanished, just as he had the night their relationship had been destroyed.

Galvanized into action at the thought, Jai hurried after his erstwhile lover. "Not this time, you little bastard," he muttered. He growled in frustration when the lift doors closed just as he got to them and then flung open the door to the stairs, pelting down them as quickly as he could. He was determined Quin wasn't going to just walk away again, even if it *was* more of a hobble right now. At least his injury would slow him down a bit.

Panting for air, Jai slammed through the door at the bottom of the stairs just as the lift doors opened. "Quin!" he called out as the other man tried to hurry away.

Quin's heart leapt into his throat at Jai's voice. He hadn't thought Jai would follow him. Jai certainly hadn't followed him that night. He tried to go faster, but one crutch skidded on the marble floor and he pitched forward. It was only Jai's strong arms around him that prevented him from falling flat on his face.

The solid, reassuring strength of Jai's arms around him, supporting and protecting him, brought home anew to Quin just what he had so foolishly thrown away. How could he ever have thought he could manage without Jai? It was as ridiculous as thinking he could walk without his crutches right now.

"Don't you bloody well dare run away from me again," Jai snapped, refusing to relinquish his hold on Quin even after the other man had recovered his balance.

"Jai, don't," Quin pleaded, his voice thick with emotion. He couldn't make himself look at Jai, afraid he'd see scorn and hatred reflected in the other man's eyes.

"We need to talk," Jai said, rubbing his hand over Quin's back to calm him without realizing what he was doing.

"You're in the middle of work," Quin protested.

"It can wait. I told them I'd need a break after seeing you."

* * *

"You *told* them?"

"Only that we knew each other and had parted ways rather acrimoniously."

Quin blinked furiously, trying to will the tears away. It was exquisite torture to be held in Jai's strong arms once more. He just wished....

"Coffee?" Jai suggested, ignoring the curious stares of the people passing by.

"Could use something stronger," Quin said, trying to muster up a smile as he finally lifted his head to look at Jai.

Jai grinned. "Not a good idea with the painkillers, mate. Don't fancy having you pass out on the floor in the middle of things."

"God, I've missed you so much," Quin admitted, his voice little more than a whisper.

"I've missed you too, babe," Jai said, brushing the auburn curls back from Quin's face. "Your hair looks good longer."

"I need..." Quin paused to swallow against the lump in his throat, ruthlessly quelling the tiny flutter of hope that woke in his heart at the endearment. "I really need to sit down, Jai, before I fall down."

Reluctantly letting go of Quin, Jai walked beside him as they made their way out of the building and down the street to a nearby café. He got Quin settled at a table and then went to place their order.

Quin stared at the cup of coffee that was placed in front of him and then looked up at Jai as he folded himself into the chair across from him.

"It's strong, with skim," Jai said as he handed Quin three packets of sugar.

"You remember how I like my coffee?"

"Remember everything," Jai said with a helpless shrug. "I loved you, Quin."

"Until I ruined it all."

"It takes two," Jai said firmly. "I shouldn't have let you walk away that night."

"I wanted you to come after me."

"I never was any good at mind reading."

"You always used to know what I *really* wanted," Quin whispered.

"Even The Amazing Kreskin can have an off day," Jai said with a wry grin. "You did a really good job of making me believe you hated my guts that night."

"I've never hated you. Could never hate you. The past two years have been an absolute hell, Jai."

"Why didn't you call me?"

Quin shook his head and smiled sadly.

"You know, there's proud, and then there's stupid," Jai said affectionately as he reached out to cover Quin's hand with his own.

"I excel at the latter."

"Not usually, but you certainly have your moments."

"I wish I could do that night over again," Quin said, turning his hand beneath Jai's so their fingers could intertwine.

"What would you do differently?" Jai encouraged. He wanted Quin back. Wanted to make the past two years nothing more than a bad dream. But he couldn't do it if Quin was still as unwilling even to attempt to control himself as he had been then. He hadn't realized how much their arguments and Quin's volatile temper had worn at him until they'd separated, even though it had done nothing to diminish his love for him.

"I would tell you how I really felt instead of finding reasons to blow up at you," Quin replied. "How scared I was of how much I loved you—still love you. I—I wouldn't just run away, Jai. I would do what I wanted to do then, what I want to do now."

"What do you want to do now?"

"Crawl into your arms and never leave," Quin whispered. "It scares the living fuck out of me just how much I need you, Jai. I know I was using the arguing to throw up a smokescreen, but I don't want to hide behind it anymore. I can't promise that I won't still be an obnoxious bastard sometimes…."

"Well, it *is* part of your charm," Jai chuckled.

"But I'm trying to do better, Jai," Quin said, smiling briefly at the interruption.

"I think it's time to get you home," Jai said, pushing his still-full coffee cup away with a trembling hand. "I'll make sure Kelly or someone else can handle your next appointment too."

The blood drained out of Quin's face as he stared at Jai, his heart breaking all over again at the thought that it was far too late, that Jai didn't believe him, even though he'd been totally truthful.

Jai helped Quin to stand up and then wrapped his arm around Quin's slim waist, caressing his face with his other hand. "Wouldn't really do to engage in a romantic relationship with a client, would it?" he said tenderly.

"Jai?" Quin breathed, his heart soaring with hope.

"I guess I can learn to live with a tantrum or two, just on special occasions: birthdays, anniversaries—"

"Jai!"

"I've never stopped loving and missing you either, Quin," Jai said, and he angled his head to take his lover's lips in the first kiss of the rest of their lives together.

* * *

JAYMZ CONNELLY is a transplanted Canadian living very happily in Australia with a supportive husband and two teenage boys who seem to have inherited her twisted sense of humor. She has worked in banking, personal management, and concert promotion and merchandising, gaining valuable life experiences to help her realize her long-held dream of being a writer.

The Road to Nowhere
Catt Ford

"Can I ask you a question?"

"Sure. Fire away."

"How did you ever end up here, in West Bumfuck, Wyoming? I mean, don't take offense, but you have a great talent. Your book is on the bestseller list; why aren't you in New York or San Francisco?"

I laughed. "Been there, like it better here." I shrugged. I didn't figure he really cared about the answer.

After a lifetime of taking my own photos my own way, having small shows in galleries here and there, and running my studio, I wasn't the only one taken by surprise when my book ended up on the *Times* Bestseller list.

It was a book of photographs, what they used to call a coffee-table book, called *Beauty in Ugly Places*, which was kind of my life's work, as I saw it—finding the little glimpses of beauty that we tend to pass by in the hurry of modern life.

It was Barry who had conceived the idea for the book, pulled together the photos, and found a publisher over my apathetic protests, so part of the triumph was his. It was he who put a name to the collection of photos, taken over a lifetime, that came together in an unlikely book that somehow hit people right and made them shell out their hard-earned dough to buy it.

* * *

And now this kid reporter was asking me how I ended up here, in South Gulch, Wyoming, as if all the folks with real talent were stuffed into the big, important cities.

"Really, I'm interested," he affirmed.

He looked interested for real. And what the hell, I'd never told my life story to anyone before. No one but Barry was really interested, and he already knew the important parts, because he'd lived them with me.

"It's a long story," I said, giving the boy an out. "I'm old."

"I've got time," he said. "I'd like to hear it."

"Okay, but if you print it, you've got to include Myrom and Dowling," I bargained, sure that the kid wouldn't buy a pig in a poke that way.

"I thought his name was Barry," he said hesitantly.

"It is. Myrom and Dowling are just a part of it."

"Tell me," he said.

"Let's go for a drive."

I STOPPED my old, rattling truck on the side of the tarmac. To the east, the sky was big and empty except for a few white, puffy clouds. There were mountains in the distance, but in front of them was a grassy field, the golden ripe grasses waving in the breeze. A dirt road was cut deep through the grasses, the dirt almost the same gold as the pasture. Everything was quiet except for the wind singing her endless, alluring song like a siren, making you yearn to see what lay around the next bend.

"This is that photo of the road," he said immediately.

"Yep," I replied, pleased that he had actually looked through my book and apparently even remembered one of the shots. It's nice to know when your work hits a chord in someone else. To me, that's the true beauty of art, communicating with someone you never met with one image, one that I had had no idea would come to mean so much to me when I first took it.

"I took that shot twenty-eight years ago," I started. "Just a snapshot, I thought."

I was gay. I'd known it ever since I had a sense of me as an entity, Jim, a boy-child. As I grew up, I knew that men interested me; I found them fascinating, irresistible. Girls were nice too, and I liked them as friends, but there was no intensity there for me.

I was a good-looking kid too. As soon as I found that out, I realized my own power to attract, and pretty soon I fucked my way through my high school, conquering even some of the straight boys who had never given a thought to man-on-man sex until they met me.

By the time I got to college, I was pretty damn well convinced that I was a prize and everyone should be trying to win me.

Went to school in New York City. Grew up there, in Queens, one of the boroughs, and to those of us stuck in the deadly bourgeois boroughs, the city was where it was at. I worked summer jobs to afford the room and board at NYU just to get out of my parents' house. I needed to be free, to live for my art. I needed to fuck around.

Barry went to school there too. First time I saw him, I knew he was gay, but a guy like him never stood a chance with me. For one thing, when they designed him, they hadn't passed up the chance to use sharp angles all over; he was a hick country boy, skinny, raw-boned, and gangly, wearing floods and a short-sleeved shirt.

He was hot for me, I could tell, but I just passed him by with a snicker. I didn't do geeks; I did the hot muscle guys. They had to be beautiful for me even to give them a second glance, let alone a date.

You'd think that he would have been picked on in school. I mean, he was an obvious rube from a small town out west somewhere, shy, quiet, and dorky. But somehow, he was hard to overlook. He was smart and funny, and he didn't *let* himself get overlooked.

It would be pretty to say that I'd come to my senses and recognized a diamond in the rough, but it was other guys who polished him up. By the time we graduated, he had a better haircut and was wearing his jeans long enough, and he'd grown into his lanky arms and legs. He now moved with a kind of loose-limbed grace that was sort of nice to watch.

Still, we were just acquaintances in a larger group of gay men who hung out just because we were all gay in a primarily straight school. After graduation, he went back to wherever he came from, and I went to San Francisco, the Mecca of the artsy gay crowd in the sixties.

* * *

I set up a studio and worked with the big advertising agencies. I had my work printed in prestigious industry publications, won some awards, and made my fair share of money.

And I fucked my brains out. The whole city was full of eye candy, gym rats whose only job in life was perfecting their store-bought muscles, refining their routines until their bodies were as hard as if they'd been sculpted from wood, rippling with muscle as they posed and strutted to advertise themselves in many a gay bar. You can imagine my private gallery; I got almost all of them to pose for me after I'd fucked them silly.

I bedded as many as I could, and as I say, being fairly good-looking myself, I made out okay. You wouldn't think it to look at me now, but back then my hair was brown and shiny like maple syrup, and I was in very good shape for a slim guy.

"YOU'RE still very handsome," the kid reporter interrupted dryly. "Distinguished-looking."

That's the compliment grey hair will always buy you. I laughed, wondering if he could be flirting with me. "Thanks." Then I got back to my story.

I'D been living with a guy, Bruce. Yeah, finally gave up my man-chasing ways. He was beautiful and useless and fascinating and selfish. Like a diamond, all sparkle but hard to cuddle up to, but I couldn't see that, not back then.

We'd been living together for over a year when he dropped the bomb on me. Actually, he didn't drop it; I caught him at home in our bed, letting some other muscle guy fuck him and without a condom.

Even then, we were starting to realize that the "gay cancer", as it was called then, was very dangerous, and that you had to use a condom if you didn't want to die. I don't know whether it was injured pride that he'd wanted someone else to fuck him or pure anger that caused me to kick him out, hot anger that covered up my cold fear that he would so blithely put my life and his at risk like that.

My heart was broken, or so I thought. After the requisite tests, finding that every bar in the city reminded me painfully of Bruce, I decided to take my pity party on the road. Alone. I gave up my studio and my apartment, put my stuff in storage, and flew to New York to see my parents.

Although I'd never actually told them in so many words, I guess they'd come to terms with the fact that I wouldn't be giving them grandchildren. Heck, I had a sister and a brother who were busy procreating, so I didn't bother to explain. It only took one week at home to convince me to get the hell out of there. For one thing, if I did happen to find someone to fuck, I had no place to take him.

I came up with the grandiose plan of publishing a monumental book of photos, documenting my travels, never doubting that everyone would want a copy. I would let my epic grief inform my art, although I was going to remain silent and mysterious as to the cause. Back in those days, the "fine art" clique looked down on those of us in commercial art. I'd show everyone; they could all kiss my ass. Bruce too.

So I rented a truck with a camper on the back and headed back across the country, determined to take the most beautiful photograph ever! Take that, Ansel Adams. Yeah, I didn't have too big an ego to get through the door. It's amazing that I didn't get a flat tire from all that dead weight.

My ideas about beauty were so different back then. I was disappointed unless there was a spectacular sunset or towering dark blue thunderclouds with the contrast of a perfect field of white daisies in front, *something* dramatic and soul-stirring. I wouldn't take my camera out of the bag for less.

As I meandered across the country, I chased after that ephemeral image, the one that would make my name famous. And so when people talked about a place, about how beautiful it was, I'd go there, hoping to see what they saw. And I saw some pretty things, but nothing that could make me forget the ache that tied my chest in a giant knot.

That was how I happened to be travelling through South Gulch, Wyoming that day. I had no idea that Barry lived here; I just barely made it into town in that damned truck, steam pouring out from under the hood. Turned out some eighteen-wheeler had thrown a rock through my radiator, and now it needed to be replaced.

Of course, the one-horse gas station didn't have the parts in stock, so I was stuck here until they could be ordered in. It was summer, hot, humid, and the town was ugly and boring. Only the one hotel, if you could call it that; it was actually more of a glorified motel.

I was sitting on the porch of the hotel that evening, all alone, feeling sorry for myself, when I heard someone call my name. Who the hell could ever know me by name out here, I wondered?

Well, it was Barry.

"Jim, what're you doing here in Wyoming? San Francisco too hot to hold you?" he asked with a big smile.

We shook hands. "Just travelling across country back to California, taking pictures along the way. I'm a photographer," I said, somewhat importantly, as if he should have heard what I was doing out there in the big world.

"And you stopped in South Gulch?" He sounded rather astonished, and maybe a little hopeful. I guess the crush he'd had on me all those years ago in college still lingered a bit.

"My truck broke down, that's all." I hated to quell his hopes, but he was still a homely man, and I didn't want to encourage him.

"Hope you won't mind a bit of a vacation," he laughed. "Parts don't come quickly here. Well, I'm in the book if you get bored and want to grab a beer sometime."

We shook hands again, and he walked away. I'd never noticed it before, but he did have a damn fine ass.

"I'M not embarrassing you, am I?" I asked hopefully.

"Nope," the kid reporter grinned as if he was onto me. "Carry on."

I DID get bored sitting around in town. There was nothing to photograph, and nothing to do, so on the third day, I gave in and gave Barry a call.

He came by that morning and picked me up. "I have to go to work, but there's a spot I'd like to show you. Bring your camera," he said.

I dragged my feet climbing the stairs to my room. I was used to this, friends asking me to take "pretty" pictures for them, and rather ungraciously, I guessed I could do that for him, provided that he was going to amuse me and get my mind off my misery for at least a few hours.

He didn't say much, just listened to me talk about myself as we drove along the highway, windows down and the breeze blowing our hair around, until we came to this very spot where I've brought you.

Barry stopped the truck and nodded to that same dirt road we're looking at now. "I've always liked the look of that road," he said. He didn't suggest that I take a picture, though.

"What? It's just a road to nowhere," I said.

"Every road leads somewhere," Barry said, the corner of his mouth quirking as if he found me amusing in that way where you're not in on the joke. "Just depends if you like where it's going."

"*Does* it go somewhere?" I demanded.

"Yep, leads to a ranch. My uncles Myrom and Dowling live there." He paused and squinted at the sky. "I have to get to work, and I thought you might like to get some exercise and fresh air. And Myrom's there; he's good company. He'll give you some lemonade and a yarn. He was in the war."

"What war?" I asked. I knew I was going to take that walk. Whatever boring job Barry had ended up with, I was sure it couldn't possibly interest me for even an hour, let alone a whole day.

"*The* war. WWII," he said, that way that people did back then, double-u double-u two.

"Myrom what?" I asked. I was ashamed that I didn't remember Barry's last name, even though I'd just looked him up in the book.

"Myrom Kessler," he said. "Tell him I said hey. I'll pick you up after five. He doesn't drive anymore."

"Right," I said grumpily. I was going to have a fine afternoon sitting with some eighty-year-old man who was too dotty to drive on a ranch at the end of a road to nowhere. I got out of the truck, feeling like Barry had tricked me into babysitting his uncle for the day.

"Have fun," he called out and started up, driving over a slight rise and out of sight.

"Fuck you," I muttered, and started walking.

* * *

It dawned on me that I didn't even know how far I was going to have to walk. What if Barry resented me for never giving him the time of day back in college and this was a trick to get me lost without water on a hot day?

"WAS it?" the kid asked.

"No, Barry doesn't have that kind of sense of humor. It was only a couple of miles. Even a city boy can manage that," I teased gently.

"Is that supposed to be a hint?" the reporter kid asked.

"Feel like taking a walk?"

"Sure."

We got out. I walked in the rut on the left; he took the right.

"Feel it?" I asked.

He lifted his face into the sun, and I could see the peace on his face. "Yeah."

"Good for you. It took me the first mile to notice it," I said dryly.

I WALKED along here, feeling the weight of my camera bag, in too lousy of a mood to notice. It was this time of year; the sky was that blue that you see at the end of summer, before it starts getting darker for fall, so blue you feel like you can see thousands of miles through it, and the grass was gold, shining like polished metal in the sunshine. The mountains were purple in the distance, and it was very quiet. No planes flying overhead, no cars on the road, just peaceful and quiet.

I walked slow and I took out my camera. There was a little water running over some pebbles by the path, glistening in the sunlight. Mud, and I was taking a picture of it. Go figure. I took a picture of the grasses, drawn by the intricate pattern of shade and light they wove as they danced in the breeze.

The second mile went faster, and before I realized it, I'd come upon a rambling, low house, built from weathered boards that had never been painted, with the history of rain and snow and sunlight scribed on the patina of their surface.

I LOOKED over at the kid reporter. He was looking around as if he'd landed on another planet. Even though the house was a bit run down now, it still looked pretty much the same as when I'd first seen it, even though Myrom was long gone.

BACK then, there had been a pole-fence corral with two horses grazing within it, their tails flicking flies off their backs. They both raised their heads to look at me, and I snapped their portrait. There was something about the way they looked at me, like two children curious to see what was under the tree on Christmas morning. Later, I found out they were hoping for carrots.

"Hey."

I turned around. "Um, hello. I'm a—a friend of Barry's...." My voice trailed off. I'd never seen a man like him, except in the movies.

He was old, his face a roadmap of wrinkles, with a patina similar to the house. He wore a straw cowboy hat and those old-folks' glasses, you know, those plastic frames that kind of come to a point by your eyes. He was bent a bit from riding, you could see his legs bowed out from a lifetime on horseback, but he was tall and skinny except for a small belly. His jeans couldn't seem to decide on whether to fall under or go over the mound, and they'd slipped down despite a handsome tooled leather belt with a big silver buckle.

He hiked his pants up and walked slowly toward me, holding out his hand. "Myrom Kessler's the name."

"Jim. Jim Folkner," I said, offering my hand.

"You're a friend of Barry's, you say. Never heard him mention you," he said, not suspiciously, just like he wanted to get me placed.

"We went to college together," I explained nervously, not that there'd been much *together* about it.

"Ah, that explains it. Doesn't talk about them days much," Myrom said. "Want a glass of lemonade?"

"Sure," I answered. I followed him to the house, and he nodded toward the chairs on the porch.

* * *

"Set a spell and take a load off. I'll bring it out here. Pretty day, shame to waste it."

I sat after I took a photo of the steps, worn concave by the passage of many feet. I wondered if Barry's other uncle, Dowling, his name was, would be coming back out with Myrom, or if he preferred to spend his days inside.

I was surprised when Myrom reappeared. I'd expected a glass of some powdered drink mix, but Myrom brought out one of those painted tin trays with a pitcher and two glasses, all pink engraved depression glass. My mouth watered when I saw the pitcher, beaded with moisture, slices of real lemon floating around in there. Ice clinked into the glass as he poured.

"Made it myself. Barry brought out some lemons from the store the other day," Myrom said proudly. "Taste it. My momma taught me how to make it when I was just a young 'un."

I drank thirstily, aware that my need was not doing justice to this nectar he'd offered. It was like I was gulping down the soul of lemons, bright, tart, and sweet, perfect after a walk on a hot day.

"That was incredible," I gasped when I'd emptied the glass.

He chuckled and refilled my glass. "Secret is to cook the peels in sugar syrup water. Captures the essence."

I watched the corrugated skin of his neck unfold as he drank from his glass.

We sat in silence for a while. It was comfortable. I got the feeling that here was a man entirely at ease in his own skin. He would never hurry into aimless conversation to fill an awkward silence. He didn't need to; he wouldn't find any silence awkward. He liked it, as if he spent a lot of his time listening to the silence.

I was the one who broke first. "So, Barry mentioned his other uncle, Dowling, I think he said."

Myrom chuckled. "Dowling don't talk much these days. 'Specially to strangers."

In spite of myself, I was getting kind of interested in Barry and his uncles. "I'd like to meet him, if it's okay."

* * *

Myrom had brown eyes, I noticed when he stared at me searchingly. Piercing eyes, dark and rich as coffee freshly brewed. Sweet and mellow, with just a hint of bitterness in their depths.

He stood up. "Well, come on then."

I followed him past the small corral to where a lone tree stood. It was an oak, I found out later, a very old one, gnarled and twisted, but the shade was welcome. As we drew nearer, I could see a stone sitting under it.

It was a gravestone, but not one of those factory-made ones. This was a boulder, with lettering chiseled into a flat face that read, "Dowling Lancaster, born 1917, died 1979." The boulder was smooth, as if it had lived in a river where the rushing water had worn it down over the years.

"I'm sorry," I said. "I didn't realize."

"Dowling, this here's Jim. He's a friend of Barry's," Myrom said, talking to the stone as if Dowling's spirit inhabited it and could answer. "Said he wanted to meet you."

Silence fell.

Again, I broke it. "So, he was your brother? Uh, half brother?" I asked, remembering that Myrom's last name was something different even though I hadn't paid enough attention to remember what it was.

"Fuck, no!" Myrom laughed. "He was my partner, my lover."

I thought I must have heard wrong and waited to hear more.

"You look kind of kerflummoxed, young feller," Myrom said, his eyes twinkling behind the old man glasses.

"You're gay?"

"Queer as a three dollar bill," he said proudly.

"How did you two ever meet? Out here?" I exclaimed as if he had mortally offended me. Everyone knew that gay life took place in cities.

"Didn't. Met in the war." Myrom looked off into the distance. "Battle of the Bulge. He fell on me."

"You were in the Lost Battalion?" I asked respectfully. Even I had heard about the Lost Battalion.

"Nope, I'm no Texan. From Pennsylvania. We were in the 141st infantry, trying to break through to them fellers. Couldn't do it. Took those brave little buggers in the 442nd to get the job done," he said.

He turned and limped slowly back to the house, sitting down heavily in his chair. "More lemonade?"

"Yes, please, and tell me how you met. He fell on you?"

"I was in a foxhole. He fell in, right on top of me. Thought he was a German. Told him he was lucky I didn't just shoot him there and then."

"And then you had sex?" I asked, eager to get to the good stuff.

"Heck no, it was freezing! If we'd taken our dicks out of our pants, they'd have froze solid and broken off. No, we huddled for warmth."

He noticed I looked disappointed. "Okay, we cuddled. Dowling wasn't the man to just jump into things. Neither was I. Wanted to get to know a man before I put his dick in my mouth."

"So you knew you were gay before that?"

"Oh, yeah, no doubt in my mind," Myrom said comfortably. "Just hadn't met too many like-minded men 'til Dowling. And even then, figured it was just a wartime thing between us. We started hanging around together. Men noticed, but no one said anything. Everyone had a trench buddy, and some friends helped each other out more than most."

"And so did you fall in love and come back here to live?"

"Nothin's ever that easy, young feller," he said with a sigh. "We had what you might call an affair. Spent some nights together when the front was quiet, but mostly we was fighting. Never said much about after the war. Seemed like a jinx, you know."

"So how did you get parted?"

"We were both wounded. Making a charge to save that damn fool battalion, and I took a bullet in the leg. I didn't know it then, but he got hit in the arm with shrapnel. My platoon withdrew, that's what we used to call a damn rout, and left me out on that field to die."

I was shocked, and I showed it.

"Didn't blame them. We were taking heavy fire. Every man for himself. I was lying there, looking up at the stars, when he came for me. Thought I was looking my last at that night sky. And Dowling, he just crawled on up to me, and said, 'I've come for you'. Dragged me a ways and then lifted me up piggyback and carried me to the Red Cross truck. That's when I found out he'd been hurt too." Myrom sighed. "Never was so glad to see anybody in all my days as when he found me. We held hands 'til they took me inside to the operating room. They dug out the bullet and sent me home. Dowling stayed on in Europe 'til the end of it."

"So how did you find each other again?"

As if he hadn't heard my question, Myrom went on. "We were… different when we came back. Just… different. People who'd stayed here in the States didn't understand. They'd had the rationing and the grief of losing their boys, and their girls too, sometimes, but they'd had it comfortable. They hadn't seen what we seen. I went back home, but I wasn't at home there any longer. I was a man alone."

He stared into the distance, a terrible suffering in his eyes.

"The arrogance of the young. I had never even asked Dowling's last name. Knew he was from Wyoming, that Dowling was his momma's maiden name, but that was it. I never heard from him through the rest of the war, never knew if he made it. When I came out from under the anesthetic, I was already on a plane, being shipped back to England, and after that, to the States.

"I tried to find him. I figured the Army or the State Department or *someone* had to be keeping track of who was who, but without his last name or serial number…."

"But you ended up here, with him?" I asked hopefully. By now, I was desperate for a happy ending for them.

His mouth softened and his face creased with a thousand wrinkles as he remembered. "He found me. He asked the medics what my last name was when they took me away. And after he was sent home, he came here first, to relieve his mother's mind that he was alive and still in possession of all his parts, then he traveled to Pennsylvania to find me.

"My folks had a little farm, dairy cows. And I was out harvesting hay for winter feed when he come up on me in the field. All he said was, 'I've come for you.'

"Well, I couldn't resist that. Or him. Went back to my house and told my folks that I was moving to Wyoming. Told them Dowling had offered me a job."

"Weren't your parents suspicious? I mean, they must have noticed you were… queer." That word did not come easily to my tongue. I'd been trained to think of myself as gay, and "queer" was a quaint, old-fashioned term, but he appeared to like it.

"Funny how folks are always mighty worried over who's fucking who, but only if the folks involved are young, good-looking or desirable. Neither of us was what you might call handsome, and my folks didn't know what to make of me after the war. Guess they was glad to wash their hands of me. I was sorta inconvenient to them, with the war sadness and all.

"I packed up and left with Dowling the next day. 'Course, it took us some time to get here, being as we stopped a lot along the way to fuck. Seemed like we just had to get that out of our systems."

His lascivious grin made me ask, "And did you?"

"Never," he declared proudly. "Not 'til the day Dowling died. We was still fucking and sucking, just not quite so often."

He sighed then. He didn't say it out loud, but I could tell he missed Dowling deeply.

"Well, didn't people in town, um, notice that you were two guys living together?"

"Some did, some didn't. Like I say, the older we got, the less they cared. Was a girl used to be sweet on Dowling, wanted to marry up with him. She always did hate me. Used to look daggers at me when we went to town, and she tried to start up some trouble, but eventually she got married and moved away.

"We lived alone a-way out here. Only went to town to trade for supplies. And like I say, nobody much wanted either one of us, so we was left to sort out our morals for our own selves."

"So you lived happily ever after," I said, like a sentimental sap.

"As much as two men can who're fond of getting their own way," Myrom chuckled. "We had some fine fights, some really great ones. So, you here to call on Barry?" he asked abruptly.

I had forgotten all about Barry in my interest in Myrom's story. "Um, no, not really."

He looked disappointed. "Looks a lot like his uncle, Barry does. He's a very sweet man, deserves to find someone who loves him like me and Dowling."

Suddenly I realized that Myrom had not only taken it for granted that I was gay, but that I knew about Barry.

"You know Barry's… queer?"

"Sure. We saw it in him when he was a little boy. Now, don't tell Marie, Dowling'd say to me, cautioning me like. Marie's his sister, and he feared she'd be mighty disappointed to find out, but he underestimated her. She up and told *him* one day that she thought Barry was following in his footsteps. He asked if she was upset and she just said, 'If he turns out to be as fine a man as you are, I'll be satisfied.'"

"She sounds wonderful," I said enviously. *My* sister certainly didn't feel that way about my way of life.

"She was," Myrom said reminiscently. "She went two years ago. Now Barry's alone with no one to look after, 'cepting me. And no one to look after him." Again, he peered at me, as if trying to read what was inside.

"You're a right handsome feller," Myrom commented. "Bet you get to pick and choose."

I preened a little. "Well, I guess so."

"But you ain't found someone to settle with, have you?" Myrom asked shrewdly. "Always looking at the packaging and not what's inside."

That stung me. "That's not true!"

"Well, you know your own business best, young feller. You're getting along in years, though."

That made me feel weather-beaten, as if I might not attract the hottest guy in a bar anymore. I was only thirty-two, for crap's sake! I didn't like that feeling, so I asked if he'd mind if I took a shot of Dowling's gravestone.

"Not at all, not at all," Myrom said. "I'd like him to be remembered. He was a great man." He hobbled down with me and watched as I took a light reading and got my shot. The shadows on the stone flickered green as the sunlight shone through the translucent canopy above.

• • •

"What did he look like?" I asked, my curiosity overcoming my hurt feelings.

"Like I say, he wasn't much to look at," Myrom said with a sweet smile. "In fact, Barry takes after him. Tall and lanky, he was, and his face kinda homely, but he had the bluest eyes. Like a summer sky, they were, all soft and smiling, with just a hint of thunder and lightning to come, if he didn't get his own way, like I said."

"Did you give it to him?" I asked curiously. I wondered if he had on more levels than just the most obvious.

"Oh, I liked having my own way too," Myrom chuckled.

In despair of my own barren life, I cried out, "How did you ever stay together?"

"Got to pick a steady man. Then you got to stick with it." Myrom squinted at me. "But maybe you're too pretty yourself to have much stayin' power. You seem like the kind to break a man's heart. Or a woman's, if you was inclined that way."

"I didn't cheat. My boyfriend did!" I protested.

"Maybe you didn't give him what he needed." Myrom shrugged.

"So that makes it okay for him to cheat?" I was outraged. I felt wronged, misjudged.

"Cheating's never okay. Makes no sense. You might as well just say you're leaving and do it," Myrom said. "But you chose a man who *would* cheat. Says something about you."

Needless to say, I wasn't any too happy with this careless delineation of my character. In fact, I kind of clammed up and didn't speak much to him for the rest of the day. Not that it seemed to bother him a lot.

I did follow him into the house, where he showed me pictures of Dowling. They were black and white and showed a man just like Myrom had described. For some reason though, I could see his eyes in color, as blue as blue could be, like the lazy summer sky overhead.

It was after five when I caught the sound of a truck bumping down the lane. Barry pulled up and said hey to me, but he got out to hug and kiss Myrom.

"How're you doing, you old sinner?" he asked.

* * *

Myrom laughed. "Never better. Took your friend down to see Dowling."

"You did?" Barry turned and looked at me with a newly speculative expression in his eyes. I might have said it was respect if I hadn't had such a rough day with Myrom.

He sat down to drink some of the wonderful lemonade. They didn't say much, just seemed to commune on some cellular level. I'd grown so used to thinking of Myrom as Barry's uncle, I'd forgotten that they weren't, in fact, related.

The sun sets late in Wyoming in the summer, so it was still light when Barry got up to go. He had a list in his pocket of things his uncle needed, and he promised to bring the supplies back out there the next day. I got the feeling that Barry made time to visit often, now that Myrom was alone.

We got in his truck with me wondering just why he'd sent me out there for the day. When we got back to the tarmac, I asked him to stop.

"I want to take a picture," I told him.

Obligingly, he stopped and even got out to watch me fiddle with my camera. I stood where I could see the majestic mountains, the grand, empty sweep of the plains and sky, and that road that didn't lead to nowhere after all.

I took that shot, and then I turned and saw Barry.

I swear, the gold of the sun slanting over the field just set him aglow. His hair was the color of wheat, and his skin was tanned. Even though he was skinny, I could see sinew in his hard forearms, bare under the rolled-up sleeves of his faded blue shirt. His jeans were worn, hanging low off his narrow hips. And his eyes matched the color of the sky, blue and full of light and soft, melting with some powerful emotion when he looked at me.

I took his picture too, because suddenly he looked beautiful to me.

And I understood why Myrom had taken me to see Dowling; he'd wanted to see if I had what it took to stay the distance. If I could understand.

Well, sir, after that day, I never did leave. The parts eventually came for the rental truck, and Barry drove with me to the nearest big town to turn it in. I sent for my stuff, and I've lived here ever since.

"SO WHAT brought me here? What kept me here? Love," I ended softly.

After a moment, the reporter asked, "That photo in the book of a man's hands—those are Barry's hands, aren't they?"

"Yes," I said. "He has beautiful hands, even now, in his sixties."

"What does he do?"

"He's a paleontologist. Studies fossils over in Big Tracks," I said proudly. "We live here because it's close to his work. I take the photographs of all the events hereabouts, weddings, graduations, family portraits. I also document his digs."

I'd walked the kid reporter down to the two gravestones standing side by side under the oak, the way the men they memorialized had stood side by side in life. The shadows were getting long on the ground. It was time to start back. We walked the two miles back to the truck in silence, because now I'm a man who's learned to like the quiet too. I started up the truck and made a U turn, heading back for town.

Eventually, the reporter shook his head. "What a waste. They could just go to Sears for family portraits, and you could be doing important work."

"It's not a waste; I *am* doing important work," I insisted. "It's beauty. It's everywhere."

"Is Barry worth giving up the excitement and fame and all you could have in the city?"

I thought he was just too young and shallow to see, but then I realized he was baiting me.

"He's worth it," I said softly. "Without him, I would never have known beauty."

I pulled up in front of the town's only bar. All of us who lived in South Gulch went there, gay or straight. In fact, it never even caused a ripple in our town when Barry and I danced together on Friday night. We were just the gay guys who lived in town.

We went inside, and I bought the kid reporter a drink. I couldn't tell if the whole story of Myrom and Dowling would make it into the piece he was doing on me. I sure hoped they would, just so they'd be remembered.

* * *

Barry came in then. His homely, lined face lit up when he saw me. The shock of white hair on top of his head was standing up in spikes, as usual, and his hands were dirty, also as usual, but his eyes were blue as the summer sky, like the day I first fell in love with him all those years ago.

He came over and gripped my arm.

"Have a good day, babe?" I asked with a smile.

"Yeah, digging in the dirt. What better job could a boy want?" he laughed. "Found some nice tracks today. We're hoping they'll lead to some interesting bones. Maybe you could come out tomorrow and take some pictures for us."

"Dr. Barry Lancaster?" the kid reporter asked in an impressed voice as he recognized Barry.

"Yes, and you are…?" Barry asked as he shook the kid reporter's hand.

"Kevin James, from the *Times*."

Typical. He didn't say *The New York Times*, making it sound as if there were only one *Times* in the entire nation. "I came out to interview your partner. I didn't realize that *you* were his…." He stopped, stuck for a word.

"His boyfriend? Yes, I am," Barry said with a proud smirk.

I put my arm around him. He looked so radiantly happy, I almost wished I had my camera so I could capture that moment forever, but I didn't really need a photo. I have taken a million pictures of Barry over the years, but I've never truly succeeded in capturing his beauty.

I guess there are some things only the heart can see.

• • •

CATT FORD lives in front of the computer monitor, in another world where her imaginary gay friends obey her every command.

She likes cats, chocolate, swing dancing, sleeping, Monty Python, Aussie friends, being silly, spinning other realities with words, and sea glass. She dislikes caterpillars, cigarette smoke, and rude people who think the F-word (as in faggot, or bundle of sticks) is acceptable.

A frustrated perfectionist, she comforts herself with the legend about the weavers of Persian rugs always including one mistake so as not to anger the gods, although she has no need to include a mistake on purpose. One always slips through. Writing fiction has filled a need for clever conversations, only possible when one is in control of both sides, and erotic romances, where everything for the most part turns out happily ever after.

Visit Catt's blog at http://catt-ford.livejournal.com/.

Snowman
Isabelle Rowan

The blackened log gave a loud crack as the flame finally bit it in two. A bright ember jumped from the fireplace and landed on the warm hearth next to the twitching paw of the sleeping dog. Although the dog barely stirred, the sound broke into the fresh dream of the man in the armchair. He glanced past the open book that had fallen against his chest and looked down to see the small orange glow fade to black as it cooled.

"Molly," he grunted, coughing to clear the sleep from his voice. "Get back here, you dumb dog, before you catch on fire."

The Border collie blinked at her name and looked up at her owner. With a snort, she stood up, shook herself and moved to settle by his feet. Caleb gave her a tired smile and dropped his hand down to scratch her ear. "Bad night out there, Molly," he muttered just as the wind rattled the glass in the windows. He knew he should take the walk up the stairs to his room, but he also knew he wasn't ready to crawl into the chilled sheets of the empty bed.

"Maybe we'll just stay by the fire a while? What do you think?" he asked, chuckling when the dog's tail thumped a few times against the floor.

Caleb closed his book and let his eyes drift shut. The gentle sputter of the fire blended with the swirl of the snowstorm as the warmth of the room lulled him back to sleep.

* * *

The sudden jangle of music didn't make sense; it jarred in Caleb's dream and didn't fit the quiet images of his mind's eye. As the music grew louder, the dreamscape vanished, and he opened his eyes to the tiny living room.

With disgusted groan, Caleb sat up and looked around for his cell phone. "Yeah, what?" he barked, his disgust obvious in his voice.

The line crackled ominously until he caught the voice of Bob, the local police officer. "Fierce storm tonight, Cal…. Didn't want to have to call you, but it looks like a tourist got caught on the road up your way."

"What the hell is someone doing out there tonight?" Caleb complained, wandering away from the warmth of the fire. He stared out through the night-darkened glass of the window and saw only a mixture of his distorted reflection and the flurry of snow. "It's coming down pretty heavy," he said, half to himself.

Then came Bob's reply: "The roads are blocked, Cal. We can't get to him."

Closing his eyes briefly, Caleb shook his head and looked down at Molly, who had faithfully followed him to the window. He met her questioning gaze with a resigned smile and asked, "Okay, Bob, where is he?"

The answer came through in disjointed syllables. Caleb scowled at the phone. "Say that again. I didn't catch it."

"He's on the road… above your place… not sure how far." There were other things said that got lost as the reception faltered, but Caleb got the gist of the message.

"What condition is he in?"

"Cold… told him to stay in the car and someone would find him."

Caleb gave a wry smile. "Someone, huh?"

Bob's laugh came down the phone clearly; he knew full well that Caleb was the only someone in that area of the high country. "I'll give you his number, but the reception is all to hell."

Caleb grabbed a pen and hastily scrawled the number along his arm. After a quick goodbye, he ran his fingers over the curve of Molly's head and said, "No more fire for us tonight."

Donning a rapidly-equipped backpack, Caleb pushed up his sleeve and keyed the numbers into his phone, hesitating when it asked for a name. He frowned, then finally entered the word "Snowman." *That'll do 'til I know who you are.*

CALEB took one step out of the door, and his breath was instantly snatched away by the icy night air. He hauled the collar of his jacket higher and jammed his hat down tight. "I wish I had your constitution, girl," he grumbled to the dog already heading to the steps at the end of the wide porch with an enthusiasm Caleb definitely did not share. With a weary sigh, he followed Molly down the long driveway.

The winter weather in the high country was erratic at best, but it had been a long time since Caleb had seen a cold snap come on as fast this. He stood at the bottom of his drive and contemplated the best way to tackle this; he could follow the road as it fishtailed its way up the mountain or head for one of the tracks. It was obvious a car had traveled past his place sometime earlier, but the tracks were already disappearing under the snow. Caleb sniffed and shook his head. "Okay, Snowman, I guess we better find out how far up you are."

The reception was, as Bob predicted, "all to hell," and Caleb had to duck down into the partial shelter of his collar to hear the voice at the other end.

"Bob said you're stuck," he called into the cell.

"Yeah, if Bob's the policeman." The voice was distant, but Caleb knew that was the storm rather than the person.

"Okay, any idea how far up the mountain you are?" Caleb asked and then realized that was a pretty stupid question for a tourist. "Forget that… are you still on the road?"

The answer came in disjointed pieces, but Caleb managed to make sense of it. The car had skidded on a sharp bend and was off the road in a ditch. There were a lot of bends up from his place, but not that many that had ditches, so that told Caleb the "Snowman" wasn't too far off and cross-country would be the fastest way to get to him.

• • •

"On my way," he said quickly and shoved the phone in his pocket. "Let's go find us a tourist," Caleb muttered and waved for Molly to follow him up the narrow track between the towering eucalypts.

FURTHER up the mountain road, Paul looked at the now silent phone. *Make it fast, okay?* He was bitterly cold and feeling more than a little foolish at needing to be rescued from his car. Pulling his thin jacket tighter around his slim frame, Paul slouched down in his seat, trying to find any warmth he could. None of this had been planned, and he certainly wasn't dressed for an interlude in a snowbound car. Next time he lost his temper, he wasn't going to throw a "typical Paul hissy fit," as his friends called it, and storm out.

CALEB'S feet skidded on the steep path, and he was force to grab at a tree trunk to keep his balance. The conditions were worse than he'd expected, and he took a moment to catch his breath. "Come 'ere, Molly," he called to the dog happily sniffing at the trail ahead. "Just need a minute, girl."

Caleb squatted in the shelter of a broad eucalypt and tried his phone again. The reception was better, and the voice of the other man came through clearly. "You're still on the way, I hope?"

"Yeah, I'm getting there," Caleb replied, surprisingly relieved to hear the question. "How're you doing, Snowman?"

Paul looked out through the spider web of the broken windscreen. *Snowman, huh?* "Not far from being a man of ice," he said and took a shivery breath. "Windscreen's cracked… drafty, but no snow coming in."

The line dropped out for a second, telling Caleb he needed to get moving again. Hauling himself back up, he groaned a little at his complaining knees and stepped back out into the wind. "You dry?" he asked, trying to assess the man's condition as he started up the slope.

"Ah, yeah… think so. Hard to tell. So fucking cold." The shivering had set in, and so had the fear. It was dark and cold in the damaged cabin of the car, and Paul was getting very scared that the mountain man wouldn't find him.

It was hard to miss the strain in the voice. There was a definite tremble that hadn't been there during the first call. Caleb knew he needed to hurry and keep the tourist talking.

"Okay, I'm gonna ask a bunch of questions," Caleb grunted as he clambered over a fallen branch one-handed, the other holding his phone firmly to his ear. "First up, how are your hands and feet?"

Paul peered through the gloom at his fingers and tried to flex them. "Um, fingers are still working, just a bit numb. My feet were sore, but they don't hurt anymore."

Fuck. Caleb cursed to himself, not liking the sound of that. "I'm nearly there, and I'll get you somewhere warm."

"Uh huh," Paul murmured softly, a sense of lethargy starting to creep in.

"You still with me, Snowman? I need you to stay on the line and answer my questions, remember?" Caleb said quickly in an attempt to keep the tourist talking and awake.

"Still here," Paul answered, and he gave himself a little shake.

"Good. So, where you from?"

"Melbourne… share a flat in Fitzroy." The answer was almost lost in a sudden swirl of static, but Caleb knew the content didn't really matter.

"Keep talking, Snowman," he said, stepping out onto the road just above the hairpin bend.

"Mmm, um, I wait on tables. Want to be a chef someday. Not yet, but someday…." The voice trailed off.

"Hey, Snowman?" Caleb asked but was met with silence. "Come on, man, don't you fucking conk out on me now. I'm almost to you."

It was Molly who first alerted Caleb to the location of the car. Standing in the middle of the road, she gave an excited yip and looked back at Caleb, who was struggling through a deepening snowdrift, urging him to hurry up.

The undergrowth on the verge of the road clearly indicated that something had gone over the edge at great speed, and only the tip of a rear light could be seen peeping above the lip of the ditch.

Grabbing at a nearby tree for support, Caleb eased himself over and skidded down to the driver's side door.

Much to Caleb's relief, a light mist of condensation fogged the inside of the glass. He tapped firmly on the window to alert the driver of his presence.

Paul fought the doze he'd begun to slip into and stared at the silhouette outside the car. It took him a moment to understand he needed to unlock the door for his rescuer and even longer to unwrap his arms and make his fingers work.

"Hey, Snowman, you gotta help me here," Caleb muttered as he waited for a response, peering through the glass to make sure the man inside was able to let him in. A small smile curled at the edges of his lips when fingers finally closed over the lock and pulled it up.

Pushing the door open seemed almost insurmountable; Paul's arms were like lead, but he could see the man outside trying to scrape away the debris of snow and undergrowth.

Finally, the door opened.

Caleb crouched, his knees resting on the doorframe, and held his hand to Paul's face. *Cold.* He quickly assessed Paul's clothes and knew they couldn't stay here until the snowfall eased again.

"You gonna tell me your name?" he asked in a quiet but insistent voice, all the while running his fingers gently over the frigid skin.

Fighting the chatter of his teeth, Paul managed to say, "Snowman."

The single word made Caleb laugh. "Cheeky bastard. I'm Caleb, that's Molly, and between us, we're gonna get you out of here. Okay?"

Paul attempted a smile and reached out to the man. His arms did their best to pull him closer to Caleb, desperate to feel the contact of another human being.

With a confused frown at the unexpected hug, Caleb held Paul against him and murmured, "It's okay, Snowman. We'll get you back home. We'll get you warm. Legs first." Caleb gently eased Paul around and out of the car. "We're gonna do this slowly because there might not be a lot of feeling in those skinny legs of yours." He grinned at the young man watching him so seriously, hoping to reassure him, and was pleased to see the hint of a smile returned.

* * *

"Skinny legs," Paul muttered, now determined to show Caleb he could get out of the car, but it was harder than he'd anticipated, and his unresponsive body seemed to ignore his instructions.

Caleb laid a gentle hand on Paul's thigh. "Take it slow, and I'll help." He straightened up with a little effort himself and bent over to put an arm around Paul's back. "Lean on me and let me take your weight."

With an earnest nod, Paul leaned into Caleb, and between them, he managed to get out of the car and upright.

Paul swayed a little at the instant onslaught of wind and snow, but Caleb held him firm. He looked Paul over: jeans, dress shirt and jacket, none of it suitable for the walk back. Caleb quickly took off his hat and placed it on the fashionably-styled black hair, then pulled a waterproof jacket from his pack. Paul's arms were carefully guided through the Gore-Tex sleeves and the front was zipped to his chin. "Time to get moving," Caleb said, whistling to Molly to lead the way.

Getting Paul up the embankment took a little time and a few false starts, but they eventually made it out of the ditch.

Paul stared down what he could see of the road. It took all his energy to get out of the car, and the thought of a long walk in the snow made him want to flop down on the bank of snow and simply give himself up to the elements. His small sound of defeat was nearly lost to the wind, but Caleb caught it and said, "It's all downhill from here, Snowman."

With his arm tight around Paul's waist, Caleb started them on their journey down the winding road.

Paul leaned heavily as he tried to get his legs moving, and Caleb knew not to rush him, even though every minute in the freezing conditions increased the danger for the young man. As a result, their progress down the slope was frustratingly slow, and Caleb listened as Paul's wheezing breaths became more torturous with each bend of the road. He tried to take more of Paul's weight onto himself, even though the effort had him sweating—sweat that rapidly turned icy in the night air.

"How you doing?" Caleb puffed as he hefted Paul's body a little tighter against him. There was no verbal reply, and Paul only managed to nod, his focus solely on keeping one foot moving in front of the other.

"Almost there," Caleb said softly, watching Molly's white tipped tail as she trotted in front of them with just the occasional glance back.

The glow of the porch light at the end of the driveway had never looked so welcoming, and even Molly broke into a run. "Home sweet home, Snowman," Caleb said, wishing his driveway were a little shorter and his legs were a lot younger.

The final stretch stripped both men of the last of their resolve, and they stood exhausted at the door. It was Molly who finally snapped Caleb back into action when she barked and scratched impatiently at the door, wondering why her human was taking so long to let her get back to her spot on the hearth.

"Sorry, girl," Caleb said breathlessly, pushing the door open. The fire had died down, but its warm glow still filled the room, and the sudden heat stung Caleb's chilled skin. He carefully walked Paul into the room and set him down in his armchair before going back to shut the front door and block out the night.

Molly had already taken up residence near the fire and was content licking at the snow between her pads. "I'll get to you in a minute, Molly; guests first," Caleb said wearily before crouching on the floor at Paul's feet.

Paul watched through the haze of exhaustion as Caleb gently removed his sodden shoes and socks. He wanted to say thank you, but he simply didn't have the energy to make his mouth form the words. Instead, he looked at the strong fingers that covered his cold feet and somehow felt safe in this man's hands.

"They're gonna hurt when they start to warm up," Caleb muttered as he enclosed Paul's toes between his palms.

It took a moment for the sentence to register, and Paul looked away from the surprisingly gentle touch and nodded.

Caleb waited for some of the focus to return to the brown eyes before he continued. "Need to get those party clothes off you now, Snowman."

Paul slowly reached up and removed the hat.

"Not quite what I had in mind, but it's a start." Caleb chuckled and then groaned at his aching knees and back when he managed to stand on his second attempt, leaning heavily on the arm of the chair. He took the hat and threw it on the nearby bureau. The jacket had kept out the wet but not all of the cold. Caleb worked quickly, with some fumbling help from Paul, to remove the remainder of his clothes, then wrapped the young man in a big tartan blanket.

Paul's shivering had returned now the effort of the walk was over, but he was gradually becoming more aware of his surroundings and the man helping him. "Your eyes are very blue," he managed to say through chattering teeth. The random comment threw Caleb for a moment, and he stood, hands still on the blanket, and stared. *It means nothing... he's disoriented, nothing more.* Caleb shook his head, unwilling to admit the words had touched a nerve, and said quietly, "I guess you're not quite with me yet, Snowman."

"Paul." There was a stutter over the P, but the word was clear.

"Paul," Caleb repeated. A smile briefly touched his lips before he cleared his throat. He wasn't used to this anymore, and the young man in his home made him uncomfortable. "Okay, Paul, I'll be back in a minute."

Standing in his kitchen, Caleb chastised himself for his reaction and set about heating water while he hunted out a hot water bottle. When it was ready, he wrapped the hot water bottle in a towel and parted Paul's blanket. "Hold this against your chest. It'll warm you up. I'm boiling more water to make you a cup of tea, okay?" Although it was a question, Caleb didn't wait for an answer and retreated to the kitchen.

The warmth rapidly seeped through the towel and spread across Paul's chest. He clutched it a little tighter, and slowly but surely, the shivering began to subside.

It was several minutes before a mug was put between Paul's hands and he was encouraged to sip the hot tea. He smiled and watched as the cushions from the sofa were thrown on the floor and arranged into a makeshift bed. By the time Caleb was done, the bed looked both comfortable and warm.

He crouched in front of Paul and pushed back the long fringe. "You look like you're with me now," he smiled.

"You're gonna stay, aren't you?" Paul asked, as if fearful of being alone.

"Ah, yeah. You, me and Molly," Caleb said and took the mug. He helped Paul off the chair and down under the quilt, but hesitated to follow him into the "bed". "Just got to see to the dog's paws first," Caleb muttered, kneeling by Molly to carefully wipe between each of her toes and pads. When he was done, he turned to see Paul's tired eyes watching him. Caleb gave an almost sheepish smile before moving to the far side of the bed and removing his clothes.

Settling in behind Paul, he said quietly, "Keep the hot water bottle on your chest and you'll soon be warm."

Paul felt Caleb's skin on his and relaxed back against him.

"You'll be okay by morning, Snowman," Caleb whispered close to Paul's ear, wrapping his arm around the young man's waist. It had been a long time since he'd had someone to hold.

PAUL recognized the ache behind his eyes long before conscious thought broke into sleep. It was that dull pain that always seemed to be there as retribution for a heavy night before. He lay still and assessed exactly what state his body was in, but as Paul rotated through his very familiar checklist, he frowned. There were some of the usual memories of drinking and dancing, but other elements of the previous night began to filter through the fog. The most insistent was skin against his and a soft voice at his ear. *Caleb.*

When Paul finally cracked open his eyes, he grimaced as the strange cabin swam painfully into focus. There was no sign of the man who'd rescued him, but he could hear the faint clink of metal against crockery and a distinct smell of coffee. Turning over onto his back, Paul stared up at the bare wooden beams of the ceiling. This was *not* how he'd expected to spend his weekend. Drinking, fucking, and actively avoiding all the outdoor recreation listed in the resort brochure had been on the agenda, not lying naked in a strange man's cabin. The fact it was a *strange man* wasn't the issue, or even unusual. Paul generally spent his nights with the latest beautiful body or in search of one, but this was a little extreme, even for him.

Paul sighed at the interesting turn of events. *Well, if he were a weird-arse serial killer, I guess he would have eaten me by now.*

"How're you feeling this morning?" The voice came from a nearby doorway.

"Ask me again when I'm upright," Paul grumbled before twisting around to see Caleb place a mug of what he assumed was coffee on the hearth next to him.

* * *

Caleb gave him a small yet serious smile. "Take it slow. You were close to hypothermic last night, and things are gonna hurt today." He seemed to hesitate when their eyes met and quickly turned away to wave his hand vaguely towards the narrow hall leading off the living room. "There are towels if you want to wash up, and help yourself to the clothes on the hamper." With that, Caleb turned and walked back out the door.

"Okay," Paul muttered to the empty room, a little surprised by the abrupt exit. He pulled himself up into a sitting position and instantly regretted not taking Caleb's advice to take it slowly. "Fuck," he grunted, wrapping his arms around his knees. "The mountain man wasn't kidding."

THE snow lay thick on the ground, but the wind had dropped, so the white covering sparkled under the reflected blue of the clear sky. Caleb blew on his mug and felt the steam rise warm over his face. Even though he knew the coffee would still be too hot to drink, he could never resist that first, sharp sip. Risking his lips, he drew in the liquid and grimaced at the inevitable burn. Closing his eyes, Caleb savored that instant surge of caffeine over his tongue. *Some pleasures are easily found.*

No matter what was planned for the day, Caleb always started it on his porch. He rarely made the sunrise anymore, but it was his way of taking the time to know that the world was still out there and maybe he was still a small part of it.

"You have really big feet," Paul said as he clomped onto the wooden decking of the porch clutching his mug of coffee.

Caleb simply looked at his work boots on Paul's feet and shrugged.

"So, I, ah, I didn't say thanks for last night," Paul said as he sat down in the spare seat. He closed both hands around the hot mug, enjoying the heat that spread through his fingers. "I was getting pretty freaked when the cop said they couldn't get up the mountain. Don't they have rescue units or something?"

After dismissing the thanks with another small shrug, Caleb answered the question. "Yeah, they have a chopper, but it can't fly on nights like that, and when I spoke to Bob this morning, he said there were skiers lost near the resort, so the team needed to get to them. He knew I'd find you."

Paul smiled, then jumped on the fact Caleb had spoken to the police. "Did Bob say if he'd told my mates I was okay?"

Caleb nodded and took a tentative mouthful of coffee.

"Awesome. So when do I get out of here?" Paul was already on his feet, signaling he was ready to leave then and there.

"Not for a day or two, I'd say," Caleb said over the edge of the mug, looking out across the snow-covered slope. "They need to clear the road."

Paul was very close to complaining before he stopped himself. Instead, he took a calming breath and asked, "Where's my phone? I better let my friends know." Once he got his answer, Paul rapidly retreated back into the house, and Caleb soon heard one side of a very animated conversation.

"I don't think we're entertaining enough," Caleb chuckled quietly to the dog at his feet, who replied with a yawn. "Thanks, Molly, I guess I bore you too."

PAUL spent most of the morning chatting on his phone or answering text messages while Caleb tried to go about his daily chores. *Tried* because he actually found it disconcerting having the young man in his home, and every time their eyes met, he'd give an almost embarrassed smile and quickly move on. Paul, on the other hand, made it very clear that the whole enforced stay was an inconvenience and a bore. He lounged on the sofa with his leg dangling over the side, talking endlessly to one friend after another.

By mid-morning Caleb had had enough and threw a spare coat at Paul with a gruff, "Come on."

It was obvious this wasn't a request, and with a roll of his eyes, Paul shoved the phone in his pocket and followed Caleb outside. "Are the roads clear?" he asked hopefully, jogging a little to catch up to Caleb's long strides.

Caleb stopped and looked at him. Paul's black hair hung in waves around the fair skin of his face now that all the product had been washed out. Add to that the darkest brown eyes Caleb had seen on a human, and he had to admit Paul was stunning, but his attitude… well, that was another issue. He sighed and said, "No, the roads aren't clear. You're stuck here, so I thought we may as well make the best of it. You can help me out with the horses."

Paul screwed up his face, but Caleb was already walking toward the stable.

There were only a few horses in the many stalls of the stable, but each gave Caleb a small whinny or snort as he entered. Paul kept himself near the doorway, unsure of the big creatures, and watched as Caleb changed the horses' rugs and let them out to trot down the walkway to their paddock.

It was all very alien to Paul, but as he watched Caleb handle each horse in turn, he slowly moved towards the stalls.

"Over here," Caleb smiled easily, recognizing Paul's fear. "I've got someone I want you to meet." He led Paul to the closest stall, where a big chocolate bay watched their progress.

"There's no way I'm going in there with that," Paul said quickly, taking in the size of the creature that seemed to be snorting steam at him.

"*Her* name is Ruth. It's short for an impressive pedigree name, but to me, she's just Ruth." Caleb stepped into the stall and rubbed his palm softly over her muzzle. Ruth nibbled gently, then lifted her head so her long whiskers tickled Caleb's lips. He laughed, and the white mist of his warm breath mingled with Ruth's in the cold air. His fingers teased the big horse's chin, scratching back until his hand came to rest on the solid muscled neck. Caleb leaned heavily against her, feeling heat and strength beneath his cheek. A sound of contentment escaped both man and horse.

Caleb looked back at Paul and beckoned him over. "Come here and meet her. She's very gentle."

Paul stepped inside the stall but made sure he kept well away from the bits that could either bite or kick. He watched as Caleb's fingers expertly worked the buckle at the front of the rug, then walked slowly to her rump, sliding his hand along her body. Each of the leg straps was unclipped, and Caleb gently pulled the rug off, exposing the very round barrel of Ruth's belly.

Caleb turned with a broad smile and held a hand out to Paul, who, surprisingly, took it without hesitation and moved next to the horse. He had no doubt he was safe with Caleb next to him.

Keeping his hand on Paul's, Caleb stroked their fingers over the soft hair of Ruth's belly, then followed the swirl of her flank.

"She's so soft," Paul whispered.

● ● ●

203

"Uh huh," Caleb confirmed, and moved Paul a little closer to the mare. "Now, do you trust me?"

Paul gave him a sideways glance and said cautiously, "I guess I have to."

Caleb chuckled and let go of Paul's hand. "Lean forward and cup your arms under her belly. It's okay; she won't do anything."

After taking a breath, Paul leaned on the mare and slowly slid his arms down. "Now what?" he said a little nervously.

"Just be quiet for a change," Caleb said with an almost cheeky grin. Paul was about to argue, but thought it easier just to do as he was told. Ruth gave a big sigh, and Paul smiled as he moved with her; she was warm and smelled surprisingly good. Caleb watched him relax into the rhythm of her breathing… *any minute now.* He didn't have long to wait before Paul jumped away from the horse and looked at him, eyes wide with surprise. "Something fucking moved… I felt something move!"

He knew it was cruel, but Caleb couldn't resist laughing and gave the mare a pat. "Your baby scared the tourist, Ruthy."

"You could have warned me," Paul scowled, then turned to run his hand over the area where he'd felt the little wriggle. There was a slight flutter under his palm. This time, Paul giggled and rested his head over the slight bulge in Ruth's belly and whispered, "Ignore the annoying mountain man. You didn't scare me; you just surprised me, is all." He hummed against the round belly, then added, "You stay where you are for a while longer, little girl, because it's too cold for you out here."

Caleb frowned. "A girl, huh?"

"Yep, she told me." Paul grinned and gave Ruth a pat.

With a roll of his eyes, Caleb moved in and put on Ruth's weatherproof rug before opening the stall to let her wander out after the others. "And now we clean," he said wickedly, tilting his head towards the soiled straw.

"No fucking way," Paul cursed. "I am not touching that."

"Fair enough." Caleb shrugged and threw a pair of thick gloves to him. "That way you don't have to touch it." Paul looked at the gloves and quickly realized there was no chance to argue, because Caleb was already pushing a wheelbarrow to the stall next door.

* * *

By the time Ruth's stall was cleared, Caleb had finished all the others and was scattering fresh straw. Paul wandered over, feeling more than a little pleased with himself, and pointed to the spotless stall.

"Good job." Caleb smiled and handed him a few biscuits of straw. "Lay some straw and then come in for lunch." This time, there were no complaints; Paul took the straw and happily separated the biscuits onto the floor of the stall.

It was still bitterly cold, but walking back to the house, Paul decided it was a good kind of cold. He blew on his hands and rubbed them together, ignoring the fact that his black nail polish was now chipped and peeling. The winter sun felt good on his face as he approached the porch, and for the first time, he noticed his headache had vanished.

"You're starting to look like you belong," Caleb commented, looking down the steps at the disheveled man heading his way.

"Shit, does that mean I'm starting to look like you?" Paul grinned and reached out to run his finger down the stubble of Caleb's chin.

The touch was unexpected, but it surprised Caleb that it wasn't unwelcome. He felt an instant flush color his face and looked down at his mug, then muttered, "There's soup on the table and a cheese and vegemite sandwich. Nothing fancy."

"Smells good," Paul said, grabbing his lunch from the kitchen. Sitting next to Caleb, Paul dipped the corner of his sandwich into the thick tomato soup. "Been a while since I had something like this."

He took a bite, and the salty taste of the vegemite seemed to burst on his tongue. "Fuck, that *is* good," he mumbled while chewing on the white bread. "Reminds me of going to the footy with my dad."

Caleb shook his head with a wry smile. "Somehow I can't imagine you at a football match."

"Fuck off!" Paul laughed and gave him a light shove. "Are you trying to say that a gay man couldn't be into football?"

The question confused Caleb until it dawned on him that there was no reason for Paul to realize *he* was gay. "I'd never say that," he murmured quietly and took a sip of his soup.

Paul didn't notice the instant change in Caleb's demeanor and carried on. "Good, because I was a huge footy fan as a kid. I had St. Kilda posters all over my wall, a Saints quilt—I even had PJs in footy colors. It was pretty cool. You know, I'd still wear them if they fit."

Caleb was only half listening as Paul rambled about classic matches and cute players, because his mind was elsewhere. Mike had been a footy fan, and he remembered enduring what seemed to be endless hours in the rain and cold wrapped in red and black scarves, watching a game he didn't understand. The memory made him smile; he didn't like the game, but he had loved the man who did.

Paul noticed the small smile on Caleb's lips and misunderstood its meaning. "So you're a fan, huh? Do you get to many matches?"

"I used to," Caleb said sadly. "My… I used to know someone who was a paid-up member, and I went with him."

Paul was about to launch into a round of questions when his cell phone rang loudly in his pocket. Raising his eyebrows at Caleb, he lifted the phone to his ear. "Hey, Stewie, man… yeah, still stuck on the mountain." With a fleeting smile, Paul grabbed his mug and walked into the house to continue his conversation.

The porch became very quiet. Caleb could hear distant chattering from the house, but where he sat alone, the only sound was Molly barking at a magpie teasing her from a low branch. "Come here, you dumb dog," he grumbled, but he didn't follow it up when she carried on bouncing around the tree trunk as if it would entice the bird down.

Caleb looked out at the property he'd bought with his lover and whispered, "It's quiet without you around, Mike. No one to give me a hard time when I don't talk enough. No one to drag me down to the city and those bloody football matches."

BY THE time Paul's phone gave the low chime that the battery was dying, Caleb had already washed up and headed back outside. From the kitchen window, Paul could see Caleb clearing snow off the driveway and briefly debated going out to help. But the thought of going back into the cold was much less appealing than seeing what he could find out about his host.

The living room didn't offer up many clues other than Caleb liked to read the newspaper and, judging by the dust on the remote, didn't seem to use the TV much. The mantle over the fire had a couple of porcelain animals, and behind the dog was an invoice for the local feed store. "Boring," Paul muttered, running his fingers over the curve of the big mantle clock. "There's gotta be more than this."

He glanced around the room before heading for the stairs. "Where's your room, mountain man?" Paul knew perfectly well that he shouldn't be doing this, but the quiet man had his interest piqued.

Caleb's room was nothing like downstairs. It was stuffed with knickknacks, books, and photos. *So many photos.* Paul scanned along a wall literally covered with frames of various sizes, some containing pictures of people Paul assumed were Caleb's family, but the majority of them were of Caleb with another man. The photos seemed to span a broad timeframe, and it was obvious from their body language that the men were more than friends. "So," Paul queried, bending to peer at one that had been taken in the city, "who are you?"

"That's none of your fucking business."

It was said in a quiet voice, but Paul couldn't mistake the anger and hurt in the words. He quickly straightened up. "I'm sorry; I didn't mean anything…. I just wanted—"

"Just go, please," Caleb cut him off.

Paul nodded and left the room. There was nothing he could say to excuse his prying, and he knew it. Consequences were never something Paul really considered; life was for living and tomorrow be damned, but the look on Caleb's face made him hesitate. He was about to apologize again when the door closed quietly, shutting him out.

AS THE day became evening, the sick feeling in Paul's stomach grew. Caleb had spent a lot of the afternoon in his room and only came out when it was time to bring in the horses. Paul wandered through to the kitchen to watch. Caleb was different from everyone Paul knew in the city. He had a quietness to him that was unfamiliar. The pauses in conversation gave Paul the space to think, and he realized that scared him.

* * *

Caleb stroked his hand along Ruth's neck and said something to her that Paul couldn't hear, but the mare responded by knocking his shoulder with her head, making Caleb laugh. Paul smiled when he saw Caleb's face creased with laugh lines and whispered, "I shouldn't have done that, and I really am sorry."

THERE was a light flurry of snow starting by the time Caleb had finished all his chores and headed inside. He kicked his boots off at the door and walked into the warm kitchen to be surrounded by cooking smells.

Paul smiled a little sheepishly from the stove and said, "I'm not used to cooking on a wood stove, but hopefully it'll be okay." When Caleb didn't reply, Paul added, "I didn't know what else to do. There's not much else I'm good at, and I wanted to say sorry somehow."

Caleb looked at him for a moment before nodding. "Smells good."

They were simple words, yet they warmed Paul more than anything had in a long time. "Grab a seat; it's nearly ready."

With another nod, Caleb sat at the table and watched the young man fuss over pots and collect plates.

Dinner started slowly, with a few comments and many silences. It took Paul a while to stop feeling that he needed to fill each silence and simply sit with the other man. However, by the time they were wiping the last of the gravy from their plates, real conversation had started and continued through several games of cards, complete with jokes and accusations of cheating.

IT WAS late by the time Paul pulled his cover up on the makeshift bed in front of the fireplace. He lay and watched the low flames lick around the last of the logs. It had been a strange day, but a good one.

Paul could hear Caleb moving around upstairs and thought back to what he could remember of the previous night. Other than exhaustion, there was one abiding memory: Caleb's hands. Paul closed his eyes and felt them, callused yet gentle on his skin. The strong arms had cradled him while he was warmed by Caleb's embrace. Caleb had held Paul all night with no expectations of anything in return.

* * *

Molly cocked her head and looked up. She glanced at Paul, then got up from her spot on the hearth and trotted up the stairs to join her master. Caleb smiled when she jumped on the bed and settled by his side. She tried it every night, and he usually shooed her off, but tonight he let her stay. With a little scratch at her ear, he said, "I think he's a good guy, Molly. He just hasn't quite figured it out yet."

A COLD nose in the face woke Paul abruptly, and he sat up to pat Molly. Caleb was already dressed and putting a flask into his backpack. He smiled at Paul, who wandered in looking anything but awake. "Get your boots on. We're going for a walk."

Paul eyed the pack suspiciously and asked, "A walk or a hike?"

"Same thing," Caleb shrugged.

"Fuck." Paul groaned, but he walked back to the living room to grab his jacket.

The track was an easy one even with the covering of snow, but Paul huffed and puffed his way up until the trees started to clear to a gentle slope. Caleb led them to an outcrop of rocks and announced, "Coffee time."

Paul heard what he said but had walked closer to the edge of the decline and stared at the view. He could see for miles in the clear mountain air. Caleb smiled, poured coffee into two plastic mugs, and joined him. "Beautiful, isn't it?"

"Yeah," Paul said quietly, taking a mug. "I think I'm starting to see why you like it here."

"One of the reasons," Caleb confirmed.

Paul turned to look at Caleb. "You said you used to go watch football with someone. Was that the man in the photos?" Although it was a direct question, Paul's tone was cautious; he wanted to know the answer, but for once, his needs were willing to take a back seat to Caleb's feelings. "You can tell me to shut up if you want."

Caleb shook his head and smiled. "His name was Mike. We were together for a lot of years before he died."

There was so much more to the story that Paul wanted to hear. Questions itched at the tip of his tongue, but he kept his mouth shut and

* * *

reached over to close his hand over Caleb's instead. They stood quietly, looking out over the white landscape, until Caleb admitted, "I still miss him; every day, I miss him."

Paul didn't know the right thing to say, so he simply twined his fingers through Caleb's and leaned against him.

"You know, I don't think I've ever said that out loud." Caleb turned and gave Paul a small smile. "Thank you."

Paul returned the smile and made his own admission. "I've never been with someone long enough to have them miss me, but I'm starting to believe that the time isn't the important part. For some fucked up reason, I'm going to miss you when I'm back down there."

Caleb laughed and gave Paul's hand a squeeze. "Maybe we both lock ourselves away from the world?"

A few days ago, Paul wouldn't have seen the logic in that question. He put himself out there all the time, always a party or club to go to, always someone willing to fuck him until he was too exhausted to even ask their name. This man was different, and there was none of the bullshit Paul had assumed was a normal part of life.

"Yeah," he said slowly, scuffing his boots in a groove he'd made in the snow. "You on your mountaintop and me... well, me in everyone's bed but my own."

Caleb carefully let go of Paul's hand and put his arm around him instead. "You sell yourself short, Paul," he said softly, keeping the young man tightly against him. "You need to give yourself time to think. Stop worrying about everyone else and think about *you*, okay?"

"Isn't that what got me into all this?" Paul muttered, none too convinced. "Being a selfish prick?"

"That's not who you are," Caleb said with a gentle smile. He leaned in to rest his cheek on Paul's head. "Well, maybe on that first night?" He chuckled so Paul knew he was joking. "I have a feeling you're running as scared as I am. Scared of being alone. Scared of not having someone to love and who loves you back. We just do it in different ways."

Paul could feel the tears prickle at the back of his eyes and took a long breath. "So what do we do about it?"

Now there's a question. "I'm not sure," Caleb replied. "Maybe we're already doing it?"

"Maybe we are." Paul nodded, quite content to stand in the cold with Caleb.

THE hike back to the cabin seemed easier, and not just because it was downhill. Both men chatted, joked, and threw sticks for Molly to retrieve, comfortable in one another's company.

When they made it to the porch, Caleb heard the sound of his telephone and left Paul kicking off his boots to answer it. It was a voice he didn't know, and it instantly asked for Paul. Caleb felt his stomach lurch as he called to Paul and handed him receiver. The outside world was there reminding him that the young man wasn't with him through choice, but necessity, and he'd be gone as soon as the roads were clear.

Caleb didn't look up from the mugs on the kitchen bench when he heard Paul come in and sit at the table. The water was poured and he was stirring in his sugar when Paul finally spoke. "That was my friend Stewart. He said they've dragged the rental out of the ditch and the roads are okay to drive on again."

Caleb nodded and set a mug in front of Paul. "I'll just have a drink, and I can take you to your friends."

"I… um, I told them I wanted to stay tonight." Paul looked up at Caleb. "I want to stay here with you for a bit longer. Is that okay?"

"It's okay," Caleb said quietly, running his fingers through Paul's hair. Paul didn't answer but slid his arms around Caleb's waist and rested his head against his stomach.

I'm going to miss you too, aren't I? Caleb closed his eyes and held the man who was no longer a tourist. *But maybe that's okay now.*

THEY spent the afternoon together, both ignoring that they'd make the drive down the mountain the next day.

IT WAS late in the evening when Caleb finally acknowledged the inevitable and laid out Paul's clothes. "You'll need these tomorrow."

They were just his usual clubbing gear, but Paul felt empty at the thought of putting them on. He walked over and fingered the fine fabric of the shirt, so unlike the flannel he currently wore, and said quietly, "I don't know what I'm going back to."

"Friends and family," Caleb stated blankly, then sighed and reached out to grab Paul's sleeve and pull him closer. "What do you want there?"

"Not what it was," Paul mumbled. "I thought my life was full of... of everything I could want. It wasn't." He looked around the room and then into Caleb' eyes. "I think this is what I want."

Caleb drew him into his arms but shook his head. "This isn't it, either, Paul, and I'm not saying I don't want you around." *Not saying that at all.* "But I think you need to be on your own for a while to sort things out."

"Did it work for you?" Paul said in a slightly frustrated voice.

"I was alone for different reasons. That was *my* way of grieving and then hiding." Caleb pressed his forehead to Paul's. "*You* worked for me, though. Got me to realize I *can* have someone around again, even if that someone is a total pain in the arse."

Paul laughed and eased back. "That's me."

"So how about we call it a night, and I'll see you in the morning?" Caleb suggested, giving Paul's cheek a fleeting touch before taking a step away.

Before he could move towards the door, Paul caught his hand. "Any chance you can stay here with me tonight?"

"Is that a good idea?" Caleb felt the need to ask, despite what he actually wanted.

Paul grinned. "Hey, mountain man, I didn't say I was gonna let you fuck me."

IT WAS so like the first night, but through comfort rather than necessity. They lay together, skin against skin, under the quilt.

"I don't think I want to go home tomorrow," Paul whispered, pulling Caleb's arm around him. He knew he had to go, but the thought of falling back into his old lifestyle scared him.

"You need to go back," Caleb murmured into the silky black hair. "You need to go and show everyone you're worth more than one night."

Paul twisted to see the man behind him. "Do you think I'm worth more than one night?"

"I think you are, but *you* need to," Caleb said with an almost sad smile. "And that means you need some time on your own."

"Can I come up and see you?" Paul asked, turning right around to face Caleb.

"When the roads are clear, you can come and see me."

"They're clear now," Paul said hopefully.

Caleb shook his head. "Not *all* the roads," he said, lifting his hand to give Paul's head a light tap.

Paul nodded, knowing that even though he didn't like what Caleb said, it was true. "Yeah, I guess not."

This time, Caleb's smile was real, and he cupped Paul's cheek to pull him into a gentle kiss. Their lips barely met, but the touch meant more to Paul than any night he'd spent in a stranger's bed. He looked at Caleb and grinned. "So, I think I'm worth a kiss and *maybe* a little more?"

Caleb laughed and leaned forward to initiate another kiss, tentative at first, but they took their time to let the kiss develop, each feeling and tasting, neither rushing.

Paul gave a soft moan, and his fingers found Caleb's hair. He needed to hold him close, almost fearful that he would stop. This wasn't how others had kissed him, like he was a hot body and kissing was a means to an end. Caleb was different. *Never been with anyone who I would miss in the morning*, Paul thought, and he opened his eyes a fraction to catch a glimpse of Caleb totally lost in the kiss. Paul's heart skipped a beat, and he knew he needed more.

This time, when the kiss ended, Paul watched the face illuminated by the glow of the fire while he slowly slid his hand down Caleb's body. It was an older body, one he didn't know, so he let his fingers explore throat, chest, belly and hair until they slipped tentatively between Caleb's thighs.

❋ ❋ ❋

Caleb barely breathed at the touch; it had been so long since any hand other than his own had been on his skin. He kept his eyes on Paul's until the slender fingers cupped his cock. "I… I don't know if I can do this," he whispered, starting to push Paul's hand away.

"Why not?" Paul asked gently.

Caleb shook his head. "I don't know."

Paul thought of the framed photos on wall of Caleb's room. "He won't mind."

He won't mind. Caleb knew he was right; he knew Mike would never want him to shut himself off from the possibility of love like he'd done. "I'm still running, aren't I?" he asked quietly.

"Time to stop and see what happens," Paul murmured, running his fingers along the length of Caleb's cock, pleased to feel it harden under his touch. "Still not gonna let you fuck me, though," he added with a giggle.

Caleb laughed. He finally felt like he'd been released, and he pulled Paul over him, trapping his hand between them. "Don't have to, to make it good," he grinned, rolling his hips against Paul's fingers.

"Nice," Paul chuckled. "But I've got a better idea." He eased his hand out and settled comfortably, cradled between Caleb's thighs. "Used to do this when I was still a sweet virgin." Paul grinned and rocked so their cocks slid along each other.

"Oh, god, yeah." Caleb laughed a little breathlessly, responding to the delicious friction. "I remember rubbing jeans to jeans and making a hell of a mess."

"Naked now though," Paul reminded Caleb, drawing him into a kiss.

When they came, it wasn't earth-shattering, but it was together, wrapped in one another's arms.

THE drive down the mountain to the town below was spent in near silence. The thought of separation hurt them both, and it was easier to leave it unsaid. As they turned the final corner and the police station came into view, Caleb could see a group of young men hanging around the main door, stamping their feet and blowing into their cupped hands.

When Caleb's truck pulled into the parking space, they looked up and shouted something neither man could make sense of, but within seconds, they were at the passenger door and pulling Paul out. "Fuck, man," one said as he clapped him on the back. "We thought you'd gone native on us." Even before Paul had a chance to reply, they'd begun dragging him towards the door of the police station.

Paul turned back to the car. *Not yet.... This can't be the end. I'm not ready.* He peered into the cabin of the car and saw Caleb lift his hand in a small, single wave. Then Paul was pulled through the glass doors.

Caleb sat and stared at the doors until the shudder of the glass stilled. "I guess that's it, Molly. Just you and me again." He gave the dog's ear a scruff and put the car into reverse.

THE little filly snatched the tuft of grass from Caleb's hands and spun around to bolt back to her mother, where she proceeded to attempt a series of awkward buckjumps.

"Really proud of yourself, aren't you?" Caleb laughed, enjoying the warm breeze and smell of spring grass.

Ruth's foal had been a girl, just as Paul had predicted, a pretty little chestnut who made her entrance in the middle of the night during the last snow of the winter. As Caleb had rubbed her down, he'd admonished her impatience to be born. "Paul told you to wait where it was warm. You should have listened to him."

Caleb had thought about Paul a lot during the first few months of spring. He missed him and found he didn't actually like being alone any more, but Paul needed to live his own life, even if that life didn't have room for Caleb. They'd had only three days together, but Caleb knew Paul had been right when he'd said that the length of time with someone didn't matter. He sighed and watched the filly trot around her mother. *Maybe the tourist finally figured it out.*

A little chime sounded in Caleb's pocket. He pulled out his cell phone and stared at it. "I have one message, and how the fuck do I find it?" Pressing buttons, Caleb finally located both the menu and the inbox. He shook his head and grinned at the message.

All the roads are clear now.

Snowman. xxx

A black cat for a witch may be a cliché, but add a whole bunch of tribal tattoos and an intolerance to garlic (seriously), and you have ISABELLE ROWAN.

Having moved to Australia from England as a small child, Isabelle now lives in a seaside suburb of Melbourne where she teaches film making and English. She is a movie addict who spends far too much money on traveling… but then again, life is to be lived.

Visit Isabelle's blog at http://isabelle-rowan.livejournal.com/.

Gambling Men: Call
Amy Lane

Quentin leaned his head back against the wall and kept his eyes shut. Jace's hands were gentle on his calves as Quent's business partner and new lover helped him toe off his dress shoes and step out of his slacks, socks, and underwear.

He was abruptly aware that Jace was standing in front of him—Jace was a little bit shorter—and when he opened his eyes to look, Jace's vodka-blue eyes were glimmering back at him.

Quentin's breathing was still not even after climaxing in Jace's skilled mouth. There was a trickle of spend on the corner of his chin to testify that it had happened, and Quentin was now locked in one of the secret fantasies he'd never given voice.

He raised his hand to Jace's chin, using his thumb to stroke away the last of his come. Jace turned his head, popped the thumb in his mouth to suck it clean, and then released it with a last lick and a satisfied sigh. Quentin kept his hand there, cupping Jace's cheek anyway, enjoying the way such a fierce competitor leaned into his touch.

Jace met his eyes again, his face shadowed in the ambient light of the city that came through the front room window. It was hard to read his expression. If Quentin didn't know better, he'd say there was uncertainty in Jace's eyes and a little bit of fear in the curve of his mouth. It was an expression Quent had never seen—not on Jace—so he wouldn't have recognized it, even in broad daylight.

"Kiss me," Jace murmured, but he was no longer commanding. Quentin would have kissed him even if he hadn't asked.

It was the first time their lips met; Quent knew he tasted like cigars and fine liquor. Jace tasted like the same thing, but mostly, he tasted like come. He plundered Quentin's mouth, taking his face in both hands and pressing Quent back into the wall until he felt the imprint of the paneling on his bare ass.

It was a kiss. It was ravishment. It was holy communion. Jace's lips were firm, and his tongue was aggressive, and their mouths tangled and merged and tasted and started all over again.

Jace pulled back and scraped his hands through Quentin's short, dark hair, and there was a half smile on his lips as he softly walked elegant fingers through Quent's trimmed goatee.

"Itchy," Jace murmured with a half-smile. He cupped one hand on Quent's cheek and sent the other on a foray under a rucked-up shirt. Quent gasped as Jace's fingers found his nipples and pinched, gently, and then firmly.

"Mind-blowing," Quentin groaned, closing his eyes because he had to.

Jace's chuckle was low and rough, and Quent's cock stirred as it dried against his thigh. "I've got a promise to keep," Jace said. The hand still cupping Quentin's cheek trembled, and he moved in for another kiss, pressing his swollen groin against Quent's body this time as he did so.

Oh. Dear. God.

The high of feeling Jace's erection grinding into his hip through his slacks was almost as high as coming in Jace's mouth. Quent groaned and pressed into the kiss hungrily, wanting all of it, the promise, the threat, and the frightening fuck.

They made it to the small bedroom on the side of what was mostly a loft apartment. The front room and attached kitchen took up most of the space; the bedroom was an intimate little corner alongside the front room, made large by another pane of glass overlooking the fairy-tale lights of the city.

* * *

Quentin wasn't looking at the city.

That curious tremble had taken over Jace's hands again, and he was having trouble with his shirt and the stays of his slacks. Quentin, who never helped Jace, never advised him, always simply sat back and let the magic man do his thing when they were at work, didn't hesitate to help him.

"I'm not a child," Jace snapped, and Quentin finally understood.

Jace, who had faced a market crash with little more than an eye-twitch and a clenched jaw and who had more bed-partners than Quent could count (double that, now that Quent knew he swung this way) was nervous.

Quentin sat on the bed and felt Jace's cock through his slacks. It was huge, thick, and pulsing, even through the wool.

"You most certainly are not," Quent said softly. Carefully he undid the trousers and slid them down Jace's fine, lean thighs. He welcomed the weight as Jace balanced to take them off with his shoes and dress socks, and then he slid his palms up the front of Jace's thighs to the waistband of his shorts. Quentin pulled them down too, and then he looked up and allowed his own nervousness to show.

"You got a license for this thing?" He held out his hand and balanced Jace's cock on his palm. It was long and fairly wide—especially at the head. Quentin explored it hesitantly, finding veins and ridges under his fingertips and skating his thumb across the head, slick with pre-come.

"It comes with the equipment," Jace muttered through clenched teeth, and Quentin felt a curious sense of power.

He smiled—the kind of smile he felt at his cheeks when he was moving in for his own kill on the market—and stuck out his tongue to taste. It was sweet… so sweet. Quentin hollowed his cheeks and made to pull the whole thing in his mouth when Jace's fingers tangled in his short hair and jerked him back.

"Lay down!" he barked gruffly. "Take off your shirt first."

Quentin gave an ironic nod. "Sure thing, boss man."

"Quent," Jace growled, and Quentin was assaulted with that sudden surge of power again. Jace wanted him—badly.

Quent dropped his clothes on the ground and backed up on the bed, propping himself up on his elbows. Deliberately he spread his knees and looked up at Jace expectantly. *Come get me, asshole. You're the one who started this.* It was time to throw down their cards, to show that they were serious, to follow through.

Jace looked at him for a moment and swallowed. With deliberate movements he stalked to his end table and pulled out condoms and lube. "Have you done this before?"

Quentin's turn to swallow. "No."

Jace glanced at him, looked away, then crawled up on the bed and leaned over, bending over Quentin until their mouths touched. He pulled back from an absurdly tender kiss and rasped, "You're going to want to turn around."

Quentin must have made a protesting noise, and Jace closed his eyes and tilted his face up to the vaulted ceiling. "Please," he murmured, not commanding, not ordering. *Begging.* "Please, Quent—I want to make this good for you. But I'm… I'm there. If I look at you, it will be over."

Quentin reached up and splayed his hand over Jace's exposed abdomen. "This isn't a one-hand game."

Jace puffed out a breath and relaxed. He almost smiled. "No, it's not."

Quentin stayed there then, his knees spread, his body wide open and vulnerable. Jace made short (or long) work of the condom, and there was an alien little click as the bottle opened. Quentin hissed. The lubricant was cool and different, and then—

"Ahhhhhhhhhh…." Jace's finger breached him, and it burned, and stretched, and felt soooooooo good. There was pressure, and stretching, and then two fingers, scissoring inside Quentin's body and making him ready.

Quent's eyes popped open in surprise at the fullness, and he saw Jace, studying his open legs, stroking Quent's cock, all of that fierce, competitive concentration bent on making it good, on wringing Quentin's body of every last shudder of screaming pleasure he possessed.

"Jace," Quent's voice was uncertain, but he wanted to see Jace's eyes.

They were every bit as fierce as Quent expected.

"Are you ready?"

Quent tilted his head back in response, saying, "No!" with enough of a smile to let Jace know he'd die if they stopped.

• • •

Jace laughed gruffly and then poised so very carefully at Quent's entrance. "I could always stop," he threatened, and Quentin whimpered.

"Don't. You. Fucking. Dare. *Gaaaawwwwddd....*"

Jace's cock was wide and thick, and it stretched Quentin, burned the rim of his asshole until he saw a ring of fire behind his clenched eyelids. Still, Jace pushed, gently, inexorably, and as his flared head breached Quent's sphincter, Quentin groaned and begged and pleaded for him to for the love of God please. Don't. Stop.

"Ahhhhhhhhhhhh...." Jace's relief at being inside was enough to make Quentin open his eyes. Jace pitched forward, held himself over Quent with strong arms, and began to shift his hips ever-so-slowly as Quentin got used to the sweet invasion. Quentin raised his hands to Jace's smooth chest and rubbed the skin greedily, thumb-teasing the hard nipples and enjoying the shift of muscle as Jace's gentle pumping grew a little more forceful.

"How's it feel?" Jace asked roughly, and Quentin grinned through the excruciating pleasure.

"Same as work—it's you, up my ass until I'm begging for mercy."

Jace laughed, but his eyes were squeezed shut as he tried to hold back. His hips jerked forward—hard—and Quentin gasped.

"Then work that ass, dammit, I need to come!"

Quentin hadn't known it was possible to laugh and moan at the same time. Jace jerked his hips again. And again. And again. And before Quent knew it, he was begging, just as he promised. "Please... dammit, Jace... God... please... fuck me. Please ohmygod *fuck me!*"

Jace lunged above him, his body sweating as he thrust again and again and again, and Quentin was in agony, poised so close to coming, but without a hand on his cock he didn't know if he could.

It didn't matter.

He'd come already, spurted into Jace's mouth, and if not coming now was the price for watching Jace come completely unglued, frenzied, naked, in his arms, he'd stay hard and aching for a week.

Suddenly Jace froze above him, his face contorted in pleasure. He gave a strangled roar and lunged one more time, burying his cock so far up Quentin's ass Quentin wondered that his lungs didn't impact as Jace came.

❊ ❊ ❊

Jace shuddered against him again and again, his balls rubbing against Quentin's flesh as he did. Quentin rubbed Jace's shoulders, nuzzled the hollow of his neck, soothing him, caring for him, surprised that Jace, who was so self-reliant, such a predator, was responding, leaning into the softness of aftermath like any lover left naked by orgasm.

"You didn't come," Jace apologized, and Quentin puffed laughter into his ear.

"You came enough for the both of us."

Jace pulled back and looked anxiously into Quent's eyes. "That's not fair."

Quentin grinned and learned another lesson about power because the expression seemed to soften Jace's rough edges, making him suddenly shy and boyish in the faint light from the window.

"Neither is poker," Quent said, still grinning. His ass hurt—in a good way—even as Jace shrank inside of him, and the rest of his body was crazy-horny-sensitized from the mind-blowing sex.

"This is better than poker," Jace said seriously, and Quentin had to agree.

In His Eyes

Bethany Brown

The stable was a lot larger than he had been expecting. In fact, it was large enough that he was starting to feel quite intimidated. How was he supposed to find one person inside a structure that big? Especially a structure that was full of horses and other stable-type creatures. Of course, the lady at the main house had said that the man he was looking for was the only one in the stable, so it shouldn't be too hard to find him.

Taking a deep breath, Ryan Matthews ran a hand through his brown hair and stepped into the building. "Hello?"

"I'm in the tack room!" a male voice called out.

"That would be more helpful if I knew where that was," Ryan muttered. Figuring if he walked in the direction of the voice he would eventually find the tack room, Ryan headed farther into the building.

The first thing Ryan noticed as he entered the stable was the smell. He was pleasantly surprised by the scent. While there was a faint aroma of manure, it was mostly overpowered by the mingled scents of leather, hay, and sweat. He had been warned about the smell of a barn by several acquaintances, but he didn't find the odors offensive at all. Ryan was also starting to think that those people were a tad stuck-up. In his opinion, there was nothing wrong with the earthy smell of the barn. It smelled real. Several of the horses looked at him as he made his way to the still-unfound tack room, and just as he approached a bright rectangle of light, hopefully from an open tack room door, a grey and white cat wound itself around his feet.

As he crouched down to pet the friendly animal, a dog came out of nowhere and demanded attention as well. Ryan laughed and gave the excited animal a few scratches behind the ears. Climbing to his feet once more, Ryan finished walking toward the rectangle of light. He stepped into the well-lit room and saw that it was full of rows and rows of saddles and bridles. It seemed as though he had successfully found the tack room. And standing in it was the most beautiful thing he had ever seen.

His back was to the door, giving Ryan an unobstructed view of a phenomenal rear end encased in curve-hugging denim. Ryan let his eyes trail down from the almost captivating sight to take in the long legs capped in scuffed cowboy boots. His eyes traveled back up, pausing to ogle the ass once more, and continued on, taking in the strong expanse of broad back and the wisps of blond hair sticking out from under a cowboy hat. Ryan cleared his throat, and the cowboy turned and revealed hazel eyes in a gorgeous face.

"Are you Max Kincaid?" Ryan gave the man a small smile. *Please, God, say yes.*

"That's me." Max smiled and tipped his hat back, revealing more of his handsome face. "You must be Mr. Matthews." He held out a hand.

"Please, call me Ryan," he remarked. Ryan walked closer to the other man and was pleased to find that they appeared to be around the same height, which would put Max at five-eleven. Of course, the boots the other man was wearing could be throwing off his estimate, so Ryan wasn't sure. He took the offered hand and found himself the recipient of a firm grip. A closer inspection of Max's face had Ryan estimating that he was in his twenties, which would make him younger than Ryan's thirty-seven.

"Okay, Ryan, did Sandy send you out here?"

"She did. She thought it might be a good idea for us to meet."

"And she sent you out here because she assumed that you would most likely run in terror from the smell and she would be able to watch and laugh from the house."

Ryan gave a surprised laugh. "I'm guessing that this happens a lot?"

"You are the first adult who has actually made it into the barn under their own power without making a face or holding something over their nose."

* * *

"Own power?"

"I don't count the parents who get dragged in here by their kids." Max leaned back against a support pillar behind him and crossed his arms, causing the muscles to flex. "So, you want to learn to ride?"

Ryan could almost feel the drool leaking out of his mouth. Hell yeah, did he want to ride. Unfortunately, he was fairly certain that Max was talking about horses. *I'd really like to ride you.* "That about sums it up."

"Can I ask you why? I mean, most new riders are younger than you."

Great, the hot cowboy thinks I'm old. "My son Tyler turns ten next week, and we're doing the weeklong trail ride for his birthday. It's going to be me, Tyler, my other son Jesse, a couple of Tyler's friends, his mother, and Greg, her new husband. I would really like it if I could ride better than Greg."

Max stared at him for a moment, and then a slow smile crossed his face. "You're here for the week?"

"Yeah."

"Then don't worry. I'll have you riding circles around Greg. Your ex will be sorry that she's not married to you anymore."

"Actually, Caroline and I were never married."

"Oh, I'm sorry. I just assumed."

"I'm gay," Ryan blurted. The minute it came out of his mouth, he wanted to take it back. He was usually a bit more tactful at expressing his sexuality, but Max first thinking he was old, followed by the assumption that he was straight, had Ryan fairly rattled. The fact that he thought the younger man was drop-dead gorgeous didn't help. He'd always been rather tongue-tied around people he found attractive. Ryan groaned and ran a hand over his face. "That came out wrong."

"Came out wrong because you aren't gay? Or came out wrong because you kinda shouted it at me?"

"The second one." Max smiled at him, and Ryan felt his knees go weak. *Holy shit, he has a nice smile. I want to lick it.* "I usually manage to say that with a bit more finesse and a tad less shouting."

"I'll let it slide, since you're in new surroundings." A glimmer of mischief appeared in Max's hazel eyes. "Unless, of course, you've been to a ranch before, in which case, I'll have to mock you."

Ryan laughed. "I've never been to a ranch before. I have driven past a stable once."

"That doesn't really count."

"Good. I guess that means I'm safe from being mocked. At least until you actually get me up on a horse. I'm pretty sure there will be mocking involved with that."

"I would never mock a student." Max stepped past him and motioned for Ryan to follow him.

"Student? Sandy didn't say that you were going to be the one teaching me."

"I'm the one scheduled for your son's trail ride, so I may as well teach you how to ride. That way I'll be satisfied with your skill level."

"Makes sense. Can I ask you a question about the trail ride?"

"Shoot."

"Is it a full seven days in the woods?" Ryan was actually a bit concerned about that. While he loved the outdoors, he didn't relish the idea of spending seven days in the woods with a bunch of ten-year-olds. In fact, despite the fact that he loved his son to bits, he was rather petrified of the coming experience.

Max's rich chuckle filled the hall they were walking down. "Terrifying, isn't it?"

"Just a bit. So, is it really seven days in the woods?"

"What trail package did you get?"

"Um." Ryan racked his brain, trying to remember which of the many different packages he and Caroline had looked at that they had chosen. "I think it was Newcomer Package A."

"No, with that one it's not a full seven days in the woods. We spend two days on the ranch making sure everyone is comfortable with their horses. Then it's a full day's ride to the camp site. We spend two days at the camp site, with smaller trail rides both mornings to see some of the sights. We ride back the next day, and then the following day you have a full day at the ranch with the big farewell bonfire at night."

"That sounds a lot better than seven days in the woods with a bunch of ten-year-olds," Ryan responded. He felt a smile cross his face as Max smirked at him. God, the man was gorgeous.

"Man, if I had to spend an entire week in the woods with some of the groups I've led, not all of them would have made it back."

"Hell, I love nature, but if I had to spend seven days in the woods, I think I might go insane."

"City boy at heart?"

"No, I just like having running water." Ryan grinned as Max started to laugh. "Bathrooms are my friend."

"You are a funny guy."

"Thanks. It's always good to be appreciated."

Max gave him a sly look. "I'll have to remember that."

Holy shit. The look that Max had sent him had Ryan's stomach twisting in knots. Was the hot cowboy really flirting with him? Or was he just being nice and Ryan's lonely brain was making it what he wanted it to be? When was the last time he'd been on a date? Ryan had to suppress a self-deprecating chuckle when he realized he couldn't remember. He almost walked past Max before he noticed the younger man had stopped.

"We're here."

"Here where?" Ryan stepped close to Max, hoping that the confusion he was certain was on his face didn't make him look like an idiot.

"This is Daisy. She's going to be your new best friend for the next two weeks," Max announced. Ryan turned away from smiling hazel eyes to face the stall they were standing before.

At first, all Ryan could see was a horse. Daisy didn't seem to be that different from all of the other horses he'd seen in his life. Then she moved forward and stuck her head over the stall door. Her ears were perked forward as she butted his chest with her nose. Ryan raised a hand to rub the velvet softness of her muzzle and instantly fell in love. She was the color of chocolate with a black mane and dark eyes. The nose she kept bumping him with had a small white patch on it. Ryan laughed as she lipped at his shirt.

"She's looking for treats."

"But I don't have any."

"Maybe she thinks you are one."

"I think I can live with that," Ryan murmured. He ran his hand up the flat plane of Daisy's forehead to rest under her forelock. He gave her a scratch, and her head lowered and rested against his chest. "I like her."

"I can tell." Max pulled a small card out of his pocket and scrawled something across it. He slipped it into a holder on the front of Daisy's stall, and Ryan could see his name written on it.

"What's that for?"

"It's so the other guides and teachers know that someone is riding Daisy. We came up with the card system after a few months of having to switch kids around when we realized that we had some horses double booked."

"Makes sense to have the cards then." Ryan laughed as Daisy lipped at his shirt once again. "Do you have anything for me to give her or should I just let her eat my shirt?"

"I'll let you give her a treat after."

"After?" Ryan removed his attention from Daisy and focused back on the handsome cowboy.

"You're getting on."

"What?"

"Hey, you want to be better than Greg, we'd better get started. Back to the tack room we go."

"Um, can I go and change first?" Ryan blushed as Max's eyes traveled from his polo shirt with his company logo on it down past his khakis to the sneakers on his feet and back up. That look sent a wave of heat through his body. When he saw what he wanted to believe to be smothered heat in Max's gaze, he had to swallow a whimper that tried to escape.

"Sandy sent you out here right away?"

"Yes."

"Did she at least give you a room before she sent you to me?"

"No."

Max laughed softly and shook his head. "I guess I can let you go back and get settled and changed before I throw you to the wolves."

"You're throwing me to the wolves? I thought you were going to be teaching me?" Ryan smiled at Max and tried to keep what he was thinking from showing in his eyes. While he was sure that Max teaching him to ride would be incredibly distracting, he wanted to spend his days with the attractive younger man.

"I am."

"So then what's with throwing me to the wolves?"

"Isn't it the thing to say? I mean, you said that you've never been on a horse before, so I guess tossing you up on one right away would be like throwing you to the wolves. Plus, I kinda like the saying." Max gave him a shy grin as he pulled his hat off and ran his hand through his hair before placing the hat back on his head. "So, need me to lead you back to the house?"

Ryan opened his mouth and then closed it before saying anything. He took a look around the part of the stable they were standing in. "I was going to say no, but I have no idea where we are in relation to the exit."

Max laughed. "Just follow me. I'll show you the way."

Oh, don't I wish. Ryan smiled and followed as Max turned and headed in what he assumed was the direction of the exit. He hoped that Max didn't turn around suddenly and catch him staring at the rather delectable cowboy ass that was presented for his viewing pleasure. The following week was going to be interesting.

Four Days Later

MAX slammed his front door as he stepped out of his three-bedroom house on the ranch grounds. All he wanted to do was crawl back into bed. Preferably with an older man who was becoming a rather decent rider. But instead, he was wearing a nice pair of pants and a dress shirt and heading to a lunch that he didn't want to go to. Max was less than pleased. While he normally enjoyed the monthly lunches with his mother, he really did not want to go to this one. All he wanted to do was stay on the ranch with Ryan.

Ryan. Even thinking his name made Max shiver in longing.

Max was having a difficult time wrapping his mind around his feelings for Ryan. After his first disastrous relationship with an older man, Max had stuck to dating men his own age or younger. He hadn't even felt attracted to an older man until Ryan has walked into his life. Not only was he attracted, Max only had to look into the honey-colored eyes to drown in desire. And he did feel desire. He wanted Ryan so much he actually ached for his touch. Every time Ryan brushed against him, he had to smother a whimper. He just didn't know what to do about his feelings.

Max sighed, slipped his sunglasses over his eyes, and headed to the stables. He had one stop to make before he left for his lunch. While he knew the stop would make him run late, he had to tell Ryan in person that he wouldn't be able to stay for his lesson. Kevin, the instructor who would be filling in for him, had offered to do it, but Max didn't want the attractive cowboy near Ryan longer than absolutely necessary.

Max made his way through the halls of the stable to Daisy's stall and smiled. He could hear Ryan's voice as he talked to the horse. While Ryan's lesson wasn't until later in the day, he could usually be found in the stable with Daisy or helping around the ranch. Max caught sight of Ryan grooming Daisy, and his heart leapt.

I am in so much trouble. "You know, she's just going to roll in the dirt when you put her in the pasture."

"I know. I'll just groom her again." Ryan put the brush down and looked at him. The honey-colored eyes widened as he took in Max's appearance. "Not that I don't like the look, but what's the occasion?"

"I'm having lunch with my mother." Max winced as he heard the annoyance in his own voice. Just because he didn't feel like having lunch with his mother that day was no reason to make it sound as though he hated eating with her.

"You don't sound that thrilled," Ryan remarked. The humor Max could see in his eyes suddenly started to fade. "You're not going to be doing my lesson today, are you?"

"No. Sorry."

Ryan ran a hand along Daisy's flank and leaned against her slightly. "So who are you leaving in charge of me?"

"Kevin. But just for today. You're mine." Max blushed all the way to his hair as he realized what he had just said. "I mean, you're my student. Kevin has his own."

"Well, it's good to know who I belong to."

Max felt his blush deepen. He needed to get out of the stable before he made a complete fool of himself. "I'll see you later." Max chanced looking up and saw a soft smile on Ryan's face. That smiled caused a feeling of warmth to flow through his body.

"Have a good lunch."

"Thanks." Max gave Ryan one more smile and then bolted. He cursed his mouth the entire way to his truck. He couldn't believe he had told Ryan that he was his. Possessive much? God, he didn't even know if Ryan liked him. He *wanted* Ryan to like him. He *really* wanted Ryan to like him. Max couldn't remember the last time he had been so attracted to someone.

Climbing into his truck, he tried to push his feelings for Ryan to the back of his mind. He did not want to have lunch with his mother while distracted. She was too observant. If she noticed a distraction, she would jump all over it until she figured out what it was. It was one of her more annoying qualities.

By the time he pulled up in front of the country club, Max was fairly certain that he had himself under control. He hopped out and tossed his keys to the valet, grinning at the affronted look on the man's face. Max knew his beat-up truck was not what the valet was used to parking. It was one of the reasons he insisted on driving the thing to the country club, even though his mother had given him a trendy sports car for his birthday the year before. He hardly ever drove it. What would be the point of driving a sports car around a ranch?

Max went to tip his hat at the doorman but froze halfway through the gesture. He wasn't wearing his hat. His mother insisted that it was impolite to wear a hat while dining, unless on a picnic, so he'd left it at home to avoid accidentally forgetting he had it on. Max turned the motion into running his hand through his hair. He hoped no one noticed the pause. Praying that he hadn't messed up his blond curls, Max headed to the dining room.

• • •

"Hello, Mr. Kincaid."

"Hey, Jefferson." Max nodded at the maître d'. "Is my mother at her usual table?"

"She's on the terrace today."

"My mother is dining outside?" Max couldn't keep the astonishment from his voice. His mother was not a fan of mixing the outdoors and eating.

"She said she wanted to enjoy the nice summer day."

"Has she been drinking?"

"Not yet." Jefferson gave him a small grin. "Do you need me to take you to her table?"

"That's okay. I think I can manage to find my mother on my own." Max smiled and gave Jefferson's shoulder a squeeze. Walking past the other man, Max headed into the main dining room. There weren't that many people inside, but he nodded at the ones he knew. He even paused to say hello to a few of his mother's friends. While the stops were keeping his mother waiting, Max knew if he didn't, the ladies would tell his mother he had snubbed them. He really hated the country club.

Stepping onto the terrace, he instantly spotted his mother. Lila Kincaid drew the eye no matter where she was. It wasn't just her looks, even though Max had to admit she was an attractive woman. Her thick hair was still naturally blonde, and there were only a few lines at the corners of her brown eyes. What made her noticeable was her presence. She was a force to be reckoned with, and it was evident even when she was sitting.

Taking a deep breath to steady his nerves, Max walked over and touched her shoulder. "Hello, Mother."

Lila looked up at him with pleasure in her eyes. "There you are, darling." She tugged on his arm until he leaned down and kissed her cheek. "I was starting to wonder where you were."

"I'm not that late." Max released her arm and sat down across from her. "I'm surprised that you're out here. I thought you didn't like dining outside."

A small look of distaste crossed her face. "I don't, but your sister keeps insisting that I need more fresh air."

"Is Tessa joining us?" Max swallowed a groan at the thought. He loved his sister, but she was a tad self-centered. And flighty. It made for some rather awkward conversations.

"She muttered something about joining us for after-lunch drinks, but you know how she is. I doubt that she'll show up."

"But you decided to eat outside just to be on the safe side."

Lila gave him a bright smile. "Exactly." She gave the waiter Max hadn't even noticed a slight nod and then turned her attention back to him. "So, how are you, my darling?"

Max watched the waiter go, hoping that whatever his mother had ordered for him tasted good. "I'm fine."

"Are you? You're not lonely?"

Max sighed and resisted dropping his head onto the table. *Here it comes.* "I'm fine, Mother. I'm not lonely at all."

"It's not polite to lie to your mother."

"I'm not lying."

"Bullshit," Lila snapped. The waiter, who had returned with their drinks, almost dropped the tray when he heard Lila swear. Max winced. If his mother was annoyed enough to call him on his bullshit in the middle of the country club, there was no way he was going to be able to get out of talking about his love life. Or lack thereof. "Well, give us the drinks, Collin, so I can continue to question my son."

"Sorry, Mrs. Kincaid." Collin hurriedly put the drinks down on the table. He gave Max a sympathetic smile before he almost ran from the tension at the table. Max wished he could go with him.

"Are you gazing after Collin because you want to run away from me or because you want him? If you're interested, I could see if he's gay. Is he your type?"

"Mother!"

"What?"

"I don't need help getting a date."

"Well, that remains to be seen. When was the last time you even had one?"

Max shifted uncomfortably. "A while."

"Before or after you dated that dreadful young man you met at the ranch?"

Max winced again. "No, it would have been him."

"Maxwell, that was six months ago." Lila focused her eyes on him with such intensity that he actually squirmed in his seat. "I have trouble believing that my handsome son hasn't been asked on a date in six months."

"It's not that I haven't been asked, it's just that I haven't met anyone I want to go on a date with." Max fiddled with the lemonade Collin had brought him. "I have trouble trusting people."

"I know you do, darling, but you can't let that get in the way of meeting someone." Lila reached across the table and grasped his hand. "I just want you to be happy."

"I know." An image of Ryan's smiling honey eyes popped into his head. "There is someone."

"Really?" Lila leaned back to allow Collin to place her entrée-sized salad in front of her. "It's not that Kevin boy you work with, is it?"

Max nearly spit out the bite of steak he had taken. He managed to swallow without choking. "No, it's not Kevin. Why would you even think that?"

"I've seen the way he looks at you."

"He looks at all men like that."

"I don't like it. You shouldn't date him."

"I'm not planning on dating Kevin."

"Then who are you dating?"

"I'm not dating anyone. I just met someone that I sort of like."

"Are you going to tell me about him?"

"I wasn't even planning on telling you this much," Max replied. He sighed and put down his fork. When his mother noticed he had stopped eating, she lowered her own utensils. "Look, I understand that you care and you just want me to be happy, but I need you to stop pushing. I don't even know if he likes me. I at least want to get things sorted before I start talking about him."

Lila smiled at him. "I understand, darling." She reached over and gave his hand a pat before turning her attention back to her meal.

They ate the rest of their lunch over pleasant conversation that had nothing to do with Max's sex life. He told his mother some of the more amusing stories from the past few weeks at the ranch. Lila filled him in on the latest gossip about her circle of peers. Max had been surprised when he first realized he liked listening to his mother gossip. Tessa never had the patience to listen to anyone except herself, and Martin, Max's father, had always spent a lot of time away on business. He was home more often now, but Max and Lila had become so settled in their routine that neither of them wanted to change it.

Collin had just removed their dessert plates when Lila's eyes locked on to someone approaching their table. "Well, it looks like your sister made it after all. And she seems to have brought someone with her."

Max turned to look and felt all of the blood rush from his face. His petite and pretty older sister was escorting a man toward them. A man who Max was quite familiar with. Intimately familiar. Thankfully, Conrad had his head bent down to Tessa and had yet to notice Max was at the table.

"Mother, I'm sorry, but I need to leave."

Lila's eyes narrowed in concern. "Darling, are you all right?"

"I'm fine." Max stood, leaned over, and pressed a kiss to his mother's cheek. "Thank you for a wonderful lunch."

"You're welcome. You should come by the house and have dinner with your father and me. He wants to see you, and since you don't golf, dinner would be a wonderful solution."

"Sounds great. Give me a call later and let me know what day works for you." Max pressed another kiss to his mother's cheek and escaped before Tessa and Conrad made it to the table. He couldn't believe they hadn't noticed him. Then again, Tessa tended to only notice the people whose attention she wanted. In his haste to get away, Max nearly knocked over an older man on his way in to the bar.

From the relative safety of the bar, Max glanced back at the table. Conrad was in the midst of kissing his mother's hand, but Lila didn't look even remotely impressed. Max smiled. If there was one thing his mother knew, it was who was trying to suck up to her and her money. Seeing through

* * *

Conrad's act would be easy for her. Unfortunately, it hadn't been that easy for Max. Oh, no. He had fallen for it hook, line, and sinker. Conrad was one of the reasons he had trouble trusting people.

Max let his eyes wander over Conrad's strong form, feeling the familiar stab of pain. It had been ten years, but Max still couldn't keep the hurt from surfacing every time he saw the older man. When Conrad ran a proprietary hand over Tessa's ass, Max felt his lunch start to rise. It looked like Conrad was dating his sister. Again. Just like he had been when he'd taken Max's virginity.

Shutting his eyes against the painful memories, Max pushed himself away from the terrace view and further into the bar. He didn't need to see any more. Seeing Tessa smile at Conrad just made him feel guilty all over again. It didn't matter that he hadn't known Conrad had been seeing his sister, he still felt guilty. His good mood completely evaporated, Max headed to the valet to get his truck. The valet was incredibly quick. It was almost as if he was afraid the truck would infect all of the sports cars around it, turning them into sensible vehicles.

The drive back to the ranch never seemed to take as long as the drive into the city. As he drove past the gates, Max felt some of his tension start to melt away. That was one of the things he loved about living on the ranch. Everything that caused tension in the city just didn't seem to matter when surrounded by nature. Max parked his truck around the side of his cottage and climbed out. He was about to go into the house but changed his mind and headed to the riding ring. As he got closer, he could see someone leaning on the fence watching the lesson. Max's eyes were caught by Ryan and Daisy as he reached the fence.

"He's looking good," a female voice commented. Max pulled his gaze away from Ryan to see Sandy leaning against the fence. "You've done a good job."

"I haven't done anything. It was all Ryan."

"He may have done all the work, but you had something to do with it. I don't think he would have picked it up as quickly with someone else."

"He wants to impress his son."

Sandy snorted. "He wants to impress you."

"What?" Max turned his body to give Sandy his full attention. "How can you be so sure?"

"The way he looks at you. It's in his eyes." Sandy gestured at Ryan. "Just look at him. He's good and he's enjoying himself, but he shines when you're the one teaching him."

Max watched as Ryan turned Daisy in a circle. "His smile is missing. He always has a smile. Even when he fell off the first time, he was smiling."

"He only smiles when you're teaching. Kevin's managed to get a couple of grins, but that bright smile is all for you."

"So Kevin hasn't been hitting on him?"

Sandy laughed. "I didn't say that. Kevin's been working overtime. Your man keeps shooting him down."

"Really?"

"Hell, Kevin's crashed and burned so often I'm starting to think I should keep a bucket out here in case he spontaneously combusts." Sandy waggled her eyebrows at him, and Max couldn't keep the laughter down. "So, how was lunch with your mom? You looked a little tense when you got here."

"The food was good."

Sandy winced. "That bad?"

"No. I actually had a pretty good time this month. It just ended on a bad note."

"How so?"

"Saw someone I really didn't want to see." Max pushed away from the fence and ran a hand through his hair. "Is there something I can do? I need to work off this mood."

"The tree that fell in the meadow behind your place is still lying there. You could start chopping it up."

"With what?"

Sandy gave him a bland look. "An axe. There should be one by the woodpile."

"That actually doesn't sound like a bad idea. I'm gonna change and then head out there."

● ● ●

"Keep an eye on the sky. It looks like there's a storm coming."

"I'll keep that in mind." Max cast a longing look in Ryan's direction and then turned away.

"I'll keep an eye on Kevin. Make sure he doesn't get fresh with your man. Of course, if he gets too out of line, Daisy may bite him. That horse likes Ryan almost as much as you do."

Max shook his head at Sandy, but he couldn't bring himself to tell her Ryan wasn't his man. He gave her a small wave and headed back to his cottage to change. He hoped that hacking apart a tree would make him feel better.

RYAN gave Daisy one last scratch before he let her into the pasture. Closing the gate, he watched as she trotted a short distance away before stopping. She turned, seemed to look right at him, dropped to the ground, and rolled in the dirt. Ryan shook his head at her antics. She rolled every single time he let her out into the pasture. "You know, I may just stop grooming you!" Daisy snorted and got back to her feet, trailing dust as she trotted farther away.

"I think she does it on purpose."

Ryan turned to see Sandy standing behind him. "I'm starting to get that feeling myself."

"I saw your lesson."

"I noticed." Ryan had also noticed when Max returned, but he wasn't about to admit that to Sandy. Although, from the way she was grinning at him, he was pretty sure she'd guessed.

"You're getting pretty good."

"Thanks. I don't want to embarrass Tyler."

"Tyler is your son?"

"One of them. He's the one with the birthday."

"I think you'll be fine." Sandy leaned against the pasture fence and sighed. "You know, I think you're the first parent we've ever had here who

● ● ●

cared this much about making a good impression on their children. Most of the parents we get can't wait to leave."

Ryan smiled at her. "I love it here. I'm really glad this is what Tyler wanted to do for his birthday. I don't think kids spend enough time outside."

"You sound like a good father."

"Thanks." Ryan blushed and ran a hand through his hair. "I try. I'm just glad they seem to like me. It's hard being a parent."

"Some people are better at it than others," she replied. Sandy tucked a strand of hair behind her ear and smiled at him. "You should head back inside. Sky's starting to look like it's gonna split."

Ryan looked up at the rather large number of ominous black clouds. "I think you may be right." He gave the grounds surrounding him what he hoped was a nonchalant look before turning his attention back to Sandy. "Have you seen Max? I wanted to ask him how his lunch went."

"As far as I know, he's still hacking that fallen tree to pieces."

"What fallen tree?"

"There's a meadow behind his cottage. A tree fell down during one of the big storms, so he's chopping it up." Sandy glanced at the sky. "You should probably go and get him. I don't want him out there with the sky looking like this. You never know when it could just open up on you."

"Thanks. I'll go find him." Ryan didn't miss the grin Sandy shot at him as he walked off to find Max. It looked like she was on to his crush. He couldn't help it. He just found Max so appealing.

It had started with him just finding Max attractive. Hell, you'd have to be blind not to notice how pretty he was. But then, as the days went by, Ryan started getting to know Max. He actually enjoyed being around the younger man. In fact, the best part of his day was spending time with Max. Max was funny and engaging, and Ryan hoped he hadn't imagined the looks the younger man had been giving him. Those looks had been fueling quite a few late-night fantasies.

Ryan passed the cottage Max lived in, spotting both a truck and a sports car parked around the side. Orienting himself at what he hoped was the back porch, Ryan started walking. He quickly encountered a worn path which led him to the meadow Sandy had mentioned. On the far left side of the meadow was a rather large fallen tree and an axe-wielding Max. Ryan smiled and made his way across the grass.

"So, does the axe mean that I shouldn't ask you how your lunch went?"

Max lowered the axe and turned, a smile lighting his face as his eyes settled on Ryan. "It means you should be careful what you ask me. Wouldn't be a good idea to make me angry."

"I'll keep that in mind." Ryan was about to ask Max about his lunch once again, when there was a loud crash of thunder. They both jumped and looked up as rain began falling down in sheets. Within seconds, Ryan was soaked to the skin.

"Come on! Let's get out of this!" Tightening his grip on the axe, Max took off for the cottage at a run. Ryan followed behind but was unable to enjoy the view due to the heavy rain. It was hard to ogle cowboy butt when it was barely visible.

The thunder drowned out the sound of their footsteps as they ran up the porch stairs. After leaning the axe against the wall, Max opened the door and ushered Ryan inside. Ryan found himself dripping on the floor of what appeared to be a mud room while Max kicked off his boots, and he started to shiver as the cool air hit his wet skin.

"Hang on. I'll grab you some towels and dry clothes." Max gave his shivering shoulder a squeeze and left him standing there. Ryan really wanted to snoop, but leaving a trail of water through Max's home would be pretty obvious. While he waited, he managed to get his boots and socks off his feet. Max came back with two towels. "Here." A towel was wrapped around his shoulders. "That should take some of the water off of you."

"Thanks." Ryan pulled the towel closer around his shivering form and attempted to warm up.

"Come on, I'll show you to the bathroom." Max grinned and led the way. He pushed the door open and moved to one side to let Ryan in. "I left you some dry clothes on the counter. Take a shower and get warm. I don't think you're going anywhere until this rain lets up."

"What about you?" Ryan blushed as Max simply stared at him. "I mean, it's your house. I don't want you to freeze while I have a shower."

"I have another bathroom upstairs. Don't worry about me," Max replied. He gave Ryan a cheeky grin and left, closing the door behind him. Ryan stared at the closed door until the shaking forced him to move.

He had no idea how he was going to shower knowing that Max was naked somewhere above him.

It was going to be an interesting night.

MAX had always been fast in the shower, so he wasn't surprised that he finished before Ryan did. Feeling hungry after all the work he'd been doing in the meadow, Max headed to the kitchen, hoping he had something that would feed the both of them. As he walked past the still occupied bathroom, he had to forcibly shove images of naked flesh out of his mind. He wanted to open the bathroom door so badly his hands were shaking.

"Get a grip," he muttered as he entered the kitchen. Just because he thought Ryan was gorgeous and the man was naked in his bathroom did not mean he wanted help in the shower. *Damn, naked Ryan. Yum.*

Max was staring out the window when he heard the water shut off. The rain was still coming down in sheets. It was starting to look like Ryan was going to be stuck with him for the night… unless he decided to brave the rain and run back to the main house. Max hoped he'd stay.

Max had his head buried in the fridge when he heard footsteps behind him. "Well, I think I've got some leftovers in here that aren't too bad. Do you like Chinese?" Max stood, turned, and almost dropped the food.

His eyes drank in the sight of a damp Ryan shirtless in his kitchen. He was standing just inside the doorway and toweling off his hair. Max watched as a drop of water ran down his chest, over the defined muscles in his torso to disappear behind the waist of the borrowed pants he was wearing. When Ryan ran the towel down his chest, Max actually whimpered.

"Fuck it." Max shoved the food back in the fridge, stalked across the kitchen, and pulled the towel from Ryan's unresisting hands. He flattened one of his own trembling hands over Ryan's chest. He could feel Ryan's heart beating. The skin beneath his hand was smooth and warm, and there was a light dusting of hair across the skin. Max couldn't stop staring. Why hadn't he known Ryan had all those muscles?

"Max?"

"God, you're so warm." Max felt fingers beneath his chin as his head was forced up. He stared into honey eyes that had darkened with desire. When Ryan's tongue slid out to wet his lips, he moaned. The fingers on his jaw tightened, and Ryan's lips moved to meet his.

When Ryan kissed him, Max snapped out of whatever weird, hot-body induced stupor he had been in. He wrapped his arms around Ryan's neck and opened his mouth to the tongue he could feel licking along his lips. Max twined his tongue around Ryan's and pulled it into his mouth, teasing until he heard Ryan groan. Hands tightened on his waist, and they were suddenly leaning back against the wall. He pulled away from Ryan's mouth to suck in some much needed air before he slid his lips down Ryan's neck. The hands on his waist tightened as he sucked on the skin under his mouth.

"Oh, like that." Ryan's voice came out husky and deep, which sent a thrill through Max. He had made Ryan's voice sound like that. Max bit down harder and was rewarded with a gasp followed by a low moan. Pulling away from Ryan's neck, he studied the mark he had left.

"You taste good." Max darted his head forward once more and licked over the red mark marring Ryan's skin. Ryan hissed and dug his fingers into his hips. Those strong hands slid up his back and underneath the shirt he was wearing.

"You feel good, Max. So strong." Strong fingers kneaded his back, leaving shivers of sensation in their wake.

"You aren't that bad yourself. Where did you get all these muscles you've been hiding?" Max shifted far enough away from Ryan's hold to allow himself room to run his tongue over a muscled shoulder.

"Landscaping. I own my own company." Ryan moved his hands back to Max's hips and pushed him away. "Max, stop."

"Why?" Max chanced a look into the older man's eyes, hoping that he hadn't changed his mind.

"We need to move. I'm leaning against a doorway and about to lose my balance."

"Oh." Max let what he hoped was a seductive smile cross his lips. "Bedroom?"

"Only if you want."

"I was kinda hoping that you wanted it too."

"Oh, believe me, I want. You're all I can think about." Ryan grinned at him. "It's not easy to ride when you're hard."

"Trust me, I know the feeling." Max pulled away and threaded his fingers through Ryan's. "Come on. Bed."

Ryan chuckled as Max pulled him to the stairs, causing Max to grin. As Ryan's fingers squeezed his, Max began to release some of the tension he hadn't even realized he was holding. He didn't usually move this fast with a prospective lover, but he just felt so comfortable with Ryan. He also hadn't lied when he told his mother he hadn't had a date in six months. Taking Ryan to his bed was giving him a thrill he hadn't felt in a long time. They reached the top of the stairs, but Max found himself suddenly unable to move. He turned to ask what was wrong, and Ryan pulled him into his arms.

Max moaned as his mouth was thoroughly plundered. He thrust his hands into Ryan's dark hair, marveling at the silky texture even though it was still damp. He trembled and pressed his body against Ryan's as the older man's tongue ran over the roof of his mouth. Leaning against Ryan, Max realized that when he was barefoot, Ryan was actually about two inches taller than he was. He liked that he had to tilt his head up slightly to kiss him. Max groaned as Ryan thrust his erection against his.

He broke away with a gasp. "Bed. You keep distracting me."

"Sorry, can't help it. You're just too tempting." Ryan pressed one more kiss to his lips before allowing him to pull away. Max grinned and pulled him into his bedroom. Once inside, he spun them around until Ryan was standing at the foot of the king-sized bed and pushed. Ryan fell onto the bed with a small grunt.

Max gazed at the man spread out before him. It was like looking at a feast. His eyes took in the strong, exposed torso and long, muscled arms; they zeroed in on the tent in the borrowed sweats Ryan was wearing. Max felt his mouth water. He had no words to express how right Ryan looked in his bed.

"You going to stand there all night?" There was a flirty look on Ryan's face, and his eyes said that he knew what was coming.

"No." Max practically pounced on him. He attacked Ryan's lips as he pressed against his strong body. Max felt hands running over his back underneath his shirt, so he drew away in order to pull it off and toss it over the side of the bed. Ryan's hands ran over his now-exposed chest and Max moaned. When the strong fingers brushed against his nipples, Max cried out in pleasure.

"Like that, do you?" Ryan asked. Max could only nod. Strong arms wrapped around him, and Ryan rolled them over on the bed so Max was beneath him. Before Max could get his bearings, Ryan's mouth latched on to one of his nipples. Max's head fell back against the pillows as pleasure lit his body on fire.

He buried his fingers in Ryan's hair and pulled the mouth that was tormenting him closer to his chest. Ryan responded by gently biting at the nipple he had trapped. Long swipes of his tongue eased the small sting. Max could feel his entire body trembling as Ryan moved to the other nipple. His fingers were clenching and unclenching in the thick, dark hair as Ryan tormented him in the most delicious way. Max moaned as Ryan released his nipple and continued down his chest.

"I love these muscles. I've been wanting to taste them for days."

"I'm not going to stop you."

"Good," Ryan replied. Max moaned as Ryan's tongue began to trace the planes of his abdomen. He couldn't figure out what to do with his hands; he loved the feel of Ryan's hair on his fingers, but he wanted to feel the smooth skin he could see on display. Leaving one hand in Ryan's hair, Max ran the other over his shoulders, loving the way the muscles moved under it. When he ran his fingers over the back of Ryan's neck, Ryan shuddered.

Max kept moving his hand over Ryan's flesh as the other man made a feast of his stomach. When he felt Ryan's chin brush against the bulge hidden behind his sweats, he gasped and dropped his hands to the bed, where they fisted the sheets as he thrust upward. Hands curled around the waistband of his sweats, and he moaned, "Ryan."

"Lift up for me."

Max obediently raised his hips and let Ryan pull the pants from his body. He looked down the length of his own naked form to see Ryan standing at the foot of the bed in the process of removing his borrowed pants. Max groaned as a fully naked Ryan appeared. The strong muscles continued in his legs, but what really caught his attention was the hard cock jutting out of a nest of curls. As he watched, a drop of pre-come slid down the shaft. His mouth watered. He wanted that cock.

"How do you want me?"

Startled by the question, Max realized he must have said the last bit out loud. "On your back. I want to ride you."

Ryan moaned and nearly landed on Max in his haste to get back on the bed. Max looked over at him and grinned. When a large hand cupped his cheek, Max turned his face to the side and pressed a kiss to the palm. He looked back at Ryan, and the desire in his eyes had softened to something that looked quite a bit like affection. Max pressed another kiss to Ryan's palm, and he turned to his nightstand and pulled lube and a condom out of the drawer. Feeling a tug on his waist, Max looked over to find Ryan holding out his hand.

"Give me the lube. I want to get you ready."

Max moaned as the words sent a spike of arousal shooting through him so fast it made him dizzy. He dropped the lube and condom into Ryan's outstretched hand and then crawled across the bed so he was on hands and knees over Ryan. "This okay?"

"Perfect." Ryan gave his nose a gentle nip. "God, sweetheart, you are so beautiful."

"No, I'm not."

"I think you are," Ryan replied. A slicked finger pressing inside of him stole Max's answer as well as his breath. "Damn, you're tight."

"Been a while." In fact, it had been a very long while, but Max wanted Ryan inside him so badly he was nearly vibrating with need. As he felt the finger slowly start to move, he forced himself to relax muscles that had tensed. Looking down into Ryan's concerned gaze, he pulled up a smile and started to thrust back. "Come on, honey, give me more."

Ryan laughed but did as he was told. When the second finger slipped in alongside the first, Max whimpered at the burn. It had been long enough that he was expecting it to hurt a bit, but Ryan seemed to be incredibly in tune with his body. The movements of his fingers stayed gentle until Max started to thrust against him, and then they began to move with more force. When Ryan's fingers grazed his prostate, Max cried out and threw his head back as the white-hot flash of pleasure shot through him. A third finger slid into him while he was still riding out the wave of pleasure from his stimulated prostate.

When all three fingers were moving easily, Max forced his eyes back to Ryan. "Enough. I want you." He hissed slightly as Ryan pulled out his fingers, then shifted so he could watch as Ryan slid on the condom and coated his erection with lube. Resting his hands on Ryan's strong chest, he allowed Ryan's hands to move him into position.

"Ready?"

"Yes." Max hissed as he started to ease Ryan's cock inside himself.

"Easy, sweetheart, don't rush yourself." Despite the soothing words, Max could see the strain in the honey-colored eyes. Ryan's hands were running up and down his thighs in a soothing motion, rubbing the strain out of them.

Smiling, Max slowly inched his way down. Even though Ryan had done a marvelous job of stretching him, Max could feel the burn as he was filled. Ryan was wider than the last person who had been inside him. With one last wriggle, Max felt his ass press against Ryan's pelvis. His breath came out in a moan as he settled. "Oh, God, so full."

"You okay?"

"Uh huh." Max nodded and looked down at Ryan. He could feel the older man's hands clenching and unclenching on his hips. From the slight twitches he could feel, Max guessed that Ryan was fighting hard not to move before he was ready. Max got his feet settled on the bed and lifted himself up. When Ryan groaned, he slammed himself back down.

"Shit!"

"So good," Max moaned. Bracing his hands on Ryan's chest, Max started a fast, hard rhythm. After a few thrusts, Ryan was rising up to meet him. Max tilted his body slightly, and Ryan was suddenly hitting his prostate with every thrust. He cried out in pleasure and increased his speed. He could feel Ryan's hands gripping his hips hard enough that he was positive there would be bruises later; he was pretty sure he was leaving marks on Ryan's shoulders, but he couldn't bring himself to care. It felt too good.

"Close. You close?"

"Uh huh." A hand closed around his leaking erection. "Ryan!"

Ryan's hand started stroking up and down his shaft. "That's it, sweetheart. Come for me."

Max could feel his orgasm building. He moaned and thrust his hips into Ryan's hold as he continued to ride his lover. A few more thrusts and he couldn't hold back any longer. He screamed Ryan's name as his orgasm crashed through him and slumped forward against Ryan's firm chest as both Ryan's hands once again took up residence on his hips. Ryan pulled him down twice more and then came with a roar. Max whimpered at the feel of Ryan pulsing inside him.

Hands began to run over his back, and Max cuddled into Ryan's arms.

"You okay, sweetheart?"

"Better than okay." Max moaned as Ryan slipped out of him. "I don't think I can move."

Ryan chuckled softly. "Where's the bathroom up here? I'll clean us up."

"It's attached. That door over there." Max waved his hand in the direction of his bathroom. He could feel Ryan chuckle beneath his cheek. Max made small protesting sounds as he was gently shifted off Ryan's chest.

"Hush, I'll be right back. You don't have to move." Ryan pressed a kiss to his forehead. "I'll be right back."

Max watched Ryan's naked rear as he walked into the bathroom. He was pretty sure he had a stupid smile on his face, but he didn't really care. It had been ages since he had felt so good. When Ryan stepped back into the room with a cloth in his hand, Max felt his cock twitch. The man was just too gorgeous for words.

Ryan crawled back onto the bed and started to gently wash him. Max smiled as Ryan pressed a kiss to each cleaned patch of skin. When Ryan ran the cloth down his crack and then repeated the motion with his tongue, Max didn't know whether to pull away or push closer. He breathed out a sigh when Ryan finally drew away. Ryan climbed into the bed, pulled Max against his chest, and tucked the covers around their shoulders.

Max snuggled into his chest. "This is nice. Stay?"

"I wasn't planning on leaving. Plus, I think it still might be raining outside."

Max laughed softly as Ryan's hands started to roam over his back. "You know, I think that I might start liking storms."

"Really?"

"Yeah. They'll make me think of you."

"I'm glad you'll be thinking of me." Ryan pressed a kiss to his head and pulled him closer. "Trust me. I don't think I'll ever be able to stop thinking about you."

"Can I ask you a question?"

"Anything."

Max bit his lip nervously and tucked his face against Ryan's neck. He really wanted to know the answer to his question, but he was also afraid to ask it. "It's about your kids."

"You want to know how a gay man ended up with two kids."

"Yes. I'm sorry if it's too personal, but I had someone lie to me about women once, and now I'm kinda paranoid."

"It's fine, sweetheart. And after what we just did, asking me about my kids isn't too personal." Ryan shifted around on the bed, settling Max more firmly against his chest. "Jesse, my oldest, was a bit of an accident."

"An accident?"

"Caroline, their mother, is my best friend, and has been since I was a kid. When I told my dad that I was gay, we got in a big fight that ended with me running to Caroline, crying, getting drunk and the two of us ending up in bed together."

"Wow." Max ran his fingers over Ryan's chest. Ryan's answer made him feel a bit better. At least he knew that Ryan wouldn't be chasing after women. "What happened with your dad?"

"We made up the next day, and we're still really close."

"That's good. What about Tyler, the one with the birthday?"

"I was twenty when Jesse was born. He was four when Caroline and Mark got married. They really wanted kids, but Mark was sterile. Caroline asked me for sperm, and I said yes. Mark died in a car crash when Tyler was six."

"How old is Jesse now?"

"Seventeen."

"So, that makes you thirty-seven?"

Ryan chuckled. "Did you ask me that just so you would know how old I am?"

"I may have."

"You could have just asked."

"It was more fun this way." Max grinned and snuggled into the arms that tightened around him. "I'm twenty-six. Just in case you wanted to know."

"I can work with that." Ryan pressed a kiss to his head. "Go to sleep."

Max smiled and flung one of his legs over Ryan's, tucking himself further into his embrace. He knew he wouldn't sleep very long, but a nap before dinner would be good. Especially a nap in the arms of his new lover.

Three Days Later

"Do I look okay?"

"Sweetheart, you look fine," Ryan soothed. He watched as his lover paced in front of the paddock gates. "I don't know why you're so nervous."

"I've never met my boyfriend's children before. I've never had a boyfriend that *had* children before."

"Calm down. They're going to like you."

"How can you be so sure?"

"Because I like you." Ryan smiled at the stunned expression on Max's face. He tilted his head beneath the cowboy hat he was wearing and gave him a kiss. By the time he pulled away, Max had stopped fidgeting. "Better?"

"No, I think I need another one," Max replied. Ryan grinned and kissed him once more. When he drew away from the kiss that was rapidly becoming heated, he spotted a car pulling in.

"Looks like they're here," Ryan said. He pulled away from Max just enough to look like they hadn't just been kissing but threaded his fingers through his lover's when Max started to fidget again. Giving Max a tug, he started to walk towards the car holding his family.

He had some introductions to make.

● ● ●

* * *

Between hiding from the snow in the winter and the grass in the summer, BETHANY BROWN ends up spending a rather absurd amount of time with her trusty laptop Desmond. Yes, she has named her laptop. She's also named her car Blue, but that's neither here nor there. While she hopes to one day be able to support herself by writing full time, she keeps herself fed with various customer service jobs, the most recent of which is at a tuxedo rental shop. Thankfully, spending the day fitting men with tuxedos helps to fuel the writing side of her brain. Other writing help includes: chocolate, ice cream, and movies with cute boys. On bad days, she can usually be found sitting on her couch with a stuffed penguin watching the Donald Strachey movies. She is thrilled to have found a home with Dreamspinner and plans to stick around until she runs out of ideas. Or the Earth's sun implodes. Whichever comes first.

Visit her blog at http://bethanybrown.livejournal.com/.

Weak in the Knees

G.S. Wiley

There are worse ways to be remembered than as the guy who reinforced Zac Efron's knees with a handful of wooden barbecue skewers.

Let me back up a little. I didn't make the legs, or any part of the epic "High School Musical"-themed cake creation, purely for my own amusement. It was commissioned by my clients, Bob and Jessica Kazmienski, for their daughter Anastasia's birthday party.

It was going to be a gala affair. I'd worked with Bob's family before, on the wedding cake for his second marriage to the much younger, much blonder aspiring actress Jessica Finver. I'd worked more with Jessica, really, and together we'd come up with a twelve-tiered creation complete with exquisite sugar flowers and a marzipan bird of paradise that was the talk of Boston society, at least for a few weeks until something newer and shinier caught their eye.

Still, Jessica was satisfied with my work. So satisfied that when it came time for the family's next gala event, my number was at the tip of Mrs. Kazmienski's blood-red gel fingernails.

"It's going to be a memorable party," Jessica told me when she came into my bakery about three days later. "Anastasia deserves a very special tenth birthday."

I'd met Bob Kazmienski's daughter Anastasia before, at her father's wedding. There was nothing sweet about her. She'd been a sullen-looking child then, and she was a sullen-looking child now, albeit one with highlights and a pair of Dolce and Gabbana skinny jeans. "I don't want a cake," she complained, but I took out my portfolio anyway and handed it over to Jessica.

We'd seen a big increase in kids' birthday parties lately. For years, ninety percent or more of our business had been wedding cakes, with the occasional bar or bat mitzvah or christening thrown in for variety. Now, at least a quarter of our clients were hiring us to make bigger and better creations for over-the-top children's birthday parties.

And these parties were truly over-the-top. Forget chocolate fountains and open bars; these pre-pubescent guests were treated to merry-go-rounds and exotic petting zoos, ten-foot balloon sculptures of the Little Mermaid and free-flowing Kool-Aid in all the colors of the rainbow.

"It's insane," my friend Ray Bianchi told me one day, shuddering over his beer. He was the head chef and manager behind Nonna Gianna's Catering, and his business had seen an increase in crazy kids' parties lately, too. "They want everything from hand-rolled sushi cones to barbecued swordfish and blue cheese pizza. I tell them, do you seriously think the kids are going to appreciate this stuff? They'd be just as happy with beanie weenies."

"Maybe you should put that on your menu," I replied, but I sympathized. Ray worked like a madman to keep Nonna Gianna's one of the best catering firms in town.

He was also gorgeous, even though every time I saw him, I itched to flick a razor in the middle of his unibrow. Not that I was likely to get the chance. Ray was straight and currently, as he liked to say, "Between wives. Not literally, unfortunately."

"If I gave it a fancy French name and charged fifty bucks a plate, maybe these mom-zillas would fall for it," he said.

It was a good term for them. Mom-zillas. Jessica Finver Kazmienski was worse than a mom-zilla—she was a stepmom-zilla, and while Anastasia sulked, Jessica flicked through my cake portfolio.

"I like this one," she said, stopping at a photo of the gigantic Kung Fu Panda cake we'd recently done for a girl's fifth birthday. It had been brilliant, but I hoped the kid went somewhere else when it was time for her to get married. There was no way we could ever improve in her mind. "The theme's a little young for you, Stace, but maybe something like that would work."

"I don't want a party," Anastasia replied. "I just want to go to the movies with my friends."

"Don't be silly," Jessica laughed, as if Anastasia had just cracked a joke worthy of Tina Fey. Anastasia turned away, and Jessica's smile evaporated. "Mr. Howard's one of the best cake makers in the city. You're lucky your father and I care this much about you."

"My mom cares about me," Anastasia mumbled in response. "She gave me movie tickets for my birthday."

"We're not discussing your mother," Jessica snapped, then looked at me conspiratorially. "I'm sorry, Spencer. You know what kids are like."

"Sure." I tried not to notice my receptionist, Leah, busting a gut behind her iMac. "Why don't I see what I can come up with, and I'll get back to you?"

"Thank you." Jessica stood up, hooking her Coach purse over her shoulder. "I'm sorry about Anastasia."

"It's all right." As Anastasia stood up, I caught her eye beneath her plastered-down bangs. I winked at her, and she looked a little surprised.

I saw the two of them to the door and then closed it behind them. I watched from behind our vertical blinds as Jessica got into her Corvette, the same blood-red color as her nails. Her mouth was working, and I was sure she was giving Anastasia an earful of abuse.

"Poor kid," Leah sighed. "And I thought my stepmother was bad. All she did was cut my hair with a pair of pinking shears."

"How could you tell?"

She raised her eyebrow all the way into her jagged fuchsia-and-black striped hairline. "Funny."

I leaned against the doorframe and racked my brains. "What do kids like these days?" It seemed like forever since I'd known.

The answer came to me later that evening, when I met Ray for drinks. *"High School Musical."*

"What?" I asked.

"*High School Musical,*" he repeated, swirling his beer in his glass. There was a Red Sox game on the TV above the bar, and he watched Josh Beckett strike out before he clarified, "My nieces are crazy about it. Especially that guy, what's his name, Efron. You know, the twink."

"The what?" I stared at him, wondering who had taken my friend Ray and replaced him with a guy who knew the word "twink".

He looked at me like I was the one who was losing it. "That's what you call them, right? Jailbait guys?"

"Sort of." It was an idea. I'd have to run it by Anastasia first. The poor kid was already stuck with Jessica. I didn't want to give her a birthday cake she hated too. "He's not really my type." I didn't know anything about the movies; I could only summon up a vague mental image of the female starlet who'd done the racy Internet pictures. Not that they'd been at the top of my Google list.

"No?" Ray drained his beer. I did the same, and he held up his hand for another round. The television changed to a commercial for Old Spice, and Ray looked down at me. The unibrow was still there, sitting like a furry caterpillar above his eyes. "Who is your type, then?"

No one, lately. I hadn't dated in months. I didn't have the time. "Butch Italian caterers with eyebrow impairments," I replied, grinning.

It was a joke, the kind of thing Ray and I said all the time. We'd been friends for years, since cooking school. We knew how to make each other laugh.

Except this time, Ray didn't laugh. Instead, his cheeks turned red. I opened my mouth to say something else, but Ray beat me to it. "I gotta hit the john," he told me, standing up.

By the time he got back, the commercial break was over, and we spent the rest of the evening engaged in the exquisite self-torture that was being a Red Sox fan.

THE next morning, I put the finishing touches on my latest wedding cake and sent Leah out to deliver it. While she was gone, I sat at her iMac and Googled the cast of *High School Musical.*

I was in the process of drawing up a rough sketch when a sudden burst of "Für Elise" told me my cell phone was ringing. I reached into my pocket and looked at Ray's number on the screen before putting the phone to my ear.

"Hello?"

"You bastard."

I smiled. "Nice to hear from you too, buddy."

"Did you recommend Nonna Gianna's to Jessica Kazmienski?"

"No." Although if she'd asked, I would have. "Why?"

"She wants us to cater Anastasia's party."

"That's good, isn't it?"

There was a prolonged silence, followed by an inordinately pained sigh. "She wants two hundred caviar dolmades. For a ten-year-old's birthday party."

"Think of the money."

"Think of my sanity," Ray complained, but I could tell he wasn't as devastated as he pretended to be. He did have some common sense, after all, and success with the Kazmienskis would mean nothing but increased bookings from the rest of the Boston glitterati.

"Think of mine," I countered. "I'm being forced to contemplate how to render Vanessa Hudgens's bust in chocolate cake."

Ray laughed. "I'll trade you jobs."

"Would if I could, Ray."

RAY was the chef I always knew I would never be. Even in our culinary school days, he was the kind of guy who instinctively knew a thousand and one uses for eggplant and who could make an elegant three-course dinner out of half a dozen potatoes and a handful of spices. I think he came out of the womb sautéing his own placenta in a nice red wine reduction.

I, on the other hand, was nothing special when it came to appetizers and main courses, but I soon discovered I could decorate a cake like nobody's business.

* * *

After graduation, Ray went to work as a sous-chef in a big, trendy seafood restaurant, and I apprenticed myself to a pastry chef at the Hilton. Ray didn't last long in the restaurant world. He was nobody's sous-chef, and everyone knew it, but Ray didn't have the requisite asshole attitude to make it as a restaurant head chef.

He started his own catering company, employing only people he wanted to work with. I left the Hilton and worked with Nonna Gianna's for a while. Mass-producing carrot cupcakes and pastel-colored petit fours for salesmen's conventions wasn't for me, and I lost interest fast. Which was fine. Getting my own cake shop probably saved my friendship with Ray, and that was worth a lot.

Once Jessica gave me the thumbs-up, and once even Anastasia had given me a weak "Okay, I guess," I started baking the cakes that I would shape into the various *High School Musical* cast members. I usually stacked the cakes to the required height and then chiseled them into shape like a woodcarver. Since it was a big project, I had Leah help me, and when our part-timer Christie came in the next day, I was going to get her on the job too.

Leah and I did as much as we could, then we locked up the bakery for the day. Leah got onto her bicycle and headed home. I was about to get into my uber-sexy white GMC van, the one with "Spencer Howard Cakes" silkscreened above our phone number, when my cell phone rang.

"Hi, Ray."

I expected more bitching about the Kazmienski order. Instead, he said, "Could you come by the kitchen?"

"Right now?" I glanced at my watch. I had a cat at home, Chairman Meow, who turned into a dictator worthy of his name if he didn't get his Meaty Whiskas in a timely manner.

"Yeah. Thanks. See you soon, Spencer," he said, and hung up.

Nonna Gianna's kitchen was in the middle of a warehouse district, about five miles from the bakery. When I arrived, I parked the van next to Ray's Mazda Miata and went up to the door.

Since Nonna Gianna's wasn't a restaurant, and Ray rarely entertained guests there, I expected the door to be locked. Instead, it swung open, and I went into his industrial kitchen.

Ray was wearing his chef's whites, standing talking to a good-looking black man I assumed was a client. I kept on assuming that until Ray turned, smiled like he hadn't seen me in years, and kissed me.

It was a good kiss, too. Right on the mouth, with no holding back. Ray tasted like expensive hors d'oeuvres, probably something involving rare cheese and expensive smoked meats. When he pulled away, he left me torn between feeling turned on and feeling like I'd been hit with a baseball bat.

Ray smiled at his visitor and said, "This is my partner, Spencer. He's a baker."

"Ah." The man smiled at us. He was wearing round, gold-rimmed glasses and a suit that looked like it had come out of a magazine—and not the Target flyer I usually shopped from, either. "Like in the nursery rhyme."

"I'm sorry?" He could have been speaking Greek, for all the sense I could get from any of this. Or Italian.

"'Rub a dub dub'," the man continued, winking, which did nothing to help matters. "'Three men in a tub'."

"Are you a candlestick maker?" I asked.

"We really need to get going," Ray interrupted suddenly. I glanced over at him. His face was bright red. "I've got a job tonight." He looked at me meaningfully. He didn't, as far as I knew, but I didn't feel in a position to argue with him.

"Of course." The other man nodded, then reached into his inside pocket. He pulled out a card, which he handed to Ray. "I'll be in town for the next few days. Give me a call if you have time." He beamed at me. "Nice to meet you, Spencer." I shook his hand and, just like that, the man was gone.

I waited until I heard the front door close. Ray and I stood in silence for another long moment after that. Finally, he sighed deeply, leaned against his work counter, and said, "I'm really sorry about that."

I wasn't. I was a lot of things, but sorry wasn't one. "What was... I mean, why...."

Ray ran a hand through his hair. "I've got to level with you, Spence."

"Please do."

He looked at me steadily. "I slept with that guy."

• • •

That didn't feel like getting hit by a baseball bat. It felt like getting run over by a bulldozer. "What?"

"It was a long time ago. After I got divorced from Monica." About three years ago. I'd known Ray three years ago. I knew Monica too. I made their wedding cake. "It was just a one-night thing. I was drunk. I was feeling down, and I thought trying something new might make me feel better."

"Did it?" My voice sounded more bitter than I'd intended.

"No. I never expected to see him again."

"So you thought you'd use me to get him off your back?" The numbness was wearing off, only to be replaced by a sick feeling in the pit of my stomach.

"It wasn't like that," Ray said.

"Okay." I nodded. "So what was it like?"

Ray didn't say anything. He stared at his wall of knives on pegs. There were a lot of things I wanted to say, but I didn't. Instead, I turned and left the kitchen, letting the door slam shut behind me.

MY APARTMENT was in Fenway, near the corner of Brookline and Park Drive. I thought about making a detour to a South End gay bar on the way home, but I decided against it. That would only make things worse.

Instead, I went home, where Chairman Meow waited on top of the kitchen cupboards, staring at me with a malevolent eye until I opened the bag of Meaty Whiskas and filled his dish.

My cell phone rang three times on my way home, and my landline rang twice when I got there. I ignored all of them. After about an hour, as I sat in front of the television with a slightly friendlier cat by my side, there was a knock on my front door.

I considered ignoring that too. It was only when Ray called, "For fuck's sake, Spencer, I know you're in there," that I stood up and went over. The last thing I needed was old Mrs. O'Malley next door or the yuppie couple down the hall getting an earful of our business.

When I opened the door, Ray was standing in the hallway, a paper bag of food in his arms. "What do you want, Ray?"

"For you to stop acting like…." He hesitated.

"Like what?" A drama queen? A screaming homo? Ray had never called me anything like that, but there was obviously a lot I didn't know about him.

"Like my ex-wife." He sighed. He'd changed out of his chef's uniform, I noticed, into his usual jeans, T-shirt and Red Sox cap. "Look, I'm sorry for dragging you into my shit, but I swear, he wouldn't take no for an answer. I only got the idea to call you when he asked if I had another guy." He held up his grocery bag. "I brought you dinner to make up for it. I know you usually eat crap not fit for the cat."

"The cat has very discerning tastes," I told him, but I stepped back and let him in. Ray made a beeline for my little, woefully underused kitchen and strapped on my Kiss the Cook apron.

He made chicken fettuccine alfredo, one of Nonna Gianna's specialties, including homemade alfredo sauce and day-old garlic bread. He'd also brought a bottle of decent white wine and a six-pack of even better beer, and after we loaded the dishwasher, we sat down in front of the TV.

There was a lot I wanted to ask him. We avoided the subject all through dinner, but now, with the baseball game on in the background, I looked at Ray and asked, "Why didn't you tell me sooner?"

He didn't take his eyes off the television, but his face turned red as he took a long drink from his can of beer. "Nothing to tell," Ray said, finally. "I was feeling down because of Monica, I did something crazy, and I lived to regret it. End of story."

There was clearly a lot more to the story than that, but I knew I wasn't going to get anything out of him unless he wanted to tell me. If I pushed, it would just clam him up further. So I let it go, just like I'd let a lot of things go in the name of keeping our friendship intact.

When we first met, I was attracted to Ray. Who wouldn't be? I never made much of a secret of it. I was young and foolish; he was good-natured and open-minded. We palled around all through cooking school, and when my parents decided to go to Hawaii one Christmas, Ray invited me to his grandmother's for Christmas Eve so I wouldn't be alone.

Ray's grandmother, the Nonna Gianna he named the catering company after, was a sweet little bun-faced old Sicilian with a tiny house in the North

End. Her entire family had descended on her every Christmas Eve since time immemorial, and most of them had already been there when Ray and I arrived.

Christmas Eve had never been a big deal in my family. Christmas itself was usually seen as nothing more than an excuse for my mother and grandmother to conduct their ongoing cold war in a festive setting, but things were clearly different for the Bianchis.

"La Vigilia", as Ray explained to me before we got there, was traditionally celebrated with a meatless meal, but that didn't hold Nonna Gianna back any. She'd made mountains of food, and I was helping myself to seafood salad and clam linguine at the buffet when Nonna came up to me.

She was about four-foot-eight, and when she beckoned me closer, I had to stoop to hear her. She said something emphatic in Italian, gripping my forearm as she spoke. She was smiling, so I wasn't worried that I might have committed some social faux pas by eating my linguine before my salad. I didn't, however, have the slightest clue what she'd said.

I smiled back, which I hoped was a suitable answer, until Ray's cousin Angie helpfully stepped in. "Nonna says she's pleased to finally meet you, and that anyone who makes Ray happy is welcome in her home."

"Thank you." I nodded at Nonna, who was still gripping my arm. Just as I wondered how to politely disengage her, one of Ray's uncles called, "Mama! Where's the cannoli?" and Nonna puttered back into the kitchen.

Ray's family was the loudest and most entertaining group of people I ever spent Christmas Eve with. It was well after midnight by the time Ray and I left, clutching the plastic containers of salad and pasta Nonna had thrust on us on our way out the door. When we got to his car, a 1988 Chevy Monte Carlo with a black plastic bag instead of a rear window, Ray put the key in the ignition but didn't start the engine.

"What's going on, Spencer?" he finally asked, looking at me.

"What?" As far as I knew, he was going to drop me off at home, and I'd get some sleep before making a pilgrimage to my grandmother's sterile, bare condo the next morning.

"You know I'm straight." I did. "So why does my family think we're dating?"

"Who?" I stared at him. "You and me?" Ray nodded. "I have no idea, Ray."

"No? Angie says Nonna even welcomed you into the family. You didn't think that might have been the moment to mention something?"

I frowned at him. "I had no idea what the woman was saying. Angie just told me she was happy to meet me."

"Yeah, well, she was. So happy, she's already planning the meal for our non-legal commitment ceremony. We're having lobster."

"That's my fault?" I looked out the window. Snow was falling onto the cobblestoned streets around Nonna Gianna's neighborhood and onto the badly dented hood of Ray's car. "They're your family. Why didn't you say something to them?"

"Oh, I did."

"Then what are we arguing about?" I looked over at Ray. He was staring out the window, but all of a sudden, I knew exactly what.

"Nothing." He slammed down the clutch and peeled away from the curb with his tires squealing, narrowly missing a lamppost.

We drove to my apartment in silence. I thought about saying something, but even then, I knew it was a bad idea to break into someone else's closet, especially if you're planning on staying friends with them afterwards. "Merry Christmas, Spencer," Ray said when he dropped me off.

"Merry Christmas, Ray," I replied. I watched him drive away; then I unlocked the door and went upstairs.

A few days later, Ray started dating Monica Hauptmann, another of the cooking school students, and we began to spend a lot less time together.

AT THE cake shop, our part-time decorator Christie rolled out the fondant while I carved three-foot teenage figures out of the piled-up cakes. Christie was an artist, a sculptor who made extra cash working in the medium of dessert. I was glad to have her around for this project; faces were never my strong point, and the last thing I wanted was for Anastasia's birthday guests to spend their valuable party time wondering why her cake was shaped like the Bee Gees, including an African-American Andy Gibb.

While we worked, Christie told me about an exhibit she was mounting in a small new local gallery. "It's a great place. The owner's an old friend of mine from New York." She glanced over at me as I whittled an approximate shape for Zac Efron's body. How they were going to dismember these people to serve the cake—and how Anastasia and her guests were going to divvy up the body parts—wasn't my problem. Most of the people who bought our cakes didn't plan to eat them, anyway. They were more like an ice sculpture: an ephemeral decoration.

"You'd really like him," Christie went on, draping one section of the fondant over the nearest figure. "He's just like you."

"Devastatingly handsome and fantastically successful?"

She laughed. "More like artistic."

Normally, I would have let the conversation go at that. But what was I waiting for? "Well, give him my number then," I said.

"Really?" Christie glanced up from her work.

I felt a slight tremor in my stomach, but I put that down to going too long without any kind of date. "Yeah," I said, before I changed my mind.

"Okay. I'll do that." She wrapped the fondant around the cake and went over to the drawers to get her decorating kit.

As well as Anastasia's birthday cake, we had two wedding cakes and a bar mitzvah cake to work on. I left the *High School Musical* cast in Christie's capable hands and spent my afternoon crafting sugar flowers and piping blue and white icing into a geometric Star of David.

One of the wedding cakes was for a small courthouse ceremony, a second wedding between a divorced bride and groom, and I dropped it off at the low-key reception venue on my way home. Since I happened to be in the neighborhood of Ray's kitchen, I stopped off to say hi before I continued on my way.

Ray was hard at work, as usual, stuffing mushrooms, rolling cannelloni, and doing all the other things that kept him in business. I waved at him from the reception area and was about to leave him to it when he called, "Wait up a minute, Spencer."

I waited, and he came out to see me. "What's up?"

Ray furrowed his eyebrows, crumpling his forehead at the same time. "I need to see you later."

"Okay." This wasn't unusual, but Ray looked like he had something serious on his mind. "Is everything all right?"

He sighed, but he said, "Sure. I'll come by your place when I'm done here."

"Sounds good."

He looked at me for a long moment, like he wanted to say something else. He didn't. He smiled a little; then he turned around and went back into his gleaming chrome kitchen.

Chairman Meow was waiting when I got home. I filled his bowl, then warmed up a microwave meal for myself. As I ate the cardboard "beef stew", I wondered what groundbreaking announcement Ray was going to make when he came over.

I didn't have long to wonder. Ray showed up at my apartment barely an hour later. I opened the door and, with a determined look on his face, Ray stepped inside, put his arms around me, and kissed me.

It caught me off guard, but not as much as last time. I pushed him away. "Is this about that guy again?"

He shook his head. There was an expression I'd never seen in his eyes, and when he spoke, there was no trace of hesitation in his voice. "No. This is about me being an idiot for way too long." And he kissed me again.

I'd like to say that I knew better, that I put the brakes on until we'd had an in-depth, detailed conversation about Ray's motivations, his sudden change of heart, and the possible ramifications to our friendship if we continued down this path. I didn't. Instead, I kissed Ray back. Then, under the watchful eye of Chairman Meow, I yanked him toward the bedroom.

I was an idiot too.

AFTER so many years of wanting what I thought I would never have, I half-expected the actual deed to be a disappointment. It wasn't. Sex with Ray was every bit as amazing as I'd imagined it would be all those lonely nights with nothing to keep me company but the cat and my pervasive sense of guilt over jacking off to mental images of my best friend. Afterward, as I lay beside him in my rarely-made king-sized bed, I felt content and at peace in a way I hadn't for a very long time.

It lasted all of fifteen minutes. Then Ray sat up abruptly, as if he'd been stabbed in the back by a spring. My heart sank. My mattress wasn't that bad.

"What is it?"

Ray didn't look at me. "I'm sorry, Spencer."

I felt an icy chill down my back, like someone had left the window open on a cold Boston morning. "What?"

Ray shook his head. He stood up, the mattress shifting as he removed his weight, and bent to pick up his jeans. "I can't do this."

The chill disappeared, replaced by a hot, pounding pain in the middle of my forehead. "Are you fucking kidding me, Ray?"

"I'm sorry." The confidence he'd had earlier seemed to have evaporated. He wouldn't even look at me. "I don't know what I was thinking. I'm straight."

"It didn't seem like that five minutes ago." Unless Ray's definition of "straight" was broader than most people's.

Ray shook his head, and his expression told me everything I needed to know. I refused to burst into tears. Instead, I was proud of the steadiness of my voice when I said, "You need to get out of here." Ray nodded. He was already half-dressed. "I mean, for good. I can't do this anymore."

I expected the words to hurt more than they did. We'd been friends for years, but Ray was damaged. He had problems I couldn't fix, issues I was in no way qualified to deal with. It was better for both of us if we stopped this craziness now.

Ray obviously knew it too. "Okay," he said. I watched as he put on his Red Sox cap. He glanced back at me. "I'm really sorry."

"Goodbye, Ray." I felt like I did when I came to the end of a favorite project, a cake I'd spent months designing or a recipe that had taken years to perfect. There was the same sense of sadness, although losing Ray didn't come with any of the satisfaction of a job well done.

I waited until I heard Ray leave and close the front door behind him. Then, with a sigh, I reached for my cell phone. I was about to call Christie and ask for her gallery friend's number, but I couldn't quite bring myself to hit "send". Instead, I tossed the phone onto my bedside table and buried my head beneath the covers.

THE Kazmienskis lived in a palatial Commonwealth Avenue townhouse, a nine-million-dollar wedding present from Bob to Jessica. They were both there when I brought Anastasia's cake over, him in a three-piece suit and her in a white Vera Wang gown that looked suspiciously like a modified wedding dress. The birthday girl was there as well, looking sullen in a red mini-dress and child-sized stiletto heels. She brightened a little when Christie and I brought in her birthday cake and even smiled when her father said, "See, princess? We told you the cake would turn out great."

It had; even I could admit that. The three-foot tall replicas of Zac Efron, Vanessa Hudgens, Ashley Tisdale and Corbin Bleu were gathered around a large orange basketball on which I'd written "Happy Birthday, Anastasia."

Carefully, we carried the cake's parts into the kitchen and assembled it on the marble counter. We weren't the only ones there; two waiters in white aprons fluttered around, and a few of Ray's people were already setting out covered trays of hors d'oeuvres. I ignored them.

Anastasia examined the cake, touching the fondant faces and the carefully piped hair, while her stepmother said, "This is truly exquisite. I can't wait to see the look on everyone's faces. Can you?" Anastasia shook her head. Jessica put one of her manicured hands, the one with the glinting diamond the size of an eyeball, on Anastasia's shoulder. She didn't shrug it off.

Before I could congratulate myself for bringing a feuding stepmother and stepdaughter together through the medium of cake, Jessica continued, "You'll have to bring photographs to show your friends at school."

Immediately, Anastasia stiffened. "I'd have liked it better if I could have invited them to my party."

Jessica laughed and shook her head, as if this were a strange, perplexing concept. "This party isn't for your friends, Anastasia. They wouldn't appreciate it."

There was a commotion in the hallway, and Bob called, "Jessica? Where do you want the string quartet?"

"In the foyer by the grand piano," Jessica replied, disappearing in the direction of the hallway.

Normally, after we dropped off the cake and set it up, our job was done. This time I felt a strange compulsion to hang around. I was endlessly fascinated by parties like this. I didn't have any children, of course, or even any nieces and nephews to compare with, but when I was a kid, a great birthday party was watching *E.T.* on VHS videocassette followed by gorging on a sickly-sweet chocolate cake and brightly-colored marshmallows in little ice cream cones. I didn't know exactly what the Nonna Gianna's team was cooking up here, but it didn't smell like marshmallows in ice cream cones.

Ray was the boss; he didn't typically come out to the parties himself, so I thought I was safe to stay for a while. I was wrong. Moments later, a familiar voice said, "Bring the caviar dolmades in from the van, Jolene."

I turned toward the French doors, but it was too late to make an escape. Ray came in, dressed to the nines in his chef's whites and black-checkered pants.

He paused when he saw me, but he didn't seem surprised. "Hi, Spencer."

I looked at him. "Hi."

We hadn't seen each other in a week. I missed him, of course. More than once, I'd left the bakery with the intention of stopping by Nonna Gianna's only to remind myself Ray and I weren't friends anymore. We couldn't be.

I had expected Ray to phone me repeatedly, the way he usually did after an argument, but there had been nothing. Now, we stood in silence for a few moments, staring at each other across the Kazmienskis' marble counters, until Ray said, "The cake looks great. Really turned out well."

"Thanks."

Around us, Ray's staff arranged hors d'oeuvres, and waiters filled champagne flutes on silver trays. "How are you?" Ray asked, moving to let one of his staff members pass with a box of canapés.

"I'm all right."

"Excuse me, boss." A woman in a white apron came up behind Ray, balancing a tray of rolled-up grape leaves stuffed with caviar.

She slipped past him, holding the tray above her head, and Ray said, "Look, can we talk for a minute?"

"I guess."

The Kazmienskis had two terraces, one behind the kitchen and the other on the roof. From the music and the voices floating down from above, I guessed the party was getting started on the rooftop terrace, and I opened the French doors to the ground-floor patio. Ray followed me out.

It was a square made from reddish-brown paving tiles. There were a few overflowing terracotta plant pots, as well as a flower mosaic made from shiny stones inlaid between the tiles. I sat on a carved stone bench next to a cherub-bedecked fountain, listening to the trickling water and the traffic on the other side of the walls.

Ray stood for a moment, then joined me, perching on the edge of the bench. "I know I was a grade-A asshole," Ray began. It was as good a start as any, I guessed. "But I've been doing a lot of thinking over the last couple of weeks." I didn't say anything. "I also spoke to my grandmother."

I looked up. Ray smiled. "What did she say?" I hadn't seen the real-life Nonna Gianna in years, not since that Christmas Eve.

"That the only man I should feel ashamed of being is one who's afraid to accept who he is."

"That's deep."

"That's Nonna."

Ray reached out, placing his hand on my shoulder. My stomach flipped a little, but I tried to push that aside. "I can't get involved with a closet case, Ray." Not even if he was my best friend. Especially not if he was my best friend.

"What if I promised you I've finally wrenched the door open?"

"Then I'd just worry you're going to slam it shut again." It wasn't like he hadn't done it before.

"If I do," Ray said, "I can guarantee you Nonna will hunt me down and do terrible things with her knitting needles." He smiled. "Worse still, she might refuse to let me use her name for the business anymore."

I laughed. I wanted to believe him. I got a little closer to it when he leaned forward and kissed me on the lips, right there in the Kazmienskis' little garden oasis on Commonwealth Avenue.

"Spencer! You'd better get in here!"

* * *

I pulled away when I heard Christie's voice from inside the house. Looking through the glass doors, I saw a group of Ray's staff circled around our cake.

With Ray following closely behind, I went back into the house and came face-to-face with a damaged cake.

"I'm sorry." A woman, the one Ray had called Jolene, looked stricken. "I didn't realize it was there." Corbin Bleu, I noticed, had a slightly squashed hairstyle, while Zac Efron wobbled unsteadily on his platform.

"There's been an accident," Christie explained, her voice as panicked as if we were talking about a child.

"That's all right." I'd seen worse. Lived with worse, in fact, when a top-heavy seven-tier wedding cake began to shift like an earthquake-stricken apartment building moments before the newlyweds came into the reception room. I pressed my hands against Zac Efron's backside, not an unenviable position, and said, "Get me some long skewers. Wooden ones."

The guilty-looking Jolene scrambled for skewers, while Ray looked at me meaningfully. "Seems like he's a little weak in the knees," he commented with one of his dazzling smiles.

Zac wasn't the only one.

The cake was saved, and Christie and I left the party soon after, just as a deliveryman brought an eight-foot tall bouquet of Mylar balloons to the door. Ray's van was parked behind ours, and he came out with us.

"Feel like a beer and a Red Sox game a little later?" he asked.

It was a risk, I thought, but so was building an extravagant cake. So was life in general. And Ray was worth it, unibrow and all.

I nodded. "See you then."

In front of Christie, the balloon deliveryman, and a couple of well-dressed party guests, Ray kissed me again.

It wasn't a passionate, adolescent-style makeout session; it wasn't a show. It was just a kiss, like one member of a stable, adult couple might give to another. I beamed all the way back to the bakery.

When we arrived, our receptionist Leah was at her desk, talking to an enormously pregnant woman in big designer sunglasses. "Here's Spencer now," Leah said, smiling as we came in. "Spencer, this is Ms. Callan. She'd like to order a cake for her son's first birthday party."

I smiled at her. "When is the little guy's big day?"

Ms. Callan put a hand on her belly. "About a year from now. My Caesarean is scheduled for next Wednesday." I blinked. "His father and I want it to be the best first birthday ever," she went on. "We've been planning it since before he was conceived. We've already booked the marching band and the magicians."

I nodded. "Of course you have." If she asked for catering recommendations, I thought as I led her to my desk, I would definitely mention Nonna Gianna's.

I couldn't wait to see Ray's face when he was booked to make foie gras puree and infant-friendly antipasto for a child not yet born.

G.S. WILEY is a writer, reader, sometime painter, and semi-avid scrapbooker who lives in Canada.

Visit G.S.'s web site at http://www.gswiley.com.

$\mathcal{S}hirt$
Amy Lane

CHAPTER ONE

Ryan hated parties. He really did.

He smiled nervously and looked around the handsome remodeled Victorian house that his co-worker had invited him to. It was a nice house—lots of niches and corners and places under stairwells, and dark paneling. Someday, when he'd gotten a few raises at the law firm, maybe he'd have enough money to buy something like this. But right now, his only hope was to flee the damned thing with dignity.

If he were really lucky, he might escape the predatory blonde with the big tits and fuck-me pumps too.

John, the partner in the firm who had invited him, handed him a beer and looked good-naturedly at the paralegal who'd nearly managed to corner Ryan at least three times.

"I thought you were going to bring a date, buddy!" John had to talk loudly over the music, and he was a little drunk, so he was shouting more than necessary. But that was okay; he was a nice guy. Built like a fire hydrant, steady as a rock, and totally in love with the wife who had decorated his home in cutting edge and red and black velvet, if there was a "party guy" at Ryan's firm, John was it. Unfortunately, he also kept trying to be cupid.

Ryan shrugged. He'd actually planned on bringing a date—really. But Tanya had been… well, they'd been dating for over two months, and she was beginning to hint that she maybe wanted to stay the night, and really, the idea wasn't doing a lot for him.

"She couldn't make it," he lied, feeling lame.

"Dude, you're a god—it's not like you couldn't find another date on a moment's notice!" John's tipsy grin was camaraderie at its best, and Ryan flushed and tried to shrug off the compliment.

"Yeah, but all work and no play leaves Ryan a horny bastard," he quipped before draining his beer, and John laughed.

"That's the truth—you leave the rest of us in your dust!"

Ryan shrugged and blushed. He was a hard worker, and he loved his job. He should—he'd worked his entire life to get through law school; he'd damned well better not lose his focus now! But talking about his ambition was not the way to make friends.

"Dude, where's the head? I've gotta take a leak!"

Best excuse in the world, and the only reason he'd polished off two imported brews in ten minutes. Unfortunately, he had to use it on John, who he liked, and not on Jonesing Jenny, who scared him. John directed him to the guest bathroom, and Ryan dodged through the adjoining bedroom and into the blissful quiet of the Monet-colored washroom with some serious relief.

He whipped out his equipment and tilted his head back as he emptied his bladder. He hadn't lied to John, and between the quiet and the long, blissful piss, he started thinking he might be able to make it through the party without making a total ass out of himself. At least that's what he thought until he heard the rustling behind the shower curtain and the bold young voice behind him.

"Jesus—that's got to be the biggest cock I've ever seen!"

Ryan was so surprised he almost whipped it around and covered the bathroom, but he managed to keep all movement to a glance over his shoulder.

"Uhhh…."

The kid was younger than he was, early twenties, maybe, and he had one of those long-haired wispy man 'dos which used a whole lot of hair-spray to hang artfully over his eyes. He had a bold nose, Slavic cheekbones, dark olive skin, and light gray eyes.

Ryan's heart rose to his throat. God, he was pretty.

The kid grinned, showing slightly crooked front teeth. "Wow. Not only is it big—I think it likes me!"

Ryan flushed, shook himself out—and yes, he was getting a little hard. Really. Two months with Tanya's hand down his pants, and this kid made him hard? Wasn't *that* interesting.

"I think it's just relieved to get away from Jonesing Jenny," he managed to say with a reasonably steady voice.

"Is that the paralegal with the short skirt and the big tits?" The kid peeked around the shower curtain some more, and Ryan managed to tuck his body away and zip up his fly.

"Yeah." Ryan moved to the sink to wash his hands and risked a look at himself. John had called him a "god," and looking in the mirror, he suddenly hoped he was at least presentable. Brown-blond hair, brown eyes, small nose, high cheekbones—pretty, in a boy-next-door way. He worked out; his body was decent. Maybe it wasn't *too* embarrassing to be spotted naked by the guy in the shower. If Ryan swung that way. Which he didn't think he did but was starting to wonder about now.

"Did she go after you?" Ryan asked after a pause long enough to be awkward. He turned around and found that the kid had climbed out of the shower after all, and was now standing eye-to-eye with him.

"I told her I was gay," the kid said with a tip of his head that let Ryan know it was the truth. "But she didn't believe me, and now I'm here."

"I...." Ryan caught his breath. The kid smelled like mint and some sort of man's cologne that Ryan had never liked for himself, but it was doing something for him now. He swallowed hard. "I should have thought of that," he said at last, lamely.

A wicked smile appeared, and a hand—tanned and long-fingered, with big knuckles—splayed under the T-shirt Ryan had forgotten to tuck in and over his trim stomach. "Is it true?"

❊ ❊ ❊

"I didn't think so," Ryan breathed, but his cock was jumping to life, and the thought zoomed through his head like an airplane banner—he suddenly had something to tell Tanya that didn't sound like a lie.

The kid leaned forward, keeping that stroking hand on Ryan's jumping stomach. His lips were softer than Ryan imagined, and his breath was sweet, even as he pulled back. "My name's Scott Davidovitch," he murmured, and Ryan tried not to make a lame sound like a whimper or something.

"Ryan Connors," he said back. Would it be too needy to kiss him back? Was there a code or a dating ritual he'd be violating? God, Ryan could barely date women… what was he going to do now that he'd found out he liked men?

Scott solved the problem by leaning in again and kissing harder, kissing until Ryan's mouth opened and Scott's tongue slipped in. Ryan groaned. Oh… oh, God… he tasted so good. Men tasted good—who knew?

"So, Ryan," Scott murmured, taking Ryan's hips in both his hands and jerking their groins into intimate contact, "want to go somewhere and see if it's true?"

Ryan groaned again, and Scott kept kissing, and somehow Ryan thought they didn't need to go anywhere but this little bathroom for his entire life to change.

CHAPTER TWO

BY ALL reports, it shouldn't have worked. A casual party hook-up, a guy coming out of a closet he didn't even know he was in—well, it was a poor recipe for relationship success, that was for damned sure.

But that one (wondrous, revealing, amazing, sensual, spectacular) night with Scott turned into two, which turned into figuring out how this whole sex thing worked and then into seeing each other most nights of the week to decide which parts they liked best. It turned into a dinner with Scott's parents and Scott moving his shit into Ryan's apartment. It turned into Scott transferring to a different Starbucks (they had medical, he said; that's why he worked there) so he could ride his bike and sell his car and maybe take some night courses in management.

It turned into clean HIV tests, sex bareback, ultimate trust, late breakfasts on Sunday morning, passionate sex some nights of the week and cuddling on others, sharing the remote, sharing the rent, and one memorable week of nursing each other through the intestinal flu. And another memorable week of vacation in San Francisco, where they saw plays, toured the bay, sat on the beach, and necked like teenagers.

It turned into a relationship, and then it turned into a serious relationship, and then it turned into Ryan asking his parents to come visit, stay in their guest room and meet the guy he was planning to spend the rest of his life with.

And they said yes. And he was picking them up from the airport. And now, goddammit, thanks to a new case and an emergency staff meeting, he was fucking late.

"I'm so sorry!" he called, running up the landing and into the apartment. It wasn't a Victorian house, but it was a little more spacious than a single one-bedroom in one of those warrens in the Howe-Hurley area, and Scott had loved it.

* * *

Right now it was too big, and his shit wasn't where he wanted it.

"Don't worry…" Scott called from the kitchen, but Ryan was already racing into their bedroom and hauling his shirt over his head before he even unbuttoned the neck or the cuffs.

"Oh, shit!" Ryan swore, toeing off his shoes while he got even more hopelessly entangled in the blue oxford shirt. "Shit, shit, shit, shit, shit… I'm *so* fucking late!"

"Don't worry," Scott said again, and his voice was closer, so he must have come into the bedroom. "Your parents called, and…."

"Shit!" Ryan couldn't move. His arms were over his head and his sleeves were mostly inside out, but the buttons at his wrists wouldn't let the damned thing off. The same thing had happened at his neck. The entire plain blue oxford shirt had suddenly turned into a straightjacket and blinding mask from hell, and Ryan was laid out on his stomach across the bed trying to wriggle out of it.

Scott was laughing his ass off.

"Oh, come on, Scotty, would you help me?" Ryan's voice was muffled through the shirt. He was helpless, barefoot, and unable even to wiggle off the bed without ending up on his knees.

"I don't know," Scott laughed. "I like you like that."

"You only like me like this when I'm naked," Ryan retorted, although, actually, he had never bottomed for Scott. They'd played with some things, plugs, fingers, lubricant, but somehow he was still in love with sucking Scotty off, licking his asshole until Scott begged, and then fucking him until they both came. Ryan had spent his entire life getting what he wanted; Scott liked that about him. So, in spite of the fact that Scott knew more about sex, it was Ryan, who knew more about life, who ended up leading.

But Scott never complained, and Ryan never asked for anything more or different. Ryan was still just surprised that Scotty—beautiful, playful Scotty, with that wicked grin and a head full of things he still wanted to be— would love a stodgy, almost twenty-eight-year-old lawyer who hadn't even known he was gay!

Which was no help now, as Ryan wriggled on the bed trying to free himself. He felt warmth, closeness, and Scott's hand made its way to Ryan's ass and rubbed it through his slacks. "I *could* like you this way," he purred, and Ryan choked off a sound of exasperation.

"Of course you bring this up now, when my parents are probably waiting at the airport," he wailed. It was close inside his shirt, and uncomfortable, and disorienting. He wanted out; he wanted freedom; he wanted air; he wanted….

Scott's hands went to his belt and dragged down his slacks and his underwear with them. Suddenly warm lips and a hint of tongue were making their way down Ryan's naked spine, and Ryan couldn't even push Scott away with a good natured laugh.

"Scotty…" he whined, and then Scott's tongue touched the dimple where his spine ended and his ass-cheeks started, and suddenly there was nothing but the whine.

"Mmmm…" Scott murmured. "I *like* this position!"

Ryan tried reason. "Scott—my parents are coming. If I don't get there, they're going to take a cab, so we need to be up and dressed before that happens, okay?"

Scott's hands cupped Ryan's ass, one on each side, and Ryan thrashed around in his restraining shirt as his cheeks were parted by two long, big-knuckled thumbs.

"Well, baby," Scott purred, "if you want to make sure you get out of this in time, you're going to have to do *exactly* what I say."

"Scott?" Oh, *shit!* Ryan couldn't fucking move. All he could see was the lamp-lit faded blue of the shirt. Scott used his shoulders to shove Ryan's legs farther apart, and Ryan's toes scrabbled hard on the carpet. He had to throw himself farther on the bed to keep from doing a move he hadn't done since he was five.

Scott's tongue—his wicked, wicked, evil tongue—traced its way down Ryan's cleft, from the top of it, down, down, as Ryan whimpered, and then….

Ryan groaned and bit down on his undershirt as Scott's tongue swiped his asshole and then went lower, to his taint and then the underside of his balls.

"Scott…" he grunted, struggling to remember why it was so urgent that he should get this shirt off and go somewhere.

* * *

277

"I told you," Scott said, his voice muffled by Ryan's body, "not—" lick—"until—" oh, God, right in his hole—"you—" up to his crease again— "come," and then back down to Ryan's hole.

Ryan's breath and mouth were making his shirt damp, and his eyes were squeezed shut in complete arousal. He was pinned, trapped; he couldn't do a damned thing about what Scott was doing—except trust him, with four months of flurried relationship between them.

There was a popping sound as Scott sucked a finger into his mouth, and then an intrusion—just a slight one—in Ryan's entrance.

Then Scott was gone, and Ryan was just laying there, his cock thrusting into the mattress, his body spread and vulnerable, and his crease tingling from drying in the air.

He couldn't see *anything,* but he could hear. Scott was rummaging through a drawer. Not just *any* drawer, but their end table drawer. Their *special* drawer, with stuff in it that they hadn't even tried yet.

Ryan heard some more rustling, and then a shadow cast itself near his head. When Scott next spoke, it was close enough to Ryan's ear for the heat of his breath to penetrate the cloth cocoon that had Ryan so imprisoned.

"Remember the word, Ry?"

Ryan's mouth went dry, and his cock got even harder. In the early days, when Ryan had known nothing about sex with a man and only the most conservative things about sex in general, they had come up with a safe word. It wasn't so much for BDSM, which they didn't do much of yet, but more for Ryan's comfort level.

"You know," Ryan said after a second date meal of pizza and soda, "last night was an anomaly. I really don't know what the fuck we're doing in bed, or what I want, or... how to have sex with a guy or anything." He was blushing furiously, but... oh, God!... their first night had been magic, and he didn't want to disappoint Scott, not now, not when he wanted so much more from him than to come once and swallow some spunk.

Scott's bleached hair was suddenly flipped out of his eyes, and his gray eyes searched Ryan's in the dim glow of the bedroom lamp.

"You know everything," he said with a smile, and Ryan rolled his eyes. To Scott, who hadn't been all that enthusiastic about college or finding a

direction, it must have seemed true. Ryan knew how to make a decision and follow through—but touching the flesh of another human being?

"I know about my job," *Ryan clarified, feeling stupid, "but not... you know...." Oh, God, would he ever stop blushing? And to make matters worse, he was getting hard.*

"Sex?" Scott asked cheekily. "Sucking? Fucking? Getting laid?"

That didn't help. "Yeah." He literally squirmed where he sat, crosslegged on the navy blue comforter on the bed where they'd made love the night before. Scott smiled, a sly smile that told Ryan he was glad to know he had something to bring to the table besides a pretty face. Ryan didn't have the words to tell him that he held everything in the back of his cheeky little throat.

"I'm going to lick you," Scott said bluntly, that wicked smile beautiful and evil in the dim light. "I'm going to take off your pants and put your cock in my mouth and suck you into the back of my throat until you grab my hair and scream. Do you have a problem with that?"

"Ungh...."

Scott came closer and grinned, and Ryan wished he had something, anything, more intelligent to say to this beautiful man who seemed to have the key to fantasies Ryan hadn't even known he'd had. As they drew eye to eye, Scott dropped his hands to Ryan's belt, undressed him smoothly, and pushed him back on the bed. Ryan was suddenly naked in front of his beguiling lover with no idea what was in store.

"I'll tell you what," Scott said with impudence, seeing that Ryan was more nervous this second night than he'd been in the heady flush of magic the night before. "How's this. Instead of saying 'no', because, you know, that comes up a lot when you don't mean it, how about 'turkey', okay?"

"Turkey?" Ryan asked, the absurdity of it breaching his tied tongue.

"Yeah," Scott leaned in for a kiss even as he stroked Ryan's aching cock. "As in, 'Watch what you're doing, turkey!'"

And that had been Scotty—by turns kind, wicked, and thoughtful. What was not to love?

"Turkey," Ryan gasped now, and Scott's soft laughter echoed on the back of his neck under the thrice-damned shirt. Then that appealing, intimate warmth was gone, only to be replaced by Scott's large hands framing Ryan's

* * *

ass again and another tingly lick from the bottom of his spine to the bottom of his balls.

Which Scott took in his mouth, one at a time, as Ryan fought for balance on the bed.

"Oh, God…" he muttered. "Scotty, I'm gonna slip and squash you."

"I trust you," Scott said, giving Ryan's testicle another lick. Ryan didn't have time to make a sound, though, because Scott's finger replaced his tongue at the pucker of Ryan's asshole again, and Ryan made an "ungh" sound into the blankets.

"You know," Scotty said, his voice all mischief, "for a guy who hasn't wanted to bottom for months, you sure do like it when I play with that."

"I'd like it better if you sucked my cock so I could come and we could get out of here!" Ryan snapped back, and was rewarded for it by a stinging slap on the flesh of his buttock. "Ouch!"

"Mmm…" Scott murmured, sounding like a psychiatrist trying some sort of new therapy. "Was that an 'ouch, you turkey!' or a 'do that again; it makes my cock harder!' kind of ouch?"

Ryan was groaning into his shirt again, trying to decide, when Scotty's hand fisted over his cock and his thumb played with the pre-come across the head.

"Have you decided?"

"Not yet," Ryan said faintly, and Scott let go of his cock and smacked him again. And again. And again. Ryan groaned into his blinding cocoon and wondered whether Scotty would grab his cock again if he begged. It was aching so hard by now, he wasn't sure it wouldn't just shoot off by itself with one more crack of Scott's hand across his ass.

"Have you decided yet?" Scott asked now, his hand rubbing at what must be one red ass, because *damn,* his skin burned.

"I've decided I want to suck you off until your eyes roll back in your head!" Ryan snapped, because he did, and it seemed safer than giving Scott a straight answer.

Scott laughed, and they both remembered the first time Ryan ever sucked him off.

● ● ●

CHAPTER THREE

THEIR first night, Scott simply kissed him, held his prick, and stroked him until he came. There had been breathlessness, then urgency, but Ryan hadn't known what the fuck he was doing, so there had been no direction.

They had slipped out of the party; Ryan hadn't even asked who Scott came with. Ryan had driven them in quiet, intense silence. It should have been awkward, but it wasn't—it was trembling and fraught with a quivering, aching tension. When they arrived, Scott had grabbed his hand and hauled him through his own apartment and then kissed him until his knees were weak. Ryan had gone willingly, hadn't questioned a damned thing, and when he came in Scotty's hard, spit-wet fist, it had felt like the world rocked under his feet just so it could be made right again when he opened his eyes. And it had been—because he opened them to Scotty's knowing smirk.

And there they were, lying side by side on the bed with Ryan's come drying on their stomachs. Scott looked at him, a hint of vulnerability in those amazing gray eyes, and said, "Is it okay if I stay?"

It occurred to Ryan that his only action in the encounter had been to kiss Scott back.

"Please," he whispered, leaning in for his own kiss. Scott's lips parted beneath his, and Ryan was suddenly hungry for more tastes of this rather amazing young man. He wanted to taste the guy who could awaken something so powerful with a kiss and a careless, snarky observation about the size of Ryan's prick.

The kiss deepened, and Ryan broke away again, panting and embarrassed. He'd been pawing at Scott's clothes, dying for the feeling of slick, smooth skin under his palms.

"Please stay," he said with a swallow. "Can... can I taste... can I...." He knew what he wanted. He had always been able to make a decision and follow through. If he was going to do this, be this person who would kiss

another man, he was going to give that man some pleasure. He would attack it with the same thoroughness with which he'd attacked the bar exam.

Scott seemed to recognize that dominance, even if it was couched in inexperience. He tilted his head back, eyes half-closed, and sighed happily. "Anything. I'm yours—explore at will."

So Ryan had, and everything on Scott's body had been a revelation: male nipples, flat and surprisingly sensitive; the silky skin of his stomach, the way it quivered when Ryan stroked it. And finally, with a few snaps and a shove at Scott's skinny jeans, there it was: Scott's erection in a nest of dark blond hair.

It was around six inches long, with a slight curve and a large flared head. It had veins and ridges and a slit at the top that was weeping a little bit of fluid. Ryan made an "oh" sound, and even as Scott laughed, Ryan kissed the head and licked the fluid, tasting it delicately.

Scott stopped laughing and moaned instead.

Encouraged, Ryan opened his mouth and carefully covered his lips with his teeth, slicked the inside of his mouth with spit, and engulfed the head, sucking as he did. Scott thrust up, the action involuntary. Making Scott do those things without planning, without warning, made Ryan feel powerful—a feeling he loved.

Oh, God. Ryan groaned again and pulled more and more of it into his mouth. As Scott's hands clenched in his hair and he grew hard again, he thought maybe he could suck it forever, just to hear his new lover whimper for more.

With a few exceptions when Scott had been "teaching," Ryan had mostly led since then.

The memory was hot and precious on the surface of their minds, but now Ryan was the one whimpering, and Scott was panting behind him as he roughly fisted Ryan's bare cock again. Ryan's thighs were shaking, and as Ryan felt Scott's chin and then his nose breathe against the skin of his inner thigh and balls, Ryan was shamed into calling, "Turkey!"

"Turkey?" Scott was obviously surprised.

"I can't hold this position, Scotty—I *really* don't want to hurt you."

For a moment, the game was interrupted. For a moment, Scott's arms wrapped around his waist, and his cheek rested on Ryan's bare back, and his lips were tender on Ryan's spine.

"You'll never hurt me, baby," he said softly, and then his arms tightened and Ryan was being hauled up onto the bed, his arms still tangled in his shirt, his head still resting on the mattress. Now, his knees were spread underneath his body, and his ass was sticking up in the air.

A stinging smack cracked across his vulnerable, bare ass, Scott's palm making contact with his hole and smarting enough for Ryan to groan.

"God, you're hot like that," Scott hissed in his ear. Up on the bed, more of Scott's body made contact with Ryan's, and Ryan could feel….

"You're naked?" Oh, shit, he *was,* and that was his cock up against Ryan's thigh, brushing his balls, close, so close….

"Oh, yeah," Scott breathed, grinding up against him. "And you know what I want to do more than anything?"

"Fuck my ass?" Ryan asked hopefully, although he'd never asked for it before. He'd beg for it now.

"Later," Scott promised roughly. "Much, much later."

Which brought Ryan temporarily to the surface of reality. "Scotty, my parents…."

"Delayed flight," Scott murmured, right before he stuck his tongue right in Ryan's asshole, and Ryan saw stars with the effort not to come.

"Augh… gonna…."

"Don't you dare!" Scotty laughed. He punctuated the order with another smack, and Ryan whimpered. Scott leaned over to whisper in Ryan's ear, his naked chest making contact with Ryan's back. "I'll tell you when to come, all right? I plan to get my rocks off at least twice before then… I've been wanting to have you at my mercy since we met."

I've always been at your mercy, Scotty. But Ryan didn't say it out loud. They both knew it was true. It had been true from the moment Scott had seen him in the bathroom and admired his thick cock. It had been true from the moment Scott had leaned in and kissed him. It had been true from the moment Scott had thrust into Ryan's mouth and come and come and come, and Ryan, who had never sucked cock before, had swallowed it because it was Scott's and he loved it.

Suddenly Scott was gone, leaving Ryan's exposed body cold without him, and there was a rustling with some packaging and the subtle pop of a bottle of lube.

"But since," Scott said happily, "one of the places I'm going to come is inside your sweet ass, I'm gonna make sure you're ready for me."

The lube was cold against Ryan's tingling hole, and then… oh, God… it wasn't the small size they'd used before—it was larger, almost as big as Scotty's cock, and it burned… it burned, and it hurt so good…. "Gawd…."

Ryan was gibbering into the hot cocoon of his shirt by the time the plug was in, but as Scott's hand went to work on his now-slippery prick, he figured none of the gibberish he'd howled had sounded like "turkey," so it must be good.

"Auuughhh, Scotty… it feels… it's so full. So good. I really want you… can't you… please?"

"Not…." Scott's voice was strained, and he moved his hand off Ryan's cock. There was a smacking sound, the kind of sound that a hand made when it was stroking full-force on a lubed, erect cock. "Now…."

There was a scalding spatter of come on Ryan's exposed ass, butt-plug and all, and Ryan almost wept into his bindings with the injustice of it all.

"God, Scotty… that's not fair. Augh!" Scott's hand splattered through the come on his ass to smack him again, and Ryan got it. You didn't get to complain about fairness when you were playing the Dom/sub game. Okay. Lesson learned.

Through the shirt cocoon and the haze of pleasant pain and aching, excruciating pleasure, Ryan heard something that almost made his raging erection die.

"Oh, shit. Is that the doorbell? That's not my…."

"Shhh," Scott whispered. "Don't worry. Not them. I'll be back."

Ryan didn't know how he knew, but he heard the rustle of fabric and the sound of Scott's feet landing solidly on the ground. He imagined Scotty hopping into his jeans, fastening them over his slick prick.

"Scott!" he moaned, feeling as naked and exposed as he ever had in his life.

"Don't worry," Scott said roughly. "No one will ever see you like this but me."

He was gone, leaving Ryan naked and bound and covered in come—and submerged in another memory.

He'd never asked who Scott had come to the party with the night they met. From their first night together, Scott had seemed so completely his. He'd had other lovers—a lot of other lovers—but from that moment on, Ryan had known there'd been no one else.

It wasn't until they arrived at another one of John's parties that it even occurred to Ryan that Scott had actually been with someone that night.

"Wow!" John said jovially, and Ryan shook his hand and introduced Scott with a blush. John raised his eyebrows in surprise. He'd known Ryan's last "date" was going to be a girl, but he obviously didn't judge.

"Nice to see you again, Scott," was what John actually said, and Ryan blinked, feeling dense. "Weren't you here with Stan last time?"

Ryan searched out the middle-aged, balding firm partner in the crowd. He'd been reasonably certain that Stan was married.

"Yeah," Scott was telling John without shame, "but we didn't leave together."

It was irrational, the terrible wave of jealousy that swept Ryan from his toes to his groin and across his tingly chest, but that didn't make it any less real.

Scott didn't know what happened; Ryan could see that he didn't. One minute they were walking down John's stairs, and the next minute, Ryan had whirled him into a secret alcove behind a bookcase in front of what had once been a connecting door, one he'd spotted at the last party. Then he was kissing Scott, fondling him, scraping his thumbs over Scott's nipples until Scott was dreamy-eyed and drunk on the promise of sex in a secluded hallway.

Then Ryan was on his knees, stroking, suckling, penetrating Scott's ass with two fingers and a hint of roughness, of desperation.

* * *

After Scott spasmed and came, shooting his wad into Ryan's mouth, Ryan looked up at his dreamy, shocked face, that fine, wide mouth bruised by the rough kisses, and muttered harshly, "No one sees you like this but me."

Scott nodded dumbly, absolutely complacent in this, absolutely willing to agree to monogamy and fierce possessiveness, and Ryan was satisfied.

And now it looked as though Scott would be satisfied as well.

CHAPTER FOUR

IT SEEMED like an eternity, but the come on Ryan's skin was still drying when Scotty returned, so it was probably no more than five minutes.

Ryan heard the rustle of clothes and knew Scott had shucked his jeans. Before he could ask who had been at the door, Scott was licking his back, licking his cheeks, tasting his own come from Ryan's skin. Ryan's erection—which had wilted a little with the wait—was suddenly up and throbbing and aching for release.

And since his asshole had never stopped feeling stretched full and burning with the intrusion of the plug, climax was one more thing Ryan was starting to hunger for in a way that was burning away reason.

"Please…" he begged as Scotty brushed his cock in a haphazard way. It bounced painfully, almost smacking against his stomach.

"Please what?" Scott asked playfully, doing that bouncing thing again.

"Oh, God… please, Scotty… please fuck me. I'm dying here. I need you. I need you… I'm so… please…."

"God…." Scott ground up against him. His erection was back, and Ryan almost wept, he was so glad. "You're so hot when you beg… you make me want to fuck you so bad…. Big, bad, Ryan Connors, begging on his knees…."

"Please, Scotty," Ryan pleaded. He was dying. He was going to shoot his load just from Scott's voice in his ear, he really fucking was.

"Want you…." Scott's voice suddenly firmed up. He was "teaching" again, promising, threatening, and Ryan wanted to weep into the mattress. "First I want to pull out that butt-plug. Then I want to lube you up. Then I want to shove my cock up your ass until you scream. Will you do that for me, Ryan? Will you scream for me?"

"Fuck, yes!" Ryan screamed for him now, the sound muffled by the fabric, and then the plug was jerked brutally from his rectum, and through the burn and the stretch and the sudden relief of cool lubricant, he knew what real screaming in pleasure was all about.

All of that was replaced by Scotty's cock—*oh*—and then he learned all over again. How had he thought the plug was anywhere *near* as big as—*ah*…. His ass was a rim of fire, and then Scotty thrust, and he was full, so damned full, and the burning was exquisite, even as Scotty pulled out.

"Fuck!" Ryan grunted, and Scott did. He pulled back, and Ryan whimpered; he thrust forward, and he groaned; and he did it again, and again, and again. *Scott… oh, God….*

"You fuck me so good," Ryan whimpered when his body was screaming for release, for climax. "So good… oh, thank you for fucking me… thank you, thank you. God… don't. Stop. Don't. Stop… *augh!"*

Scotty had reached around and grabbed his cock and was stroking, hard and sure and almost roughly, and Ryan was suddenly coming, coming until his eyes rolled back in his head, spattering so hard the front of his shirt was coated in semen. Then Scotty was jerking into his body, and he felt it. Hot come inside his ass… oh, *fuck*, it felt so good.

Scott lay over his body for a few minutes, both of them panting, both of them dazed and numb and high from the sex. And then, "Scotty?"

"Yeah?" Scott was definitely out of it.

"Will you *please* help me out of this damned shirt?"

Scott laughed then—long and hard and wickedly. But he also pulled the shirt down and unbuttoned it tenderly, even the wrists. Ryan's hair was sopped through with sweat, and Scotty laughingly rubbed the shirt over his face and his neck to dry him off.

Then he kissed Ryan so sweetly, so softly, that Ryan was brought back to that first kiss, the magical one in a friend's bathroom that had started all of this.

Ryan sighed, then collapsed sideways on the bed, facing his lover who followed him. "Scotty?" he murmured, rubbing that wide, wicked mouth with his thumb.

"Yeah?"

"Where the hell are my parents?"

Scott laughed some more. "Their flight got delayed. They'll be here early in the morning. I was going to tell you, you know, but you just came tear-assing through the apartment and then…." He smiled dreamily. "There you were. All spread out for me. Mmmmm…."

Ryan chuffed out a little bit of laughter. "So you'd been dreaming about this for a while?"

Scott shrugged, and suddenly that wicked curve to his mouth changed, became vulnerable, naked and soft. "You're always so… so together, Ry. You never have any doubts, never… you know. You never seem to really need me. You just take care of me. I just…." Scott looked away, embarrassed now, after the things he'd had Ryan begging for just moments ago. "I wanted you to need me. I guess I just… I wanted you to beg for me the way I want to beg for you every day."

Ryan cupped his cheek, rubbed his high, planed cheekbone with a thumb. "You moron—don't you know how weak I feel when I'm with you? You… you *love* me. You make me laugh, and you make me young; you make my knees wobble, and you *love* me. You're… you're like the most powerful person I've ever met."

They stared at each other, breath mingling, come and laughter, sex and magic, all of it, scenting the air.

Scott smiled again, a little of that wickedness creeping back. "So… does that mean you don't want to do that again?"

Ryan flushed, probably all over his pale body if he'd cared to look down and see it. "I didn't say *that,*" he mumbled, and Scotty laughed for real. Then, something else occurred to him. "Hey, Scotty, who was that at the door?"

Scott's gleeful grin was truly a thing of beauty. "Pizza!" he crowed. "When I found out your parents weren't coming, I ordered in!"

Ryan couldn't help it—he lay on his side and laughed until Scott's wicked, wicked mouth shut him up. They kissed, happy, tender, until Ryan rolled Scott underneath him and kissed him harder. Scott gave a grumble of discomfort and pulled back a light blue wad of cotton chambray, sweaty and spattered and sticky with semen. He grunted and made to throw it across the room (where it would surely miss the hamper), but Ryan took it from him and crushed it fondly against the bed.

"Baby—we're *framing* this shirt!"

Scott kissed him playfully and rolled away. "I don't know—let's take a shower and eat, and maybe we can think of better things to do with it than frame it!"

It turned out that they had more than a few ideas.

The Neighbors

Janey Chapel

She liked the new guys who'd moved in down the hill behind her.

One of them seemed to own a landscaping company. She thought of him as The Babe—tall, a little on the skinny side, with great, long legs and a big smile.

The other one worked in construction. He was fine, too, in a wife-beater, retired jock kind of way, all broad shoulders and muscle, his voice a rough rumble she felt as a vibration in her chest across the stretch of yard. She called him Muscle Man.

The house had been sitting empty for a couple of years. When the trucks had first pulled in the driveway, offloading piles of mulch and lumber, she assumed the guys had been contracted to spruce the place up, but then the trucks stayed, and lights went on at night: they'd moved in. The mulch and lumber piles got smaller, and a basketball hoop went up over the garage door. Most nights, she fell asleep to male laughter, the low throb of Muscle Man's voice, and the sound of the ball smacking pavement.

Muscle Man and The Babe lived their days and nights like they loved their jobs, their house, their backyard, and each other. They never tried to hide it, and for someone who'd hidden a lot in her life, that made watching them even better. No matter how sucky her day was, most nights she could look over the fence at just the right angle, and something she'd see would make her feel better.

• • •

She didn't spy on them, not exactly. More like one of her kitchen windows looked out on their kitchen window, and so over time, she learned their routines. Okay, so she had to sit in one certain spot to see their house, and lean a little bit, and yeah, sometimes she left the lights off—no point advertising her interest—but it wasn't like she was *stalking* them.

She just liked watching them.

Before they moved in, she'd had no idea that seeing two guys together could turn her on, but, wow, it did. It *totally* did.

She'd noticed that Muscle Man was especially prone to jumping The Babe after they'd been playing ball. He'd run his hands up the back of The Babe's sweaty shirt, tossing the ball away as he dragged him around the corner of the house, out of view of the neighbors. Well, *most* of the neighbors.

She'd love to know what they did in the rest of the house, given what they were willing to do in the backyard. Obviously, they had no idea anyone could see them. Otherwise, she was pretty sure The Babe wouldn't have let Muscle Man give him a hand job right there on the back stoop that one sunny Saturday, The Babe leaning back on his hands, legs twitching, while Muscle Man took his dick out of his shorts and yanked on it 'til The Babe turned red from his chest to his hairline and came all over Muscle Man's hand.

She'd stayed still as a little mouse, afraid to move from her perch until it was over, squeezing her thighs together in the same rhythm as Muscle Man's hand. It took a while to get her breath back after that one.

There was that other time, too, when Muscle Man stretched out on a big lounger near the dwindling mulch pile and The Babe laid down right on top of him, and they'd surfed some tide only they knew, waves crashing. That time, she'd actually come when The Babe reared his head back and pushed his thighs between Muscle Man's legs, lunging up and down on him. He'd looked so strong, so *gone*.

But nothing beat tonight. Tonight, with the dinner Muscle Man had spent an hour making and The Babe spent about a minute cleaning up before he got pinned to the counter from behind and groped right there in front of their big kitchen window.

She congratulated herself—she'd figured The Babe for catching and Muscle Man for pitching, and given the way The Babe seemed to surrender the minute Muscle Man shoved up against his back, she'd been right on the money. Oh, yeah, this should be good.

She settled in her chair and vowed to keep her hands off herself, at least until things really heated up.

But, hey, wait a sec.... Muscle Man turned The Babe around, started talking to him. She squirmed in her seat, disappointed. The Babe started to drop down, but Muscle Man pulled him back up, hugged him. There, that was better.

Then, all of a sudden, The Babe started stripping Muscle Man like his clothes were on fire, taking his own clothes off, too, and within a few seconds, as far as she could tell, they were both standing there stark naked.

Naked!

In the kitchen!

Damn, she wished she had binoculars. Or a telescope, even.

She could only see them from the waist up; they still managed to shock her, arouse her. God, they seemed to be having so much *fun* together, like they didn't have a care in the world. She wondered if their lives were really as golden as they seemed from where she was sitting.

They'd switched places; now Muscle Man had his back to the window, and she had a nice, clear view of The Babe's gorgeous face. Whatever he was doing to Muscle Man, he was enjoying it, that was for certain.

The Babe's head disappeared, and she thought, *Ooh, he's gonna blow him, just watch*, but then Muscle Man pushed him away and turned around, staring straight at her through the window.

Her heart, which had started racing right about the time she saw The Babe's bare chest come into view, skipped three beats in a row.

Muscle Man could see her, she just knew it. He was looking *right at her*.

She'd lifted her hand before she could stop it. A wave? A salute? Some acknowledgement that she'd seen them? She didn't know, couldn't think or even breathe.

He didn't do anything. Didn't wave back, didn't turn tail and run; he just stood there, staring. Then he shrugged, a little movement of his shoulders, and her heart started its frantic beat again.

If he'd seen her—*if*—surely that shrug said all was well? *Go ahead and look, lady—he's fine, ain't he?*

• • •

Muscle Man braced himself with his hands set wide, and The Babe did something behind him.

No.

Surely not?

Was The Babe hitting the mound?

Was that big Man o' Muscle getting himself ready for a fastball?

It skewed her view of them. Not literally—she could still see them just fine, thank you. But her view of who they were changed in that moment. It had seemed so clear, watching from her shielded nest, that in their world Muscle Man drove and The Babe navigated. But here stood The Babe, putting it to Muscle Man something fierce, if the way Muscle Man dropped down to his elbows told her anything, and Muscle Man looked really, really happy about it.

Huh.

The Babe's hands moved out of view. Touching Muscle Man's cock? She hoped so. She liked imagining what was happening just out of sight.

Muscle Man's head dropped, and The Babe stood stock still behind him. Shit. Was he in? Was The Babe *inside* him?

Fuck, that was hot.

The Babe started to move, and then it moved past hot and into incendiary, panty-soaking, and no way could she keep her hands out of play, not with their rhythm seeping into her body, dragging her down with it. She let her hands slide between her legs, over her panties, gently nudging the fabric against her clit, drawing out the pleasure, determined to come when they did.

The Babe had some kind of beat going now, rocking so hard he shook them both, bending across Muscle Man, rubbing his head on that broad back.

He seemed to be trying to say something, or hold on, or something, but whatever it was, it didn't work, because he lost it, just about lifting Muscle Man off the ground, he was ramming him so hard, and suddenly, a wet streak splattered against the window. Sweet Jesus. Had to be Muscle Man, coming so hard he shot that far.

* * *

She shoved her hand into her wet panties and rubbed quick and hard, catching the orgasm just as it started and sending another close on its heels. She gasped to the glass between them, "Babe."

They fucking blew her mind.

Their *fucking* blew her mind.

Muscle Man and The Babe ended up bent over the sink, The Babe holding Muscle Man around the chest. She could imagine their thundering heartbeats, their sweaty bodies sliding together, the kitchen smelling of come and wine and whatever delicious thing Muscle Man had made to seduce The Babe, like he needed anything beyond his handsome self and the crook of a finger.

She gave herself one more climax, a slow, sweet one, to the sight of The Babe pulling back and Muscle Man turning around, reaching for him, pulling him close.

The Babe caught Muscle Man's chin in his hand, grinned, and kissed him. Muscle Man leaned over, put his face in The Babe's neck, moved up to his ear. He must have said something, because The Babe nodded, then kissed him again.

God, they were good.

She stretched, satisfied, warm inside and out.

They'd ruined her, she was sure of it. Ruined her for boyfriends *and* neighbors.

Oh, well. They looked pretty settled there, in their house with its yard full of mulch and lumber, their basketball hoop sturdily mounted, and she didn't plan on going anywhere. Maybe they could stay as they were, the three of them: two together, enjoying each other; one apart, enjoying the view.

• • •

JANEY CHAPEL found a paperback romance in her grandmother's bookcase at the age of eleven, inhaled it in one sitting, and then proceeded to devour thousands of romance novels in a variety of genres over the course of several decades. Eventually, her husband said, "Stop reading! Start writing!" After a lifetime in the South, Janey now lives in the Northeast with her husband and daughter, where she volunteers with the PTO, struggles to adapt to actual winter, and writes fiction in her spare time.

Visit her blog at http://janeychapel.livejournal.com/.

Gambling Men: All In
Amy Lane

en fall asleep after sex—it's a fact of life.

Quentin dozed off after Jace slid out of him and to the side. His last conscious thought was that Jace's stubble tickled his shoulder.

When he woke up, probably no more than a few moments later, Jace was gone. Quentin looked around blearily—he was never good at waking up—and saw him.

He had grabbed a handful of sheet and slung it around his waist, and he stood in front of the window, staring thoughtfully out at the city below them. His body—and now Quentin knew firsthand how good that fine body felt under his hands, against his chest and thighs, inside of him—was silhouetted by the lights, his shoulder blades and the muscles of his back thrown into shadow.

Quentin swallowed. That pose could mean a lot of things. He was hoping one of them wasn't regret, but he feared asking. After a moment of watching Jace, deep in thought, he squared himself to ask. You couldn't win if you didn't play.

He stood and grabbed his own blanket, walked to Jace, and wrapped an arm around his waist, turning his chest to Jace's shoulder. Carefully, he placed a kiss on Jace's neck, and another one along his collarbone, and another one on the edge of a round, smooth shoulder.

● ● ●

Jace tilted his head and accepted the kisses, closing his eyes against the brightness of the city. "What now?" he asked.

Quentin looked at his profile and then leaned in and kissed his jaw. Jace made a little "Mmmm…" sound, and Quentin smiled against his neck. "'What now?' You mean where do we go from here?"

"Yeah." The syllable was soft in the darkness, as uncertain as anything Jace had ever said.

"You mean… I don't know… do we out ourselves at the office? What?"

Jace nodded and searched out Quentin's brown eyes in the darkness. "Exactly—what? Do we move in together, have quickies in the broom closet, go to poker night holding hands? What?"

Quentin blew out a breath. Nope. He hadn't thought of this either. He had a sudden thought, though, that he wouldn't go back to before. He wouldn't go back to stuffing these fantasies to the back of his head and spending more time at the office than at home because Jace was there.

"Jace?"

"Yeah?"

"Why'd you do it? Why'd you show your hand? We were just at the gym. Been there a thousand times. Why'd you… you know. Suddenly decide I'd be receptive?"

Jace smiled and looked away, and Quentin knew it wasn't his imagination. The gesture had been shy.

"You blushed," Jace said.

"Blushed?" Quentin tried to remember.

"I told you I never let anybody win, and you blushed." Jace smiled again, and this time the shyness was gone and the shark was back. "I smelled blood. I took a gamble."

Quentin nodded and pulled Jace's far shoulder to him, so they were standing chest to chest in front of the diverse, throbbing city that could either welcome them or eat them alive. "It paid off," he said quietly. "You want to take another?"

Jace nodded, accepting. "What are the stakes?"

"Nothing big. How about I stay the night?"

Jace rested his forehead on Quentin's, and their breath mingled in the quiet for a moment. "You can borrow one of my suits for work tomorrow, if you can explain why I'd let you."

It was Quentin's turn to laugh. "I'll tell them you let me win a bet."

Jace raised his head and murmured, "Maybe, this once, I could let you win," before going in for a kiss.

Illustrations by Paul Richmond

http://www.paulrichmondstudio.com

Dreamspinner Press
For more of the
best M/M romance,
visit
Dreamspinner Press
www.dreamspinnerpress.com

LaVergne, TN USA
12 May 2010
182423LV00004B/109/P